Homo Jihad

Timothy Graves was born in 1969 and studied Drama and English Literature at Exeter University. He currently lives in London. 'Homo Jihad' is his first novel.

ISBN: 9781904585152
Published by Paradise Press 2010
BM5700
London
WCIN 3XX

First published in the United Kingdom in 2009

Homo Jihad

Timothy Graves

'My mouth tastes sweet
With your name in it:
I turn my face to you,
And into eternity:
There is a growing taste I prefer
to every
Idea of Heaven.'

(Jalal al-Din Rumi 1207-1273)

For Oren

Chapter 1

I got out at Euston, made my way to the Northern line and stood on the platform, reeling from the overhead lights and sudden tannoy announcement - defective train, severe delays expected. Swigging the last gulp of luke-warm mineral water, I managed to make it to the far end of the platform and last available seat, squeezing next to a middle-aged woman in a lime-green shell suit. The carrier bags she'd lugged from the local branch of Tesco displayed a range of goodies at her feet: a bumper pack of Marlborough Lights, microwave dinners for one, and a host of trashy T.V mags. She was staring blankly at the tunnel wall – at a billboard poster, somewhat torn at the edges, of a tropical island out in the Indian Ocean: palm-fringed stretches of coastline, sun-kissed beaches and endless turquoise blue sea. On the other side of me, a Japanese cyber-punk, plugged into his i-pod, adjusted his boot straps - a red Mohican bobbing up and down to the screeching of electric guitars inside his headphones. He didn't seem to notice the rat. Appearing from nowhere, it darted between his legs, scuttled across the platform and fell off the edge - disappearing into a subterranean world of tube carriages zigzagging deep underground like the electrical impulses in the drug-addled neural pathways of my brain.

I looked shiftily at both my fellow passengers and a growing paranoia began to take hold: my clenched jaw, over-dilated pupils, how I must have swayed as I walked in their direction – all tell-tale signs if you knew how to read them. Huge fuck-off sunglasses and a baseball cap, so I could tilt it downwards and deflect unwanted attention, would have been a godsend right now - that, a ready-made spliff and a couple of valium. I leant forward and looked down at the frayed ends of my jeans covered in dirt, chewing gum firmly stuck to one of the trouser legs. I began picking at the paper on my empty bottle of Evian water, slowly peeling away the pink and blue outline of the French Alps, and noticed the rubber was coming apart at the sole of my left trainer. Could they tell I'd been up half the night fucked on a Molotov cocktail of drugs? Still, not as fucked as I'd been earlier, just minutes away from MI6's headquarters, 'Babylon-on-Thames', down on my knees in some back-street, after-hours club in the Vauxhall village, that out of it, I couldn't see the coke for the toilet seat and ended up spilling half the gram down the pan. I glanced across at both of them. The woman still staring vacantly at the tunnel wall plastered with advertisements for luxury foreign holidays, women's deodorants and twelve week courses in Western philosophy - the Japanese kid lost inside the music; they hadn't noticed a thing.

The platform was beginning to fill up. I closed my eyes and wished myself back to last Sunday morning: the sun gently filtering through his bedroom curtains, the kiss of his breath on my chest, his warmth as he curled himself into me and the pine tree outside his bedroom window as it gradually came to life with a chorus of birdsong. Now, all I could hear was the mindless thump, thump, of some dirty electro-house number that had been played to death over the course of the last eighteen hours - a mantra to unadulterated hedonism and the path of excess. I'd fucked up big time and I knew it.

The tannoy crackled, suddenly emitting a high pitched screech, then nothing. It crackled again and a voice in a thick Jamaican accent announced that the defective train had been taken out of service. Minutes later, I heard the familiar roar of a tube hurtling through the tunnel and got to my feet as fellow passengers jostled and positioned themselves behind the yellow line. The train had arrived and I was pushed on all sides as the carriage doors opened and out spilled out-of-town day trippers, backpackers and a group of girls, all cleavage and fake tan. I just caught the tail end of their conversation – something about dumping Gary – as I pushed my way into the carriage and made a beeline for the prized corner seat. I sneaked a glance at the tube map opposite - five stations to go and planned each leg that remained of the journey with military precision: get out at Archway, climb the escalators, walk to the bus stop, wait for the number 27 or 43 to Highgate Hill, and get out on Hornsey Lane. It seemed more manageable when I broke it up like that, and less likely that I'd end up passing out, puking up, or waking up dazed and confused at the end of the Northern line.

Somehow I made it out of the tube station, onto the bus, and was now walking up the gravelled forecourt to his apartment block. A smudge of moonlight appeared to play peek-a-boo through the branches of the pine tree and stopped me in my tracks. What was this chunk of cratered rock that in turn masqueraded as a man's face or silver hook and now seemed on the verge of slipping away altogether - as if the gravitational pull of some greater celestial body had just laid claim to it? And the pine tree, that, in its branches held the early morning secret of my love for him, was now transfigured by the moon into some strange totem pole with closely guarded stories and genealogies hidden deep within its sap. My head was reeling as I scanned the top floor for his one bedroom apartment. I felt sick. The sash windows were now shut, and inside, complete darkness. He wasn't in. I'd come all that way and he wasn't at home. I couldn't go back, not in this state, and not without letting him know how I really felt. I had visions of myself camped outside his flat, walking the streets at three in the morning, trawling the local pubs and restaurants to see if I could find him. I couldn't face the prospect of going home, not now - back on the tube, back to East London, with only Monday morning to look forward to.

Luckily, the door to his block was open and I walked

through and waited for the lift. The doors opened and I stepped in, breathing heavily. The pulleys above the lift slowly cranked it towards the top floor and I stared at red digits on the dial to the side of me – five, six, seven. They soon turned to double digits and I imagined them flickering with increasing tempo, the fuse box beginning to fizz, sparks flying in all directions until the lift burst through the roof of the building like a jet-propelled rocket launching into space and I floated in a sea of tranquillity. A sudden jolt brought me back down to earth and the doors opened.

There he was, holding onto the door frame to his apartment, barefoot, in an old pair of khaki shorts. I felt that familiar hollow burning sensation in the pit of my belly. For a moment we both stood there, unsure of each other. Then I noticed the dark circles under his almond-shaped eyes and that he hadn't shaved. His face broke into a smile and I was suddenly overcome with an overwhelming feeling that I'd done the right thing.

'It's good to see you. Come here,' he said.

The crazed clubbing session in Vauxhall, the fact he hadn't returned any of my messages in over a week, none of that mattered now. He hugged me and I felt his lips brush against my neck, the familiarity of his smell and his body as he pressed himself closer into me.

'I've missed you,' I whispered.

'Me too.' Then I felt him tense slightly. 'You have no idea.'

He switched the light on in the hallway and I took off my shoes. The painting of an enlarged fingerprint encircled by Arabic writing greeted me like an old friend. As did the framed black and white photographs of life in his home town in the Emirates which had formed part of his portfolio in his second year at St. Martin's Art college. But walking into his open-plan living room and kitchen, I was shocked by the transformation. On the coffee table, where art and photography magazines were usually neatly stacked, lay empty coffee mugs, takeaways and an ash try overflowing with cigarette butts. The kitchen area, usually immaculate and spotless, was piled high with dirty plates and saucepans, and spread over the chesterfield sofa and oak wooden flooring were pages of the dissertation he'd been working on.

He lit a cigarette and sat down on the sofa. I stood, surveying the damage.

'Sorry about the mess,' he said.

'Are you ok?'

He didn't answer and leant forward to flick his ash.

'Did you finish your painting?'

He shook his head. 'Giving it a rest for a bit.'

'But you were so excited about it! The centre piece for your next exhibition. That's what you said.'

'Things change.' He patted the sofa and smiled. 'Come here, mister.'

I sat next to him on the sofa, leant my head on his shoulder, and looked out across leafy, suburban Highgate and neighbouring Muswell Hill. The silhouette of detached houses and blocks of flats cut into a sky streaked in hues of deep purple. And stretching their leaves towards the fading light outside - his collection of yucca, succulents and cacti plants crammed onto the window sill. A reminder of his childhood back in the Arab Emirates, where even the wind is searing hot, and sand storms descending from nowhere will just as quickly disappear. For me, they were a piece of him. Only a few weeks ago he'd given me a prized selection of cuttings from these same desert plants and a carrier bag so I could carry the pieces back home on the tube with me. I smiled to myself as I remembered planting the cuttings on my balcony that evening, sprinkling some root powder, making my wish. From the minaret at the East London mosque just down the road, the crackled recording of the call to prayer had risen above the overcrowded tower blocks and sprawling council estates: '*Allah u Akbar, Allah u Akbar*'. It was as if I'd been called to my own prayer and on that cold February afternoon had dared to whisper his name: *Ahmed*. It was his voice that suddenly broke the spell.

'You've been there haven't you?'

'Sorry?'

'I don't know. *Fire, Beyond...* wherever gay people go who take drugs.' He leant closer. 'Your pupils – they're enormous. You've been to Vauxhall, haven't you?'

I paused for a moment, anticipating the possible fall-out from his reaction but it was pointless trying to cover my tracks. I simply nodded.

He stood up, walked over to the window then turned to face me. 'I don't believe it! I thought you hated *Fire*. More than a whiff of death about the place. That's what you said. Vauxhall in its final death throes. Goodness knows the place should have been raided before now. From what I hear it's full of cocaine-fuelled sexual robots and guys passing out on G.'

'Well, I guess that's one way of putting it.'

The door to his bedroom was slightly ajar and the orchid I'd bought him at Columbia Road flower market was still there, flowering next to his side of the bed. Its velvet petals etched by a web of blood red capillaries, an entanglement of roots pressing hard against the glass vase.

'I didn't think you wanted to see me again,' I said.

'That whole scene. I thought all that was behind you.'

'You wouldn't return my calls.'

'So the first excuse you get, you go out, take goodness knows what then turn up like this, on my doorstep, off your face. I can't believe you'd bring drugs into my house. This is my home, David. For heavens sake, this is where I pray.'

I looked at his copy of the Koran on the wooden stand on

his book shelf and could feel his eyes boring into me. I longed to take his hand and trace a veritable landscape of hard ridges, mounds and crevices that would reassure me with their familiarity. But I held myself in check.

'It's your body.' His voice seemed to soften. 'But that stuff you take – you're not getting any younger, David. And you still...I just want you to be happy. That's all.'

All I could feel was a growing tightness in my throat and the burning sensation in my chest from having chain-smoked my way through two packs of cigarettes.

'It was Michael's birthday. What did you expect me to do? Stay at home and leave my best friend to it?'

He came and sat back down, placing a hand on my thigh. 'I'm only telling you because I care about you. I hate to see you like this.'

'So why didn't you return my messages? I called you twice a day, every day.'

He looked away.

'Look, I know how you feel about drugs. I know I slipped up. But I had to see you. I had to see that you're all right. And I wanted ...' I couldn't say it. I wanted to tell him but not now. Not like this. 'It doesn't matter.'

Tears were welling up in his eyes as he slowly turned and cradled himself into the corner of the sofa, his chin curled into his chest. I stared at the nape of his neck and was taken by the way the two bands of muscles on either side reached up to the ridge of bone at the base of his head. It was as if I was seeing part of him for the very first time and for a moment I felt the miracle of him before me: the contours of his shaven head, his slender frame, the way the outer ridge of his ears curved and dropped to the soft flesh of his lobes - at once only too familiar and yet at that precise moment, a complete revelation; I felt him without touching him. I could smell him, not just his sweet musky odour, but his being, his essence, distilled like a drop of perfume carrying the imprint of a distant memory I couldn't quite fathom. And as I struggled to remember something that flickered on the edge of my consciousness, refusing to yield its secret, I suddenly thought the unthinkable.

'Are you breaking up with me? Is that why you didn't return any of my calls?'

He didn't answer. I inched closer to him on the couch and tentatively reached out to touch his fingers but his arm made a sudden retreat for the back of the sofa.

'I'm sorry. I can't,' he said.

'What is it?' The wind was gently rattling the window. 'Ahmed, what is it?'

He sat up and turned to me. 'My parents.'

'Yes?'

'They're in London.'

'Why didn't you tell me? You know I would have met them.'

'Oh, hi Mum, Dad. This is David, my lover. Don't think, given father's track record, it would go down that well, do you?'

'Where are they staying?'

'Where they usually stay. The Dorchester.' He paused. 'Only this time they came with Fatima's parents.'

'Your sister's friend from Saudi?'

He paused. 'Honestly, I was going to tell you before. There just never seemed to be a good time. I'm sorry, David.'

'What do you mean?'

'Look, I don't quite know how to say this.' He averted his gaze.

'Say what?!'

'Of course – you should know. I never meant to keep it from you. I would never intentionally hurt you, you know that.'

'Jesus, Ahmed. You're scaring me. What is it?'

'They want me-'

'Go on.'

'They want me… They want me to get married.'

It took a while to register. 'This is a joke, right?'

'Please, don't make this any harder.'

'Married?'

'That's why Fatima's parents were over here as well.'

'Fatima?' Her name stuck in my throat. 'You're marrying Fatima?'

'Not seeing you, I thought it was the best way.'

'Why on earth would you marry Fatima? Have you gone completely mad?'

'I didn't know how to tell you.'

I looked across to his sash windows and the darkness outside. Specks of rain had hit the glass intact and stuck there, perfectly formed, reflecting the white light of the street lamps, glistening like tiny jewels. 'I came here … I just thought -' I stood up rather too quickly, nearly keeling over with a major head rush and had to steady myself for a moment on the arm of the sofa.

'Are you ok?' he asked.

'I can't believe you would have kept something like this from me.'

'What do you expect me to do? They're already planning the big wedding out there. Hundreds of guests, my mum's family from Egypt, father's friends in government.' For a moment I thought he was going to start crying.

'You're going back home?'

'For the wedding.'

I knew if he went back to the Arab Emirates he wouldn't be coming back. Once he was married off, that would be it. He'd be shacked up with Fatima in next to no time. She'd be up the duff in some palatial villa on the edge of the desert and he'd be making clandestine excursions to Abu Dhabi or Beirut or wherever it was a gay man in the Middle East went for a bit of man to man action. I wouldn't see him for dust.

'I should have told you before. I know that. It's not the first time they've tried to persuade me to marry. I told them I need to be really focussed on my career, that I'm not ready, that I *will* get married – just not right now. They didn't listen. I honestly thought I had a few more years left.'

'I'm –' I nearly choked on the words. Every time I'd said it before it had ended in disaster. There'd be an awkward silence or half-hearted 'ditto' or maybe a 'me too' and weeks later the relationship would be finished. But I couldn't stand by and let him make one of the biggest mistakes of his life. I couldn't let him walk away without him knowing how I'd felt all along, how I'd been longing to tell him for months.

'What is it?' he asked.

Again, that sense of strangulation in my throat and then a sudden release of tension and the words were out.

'I'm in love with you, Ahmed.'

That feeling that had been bubbling up for the whole tube journey, that secret I'd kept for nearly six months; it was out in the open. That was everything I had to give. I stood there waiting for a miracle, waiting to hear my name, to feel his touch. I wanted my words to magically change everything, to give him the hope that anything was possible if we loved each other.

'I feel the same way, you know I do, it's just what with everything happening right now and you turning up like this...' I'd never seen him cry before and went to hug him. He pulled away. 'I'm sorry, David. I think it's best that you go.' Then he eased himself off the sofa, stood up and walked towards the hallway.

I sat and held on to the edge of the sofa, stunned and

confused – staring into the abyss at Dumping Ground Central. Our weekends away: Barcelona, Sardinia, Rome - waking up in the same bed together, realising that finally I'd found a man I really wanted to be with. Had I lived the last six months under some kind of grand illusion? Had he known about this all along? I stared at Ahmed waiting for me to leave, completely dumbfounded. 'So that's it?'

'It's better this way.'

'Who says? Your father? You can't let him control you like this. If you can't think of me or yourself, think of Fatima. What sort of life will she have married to a man who can't give her what she wants? She's twenty two years old, for god's sake! She deserves happiness. We all do. You can't go through with it.'

He wouldn't look at me. 'Please, just go.'

I stood and followed him to the front door where I knelt down to tie the laces on my trainers. The last thing I saw before I stepped outside was the gift from his grandmother hung on the back of the front door – a ceramic artefact from Ras al-Khaima. Arabic lettering laced the contours of each finger and a black eye in the open palm stared blankly back at me- *The Hand of Fatima*. So much for warding off evil and misfortune; it felt like a curse. I waited for the lift and could feel another pair of eyes on my back. I turned round. He was still standing at the doorway.

I waited for what seemed like an eternity as the familiar clunking and strain on the lift pulleys eventually brought the lift up to the nineteenth floor. The lift opened. My back still towards him, I stepped in. The door closed. I imagined the pulleys above suddenly snapping and sending the steel capsule plummeting in a matter of seconds to the bottom of the shaft. I heard his voice calling my name as the lift made an orderly descent to the ground floor.

Outside, the smell of fresh pine needles perfumed the air,

and the moon, no longer a ghostly imprint imprisoned behind branches, had risen from the furthest reaches of the pine tree to proclaim the night sky as her own. In my absence, she'd hacked away at the black canvass with her curved blade - a white light now seeping through, casting strange shadows across the lawn and gravelled forecourt. My own shadow, somehow severed at the waist, bewitched by the great scythe in the sky, began to run: away from his towering apartment block and the four by four parked in the drive, away from the *Hand of Fatima*, desert plants and pine tree - away from the man I loved. I didn't look back until I found myself out on the street.

I looked up and could just make out his silhouette at the window and for a split second I wanted to shout out his name and make a mad dash in the opposite direction. For him to be standing there at the doorway just as he had before, when I'd felt a potent mixture of relief and desire and belief – in him, in us, in our future together. I wanted to hug him and hold him and never let him go. The thought of not seeing him again, of possibly never seeing him again, ever, suddenly hit me for the first time and I found myself staggering across a flower bed and steadying myself against a brick wall. A wave of nausea passed through me, then a sudden burst of anger and pain as my knuckles smashed hard against the brick. I stared at my knuckles, scuffed, beginning to draw blood and all I could think of, all I wanted, more than anything in that moment, was to hold him, kiss him and tell him everything would be ok. But it wasn't. Nothing could be further from the truth. He was about to accept Fatima's hand in marriage and I'd blown any chance I might have had of persuading him not to waste the rest of his life just to placate his domineering, homophobic father.

I was suddenly filled with a crushing sense of my own stupidity. What if I hadn't gone round there still reeling from the effects of Class A's? What if I'd gone home instead? Is there a chance, no matter how small, that he might not be considering an arranged marriage to Fatima? I turned away and walked to the bus stop that would take me back to Archway station. It might as well have taken me to hell.

Chapter 2

'Sweetheart, he's not worth it. He's a complete and utter arsehole. Mind you, most men are. Present company excluded, of course!'

Caroline took a sharp drag of her cigarette and turned to watch as a parent, burqared-up to the eyeballs, walked through the car park at the back of the school. Usually it was Caroline who'd turn heads, completely oblivious to the fact another hot guy had seriously checked her out. She was petite, but more than made up for it with a god-given talent for giving as good as she got and a collection of seriously high-heeled shoes fit for any occasion. In fact, her Achilles tendons had compressed to such an extent it was practically impossible for her now to wear flats. A shock of blonde hair, strands of it now dyed strawberry pink, feathered towards her elfin features that, every now and then, would contort into an unexpected and exaggerated facial expression.

I'd got the text that morning. My mobile had beeped when I was in the middle of reading the kids a classic gender-reversal story about a feisty princess who is quite happy slaying her own dragons and rescuing cowardly princes in distress: 'David, I'm going ahead with the marriage. I never meant to hurt you. Take care of yourself. A.'

With both hands shaking, I'd deleted the text message and his mobile phone number immediately, expecting, as if by magic, that I could delete every last detail of the last six months I'd spent with him. But who was I kidding? The damage was already done and the corrosive content of that virtual yellow envelope was seeping through every cell in my body like toxic chemical waste. I was seized by an uncontrollable desire to lob my phone out of the window like a grenade or submerge it in a sink full of water. I felt compelled to erase any trace of his message, any memory of every last digit of his mobile phone number. I had every intention of inflicting serious grievous bodily harm on Nokia's feat of modern engineering and technology but carried on stoically until morning break with the twists and turns of fairy tale fortune for the 'Paperbag Princess' and her undeserving suitors.

'Look at it this way. If the guy's still tied to his mother's apron strings at the age of twenty five, you're better off out of it, darling. It's his loss.'

'But he was different. I really thought it might work out. I thought he was the 'One', Caz.'

'Oh darling, you always think they're 'The One.' What century are you living in? There's no such thing as 'The One.' It's the stuff of fairy tales.'

'Thanks. I feel a whole lot better!'

'You know what I mean.'

She took a puff of her cigarette, tilted her head, and blew the smoke upwards.

'Jesus, I don't know about you but I'm fucked. I've had about three hours sleep and they've been absolute shits all morning. It's frustrating having to stop and start the lesson every couple of minutes. They just don't shut up. And all this cortisol flowing through my blood stream can't be healthy, can it?'

I noticed there was a distinct lack of her usual war paint - dark red lipstick, green, sparkly eye-shadow and heavy mascara. Something had to be up; she hadn't even done her nails.

'I'm sorry. I shouldn't go on. Here's me droning on about not sleeping. Honestly, I swear I bore myself about it half the time and you've just been chucked by the love of your life. I guess your sleeping patterns are shot to bits too.'

'They've been better.'

'David, you do look awful. Are you going to be alright?'

'Yeah, I'll be fine.' I was anything but. 'Caroline, he was

different. Didn't take drugs, hadn't been to prison, wasn't a drug dealer or prostitute and hadn't, as far as I know, cheated on me. He had this amazing passion for his art, for life. I never dreamed it would end like this. Maybe if I hadn't fucked it all up by going behind his back and getting trashed in some backstreet sleaze-pit, he'd still be with me. '

'Hello? You going to your flat mate's birthday bash had nothing to do with him binning you. Do you hear? It's not your fault he's a closet case, contemplating an arranged marriage to some poor unsuspecting girl from Saudi, who, believe me, has no idea what she's getting herself into. Just you wait, gorgeous. One day you'll meet someone who deserves you. You'll see.'

'Like Ricardo you mean?'

'Which one was he again?'

'Had a photograph of his ten inch cock spread across the back pages of QX magazine.'

'You weren't to know.'

'Come on. How many gay Brazilians with ten inch cocks and visa issues do you know who aren't on the game? And how long did it take for me to wake up and smell the coffee?'

'Oh my god, now you've reminded me. Who was that guy - what was his name? You know, the one on day release from the psychiatric ward in Mile End.'

'Francoise. Now why did he have to go and spoil it by obsessing over the idea of me jacking off into his apple pie and custard?'

'Spare me the visuals!'

'I tell you, I'm jinxed.'

'Still, credit where credit's due, darling, at least you got shot of that one pretty quick.'

'And Ibrahim and Roberto and-'

'Chalk it up to experience. Just a spell of bad luck, that's all.'

'Oh come on, it's more than that, Caz. There's a whole host of them. Let's face it. I'm a man-magnet for the fucked-up, screwed-up users and abusers of the lower echelons of gay society. Ahmed was different.'

'Yeah, he's an upper class wuss. I mean it. That boy was born with a silver spoon in his mouth. You'll see, you'll meet someone when you least expect it. Someone your own age, similar background… and dare I say it – English?' She had that far off dreamy look in her eyes. 'I can just see you settling down with a nice man from Surrey or Herefordshire. Late thirties to early forties, own house, couple of dogs, walks in the countryside-'

'I know. In bed by ten o'clock on Saturday night after a night of crap T.V and a cup of hot coco. Why don't you just put me in a retirement home and throw away the key!'

The thing was I didn't want to meet anyone else. I wanted Ahmed, to wake up early in the morning and watch him as he slept: the slight curl to his eyelashes, the fullness of his lips, the gentle rise and fall of his belly. I longed to hear his voice, full of a quiet, self assured confidence, and his laughter that would dispel any doubt or worries I might have been harbouring. I wanted to hear him enthuse about new ideas for paintings and photography projects, to watch him as he prayed before climbing in bed next to me. I dropped the butt end of my cigarette into the gutter and suddenly couldn't bear the thought of life without him.

'You're wrong – about Ahmed. You know he hasn't had it easy. Living under the shadow of a father who thinks homosexuality is a mental illness. The eminent Emirate psychiatrist who thinks injecting his gay patients with shit loads of hormones will cure them of their perversion.'

Her face softened. 'Oh darling, you've got yourself into a bit of a pickle, haven't you? Don't you see? I'm helping you get over him, sweetheart. That's what friends do. Come to Mamma.'

She reached out and held my hand. 'Let's just say you've got to kiss a lot of frogs before you meet your prince. I know you thought he was the 'One', the romantic artist fleeing from a draconian father and all that. I can see how that would be a powerful aphrodisiac, really I can. But face facts. He led you down the garden path, and for what? To show you a pond teeming with heartache, let downs and disappointments you already knew existed.'

'You're wrong, Caroline. I know you are. I don't want anyone else. With him it's different. Maybe he won't marry her. Maybe I should just go round there. Maybe...'

'Maybe all three of you can go play happy families in Highgate village? Get real! He dumped you. For a woman! That's all there is to it. Finito!' She gave me one of her looks. 'And don't you dare. Don't you dare phone him. Do you hear me? The only thing worse than being dumped is being dumped and unwilling to accept it's all over. Ditch the drama! The knife's already in. Don't torture yourself by twisting it even more!'

I looked down the cobbled street that backed onto the school. A lone figure with a dowager's hump was shuffling along, wrapped up in a thick winter coat, dragging a battered shopping trolley behind her. On nearly every fag break we'd spot her shuffling along the cobbles in her black clumpy shoes. Caroline once told me she longed to go up to her and give her a good prod - just to see if she was real. I always wondered if she knew she was following in the footsteps of prostitutes, past and present, even the great serial killer himself – Jack the Ripper.

Somehow I got through the afternoon, but the drug-fuelled excesses of the weekend were beginning to take their toll and the come-down had come early with a comeuppance that left me washed out, washed up, hung out to dry. It was dark when I left but on the other side of the playground the school flood lights lit up a number of well-known fairy tale characters on the brick wall. They reminded me of the story-book characters you might see in a children's hospital ward - Peter Pan, Robin Hood, or Pinocchio - a splash of colour intended to bring a little cheer in an otherwise sick and depressing environment. Only on this brick wall, the paint work was beginning to fade and peel, so that all that was left of Little Red Riding Hood was her basket and cape – a headless reminder of the dangers inherent in straying from the path. Dick Whittington now stood on one leg and Cinderella's fairy godmother was missing her wand and half of a wing.

When I got home that evening I rummaged round in my kitchen drawer, found the piece of paper where I'd first scrawled Ahmed's number all those months ago, grabbed a lighter and watched as it disappeared into a long stream of black smoke.

Chapter 3

After being dumped from a great height by Ahmed, I hadn't been out on the scene for nearly two months. It was all I could do to get out of bed in the morning and make it into work each day. And even though my flat mate, Michael, had done his level-headed best at the weekend to get me out of the flat and drag me back onto the dance floor, I just couldn't stomach it. The very thought of getting back on that Gay Merry-Go-Round of shagging, drugs and more shagging, just made me feel queasy: Coming up, coming down, spinning round in a haze of Muscle Marys, pre-op transsexuals or 'chicks with dicks' and dealers with a side line in 'escorting'. I just couldn't deal with it. Instead I stayed at home and drowned my sorrows by tuning in to repeats of *Sex and the City* and, much to the annoyance of Michael, rediscovered my vinyl record collection from my adolescence. *The Smiths* and *The Cure* featured pretty heavily through those long dark months of February and March, as did Sinead O Connor's '*Nothing Compares to U.*'

Yet here I was again gagging for more, down in the Vauxhall village or '*Vauxhell*' as Michael now liked to call it, standing alone in the same queue outside *Fire* at eleven in the morning. He'd finally persuaded me to leave the house after threatening to call a colleague of his who doubled up as a psychosynthesis counsellor at the weekends. I certainly didn't need someone raking through my dim and distant past, probing into my psychic nether regions, thank you very much, least not by some well-meaning ex hippie from the sixties who practiced from her front room in Stoke Newington.

I looked up at the drizzling rain lit by the yellow glow of a street lamp. Michael had disappeared hours ago from the previous club at The Coliseum, and was no doubt, right this very minute, being shafted by a 'Sarf' London skinhead in some run-down council estate in Elephant and Castle. He liked to think of himself as a bit of an intellectual, a bookish type, but when it came to sex the only book he was interested in was one plastered all over with pictures of half naked chavs, scallies and convicts caught in compromising positions. His porno collection was littered with titles like 'Shoplifting Cunt', 'Danny, it's Hard up North' and 'Fuck a Hoodie'. He'd always been partial to a bit of 'how's your father' and liked it rough 'n ready, preferably with a bit of a bruiser.

Fire had only opened up at the beginning of the year, but was already a phenomenal success. Michael had aptly renamed the Sunday morning session *The Church,* which would attract a diverse crowd of muscle boys, club kids and the odd transsexual waiting in line for their very own form of salvation. We were like moths to the light, lured by the late night prospect of getting trashed with kindred spirits, and as the night, and sometimes the next day, drew to a close, everyone and everything would get steadily more twisted and deranged.

Under the purple neon glow at the entrance of the club, a meat-head of a security guy felt right up my inside leg, around my groin and under my arse. We were all getting frisked a lot more intimately since GHB had started to hit the gay clubs. It was surprising what lengths certain Gina devotees would go to, to smuggle the rancid liquid into the club, stuffing vials of it under their pants, or even up their arses, to get it past security and into the venue. They'd even come armed with their own plastic pipette to measure out the dose. A mate of mine, a litigation lawyer and recent convert to the delights of Gina, had done the dirty deed in a toilet cubicle a few months back. I watched, mesmerised as he pulled a bendy pipette from his crotch and squinted under the neon light to measure an exact 1.5 millilitres of the stuff. It had more than a whiff of a laboratory experiment about it, bringing back schoolboy memories of the periodic table, Bunsen burners, and the rock hard boner I'd get perched next to Thiago da Silva, the one and only Argentinean hunk in the school. I didn't touch the stuff myself. If I'd wanted to swallow loo cleaner or whatever it was, I could quite easily do that in the privacy of my own home. But somehow I'd never quite seen the appeal in an 'Ajax' aperitif. But I had seen a number of semi-naked gay boys start fitting and vomiting on the dance floor, only to be rushed away by ambulance to the nearest Accident and Emergency department. Not exactly my idea of a night out on the tiles. But I do admit to a morbid fascination seeing them back in the club a few hours later, cavorting on the podium like it was going out of fashion.

The Door Whore, 'Zsa Zsa La Hore', a fine figure of a woman with legs up to her armpits and broad shoulders to match, was sporting a blonde beehive wig and heavily caked in foundation. 'You do know this is a fucking gay club, and only the glamorous and seriously perverted may enter into my domain?!' she called out to the long line of punters queuing up outside.

Gesticulating dramatically in a sudden flash of perfectly manicured two inch nails, she strutted up and down the queue in thigh length PVC boots with killer heels. A guy who must have been at least in his mid fifties, looked like he'd just come from the opera and was wearing a long black coat and bow tie. He just laughed in a knowing way, paid his twelve quid and was ushered in. She blew a kiss after him, hands on hips, wildly exaggerating her facial expressions to the rest of us still queuing.

'Not the usual Riff Raff, Tom, Dick or Harry, are we, gorgeous? And while we're at it, can daddy buy baby doll a brand new vibrator?' She bent over to mime the parting of arse cheeks, her expression fixed in feigned shock and innocence.

Inside, the place was heaving and I was running on empty as I found myself pushed and prodded like a cow in a cattle market, squeezed on all sides by male Barbies dripping in sweat. I pushed my way to the bar and waited in line to be overcharged for yet another tiny bottle of mineral water. You knew you weren't high anymore when you started to resent paying two quid for a bottle of water you could quite easily get for a quarter of the price down at the corner shop. I had to find a dealer and fast but I was seriously beginning to zone out and couldn't face scouting round for more drugs. At that point, all I really wanted to do was find the nearest exit, collapse in a cab and maybe wake up hours later in bed, pleased I hadn't pushed it to the max.

Instead, I found myself pushed along in a sudden tsunami of beefed-up, naked torsos. I couldn't help thinking if half these guys managed to lose a few pounds of muscle between them then maybe there'd be a bit more room for manoeuvre. But I guess hours of dedication at the gym and weekly steroid injections in the gluteus maximus made the wait all the more worth while, when you could show the goods off on Saturday night, T-shirt tucked down a pair of the latest designer underpants, stripped to the waist. A sudden rush of cold wind and smoke blasted out from the smoke machine and someone's cigarette butt burnt my forearm. Arsehole!

I spotted the Chinese guy in the corner of the dance area near the bar. His fringe fell over his left eye in streaks of mousey pink, and protruding over his sarong were layers of pale, hairless fat, lending him more than an air of androgyny. A tattoo of a spider was sprawled across his left shoulder and even with all the lasers and strobes, his skin, especially round his neck and shoulders, was clearly badly pot-marked. He reminded me of a modern-day witch, a practitioner of the dark arts of artificially induced states of euphoria, dishing out pills and potions through a haze of smoke and strobe lighting, casting his spell that would keep you coming back for more.

'How many you want?' he asked, looking furtively around.

'Any good?' I asked, not especially keen on the thought of monging out on the sidelines for another couple of hours, any potential pulling power zapped by crap pills.

'Look, you not happy, you come back, right? I give money back.'

I'd heard that one before. He handed me four pills and I handed over twenty quid. Half an hour later, the pill began to work its wonders - a gentle tingling sensation rose up my spine - and I began surrendering to the first rushes of ecstasy. I was back in the fray and didn't seem to mind so much getting pushed and prodded as I made my way to the next room, squeezed on all sides by beefed-up Muscle Marys in military drag and Hairy Bears with fatittude. Some were sporting the latest tribal tattoos, ancient symbols bequeathed by warrior tribes as far afield as Tahiti or the south pacific islands of Papua New Guinea. Now they'd been adopted by urban queer warriors from the West fighting an entirely different enemy: the four horsemen of the gay apocalypse – homophobia, faith hate, HIV and drug addiction. I suddenly found myself back in the toilets tightly jammed on all sides - a drag queen to one side of me, gurning grotesquely while manically waving a toy wand - to the other side, a little Latino guy seriously checked out my shrunken dick whilst I huffed and puffed desperate to pee.

It was there, just outside the entrance to the toilet at the back of the club, that I saw him. My eyes tried to focus on the blue lettering on his tight-fitting white T-shirt but the letters seemed to morph into an alien alphabet. Either that or I was completely twatted. He stopped me before I'd even got to the urinals. Even though he was a bit fuzzy round the edges, I took in his dark olive skin, brown eyes, full lips and square jaw line: a wet dream straight from my adolescence. He looked Arabic and was leaning against the wall, a can of Red Stripe in one hand, cigarette in the other, with a slight curl to his upper lip.

'*Shalom.*'

'Come again?'

'I saw you earlier. You don't stop still for very long, do you?' he said, smiling.

'This yours?' He handed me a bottle of Evian water.

'I must have dropped it. Thanks. I like your T-shirt. What does it mean?' I asked.

'Never mind that.'

He grabbed me by the arm and pushed himself onto me. It was the first time that night I'd touched or kissed anyone and it was sheer relief to let go, as I pressed my body onto his. He was shorter than Ahmed and stockier, with large, square shaped hands that grabbed mine firmly and led me away. I noticed he had a full arse and I couldn't wait to bury my face in it later on, given half the chance.

'Let's go and sit down,' he said.

We went to the *Red Room*, a designated recovery area for those trying to recuperate from the mayhem outside. But inside, under red lighting, a car crash of bodies sprawled over red cushions and sofas in unusual and twisted positions. Some had heads lowered between their knees presumably bracing themselves for the impact of the crash, whilst others looked wide-eyed and startled, obviously unprepared for a sudden screech of brakes and headlong collision - casualties from excessive drug taking or the wrong cocktail of drugs.

I'd been there myself in a K-hole, virtually paralysed from the neck down, or, having convinced myself that one more little line of Charlie would do the trick, had stumbled onto the dance floor, paranoid the pain in my shoulder, neck and chest would lead to a full blown heart attack. And each time I'd had a really bad drug experience, I'd sworn to myself there and then, never again, but that didn't stop me from doing it the following weekend, or the week after that, once the memory of how awful it had been had worn off.

Part of me still hoped that each time I fell down the rabbit-hole I'd climb back out and inch closer to my ultimate goal - of eventually recognising it, walking round it and crossing over to the other side. But each time I went out on a bender of a weekend, I just seemed to slide ever further on that drug-induced helter-skelter joyride, round and round and back on in to – 'All The Fun of The Fair': blinded by the illusion - a kaleidoscope of coloured lights, giant disco balls and silhouettes shifting staccato-like on the dance floor. There I was - back again like I'd never been away - back in the hall of mirrors where you don't even recognise your own face staring straight back at you – lost in a maze of my own creation where a thousand dreams vanish in a haze of dry ice pumped from a mother of a smoke machine.

Sitting at the far end of the red room, one guy didn't look at all well. Breathing heavily, he was beginning to look extremely agitated, his T shirt already drenched in sweat. Suddenly his arms and legs started jerking uncontrollably. His friends were trying to restrain him and give him water. At that point, two security guys lifted him up and carried him out of the *Red Room*. He'd be taken to the back of the club, just like the other drug casualties, where he'd receive First Aid before the ambulance was called, much to the annoyance of the club owners and promoters. They risked police raids, and possibly even closure, if they exceeded their quota of ambulances in any one weekend.

'Too much G,' I said.

'What's that?'

'You know. Liquid ecstasy, Gina, GHB. The stuff they use to unblock drains, clean ball-bearings with... fuck knows, mate.

You hear so many stories. You don't know what to believe.' Was it a coincidence that changing the position of just one letter gave you GBH.

'You mean 'Goodnight Cinderella'?'

'Never heard it called that. It's got a sort of tragic campness to it. Very Judy Garland!'

'That's what my friends call it back home.'

'I can't see it catching on here! It's all about proving your macho credentials.'

He leaned back against the wall and smiled.'You're funny. What's your name?'

'David. Yours?' My eyes were beginning to loose their focus, as the E really started to kick in.

'Yossi. I'm from Israel,' he paused 'but I'm flying back tomorrow evening.'

I knew there had to be a catch somewhere. There always was. He told me about his life in Israel: apartment in central Tel Aviv near the sea, worked free-lance as a stylist and costume designer. He was in London as they were filming a new commercial for an Israeli fashion label in Nottinghill.

'If you ever fancy a trip to the Holy Land, let me know,' he said.

'I don't need to travel to the Middle East for that. Take a look around you. We've journeyed far and wide, mate. This is the gay Mecca. The New Jerusalem. I mean some of these guys are so pumped full of drugs they already think they're in seventh heaven.'

He started laughing and ruffled my hair.

We stayed chatting for another hour then left the club in a minicab, high and horny on a cocktail of chems. Crossing Tower Bridge, I looked out of the cab window and saw the now familiar landmarks of Bishopsgate and East London - UK-style skyscrapers proclaiming themselves as part of the new London skyline: Tower 42, the phallic shaped Gherkin and Canary Wharf with its flashing pyramid-shaped roof that looked like it had just landed from outer-space. The sun was streaming into the cab window and I closed my eyes. Further east, its rays would be slicing through the vertical gaps of the great monoliths to capitalism: Barclays bank, HSBC, City bank and Canary Wharf tower - our very own twenty-first century Stonehenge.

It was nearly eight in the morning and I was still buzzing. My trainers were filthy, there was chewing gum stuck to one of the soles again and I was in desperate need of a good shower, but everything felt right with the world. I'd met one of the sexiest guys in the club, and even though he lived in Israel, none of that seemed to matter now. The least I could do was return his invitation to Tel Aviv by inviting him back to my neck of the woods – to my humble abode in Whitechapel. It didn't seem to matter that I kept forgetting his name and he was looking slightly hazy around the edges. I intended to make the most of it, seeing that he was flying back tomorrow evening and I hadn't had sex for over two months.

Chapter 4

The taxi passed Aldgate tube station and I pointed out the primary school I'd worked in for the last five years: *William Booth Community School* – an imposing five storied Victorian building, set back from the main road, and surrounded on all sides by the standard high-security, electronic-gated fence. The glassy eye of a CCTV camera scanned the empty playground and school entrance. On the other side of the road – a billboard poster advertised the latest mobile phone. A couple of months back the Met. had plastered the same billboard with a massive rainbow-coloured poster against homophobic hate crime. It lasted a day before it was ripped to shreds and all that was left was a spectrum of part of the rainbow and the word 'hate'.

As we turned into Whitechapel Road, I pointed out the domed and turreted East London Mosque that dominated the skyline and rose high above the rows of Asian clothing stores and fast food joints. Being Jewish and Israeli, I was interested in Yossi's take on the area and pointed to a shop window on the other side of the street with faceless mannequins dressed in tailor-made suits. In years gone by, it had been the office of the *Daily News* and still bore the emblem of the Star of David above its doors. Further along was the *Islamic Bank of Great Britain* which had recently opened up for business, operating on the principle of not charging interest and only investing in products and services that are not forbidden by Sharia law.

'It's like home from home. We could be somewhere in the West Bank,' Yossi said, laughing as he squeezed his hand between my legs and began to kiss me. Then he stretched out and laid his head in my lap, a huge smile on his face. I checked the cab driver's rear view mirror and he suddenly caught my eye. I smiled back but he quickly averted his gaze, looking at the road straight ahead of him. What did I care what he thought anyway? If he had a problem with two blokes high and horny in the back of his cab, what on earth was he doing working for the gay clubs down in the Vauxhall village?

Looking out of the cab window, I couldn't quite believe I'd lived in this corner of Tower Hamlets for coming on for ten years. We passed the Whitechapel bell foundry which had been in business for centuries and had made the original bell Big Ben; and headed towards the tube station and Whitechapel market, now deserted of the many stalls which, on any other day of the week, would be selling cheap household goods, Bollywood porn or glitzy pictures of Mecca and Hajj. Opposite the market was the 'Royal London Hospital' or 'The London Infirmary', as it was known in a by-gone age, when barbers, who had the sharpest instruments, would practice surgery, and body parts and excrement would be taken out each night to be dumped on the streets. Now, the streets were cleared of amputated limbs, but on the odd occasion you might see those knocking on death's door congregating outside the main entrance in wheel-chairs or elbow-crutches, limbs in plaster, holding a drip in one hand, fag or can of Special Brew in the other, escaping the tedium of an overcrowded and understaffed NHS ward.

The taxi slowed down and stopped outside my block of flats that belonged to 'Tower Hamlets Community Housing'. I got the flat for being a 'key worker' and was lucky enough to get a cheap rent deal. The drawbacks were the noise and the neighbours. Whitechapel aint no Highgate Village, and certainly not for the faint-hearted. I'd moved from a previous flat, just off Brick Lane, because gangs of youths would shout 'battyman' and block the stairwell that led to my flat. It was like going from the frying pan and into the fire. One of the neighbours, second floor up, would surely have qualified to make a guest appearance on

'Neighbours from Hell.' White trash, two kids, alcohol and mental health problems, she had it all going on. Every now and then, she'd invite the local drunks and homeless from the Salvation Army into her flat, and at three or four in the morning, you'd suddenly hear raised voices, effin and blinding, and banging doors to the accompaniment of drunken singing on the stairwell. We were in the process of trying to evict her, and right now she was the last person I wanted to bump into. Getting out of the cab, Yossi offered to pay the fare, but I got there first and shoved a scrunched up twenty quid note into the cabby's hand.

In the park across from the flats, a small group of Bangladeshi lads, impressing each other with gestures of street bravado, were hanging out smoking pot, their trackie bottoms slung low on their hips to show the parting of the arse cheeks. The irony of it. If only they knew the idea first took off in certain jails in the U.S - low hanging trackie bottoms meaning you were the bitch and up for some behind the bars, rear-guard action. For now, I decided against taking Yossi for a stroll in the park and fumbled in my jacket pocket for my keys.

As we climbed the stairs to my flat on the third floor, I couldn't help but wish I was bringing him back to somewhere a bit more upmarket. But I guess that's what you get for being a key worker for the local community. If I'd wanted to do a really useful job like investment banking or gambling on stocks and shares, no doubt I'd be living in my dream penthouse apartment further east in Docklands rather than making do with social housing in Whitechapel. As it was, I put up with local Bangladeshi kids each night, high on skunk, spray painting the name or motif of their gang all the way up to the third floor. 'Brick Lane Massive' or 'Cannon Street Posse' usually had their stamp somewhere on the white walls of the stairwell, which were continually being repainted by the hard-pressed Housing Association site manager.

I'd see them disappear late at night, Hansel and Gretel-like, leaving a trail of beer cans, empty packets of rizzlas and crisps behind them. Michael said it didn't bother him, that this was London and to be expected. I wasn't so sure and had recently caught myself in flights of fancy, dreaming of taking up residence in the gay Mecca of Vauxhall - the high life or the low life, depending on how you saw it, right on my doorstep.

The flat was a pigsty. Neither Michael nor I had bothered to tidy up before we ventured out into gay club-land south of the river. A couple of half drunk flutes of champagne, and Michael's rizzlas and tobacco lay scattered on the Indian wooden table next to the floor cushions. Discarded jeans, underwear and T shirts lay strewn around the entire flat, deemed either not trendy or fetching enough to make it as the outfit of the night. In the kitchen half eaten mounds of sticky pasta had stuck overnight to the dinner plates, and rubbish was spilling out of the cheapskate swing-bin we'd bought in Pound Land.

I apologised to Yossi for the mess. He just smiled, unbuckled his belt and took off his jeans then sat on one of the kitchen chairs in his black jock-strap. I poured some orange juice into two glasses and chopped two smallish lines of coke from what was left of the gram from last night. I didn't have any notes left, so I tore part of a club flyer, rolled it as best as I could, then snorted the few crumbs of coke into my left nostril. I handed the rolled piece of card to Yossi and knelt down, feeling for his cock and balls under his jock. He wasn't hard but I put it down to taking too much ecstasy. Then I looked up.

'What's wrong?' I went to hug him and he flinched. For a moment I wondered if it had something to do with him not getting a hard-on. He didn't answer.

'Is it something I've done?' I asked.

He wiped the tears with the back of his hand. I reached for

his forehead and kissed him.

'I'll put the kettle on. Would you like a cup of tea?'

He nodded. I poured water into the kettle and waited for it to boil, staring out of the kitchen window at the clock on top of The Royal London hospital. It had stopped months ago and was still showing quarter past four. A double-decker bus was parked in the bus depot behind Whitechapel tube station, vibrating ever so slightly at the edges a bright, blood-red. I stood waiting for the kettle to boil, my ears still ringing and some mindless tune stuck on replay inside my head.

He looked handsome and vulnerable, sitting there in nothing but his underpants, more muscular than Ahmed, but older and with a belly that hung over the top of his jock-strap. I wanted to tell him that it was ok to cry, that the bad stuff never lasts for ever, when the sun suddenly disappeared behind a cloud outside, casting the kitchen into shade.

'I don't know what came over me,' he said.

'Look, there's nothing to be sorry for. And you don't have to tell me, not if you don't want to.' I gave him his cup of tea.

'Thanks. You're very sweet,' he said.

'Look, why don't I run a bath. We could both do with a wash and it'll help us relax.'

'Good idea. And no more drugs. I have a plane to catch, remember?'

I went into the bathroom, turned both bath taps on and poured in some bubble bath. I then lit a couple of candles and looked in the mirror. Dark circles and massively dilated pupils stared back at me. My cheeks had more of a sunken look than usual but my arms were looking pretty pumped. Poking out my tongue, I noticed a thick, yellow coating had sprouted right down to the tip. Pulling at the corner of my mouth, I examined the inside of my cheek where I'd accidentally chewed it earlier on. I'd seen better crystal meth before and after pictures! I looked completely washed out, but then it probably wasn't such a good idea staring at myself in the mirror when I was off my face. I touched the scar on my forehead above my left eyebrow, a permanent reminder of being queer bashed in Kings Cross.

I still saw him at night when I closed my eyes- the swagger as he approached me, the tattoo on his left forearm, his gesture to follow him down the side street. It had all happened so quickly, I didn't realise I was bleeding until I put my hand to my face and felt it cold and wet. But now, staring at myself in the bathroom mirror, I felt completely removed from it – as if it had happened to somebody else.

Suddenly feeling a bit light-headed, I sat down on the edge of the bath. What was I doing? I was going to be thirty five in a few months time, and here I was again, off my face, barely able to stand up, with a virtual stranger in the next room. Michael said I had a knack for attracting all the waifs and strays, the down and outs, down right deranged or slightly unhinged disco bunnies of gay club land. Damaged goods - that's what he called them. Said they could smell me a mile off. But then aren't we all a bit damaged in some way, don't we all bring baggage from our past? I thought of the guys I'd met in the last few years which included a homeless rent boy from Brazil, a crystal meth induced schizophrenic from Morocco and the ultimate bad boy - a drug dealing illegal immigrant from Turkey who I'd visit every month in Holloway prison.

The bathroom door opened. Yossi was carrying two flutes of champagne and looking a lot happier. 'I found it in the fridge.' He knelt down and put the glasses down at the end of the bath, near the taps. 'Just so you know. I don't make a habit of crying in strangers kitchens,' he said.

'I'm hardly a stranger. We've known each other for the best

part of a few hours! In gay terms, we're practically engaged! Come on, get in.'

We both stripped off and clambered into the bath rather awkwardly. I let him have my end, whilst I sat hunched over by the taps. The water suddenly rose to the brim and splashed over the bathroom floor. Yossi just laughed and for the first time I noticed two silver, interlocking triangles, nestling between the dark hairs on his chest. I held the Star of David between my fingers.

'He had a male lover, you know,' said Yossi.

'Who?'

'King David. You should read the books of Samuel in the Old Testament.'

'I'll get my Bible out now shall I? And today's sermon is – 'god's gift of infinite variety in human love." I passed him the champagne.

'When Jonathan's slain by the Philistines, David says 'thy love to me was wonderful, surpassing the love of women."

I couldn't help laughing. 'Well this is a first. I've never shared a bath with a guy who quoted scripture before. Next you'll be telling me Jesus was gay.'

'Ever read the secret Gospel of Mark?'

'Oh, come on! Maybe one or two of the disciples. You know what they say. One in ten and all that, but J.C? The main dude? I'd like to see those po-faced Christian types put that in their pipes and smoke it, not to mention the God Hates Fags brigade.'

'You don't think I'm serious? You won't find it in the Bible. But someone did find a letter at a monastery near Jerusalem. It refers to this secret gospel where Jesus spends a night with a young man who appears wearing a linen cloth over his naked body. It's written that he shows him the mysteries of the Kingdom of Heaven.' He shot me a mischievous grin. 'Shall I show you the mysteries of my Kingdom of Heaven?'

He stood up, saying something in Hebrew, and droplets of water caught the light as they rained down over me in a baptism all of my own. I took him all in: his muscular hairy thighs, his manly belly, each part of him breathing new life and a sexual awakening into my tired and spaced-out body beneath him. I closed my eyes, took a deep breath and fully immersed myself in the bath water. When I resurfaced he was lathering himself up, looking down at me, and I felt his hand gently guide my head to his beautiful circumcised cock.

It must have been hours later when I heard the front door close and glanced at the clock. It was nearly midnight and Michael had only just got back. My mouth was dry and I was covered in a cold sweat, but I forced myself up and staggered out of bed. Creeping into the kitchen, I saw him sucking the life out of a cigarette, and scouring the pages of the latest edition of QX magazine – one of London's gay freebies, full of photos of guys off their faces out on the scene and Latino escorts with bubble butts and monster cocks.

'Why is it always the same guys off their faces who get their chiselled mug shots and six packs in here week in week out?' he asked.

''Aint it obvious? This is what we're all meant to aspire to – the dizzy heights of the gay glitterati in club-land - six packs, massive pecs and perfect model looks – oh and don't forget that obligatory tribal tattoo that seemed like a good idea at the time back in the early nineties.'

Michael pursed his lips into a trout pout and pulled back the skin on his face. 'Strike a pose, there's nothing to it!'

'Very fetching! I can just see you on the front cover of next week's QX. Her Madgesty would be proud! But come on, mate, fess up, what was with the big disappearing act last night?'

He leant back in the chair, his black leather jacket unzipped, and blew a smoke ring into the air. In the half light of the kitchen, with his mass of dark curly hair and his goatee beard, there was something of the faun or satyr about him.

'I tried to find you before I left *Beyond*. I looked everywhere. Honest. Then I met this guy.' He smiled apologetically and I sat down at the table opposite him.

'I'll forgive you dear friend, but next time - try a bit harder to find me before you leave ok? You're not going to turn into a pumpkin or anything at the stroke of midnight. I was worried about you.' I took one of his cigarettes and lit up. I decided to add giving up the fags to my list of things to do next week.

'I lost my new top, the Diesel one.' He paused, glancing down and I noticed the thin line of body hair that rose from his belly to spread across his chest.

'Don't tell me. It was discarded in the throes of sexual passion in a toilet cubicle at *Beyond*.'

Michael sang a line from the Elaine Page and Barbara Dickson duet. 'You know me so well!'

'God, you're camp - and showing your age! Anyway, it wouldn't surprise me if your bit of trade saw his chances and made off with it. Remember that arsehole who took my jacket a couple of months back?'

'Guess it's a fag eat fag world, honey-child.'

'So tell me about the guy. What does he do? Gonna see him again?' I asked.

'He was ok. Oh, you know how it is. You meet them in the club off yer tits, think they're some tough guy who'll give you hot, nasty sex, then you go back to their place, and somehow the fantasy falls apart. To be honest, he was pretty camp. Should have seen his bathroom - beauty products everywhere, and this camp little doll thing sitting on a roll of bog roll. Jesus, I nearly fled for the hills when I saw that!'

'Sounds like a match made in heaven to me!' I said.

Clearly, Michael wouldn't be seeing *him* again. In fact he rarely saw anyone more than once. I put it down to the *Goldilocks Syndrome*: Too tall, too short, too fat, too thin, not tough or manly enough, too much of an arrogant arsehole. There was always something better just round the corner.

'Anyway, enough about me. What little escapades did you get up to?'

'Ssh...not so loud. He's asleep.'

'You bought someone back? You old hussy ! Tell me more. I want all the gory details.' Michael leant forward, his cigarette poised between thumb and forefinger. He'd perfected the art of holding his cigarette like that because he reckoned it looked more manly.

'His name's Yossi,' I said.

'Do I detect a hint of foreign? A calling to some far away land full of Eastern promise? No, don't tell me. He's from the Home Counties, has a perfect English accent and very pale, peachy white skin.'

He knew it had been years since I'd slept with or dated anyone remotely English. It's just the way it was. Most people have a type they're attracted to and for some reason, unbeknown to me, mine wasn't of the English Rose variety. I'd heard of the 'gay gene' theory some time ago, but was sure I'd also inherited a rather rare and exotic gene from some distant relative, long since deceased, which compelled me to fall overwhelmingly for foreign men.

'Well, at least I'm not like some gay men, only happy with a carbon copy version of themselves. Bear seeks bear, Shoreditch type seeks similar. Same, same, same, only possibly a slightly more upmarket version! I can't think of anything more narcissistic! Isn't it enough that we all have a penis in common!'

'You don't get away with it that easily! Come on lover boy, where's he from? And more to the point, does *Easy Jet* fly there or are you going to have to fork out a small fortune to fan the flames of an LDR?'

'If you must know, he happens to be Israeli, lives in Tel Aviv and… leaves tomorrow,' I replied, suddenly remembering the fact of his imminent departure.

'Perfect! Unavailable, unattainable and pining away in the Holy Land. How romantic! I can just see the American blockbuster. Sort of *Romeo and Romeo* with a Middle Eastern twist!' He took a drag of his cigarette. 'Just don't go falling in love with this idea of the ideal man. I know you. Remember, love is what you do when the shit hits the fan.'

'Thanks, I'll bear it in mind.'

'Well, to be honest, I'm glad. About time. I was beginning to think you were doing a Kenneth on me. Turning all asexual,' he said.

'Thanks for the vote of confidence.'

'So, I take it this means you're finally over Ahmed?'

'Michael, I've just met the guy.'

'Well, he sounds your type, very you. Foreign, no doubt of dark complexion - '

'If you must know, he's invited me there for a holiday.'

'Oh my God! Stop! This is so you!' He was cracking up with laughter. 'Don't tell me. Before you know it, you'll be learning Hebrew, getting the snip down below and converting to Judaism. *Mazel tov* ! When's the wedding?'

'You're a fine one to talk. You're the one who's big on religious conversions, not me.'

Last year Michael had become a fully paid-up member of the local Buddhist centre in Bethnal Green, dutifully paying his fiver every Tuesday evening to sit cross legged, chant 'Om Shanti' and indulge in some pretty full-on navel gazing.

'Yeah well, I don't think the transformation's entirely complete do you? And I'm sure Buddha wouldn't exactly give his seal of approval to my drug-fucked excesses of the weekend. In fact, if I were a proper Buddhist, I would dutifully recognise that, having broken the precept of refraining from all intoxicants, I will, no doubt, be reborn in my next life as a worm. No, wait, not a worm. Pond scum.'

'No Michael, not pond scum. The scum that feeds off pond scum!'

I'd known him for years. He was my first ever boyfriend - I'd met him about fifteen years ago, when we were both still at Uni in Manchester. Me reading History, him Sociology. And now here he was, doing his Masters in comparative religion and going all 'New Age' on me. I mean, I know Boy George turned to Hare Krishna, post smack and everything, when things got out of control, but Buddhism! It just seemed so nihilistic! Michael had dragged me to the centre once and everyone was incredibly intense during the tea break, sipping their luke-warm camomile tea and discussing how best to transcend Desire. God, you may as well be dead! Life *is* desire! I didn't want to transcend it, especially right now, when I was in mid-flow and in my prime. Without desire and passion, what's left? Maybe I got the wrong end of the stick, but I left the centre disillusioned with the whole shebang, and determined to get twatted that very weekend.

'Seriously Michael, I wouldn't give yourself such a hard time. You're just having a little break from it, that's all. Anyway, who was it who said 'the road to excess leads to the palace of wisdom?'

'Search me. Someone who obviously hadn't been to *Fire*!'

I left Michael in the kitchen pondering the philosophical tenets of hedonism and went back to bed. Yossi was already propped up on the pillow and I wondered how much of our conversation he'd heard.

'I wish you didn't have to go back to Israel tomorrow,' I whispered.

'You're not the only one,' he said.

I still wasn't a hundred percent sure he felt the same way. You never can tell. I half expected the usual outcome - a half-hearted promise to stay in touch the following morning, followed by an awkward exchange of telephone numbers.

'No it's a crazy idea -'

'What is it?' I asked sitting up in bed.

'Well, I was thinking… maybe I could extend my stay. Delay my flight. Just for a day or two though.'

I was stunned. Nobody had offered to delay their flight for me before. It was impulsive, romantic – a grand romantic gesture in a city where sex is on tap and romance is a free gram of coke.

'No, it's a silly idea. I've scheduled a meeting for tomorrow evening.'

'Can't you reschedule?'

'It's with the director of a play – 'Bent'. It's playing at a theatre in Tel Aviv. I'm designing the costumes. Forget I said it.'

'The play by Martin Sherman? The one about two gay lovers in a concentration camp?' I'd seen the play as an undergraduate at University. It had made a serious impression on me. 'Fuck, I love that play. The scene where they're standing next to each other but can't touch – and they say all the things they want to do to each other but can't. Then they each cum in their prison camp uniform.'

'Love will find a way – even if it is between two gay Jewish men in a concentration camp.' He paused. 'I guess you're right. I could reschedule my meeting. I'll phone him in the morning.'

I clambered on top, straddled him and kissed him all over.

'I'll take that as a 'yes',' he said.

Smiling, he kissed me back then stretched and turned over so we were spooning each other. He soon drifted off to sleep again but I couldn't stop thinking about what we might do together now he was extending his stay. I wanted everything to be perfect. I propped myself up on my elbow and lay watching him, mesmerised by the way his Adam's apple climbed to a sharp peak. My gaze followed down to the dip below, a small hollow, formed by the two collar bones on either side, and below that, his silver star. The moonlight was shining directly into the bedroom and it seemed that each point on the star was emitting its own light. He looked so peaceful lying there asleep, as if all the drama of a lifetime had just slipped away, as if the slate had been wiped clean. I found it hard to believe that only hours earlier on the kitchen floor I'd lifted my head from his lap to see him crying inconsolably.

Chapter 5

Yossi had been to London countless times before, so I decided against playing the conventional tour guide and showed him Brick Lane instead. Brick Lane or 'Bangla Town' was only a ten minute walk from where I lived and the hub of the Bangladeshi community. Even the names of the roads were written in Bengali script. Indian restaraunts, where you'd usually have to bring your own beer, lined both sides of the street, but it was too early for anyone to be touting for business; it was just before midday. A blue van parked outside the 'Taj Mahal' and men in blood-stained white aprons, carrying carcasses of halal meat slung over their shoulders, got out and made their delivery. The great hunks of meat would be hacked, chopped and fried, for the hordes of hungry customers – mainly Brits on the look out for a cheap curry and beer, who'd pass through Brick Lane later in the day. Continuing on, we passed manikins in shop windows, decked out in brightly coloured silk saris and sporting 1970's beehives then came to a stop on the corner of Fournier street.

We looked up at the building, which was now 'London Jamme Masji', a local mosque. On Friday, the shoes of worshippers would literally spill downstairs and out onto the street, but different groups of immigrants in the past had turned the building into their own place of worship. The French Huguenot community had worshipped here when it was a Protestant church, and over a century ago, the local Jewish community transformed it into a synagogue, before moving to the 'bagel belt' in the sixties, to Golders Green and Hendon. And now it was one of many mosques in this part of the East End.

'This used to be a synagogue?' Yossi asked incredulously.

'Look up there. Can you see the sundial? Read the inscription.'

'*Umbra Sumus.*'

'It's Latin. 'We are shadows'. I guess nothing stays the same. Maybe in another hundred years this place will change hands again and become a Hindu temple or Gurdwara.'

Yossi was smiling.

'What is it?'

'It's you. I can just see you in the classroom.'

'Oh my god, I'm boring you! How could you let me drone on and go all geeky!'

'Don't be crazy. This place looks like it's steeped in history. But wait till you see Tel Aviv. It's a UNESCO World Heritage Site for Bauhaus.'

Earlier on, I'd shown him the men's clothing shop in Whitechapel, which had originally been the office of the 'Jewish Daily News', and 'Burger King', just by Aldgate East Station, which had once been a Kosher restaurant. On the odd occasion you still might see an Orthodox Jew, dressed in a black suit and wide brimmed hat, walking along Whitechapel road, but the Jewish market traders, tailors, leather workers and boot makers that had settled here at the turn of the century were ghosts of a bygone era. Now there was only a scattering of synagogues, and of course, the well known bagel shop at the North end of Brick lane, open twenty four hours a day.

We stopped for coffee just under the Old Truman's brewery, near where the plastinated 'Body Worlds' exhibition had been displayed - human and animal corpses, drained of their fluid, preserved, and then resurrected in your very own twenty-first century freak show. Not far from here, the same crazed German professor, who'd exhibited 'Body Worlds', had performed a televised live autopsy. Members of the public flocked to witness a macabre spectacle - the drilling and chiselling away at a cadaver, just as trainee surgeons had done over a couple of hundred years ago, when graves were dug up and ransacked to provide enough corpses for them all.

There was a chill in the air and we carried our two steaming coffees outside. We sat down at one of the tables facing Brick Lane and watched students, delivery men and local Bangladeshis go about their business, our knees pressing into each other, holding hands under the table. The skin on the pads of flesh, just below each of his fingers, was rough and grainy. I traced my finger along them, as he circled his, around my wrist and drew a faint line along the inside of my forearm to the crease of my elbow. It felt strange sitting here in Brick Lane, just around the corner from my school, which was now locked up and deserted for the Easter holidays. I looked at the posters on the wall opposite, advertising local bands, or the various club nights at the 'Vibe Bar' and '43 Feet East', and wondered if drugs were as readily available on the straight scene. I guess, in certain bars and clubs they were but I'm sure gay men on the whole carried on taking more drugs for longer, tripping the light fantastic, reluctant to trade in their Peter Pan lifestyle for a pair of slippers and a good book until they absolutely had to.

It felt good to be out of the flat and away from the Vauxhall club scene. To be honest, I was tiring of the same faces, the monotonous drone of commercial house music and chasing after crap drugs that cost the earth in some converted warehouse, where we were all packed in like sardines. Even after a long break from it, nothing had changed. It was still *Groundhog Day Central* - the blind leading the blind in a drug-fucked stupor, no-one able to find a way out of Muscle Alley or that mythical door rumoured to exist which would lead you out of the labyrinthine passages of cock-struck chemical encounters for good.

'Are you still coming to Tel Aviv?' he asked.

'Try and stop me.'

'It would do you the world of good. Get away from these grey skies, lie on the beach, feel the sun on you. I dare you. Go on, come with me tomorrow?'

I wanted to jump at the chance but held myself in check. 'I'd love to. But the school has an inspection coming up. I was going to catch up on some paper work. Plus there's a bit of a cash flow problem at the moment. This is Britain, you know. I don't know what it's like in Israel but over here we're all maxed out on credit cards and personal loans. Maybe the summer?'

'That's settled then. You can stay as long as you like. It's the gay jewel in the Middle East. You'll love it.'

We walked back and turned left towards Liverpool Street as I wanted to show him the rows of Georgian houses with old French shutters. They'd been built by the Huguenots over two hundred years ago after fleeing persecution from France when Protestantism was outlawed. We then walked to Spitalfields and lunched in 'Spitz', over a bottle of cold Chardonnay, later crashing out back at the flat for the afternoon. In the evening, I took him to *Lounge Lover*, a trendy cocktail bar in Shoreditch, and we sat on a chaise-longe near the window, surrounded by an eclectic mix of eighteenth century furniture, anatomical drawings and chandeliers, drinking 'Endless Love' cocktails, a delicious mixture of amaretto and champagne. When Yossi walked into the place he was hit by a strong sense of déjà vu, then realised where he'd seen 'Lounge Lover' before - on the pages of an Israeli interior design magazine back in Tel Aviv. I never knew Shoreditch had such international appeal.

Later that night we were lying on the futon, Yossi with his back to me. I stared up at the ceiling.

'Why won't you talk about it?' I asked.

'We have a saying in Hebrew. If a word be worth one shekel, silence is worth two.'

'Look, it happens to loads of guys. You're probably just tired from the weekend.'

It was the second time it had happened though. The first time, I tried to give him a blowjob in the kitchen and he wasn't hard. Not even a semi. He turned to face me.

'It happens David, from time to time. That's all there is to it. Just remember, I like you. That's the most important thing. It's not because I don't fancy you. It's just the way it is sometimes.'

I looked down at his flaccid penis. We'd had sex, oral sex anyway, in the bath on Sunday morning and he'd shot his load all over me. Maybe he was just one of these guys that has to get out of their head to get into the sex. Needs an assortment of class A's to really get off. Or maybe it was just a phase? I'd heard a lot of guys get it at some point in their life. Although having not personally been afflicted, it remained somewhat of a mystery. Was it because he was slightly overweight? I'd heard that could be a contributing factor. Or did he have diabetes and not know it? Then again was it psychological rather than physical in nature? I lay my head on his chest and pondered the myriad of possibilities that could have given rise to his semi-impotency.

Eventually I turned on my side, closed my eyes and thought of Ahmed. I still thought of him, usually just before drifting off to sleep. I'd pull the duvet right up, curl myself into the pillow and remember when we first met at that art exhibition in Shoreditch. How he'd seriously caught my eye so I couldn't help but look and look again whilst a friend of mine, who taught art at a secondary school in north London, rambled on about the influence of Jackson Pollock and Andy Warhol. Or I'd picture him, half naked at five o'clock in the morning, having risen early because he wanted to pray or was suddenly inspired to paint. I'd try and recapture the time with him at Kew Gardens, in the greenhouse looking down through the fine mist at the tropical plant life below, his kiss - that feeling of disappearing into the light, of standing at a precipice about to fall into a moment of almost unbearable joy and happiness. But memory is a blunt instrument. In trying to recapture that lightness of being I felt with him, that exquisite, all consuming feeling, all I managed to summon up were echoes from the past, fragments from my own febrile imagination, hastily assembled together and mocking me from an insurmountable distance. Out of sheer frustration, I'd find myself furiously tossing off, only to feel a greater sense of emptiness once I'd cum and I'd begin to wonder if he'd gone through with the arranged marriage, if he was with Fatima back in the Arab Emirates, if I'd ever see him again. I hadn't heard anything from him for nearly three months - nothing, and just recently the detail was beginning to fade; the picture of his face was loosing definition, and I knew, that in time, most of my memories of him would fade and eventually it would be like we'd never met.

I turned towards Yossi who was now fast asleep and wondered if this too would fizzle out, just like everything else seemed to - whether I'd ever see him again, whether he'd even bother to contact me when he got back to Israel. I drifted in a sea of questioning but felt certain of one thing. Happiness is fleeting - and in trying to recapture even a moment we kill the very essence of it. But knowing all this didn't help. Inside, it still cut like a knife.

Chapter 6

The taxi arrived at 10.30am to take Yossi to Heathrow airport. I decided at the last minute to go with him and waited until he was ready to board his plane. Just before he left to go to the departure lounge, he hugged me and reminded me of my promise to visit him in Tel Aviv. Then he unclasped the chain at the back of his neck and pressed his Star of David into the palm of my hand. I tried to give it back but he'd already turned and disappeared through passport control. He didn't look back.

Trudging up the steps from Whitechapel tube station I was greeted by a thick, grey covering of cloud and the usual fixtures - the old woman humming tunes on grease-proof paper folded over a comb, and the guy in his drab winter coat, matted hair and beard, holding onto the perennial whisky bottle for dear life. Once I'd walked up the stairs and was on street level, the usual ticket touts and beggars accosted me, and it was here that the journey back home really began - through Whitechapel market. But at least the teenagers in traditional Islamic dress, inspired by a firebrand version of political Islam, weren't there on their soap boxes, loud speaker in one hand, leaflets in the other, denouncing Blair as a terrorist and condemning homosexuals as paedophiles and dogs. But in their place, members of the 'Respect' party were out in full force - handing out fliers, collecting signatures and canvassing for the Muslim vote to get Saddam Hussein's sole friend in Westminster, George Galloway, into the Bethnal Green and Bow constituency. I knew they were a force to be reckoned with because even the kids at school had started to wear 'Respect' badges on their school uniforms.

It was always mayhem right outside the tube station as you dodged prams and push chairs, the elderly and the young, the drunks who'd escaped from the Salvation Army further up the road and those who, only a couple of decades ago, would have been locked up in a psychiatric hospital, but were now part of 'Care in the Community'. Discarded KFC and McDonalds food packaging littered the pavement and men whose beards had turned white, or who'd dyed it with henna, waited on the corner, selling cheap international phone cards for those with friends and families back in Bangladesh. As I passed the bus depot and into my street, the heavens opened.

Once inside my flat I poured myself a generous glass of red wine (somehow when the weather's shite I always seem to drink red) and went online. I thought I'd just check how much the flights were to Tel Aviv, out of curiosity. By the second glass of wine, I was entering into the spirit of things, comparing prices and dates, looking at photographs of Tel Aviv and Jerusalem, imagining myself lying on the beach or rambling through the streets with Yossi in the old city of Jerusalem. And I thought about the rest of my holiday, stuck here in London with a mountain of paper work still wondering if Ahmed had been dragged down the aisle kicking and screaming. It was still pissing down with rain outside when I decided to throw all caution to the wind – and bought a return flight to Tel Aviv for later that week courtesy of El Al Israeli airlines.

'I can't believe you're going. You'll give him the shock of his life. You only met the guy a few days ago.' Michael was still in his work clothes. He worked as an administrator at the Metropolitan University - another bedrock of Islamic radicalism. He'd told me the men's toilets were full of anti-Semitic graffiti and verses from the Koran. It didn't surprise me. A girl in my class, just the other day, told my teaching assistant that she hated Jews. Not that she had a clue what she was saying but her parents certainly did.

'You're just jealous. I've never been and the invitation's there. Why shouldn't I go?'

'Let me see. Maybe it's because you hardly know the guy, or is it because you haven't even told him you're going and then of course there's the odd suicide bomb to contend with.'

'I'll be fine.'

'David, it's bloody dangerous.'

'I just won't use public transport. I'll get taxis.'

He gave me a dubious look. 'You do know it's not just buses they target? It's indiscriminate. Shopping malls, cafes, nightclubs. Anyway, when are you going to tell him?'

'I'm not. It's going to be one big surprise.'

'Oh, it'll be that alright. He won't know what's hit him. You do know this is stalking on a global scale!'

'What's wrong with you anyway? I thought you'd be pleased.'

Michael slumped further down on the sofa. 'It's just a shock that's all and to be honest, the weekend really took it out of me. I don't know about you but I'm still in recovery. Come down from hell. Why do we do it to ourselves?'

'Don't go down that road again. You always say this.' I didn't need reminding of it myself. My mid-week come-down was just kicking in but unlike Michael I preferred to postpone the post mortem indefinitely. If I was going to do drugs I didn't want to be guilt-tripping about it for days afterwards. What was the point?

'I mean it. We make ourselves sick by putting that shit into our bodies and suffer for it the whole bloody week. I had a terrible day at work. And to top it all, now you're disappearing to the Middle East. Who knows when you'll be back?'

'Don't be such a Drama Queen! I'll be back by Tuesday.' I decided a positive spin was called for. 'You're always complaining you never have the flat to yourself. Now you can go out, get absolutely trashed and drag some poor unsuspecting guy back and shag him senselessly.'

He smiled wanly. 'As if I would. Open another bottle of red

would you?'

That night I lay awake thinking about what I'd done. I should have been catching up on marking a backlog of past SAT's papers, but instead I was flying to a country I'd never been to before, to see a man I didn't really know, who didn't even know I was coming. Maybe Michael was right; I was crazy. That evening I waited for the phone to ring, expecting Yossi to call and say he'd got back safely, but it never did.

On Friday morning I arrived at Heathrow airport for the second time that week and picked my ticket up at the El Al Israeli Airlines ticket collection desk. A poster, advertising Israel as a holiday destination, caught my eye. 'Tel Aviv, the nearest you'll get to a Mediterranean city!' and 'Welcome to the White City: Tel Aviv, Unesco World Heritage Site 2004'. The sea was a sparkling turquoise blue and strange white buildings rose up under a cloudless blue sky. Next to it was a poster of Jerusalem, with Jews praying before the Wailing Wall and the golden Dome of the Rock gleaming in the distance. I made my way to the check in. It all felt very déjà vu being back here again only after a few days and I was a bit spaced out as I hadn't slept that well. I'd spent half the night worrying if I was doing the right thing and when I finally did get to sleep I dreamed I was somewhere in Israel as a suicide bomb went off in a crowded marketplace.

Right at the end of Terminal One, two armed Metropolitan police officers were still guarding the entrance to the El Al check in. A large family of Hassidic Jews waited in line to check their belongings in: large parcels and boxes tied with string, several suitcases and even a microwave oven. And I couldn't help but wonder, was it true? Did some orthodox Jews have sex through bed sheets without touching each other? A little boy ran around the luggage trolley, dressed in a little black suit and waist coat, pale white skin and long spirals of hair that curled down to his chin. A handsome, young Israeli security guy in his early twenties stepped forward.

'*Shalom*. Good morning sir. Would you mind stepping aside for just one moment? I'd just like to ask you a few security questions. What is the purpose of your visit?'

'I'm visiting a friend.'

'So, what is your friend's name and where in Israel does he live?'

I wasn't expecting any of this. I should have quizzed Yossi more about the procedure for travelling to Israel. I told him Yossi's full name and address in Tel Aviv. He then proceeded to ask what Yossi did for a living, where I'd met him, was I intending to visit the West Bank, and did I know any Palestinians there or in London.

'And what is your religion Sir?'

I nearly told him I was C of E then thought better of it. 'I don't really have one,' I said.

Eventually he let me go and I had all my luggage put through a huge electronic scanning machine. Then I had to unpack all my belongings from my rucksack in front of everyone and put them back in again. Finally, I was taken off to a little room and I began to wonder if they suspected I was drug smuggling but they were more interested in my shoes which were scanned and inspected, before I was free to proceed to passport control. I never guessed all this had to happen but who could blame them? It wasn't just suicide bombers from Gaza or the West Bank they had to worry about. Yossi had told me that a few years back, a couple of British-born Muslims had targeted a bar on the seafront in Tel Aviv, only one of them had backed out at the last minute, dropping his bomb belt before disappearing into the sea.

I forked out on a pair of new sunglasses at the duty free shop, not exactly Prada or D & G but they'd do the job. I also splashed out on a bottle of champagne for Yossi. I'd already bought him a book on the history of the East End but was in holiday mood and feeling extravagant. Lord knows I couldn't afford it on a meagre teacher's salary but it was a couple of years since I'd been on holiday so a little recklessness was to be expected. Or that's how I justified it. So what if I had a temporary cash-flow problem at the moment? Didn't everyone? That's what credit was for. I waited in line at gate 56, the last gate in terminal one, before going behind another screen, and being searched and questioned again.

I sat by the gate waiting to board and watched the planes taking off as a Hassidic Jew rocked back and forth, holding a copy of the Torah with both hands, the fringes of his shawl dangling from under his black suit jacket. Eventually we were allowed to board and took off to rapturous applause from my fellow passengers.

Halfway through the flight I began to wonder if I was doing the right thing, arriving unannounced. Why couldn't I think things through for once, before acting on a whim and a prayer? Then the panic really set in. What if he wasn't there for some reason? What if he already had a partner who he lived with, and I'd just been a bit on the side while he was in London? Then it dawned on me that he might even be married. God forbid he was like Ahmed and under family pressure to marry. For all I knew he might be from an ultra conservative, orthodox Jewish family. He could have given me the wrong address and really be a Zionist settler in the West Bank with ten kids! The possibilities were endless. God, I needed a drink! After a couple of double gin and tonics I sank back in my seat, closed my eyes and remembered when we'd both stood by the mosque on the corner of Brick Lane, and I'd pointed out the sundial with the inscription 'Umbra Sumus.' I laughed to myself in a post gin and tonic haze of merriment. I certainly didn't feel like a shadow, hurtling towards the Middle

East at 35,000 feet above sea level in a Boeing 747.

A couple of hours later, the pilot announced we were beginning the descent into Tel Aviv. I looked out of the window and saw the faint glow of yellow lights that marked out the coast from the pitch black of the sea. Suddenly we swerved to the left, and for a moment, the aeroplane wing obscured the approaching coastline and I turned my attention to the map and the alternating English and Hebrew names of neighbouring cities and countries flashing on the overhead screen. I noticed with some confusion that Tel Aviv appeared as Tel Aviv-Yaffo on the map and looked out of the window again as the darkness of the sea gave way to a trail of lights, and cars weaved their way along a network of roads in the interior. As we made our descent to Ben Gurion airport, I could just make out the odd palm tree and swimming pool below and a few high-rise buildings in the distance.

Stepping out of the plane, I followed the other passengers into the airport, where we had to queue for what seemed an interminably long time - Israeli nationals on one side, foreigners on the other - again the same barrage of questions from Israeli immigration. No, I was not Jewish. Yes, I was visiting a friend. No, I had not been to Israel before and had no intentions of visiting Gaza or the West Bank. No, I did not know any Palestinians back in London. Yes, I packed my own bag and yes, I had met Yossi in London, in a nightclub. I thought it was best to tell the truth, in case I slipped up telling lies. I think the female immigration officer could probably tell I was gay, probably suspected that Yossi was my boyfriend and eventually let me pass through. I guess few profiles match that of the queer Jihadi terrorist, although never say never. Who knew the myriad of temptations that might lure the potential gay suicide bomber? Would it be seventy two muscle Marys sweating it out in *Disco Heaven,* a paradise island of sexy Middle-Eastern boys or something with a more military bent?

I just wanted to see Yossi and was half expecting him to be waiting for me at the airport, which was, of course, ridiculous. Eventually I found the taxi rank outside and gave the driver Yossi's address. I didn't have a clue where we were heading, as we drove away from Ben Gurion airport and onto a motorway, where the headlights from the taxi would suddenly light up the odd palm tree or a huge bill board covered in the indecipherable Hebrew script. The window of the taxi was wide open and I felt a rush of exhilaration as we sped past road signs in English, Hebrew and Arabic showing the direction to Haifa, Jerusalem or Gaza. We soon hit the outskirts of Tel Aviv then travelled down a wide tree-lined boulevard, passing flat-roofed white boxes of three or four storeys and eventually trawled along a street I now know to be Shenkein Street; a place, I later discovered, to see and be seen in, and regarded by some Israelis as a more bohemian and smaller-scale Hebrew equivalent of Old Compton Street in Soho or Greenwich Village in New York. It was a narrow street full of shops still open, juice bars, coffee bars and restaurants, packed full of young people just hanging out or heading down to the seafront.

The taxi turned down a side street and we passed a synagogue bearing the Star of David just below its flat roof, then into Yossi's street. I paid the fare and fetched my rucksack out of the boot. My hands were trembling as I took the scrap piece of paper with Yossi's address on, out of my wallet. I rang the buzzer. No answer. I buzzed again and waited - still no answer. I stepped back onto the street and tried to guess which apartment was his. Was it the one in complete darkness or the one at the top with washing on the balcony? I sat on the wall next to the giant leaves of a banana tree and dialled his number. It went on to voice mail and I left a short message asking him to phone me. I still didn't want to ruin the surprise.

He lived in one of the flats at the end of a quiet residential street, lined on both sides with flat roofed apartment blocks, some painted pristine white with carefully tended front gardens, others looking in need of renovation, stained an off-yellow with hairline fractures in the plaster spreading over the façade, tributaries to the deeper cracks closer to the ground. On one side wall of a building, just above a network of exposed pipes, the plaster had completely peeled away, leaving wafer-thin flakes of white paint which had bubbled up as if a blow torch had been applied to the surface. And stretched across the length of the street, a forest of thick black cables hung over the multitude of banana trees, palms and flowering bushes.

Many of the apartment buildings were built on grey concrete plinths with narrow flower boxes crammed with geraniums fixed on ledges outside. The full moon had climbed higher overhead and the sky was now covered with a scattering of stars. I looked at my watch. Ten thirty. A dog started barking. I looked down the street. Below a ceramic street sign in Hebrew, bordered with flowers, the letters 'USA' had been spray-canned on the wall underneath. On the other side it looked like they were busy renovating an apartment block. A shoot from the third floor had emptied bricks, plaster and debris into a large skip below. A cyclist passed me on the pavement and I watched as people passed by talking in a language which seemed a strange mix of Russian, German and Arabic. I noticed an Israeli flag in the apartment block opposite - two interlocking blue triangles against a white background. Before I left for Israel, Michael had pointed out that the Star of David actually has seven points: six points that form the outside of the star and one point right in the centre of the hexagram, formed by the two interlocking triangles. He said that each point represented an angel from The Old Testament: Gabriel, Uriel, Michael... I can't remember the others. I looked down at the Star of David around my neck and remembered when Yossi had pressed it into my hand before leaving to board his plane.

A tabby cat suddenly jumped onto my lap and started purring. I began worrying again and weighing up my options. Should I just leave another message and tell Yossi I was already in Israel? Maybe I should just try and get a hotel for the night, sleep on it and come and see him tomorrow morning. But what if he wasn't in town? For all I knew he might not even be in the country.

At that point, a car drove slowly up to the drive outside the apartment block. It was Yossi and he was staring right at me. He leant out of the window.

'David, is that you!' I jumped off the wall and ran to the car. I didn't say anything. He leant over and kissed me through the open car window.

'I don't believe it! *motek*, I don't believe it! This can't be happening. Wait. Let me park the car.' He drove the car into the driveway, opened the car door and gave me a big hug. 'You're in Israel! Why didn't you tell me?' He could hardly contain himself. A wave of shyness suddenly overcame me.

'I just wanted to surprise you, that's all. Where were you?'

'I was at a friend's house. It's *Shabbat*. Anyway, never mind all that. You've come all this way! My God, David! Come in.' He opened the door to the apartment block, muttering that he couldn't believe it.

'No one's done this sort of thing for me before.'

'Well, no one extended their air ticket for me before.' I reached under his T shirt and kissed his chest and nipples as the lift went up to his floor. He tasted hot and salty. The lift suddenly opened and on the front of his door, to the right hand side, hung a ceramic object with Hebrew or Arabic lettering. I was suddenly reminded of Ahmed and the Hamsa that hung on the back of the door to his flat. But this was a mezuzah, something Jews placed on the front of the door, inscribed with verses from the Torah. I looked closer and saw the menorah and Star of David. What was it about walking through a doorway that made it necessary to reflect on God?

'I thought you weren't religious?'

He started to laugh. 'I'm not. You don't have to be religious to hang a mezuzah on your door.'

His flat was open-plan and the walls completely bare. Sash windows, framed by drape curtains which had frayed and torn at the edges, were open and looked onto the street below. I noticed two large porcelain figures of the Virgin Mary standing on the marble floor. Rosary beads dangled from her waist and *Bethlehem* had been inscribed on the base in turquoise. For a moment I suspected Yossi of harbouring closet Christian tendencies.

'Sorry about the curtains. I've been meaning to get new ones.'

'Don't be silly. I've come to see you, not your curtains.' I gave him the champagne and the book about the East End of London.

'You're too much, you really are. What have I done to deserve you, hey?' He paused and looked at me. 'I'm so happy you're here, David.'

So was I. It had only been a few days but I'd really missed him. He asked me about my flight and I told him about the unexpected security checks.

'Yes, it's quite common. Nothing to worry about. The main thing is you're here, *motek*. When are you flying back? Not that I want you to of course.'

'Tuesday.'

'So soon? You're crazy. You should have come for the week.'

'I didn't want to outstay my welcome.'

'Rubbish. Tomorrow is Saturday. I'll show you Tel Aviv. Let me know what you'd like to do. I'll try my best to take Sunday off work as well, seeing that you're only here for a few days.' This was the most excited I'd seen him.

'Can we go to Jerusalem?' I asked. 'I've always wanted to go.'

His face suddenly changed. 'What do you want to go there for?'

I was caught off-guard. 'I just thought – '

For a moment, he seemed lost in thought. 'Walking through those dark, twisting streets…it's like stumbling through an archaeological museum.'

'But I looked in my guide book. It's only 50 kilometres.'

'It's full of religious maniacs David, from both sides. Nutters! It's stuck in the Middle Ages. Tel Aviv *is* Israel!'

There was an awkward silence. He poured the champagne and all I could hear was the loud ticking of a large clock mounted on the wall, its circular white face discoloured by the sun. He saw me looking at it.

'Belonged to my grandfather. Anyway, *L'chaim!* To Life! '

'I think I have some coke somewhere. Would you like some?'

'Never been known so far to decline a cheeky white line.'

I perched on the sofa and Yossi sat down on the brown leather Art Deco arm chair near the window and proceeded to chop two thick, white lines. What Caroline would have called a 'bit of nose', or 'bit of bugel'. He snorted first then handed the rolled shekel note to me.

'Makes me horny – a line of coke. I'm sorry I didn't tell you in London. Somehow it didn't feel like the right time,' he said.

'Tell me what?'

He reached across the glass table for a cigarette.

'The reason I sometimes find it hard-'

'It's ok you don't have to tell me.' I thought I wanted to

know but maybe some things are best left unsaid.

'I'm on antidepressants. They lower your sex drive. But it's strange, when I take coke, not too much, it's like taking Viagra. I get really horny.'

'Why are you taking that stuff?'

'Come and live in Israel for a few years and ask me the same question. You need all the pick me ups you can get. I can assure you.'

I was surprised. I'd never heard him talk like that back in London but then we'd only spent a couple of days together – hardly enough time to really get to know someone. He looked fine but I knew that on the inside he must be on serotonin overload. Michael had been on Prozac a few years ago when he was trying to cut down on the drug binges. He just ended up not giving a shit about anything and partied even more. He told me Prozac was like ECT in the form of a pill; it took away your soul.

Yossi led me to the bedroom, took of his pants and sat on the edge of the bed. I knelt down and placed myself between his two muscular, hairy legs and admired the view: two low hanging balls, a hairy crack and his cock which was now thick and turgid and ready for swallowing. I felt his hand pressing down firmly on my head and my gag reflex kicked in as I went too far down. I felt my wrists being grabbed and my arms twisted and shoved roughly behind my back. He was in control and definitely got off on it. Eventually, he groaned and shot his cum to the back of my throat. I'm glad, for both of us that he could get it up, but after I'd cum, I remembered the sex I'd had with Ahmed - the feeling of intimacy when he looked into my eyes as I was fucking him. I wondered what he'd make of it, me being here in Israel with Yossi? Not that he'd call it Israel. To him it was the Zionist entity, on a par with South Africa in the old days of apartheid. He'd even taken to boycotting Marks and Spencer's on account of their links with the Jewish state.

Lying in Yossi's bed, I could hear the sound of footsteps upstairs and voices conversing in Hebrew outside on the street. I rather liked it, listening to a language but not understanding a word of it, letting it wash over me, just aware of the rise and fall of the voice somewhere in the background.

I was still holding onto Yossi when I woke and noticed particles of dust dancing in the early morning sunshine. For now, this was home. Somewhere in central Tel Aviv, in the arms of an Israeli Jew, who, for some reason, wouldn't or couldn't tell me why he was taking antidepressants nor why he'd baulked at the very idea of travelling to Jerusalem.

Chapter 7

I could've stayed in bed with him all morning. It was warm and safe, my ear pressed to his chest, the sound of distant traffic outside. There was no need to say anything to each other and I relished just lying there, doing nothing, an overwhelming sense of peace and contentment. He then yawned, rolled over and kissed me.

'What's that mark on your forehead?' he asked, getting up and putting on a pair of shorts. 'I've been meaning to ask you.'

Instinctively I put my hand to my face. 'It's nothing,' I said.

'Well, I think it makes you look even more handsome.' He smiled back and left the bedroom.

I didn't move. I fixed my gaze on a hairline crack in the ceiling and followed its trajectory along the wall. That's when it got me, when it always got me – whenever I was off-guard, least expecting it. It was Yossi's remark, full of kindness and intended to make me feel better about myself, that made it that much worse and brought it all back: the sudden blow to my stomach, falling onto the pavement, shielding my face as his boot repeatedly kicked me in the ribs, the shower of spit and torrent of abuse before he left – 'You dirty fucking queer bastard!', 'You piece of shit!', 'I bet you've got fucking AIDS!'

When I got out of the hospital - that's when the drug taking started to spiral out of control. I didn't care. Maybe I should have beat the living shit out of someone myself. Learnt karate then hung outside some straight club in eager anticipation of my first victim. Instead, I went out, got fucked up on a cocktail of chems and got some serious cock action into the bargain. I guess it was my way of saying 'fuck you, you sad bastard! Whilst you're out there getting off on beating the crap out of gay men, I'm in here getting off my head and getting my cock sucked.'

I turned over and lay on my side staring at the window - a large trapezium of frosted glass, cut into an array of geometrical shapes and splashed from the outside in splatters of white paint. Eventually I got up and stood at the door to Yossi's kitchen, watching him scramble some eggs and make coffee. He smiled at me.

'*Shalom! Boker tov!* Good morning! I'm not renowned for my culinary skills by the way.' He was dressed in pyjama bottoms and looked the perfect husband.

'Eggs are great. Thanks.' I hugged him and he felt deliciously warm. I felt my tears warm against the back of his arm.

'Hey, what's wrong?'

'It's nothing,' I said. 'I'm just really pleased to see you again.' The sun was streaming in through his tattered net curtains and I was relieved he didn't press me on the matter.

After breakfast, we walked down the tree-lined boulevard of Bograshov street, passing the main shopping Mall, where people were waiting to have their bags checked by security guards, and down to the sea front towards the Plaza Orchid Hotel. Before crossing the main road to reach the promenade, we passed through a memorial garden. I read one of the plaques.

'London Garden 1942 dedicated to the city of London as a token of identification of the inhabitants of Tel Aviv with the British Nation, who suffered from severe, intensive bombing at the time of the Blitz during the Second World War.' The path zigzagged with carefully tended flower beds down towards the sea and at one point formed the shape of the helm of a ship. Old black and white photographs had been mounted along the wall. I felt an arm on my shoulder.

'*Aliyah Bet* or *Ha'apalah*. Look - ships crammed with Jewish refugees after the Second World War. You need to learn a few things about Israel, David. Israel was a nation forged in refuge.

This was a time when the British were trying to blockade the ships and establish detention camps in Cyprus.'

I studied the photographs carefully. The ships were crammed with people but their faces were jubilant and so too were the faces of the people on the shore running to greet them. I turned and looked the way we'd come. To one side was McDonalds and KFC and in the distance the skyline, broken by a series of V signs tilted at various angles, cranes busy constructing the outskirts of the city.

The air was warm and the sea sparkled in the late morning sun as we walked along the promenade passing joggers and cyclists. All the big hotels were here: the Sheraton, Marriott, Olympia. A few looked like they'd come straight out of some Eastern Bloc communist regime, grey monoliths rising up on towering concrete splints, and had been plonked slap down in the middle of this particular Middle Eastern stretch of the Med. I wasn't so sure about Tel Aviv, 'The White City'. In parts it was too much like an ugly duckling trying to pass as a swan.

Yossi would keep stopping and marvelling at the apartments built in the modernist Bauhaus style of architecture. Last summer, UNESCO had declared Tel Aviv, or 'The White City of Tel Aviv', a world heritage site. 'All this used to be sand dunes. The first Jewish settlers turned it from a wilderness to the first Hebrew City and now look. We're the world capital of Bauhaus,' he proclaimed proudly.

He told me how, in the 30's, Jewish emigrants from Germany who'd settled in Tel Aviv, had imported the Bauhaus or international style of architecture as Hitler later set out to destroy it in their native homeland. The white Bauhaus apartment blocks were simple and functional, typically with small round balconies. Personally I preferred the older style of architecture in southern Europe - the Baroque and Moorish-influenced architectural style in Spain, or the Renaissance and Roman architecture of Italy. But I kept my preferences to myself as Yossi clearly enjoyed playing the tour guide and showing me the historic roots of his city with pride.

A fighter jet came from nowhere, the roar of its engines blasting it across the sky. Then it was gone. Yossi had led me past all the big hotels to a narrow strip of beach near the Hilton Hotel, where Israeli gays would tend to migrate and hang out when the weather was warm enough. We lay on our sun beds, drinking beer and looked on while a group of athletic looking Israelis played volleyball. Out at sea, surfers in their black wetsuits were bobbing up and down, lying on their boards, paddling into deeper water or performing a delicate balancing act as they glided miraculously for a few moments on the crest of a wave. Further out were the windsurfers and their fluorescent yellow sails, and coming in the direction towards Jaffa, a hum that gradually became louder and louder; a swarm of Apache helicopters, the flashing light on each grey underbelly barely visible against the sharp glare of the midday afternoon sun. I closed my eyes and drifted in and out of sleep, lulled by the waves crashing on the shore and the constant beeping of a small bulldozer shifting sand.

After lunch, Yossi took me to Jaffa or 'Yafo' and we passed *The David Intercontinental Hotel* where Madonna had stayed during her visit as a student of Kabala. We walked through cobbled alleyways of art galleries and cafes in the old part of Jaffa until we came to the sea again. This was where Jonah set sail for Tarsus. And not far from the coast, Yossi showed me the rock to which, according to Greek legend, Andromeda was chained as a sacrifice to the sea monster. All there was now was a scattering of rocks near the shore with an Israeli flag claiming Andromeda's rock as her own.

Later that evening, we went to Laila's home. She was an old

friend of Yossi's and had invited us both to dinner. By all accounts, she'd been a top model in Tel Aviv about twenty years ago but now preferred to stay at home and make homemade purses and handbags which she'd sell to trendy boutiques in Shenkein street. She lived in a first floor apartment with its own terrace, which looked onto a tiled courtyard filled with bright yellow and purple flowering plants climbing the outside walls. Her own apartment inside was enormous and open-plan. Abstract paintings splashed in reds, oranges and yellows were hung on pristine white walls. Handmade purses and handbags decorated with large flowers and sequins, her own hippie-styled creations, lay strewn across the floor by the sofa. Laila herself was a giant and her long bony arms were in the sink washing up when we arrived. She had a shock of peroxide blonde hair and unnaturally white skin to be living in such a hot climate.

'What is taking you so long? I thought you are coming at seven? *Shlika*, my house, it is a mess.' She kissed me on both cheeks.

'So *shalom, barukh ha'ba l'israel. Eretz Yisrael HaShlema!* The Greater Land of Israel. How do you say? The land of Milk and Honey?' Her voice was ironic and cutting. Yossi had told me that she'd recently been diagnosed with breast cancer.

'Here is falafel and hummus with tahini. I am making the schnitzel and cooking the vegetables. There is one man we are waiting for. A journalist, Daniel Rosenbaum. He is also coming tonight.' She looked at me. 'You will have plenty to talk about. He lives in London, darling. Which paper does he work for? I keep forgetting.'

'The bastion of Britain's anti-Israeli, left-wing establishment. *The Guardian*. Who else?' said Yossi.

'So, what do you think of Israel, David?' She leant her arms back against the kitchen wall for support.

'The view of Tel Aviv from Jaffa's pretty fantastic.'

'I mean – does it seem racist in some way?'

Yossi gave her a look.

'Laila, please -'

'You have to understand most of the jobs no one else wants to do are done by Ethiopian or Sudanese Jews. And then of course, there are the Russians who find it hard to fit in here and the Arabs who are treated like second class citizens. We could be living in South Africa in the old days of Apartheid.'

'Hey, you'll put him off before he's even seen the place. I *would* like him to come back.' Yossi went over and gave her a hug but she brushed him off.

'Leave me alone. I'm fine. You two boys go and sit outside. The food won't be long.'

I watched as two children played together in the courtyard below, falling down and chasing each other, laughing and shouting, apparently without a care in the world. Yossi took my hand.

'She doesn't mean to be so brusque. It's just -'

'It's fine. It's good to meet some of your friends.'

Yossi had briefed me before we arrived. He'd met her fifteen years ago when he started working as a fashion photographer's assistant. Laila was a bit of a party girl then by all accounts, often hanging out at celebrity parties in Tel Aviv enjoying champagne, coke and gossip.

At that moment, a slightly hunched guy with unkempt hair, wearing NHS style spectacles, arrived on the terrace with a bottle of red wine. Laila came out to greet him and introduced us. He spoke in a very quiet voice, with a slight American accent. We all sat down and there was an uncomfortable silence.

'So what brings you to Israel?' he asked.

'Sorry?'

'The Land of the Jews. What brings you here?'

Homo Jihad

I told him that I'd come to see Yossi and left it at that. Somehow wherever I was, here or back home, discussing Israel felt like a minefield. It was probably best to keep a low profile when it came to politics in the Middle East. Eventually Laila came out with the food - asparagus, schnitzel and potatoes, then sat next to Daniel who poured the wine. He looked at Yossi.

'So how's the therapy going?'

Yossi didn't look up. 'It's going fine.'

I knew he was taking antidepressants but he hadn't told me he was seeing a therapist.

'Have you seen much of Moshe's parents?' asked Daniel.

'I don't mean to be rude but I'd rather not talk about it whilst we're having dinner.'

'Yes of course. I didn't mean -'

Laila leant across the table and touched Yossi's hand. There was another awkward silence. '*My* therapy is actually going very well. In fact, it's going so well, I'm practically in love with my therapist! She's the most amazing person I've ever met! '

'That's fantastic, Laila.' Daniel put his arm around her.

'You know, why can't they just do away with religion and make everyone have therapy? No more mosques, churches, synagogues. Let's face it. The world would be a happier place,' she said.

'But you can't tar all religion with the same brush, my darling. Or even one religion. I mean take Reform and Orthodox Judaism. A world of difference. The danger of religion is if it doesn't evolve or seek to renew itself. If it denies the spirit,' said Daniel.

'Nonsense, everyone should have therapy. Simple. It should be made compulsory for everyone and those who can't afford it should be given help by the state. Religion has passed its sell-by date.' She looked triumphant. I thought to hell with it and decided

75

to speak up.

'I'm not so sure.'

'Oh and why's that?'

'I think it's more about promoting tolerance. It's good for Muslim kids to learn about Passover or for Jewish kids to know about Eid.'

'But they're all going back to their own place of worship. They will only ever worship their own jealous God. They'll forget about difference and tolerance and understanding. Religion will always cause division.'

I should have left it there but she sounded so adamant she was right, it irked me. 'Don't get me wrong. I'm not a believer, far from it, but you have to work with what we've already got. You have to be practical. You'll never dismantle ways of seeing the world that are thousands of years old overnight. You have to change things in small ways.'

'A pragmatist! The politics of the English! So David, what do you do as a teacher to change things, in *small ways* as you say? What do *you* personally do?'

I was stumped for an answer and felt ensnared in her gaze.

'I'm not letting you off the hook. What is it you do to change things, in small ways, as you put it?' asked Laila.

'I don't know. I try to get them to understand why -'

'No. Not what you try to achieve. What do you do?'

For some reason an image of the children dunking their own ten commandments in a bowl of cold tea bags came to mind. 'They made some scrolls. Wrote their own commandments then came up with ideas to make the world a happier place.' I looked at Yossi for support but he seemed to know better and was staying out of it.

'Commandments. The Ten Commandments?' She laughed. 'We all know Moses was high on the bark of the acacia tree on

Mount Sinai when God gave him that little rule book and if he wasn't completely stoned when he saw the 'burning bush', I must be a Hasidic Jewess.' She leant forward on the table. 'Shall I tell you what my therapist does with me? Shall I? She gets me right here.' She touched her chest. 'I feel the pain of my childhood. I know I can never make it better but I feel it and now I can take care of her. What is it that you do that touches your children emotionally? That heals them of their pain?' She was leaning across at me, her eyes filling with tears.

I knew this was no place to enter into an intellectual debate about the merits of religion and psychotherapy. 'Laila, most of us spend a lifetime searching for something that will help us make sense of all this. I'm just glad you've found something that works for you. Really, I am.' I offered to clear the dishes away, relieved to be out of the way, even for just a few minutes. I wasn't used to open demonstrations of emotion with people I didn't really know.

When I returned, Laila seemed to have cheered up and had brought out a home-made fruit tart and a jug of cream. She asked everyone to close their eyes and make a wish, so we did. I wished for Yossi to come and visit me in London again. After desert Daniel talked to us about working for The Guardian, and how anti-Semitic BBC reporting of issues in the Middle East was, then we made our excuses and left.

It was a clear night sky and the wine had left me feeling rather light headed as we reached the main boulevard and headed in the direction of the seafront. Despite the political situation, I felt more relaxed and at ease out on the streets here than I ever did in London. There were no gangs, sink estates and all that goes along with it: low level street crime, anti-social behaviour, Asbos, getting the shit kicked out of you. Maybe when you have a common enemy, the people don't turn on each other.

'He clearly fancies you,' said Yossi.

'Well, I think it's safe to say I won't be going there. Not my type.'

Yossi stopped to light a cigarette.

'Who was Moshe?' I asked.

'Not now David, please.'

'What do you mean, not now?'

He looked pained. 'It's not something I want to go into right now.'

'I just want you to open up and trust me, that's all.'

'Open up? I'm dealing with it, David. I just can't -'

'Dealing with what?'

'It has nothing to do with you.'

'I've come all this way. I spent the last bit of money in my account to fly here and see you. Why can't you just meet me half way?'

'Meet you half way? Did I ask you to spend your money? Did I ask you to come here?'

'You invited me. You gave me your Star of David.'

'I didn't think you were going to hop on the first plane out here.'

'I did it for you! You extended your ticket. I wanted to surprise you in the same way. I thought that's what you wanted. I thought you'd be happy.'

'Listen to yourself. You're hysterical. You don't even know the first thing about me.'

We walked back to his flat in silence. Maybe I shouldn't have asked. It was completely up to him what he told me but I couldn't help but feel certain topics of conversation were just off limits - Jerusalem, ex boyfriends, losing erections. At that moment it felt like I'd come all that way for nothing and all I really wanted to do was get on the first plane back home.

Chapter 8

As soon as we got into bed Yossi turned his back and, minutes later, was sound asleep. Staring up at the ceiling, listening to the gentle rasping sound at the back of his throat and occasional splutter, I couldn't stop replaying the conversation over dinner, the argument and awkward silence on the way home. Who was Moshe and why had Yossi reacted so defensively when I asked about him? What was I even doing here, miles away from home with a man I barely knew? I slowly lifted the bed covers, crept into the living room and tried to make myself as comfortable as I could on the sofa. Now all I could hear was the ticking of his grandfather's clock, and every time I opened my eyes, the minute hand had inched only a fraction of the way round the clock face. I tossed and turned and my thoughts drifted to Yossi's family. Yossi didn't call it the 'Holocaust'. He simply used the Hebrew word 'Shoah'. His grandfather, on his mother's side, had died at Auschwitz. And I was beginning to learn that most of his friends had family members who'd been part of 'The Final Solution', stripped not only of their clothes but also of their names, meeting their end in the labour and extermination camps of *Dachau, Bergen-Belsen, Himmelstrasse* or *Treblinka*. I curled up in a semi-foetal position, drifting in and out of sleep until the first light added a touch of green to the huge banana leaves outside in the garden and birdsong heralded the start of a new day.

Some hours later, I woke, just as a woman with short hair was about to jump overboard a ship crowded with Jewish refugees. She looked up, still clutching a small suitcase of belongings, but the ship and her expression of determination disappeared as I felt the warmth of Yossi's breath and his lips as they brushed against mine.

'I have to go into work for a few hours,' he whispered. I

must have fallen asleep again once he left because it was half past ten when I eventually peeled my sweaty body from his leather sofa. I stood up slightly dazed and went over to the kitchen. Propped up against the milk bottle was a note:

'Sorry about last night. Popping into work for a bit. Chat later. Love Y. xxx.'

I ate breakfast, showered then went into the bedroom. A sepia coloured photograph of two naked youths standing against a rock was framed, yet standing on the floor against the wall. I knelt down. One of the boys was wearing a wreath on his head like an Athenian youth, the flesh of his belly still round and soft. An innocence and beauty smiled back that seemed to belong to a different age. Above the photograph were shelves full of hard-back art, fashion and photography books all in English: Picasso, Van Gough, Mapplethorpe, Herb Ritts, Cindy Sherman. Paperback novels in Hebrew were stacked on the next shelf higher up and lodged in between the hardbacks and paper backs was a stack of old papers and fashion magazines. Peering closer, I noticed a pack of photographs in the middle of the pile. In normal circumstances I wouldn't even have considered it but I needed to know. I needed to know why he would suddenly just close down like that, shut me out. Why the mere mention of Moshe's name would end up in an argument or stony silence. I knew what I was doing was wrong but I couldn't help myself.

I pulled the pack carefully from underneath the stack of papers and fashion magazines, making a mental note of which magazine had been on top. For a moment I hesitated. It wasn't my place to go snooping amongst his things. But it was too late. I'd opened the pack and was sliding out the first photograph, careful not to get fingerprints all over it. A much younger version of Yossi and Laila at her house smiled back at me. She had her arm over his shoulder, towering above him in a low-cut purple dress, looking radiant. Lots of black and white photos of models, male and female, presumably of his work and then a photograph of a handsome looking man with sunglasses, reading a copy of *Ha'aretz* on the beach. It looked like Tel Aviv; I could just make out the Sheraton hotel in the distance. He was shorter than me, dark like Yossi, and older, late thirties to early forties. I was mesmerised, any lingering sense of guilt or anxiety long since gone, and laid the photographs on the floor. My eyes darted from one to the other, trying to piece together those parts of Yossi's life he'd rather keep in the dark. The same man again – this time without the sunglasses. Who was he? There was one of them sitting together in the same café on the corner of Diezengoff street Yossi had taken me to yesterday, another one of him sitting on the edge of the bed, in what looked like this bedroom (was that the same picture on the floor?) smiling up at the camera. I began to wish I hadn't opened the pack but a morbid fascination had taken hold: Photographs of them in London on the London Eye, outside the Houses of Parliament, at the Wailing Wall in Jerusalem, naked shots of both of them.

Suddenly I heard the key turn in the lock. What was I doing? The photographs, his private photographs, were spread all over the floor. Seconds later, the door to his bedroom opened. I looked up from kneeling on the floor to see Yossi standing in the doorway. I froze.

'David, what on earth are you doing?!'

'I didn't mean -'

'I don't believe -' He snatched a photograph from my hand. 'Have you completely taken leave of your senses!? They don't belong to you!'

'I'm sorry. I just -'

'You just…. Nothing! You had no right! They're personal photographs. My photographs.' He crouched down. 'Did you find what you were looking for?'

'I don't know what came over me.'

'*Nishbar li, mimha!*'

'Sorry?'

'Just get out!' He didn't even look at me in the eye.

'Yossi, please I can explain -'

'What word do you not understand? I said GET OUT!'

'Fine. You know what? You were right. I don't know you. You make it impossible because you won't let me in. I was just trying to find a way in, that's all.' I grabbed my wallet from the kitchen table. He called after me.

'David!'

I didn't want to hear it. I slammed the front door behind me and headed towards Bograshov street, stooping every so often under the umbrella of an overgrown shrub or banana leaf. Eventually I found myself in Shenkein Street, disorientated, with a pain that had stuck in my chest and had lodged itself in my throat. All I could hear inside my head was Yossi telling me to get out, shouting at me in Hebrew. I kept replaying the moment when he opened the bedroom door and snatched the photograph from my hand, when he crouched down and asked me if I'd found what I was looking for. What had I done? I'd ruined everything. It was all that I could do to keep walking, to hold back the tears, to stop myself from thinking that this is what always happened, that my love life was just one big disaster after another.

The street was packed with hordes of pushy shoppers and house music was being pumped out of every other shop door. I pushed my way through a small crowd that had gathered under a billboard advertising the latest pair of Levi jeans. A street juggler, barefoot and bare-chested, was juggling with huge metal rings, and next to him a make-shift stall had been set up. A group of young Israelis had organized a petition and were handing out leaflets and calling out in Hebrew. Above the stall, under Hebrew script, the words 'Stop the Israeli Occupation in Gaza' had been painted onto a piece of fabric and fixed to the wall. I stopped at a juice bar, ordered a large banana juice and gulped it down in one. I then lit a cigarette, my eyes straining from the brilliance of the midday sun. Why did I always fuck things up? Why did it always go pear-shaped? I inhaled deeply on my cigarette and considered my options. All I knew was I wasn't ready to go back yet.

As I got up to leave, a middle aged woman with two small children in tow began to shout and scream at the youngsters who'd organized the petition. The juggler suddenly stopped juggling, catching the clanging metal rings one by one and a young man in the Jewish kippah, who up until then had been watching the juggling, turned and walked up to the woman, shouting and waving his hands aggressively. Then an elderly woman in the crowd started up. I left them to it, finished my juice then walked back to Bograshov street and carried on down to the sea.

I passed the memorial garden and the black and white photographs of the Jewish migrants who had settled in Tel Aviv shortly after the war. Crossing the main road that cut the beach off from the town, I carried on until I came to a semi-circle of pebble-dash covered concrete and sat down. I stared at the horizon where the pale, hazy blue of the sky met the deep green-blue of the sea and tried to imagine how it must have been – a refugee on a ship from Europe, overcrowded with survivors of the holocaust, desperate to forge a new life for themselves in the British mandate of Palestine.

There didn't seem to be as many people on the beach today and I watched as a woman twisted her body into a new yogic position. I was going home the day after tomorrow and things had taken a definite turn for the worse since the argument on the way back from Laila's. And now the sordid business of the photographs. Not exactly what I had in mind when I'd boarded the plane at Heathrow.

Everything had been a lot easier with Ahmed, until the end anyway. I closed my eyes and pictured his hazel brown eyes laughing back at me, promising the world. Then I remembered the last day I saw him, when he wouldn't even touch me, when he'd told me about Fatima, told me to leave his apartment, and I'd caught the last tube back home still wasted, unable to believe it was really all over. I opened my eyes to blurry shades of blue and yellow, of sea, sun and sky and was left with a strange yet too familiar feeling. I could keep it at bay most of the time, but it had found me even here, sitting on the sea front in Tel Aviv - a ghostly reminder that I hadn't found who or what I was looking for and probably never would.

I wasn't sure how long I'd been there, but my arms were turning a delicate shade of salmon pink and I was beginning to feel slightly dazed. An Orthodox Hasidic Jew walked past in a long black dress coat and high fur hat.

'David!'

I turned round on the bench and saw Yossi waving at me from across the road. I raised an arm then turned back and faced the sea, fixing my gaze on the perfusion of yellow, gold and orange marigolds, planted neatly in flower beds on top of the promenade wall. He sat down next to me on the bench.

'How did you find me?' I asked.

'Calculated guess. I always come down to the sea myself if I need to do some thinking.' He paused. 'David, I didn't mean for you to leave the flat like that.'

'I'm really sorry I looked at your photographs. I never meant-'

'I know. Listen, I don't know how to put this.' A pause. 'Something happened last year. I should have told you.'

'I should never have pried.'

'Since then-'

Not far from the shore the waves crashed into a cluster of rocks, suddenly sending a white spray high into the air. Further out, a naval ship slowly made its way towards Jaffa.

'Yossi, you don't have to tell me. You were right. Some things are best left unsaid. Let's just try and enjoy the last few days together before I head back to London.'

'Before I met you- '

'Look, there's no need. It's really none of my business.'

He carried on looking out to sea. For a moment it looked like he was having second thoughts. Then he spoke, calmly, without emotion.

'It happened at the Hillel café, East Jerusalem, 9th September, Tuesday night. Forty people injured. Seven fatalities. He was sitting inside drinking a coffee with a friend. They were making plans to develop the botanical gardens in west Jerusalem, near the university.'

He didn't need to say any more. Not even his name. I remembered how his face had changed when I first suggested going to Jerusalem, how he'd avoided the subject when Daniel had asked him over dinner, how he'd turned on me when I asked him who Moshe was.

'He lost both legs and was taken to hospital with third degree burns. On the way he suffered two massive heart attacks. He didn't make it.'

For a moment I felt nothing, then a stinging numbness. I tried to speak but couldn't even think. His words – spoken so matter-of-factly, were all I could hear, but jumbled, scrambled up, each word or phrase clamouring to be heard, repeating itself at random over and over so none of it made sense. The white glare of the sun slowly gave way to a sickly, yellow light that seemed to bristle with the memory of burning sulphur, burning flesh and suddenly everything seemed a long way off: the flowerbed, people passing by on the promenade, the sound of the waves crashing on the beach. Yossi looked down and pressed his hands hard onto the pebbledash. Why hadn't I listened to him? Why couldn't I leave well alone? He must have been through hell and back and there I was pushing him to tell me about Moshe, to open up, to talk about his past.

'I'm a mess, David. I just used to block it out before. I didn't want to know about any of this - the violence, the intifada, the hatred. I just shut myself off from it. Like most Israelis I lived in the *bu'ah*, a bubble, to avoid thinking about the situation here, went to work, partied at the weekend and then this.' He took my hand. 'Are you ok with all this?'

I struggled to find my voice. 'I'm glad you told me. It was the not knowing. That was worse.'

'I have a recurring nightmare. There are bits of glass everywhere - and parts of bodies: someone's leg, a hand, people screaming but no sound coming out, and I can't find him. Moshe's not there. He's not there, David.'

For a moment, I glimpsed the depth of despair and mental anguish that lived inside him. 'I'm so sorry.'

'When I arrived at the hospital he was dead. I didn't even get a chance to say goodbye.'

His whole world must have fallen apart that day. I looked at Yossi, crushed by the devastating effect of one single act of terror and knew they hadn't just killed Moshe that day.

'Yossi, it's not your fault.'

'I should have been there.'

'You were in shock. You were grieving. It's not your fault.'

'I should have been there. I was meant to go to Jerusalem. If I'd been there - '

'It's not your fault.'

He stood up and walked towards the flower bed. '*Ani shone at haim hamehorbanim!*' God, I hate this fucking life! I hate this fucking life!'

I stood up, walked over and put my arms around him. 'You loved him.'

He broke away and turned round. 'If I loved him, I would have been there. If I loved him, he'd still be alive.'

'If you were there, don't you see, you'd have been killed as well.'

'I wish I had been! I wish it had been me instead of him. I wish to God it had been me sitting in that café!'

'You don't mean that. Would you really want Moshe to go through what you're going through right now?' I wanted to fix it, say something that would take away some of his pain, but I realised there was nothing I *could* say, so I kissed him gently and he started to cry. In that instant, I made a promise to myself. I would be there for him - no matter what.

'A month after Moshe died, I took an overdose. Laila found me.' He pulled back. 'Just let me know if any of this is too much. You don't have to stay. I'll understand.'

'I'm not going anywhere. I'm right here.' I held him tighter and kissed him again, aware that in just a few days time, I'd be heading back to London.

*

'So he told you about Moshe then?'

I was sitting on the balcony outside Laila's flat drinking tea. We were on our way back to Yossi's to see a documentary about a gay Palestinian who'd asked the Israeli High Court of Justice to grant him asylum. Yossi was inside checking the time the film started and Laila was sewing a yellow flower onto one of her denim handbags. The air was stifling hot that evening and I listened to the shouts of children playing football in the courtyard below. It reminded me of the noise in the playground back at school in East London: happy, jubilant voices, a vital, irrepressible energy asserting itself.

'The doctor prescribed antidepressants after it happened. That's how he ended up overdosing. Not that his parents wanted to know. They've never accepted he's gay.' She put her sewing down. 'It's so hard for him. But he did the right thing by telling you. It's good for him to talk about it.'

'I didn't know what to say to him.'

'*Im takshiv, tilmad.* If you listen, you'll learn. You don't have to say anything. Just be there for him if he wants to talk about it. You know he's very happy you came to see him. He's just going through a really difficult time right now.' Laila was completely different, relaxed, more at ease with herself. Maybe her mood swings were down to the chemo she was having.

'He told me you found him after he'd taken the overdose. Do you think, in time, he'll ever get over it?'

'David, he's devastated. He'll never get over it. You don't get over something like that. It becomes a part of you. Moshe was the love of his life. And he'll always love him and think of him. We all will. We have a saying in Hebrew. The only truly dead are those who have been forgotten. But I'm glad he's met you David. Take care of him for me.'

'I can't see how I can do that, living in London.'

'You'll find a way.'

'You know, I just can't get my head around it. How can anyone in their right mind do that - blow themselves up, murder innocent civilians?'

'The situation here is a mess. But for now, there is no chance of peace. The best we can do is manage a bad situation. It has to be endured.'

'But violence doesn't solve anything.'

'Tell that to the Palestinians who've had their homes raised to the ground by the Israeli military, who face army check points every time they enter or leave a city in the West bank, who are 'accidentally' caught in the cross fire when Israel is targeting Hamas.'

At that point Yossi walked in. 'Hamas? I leave you two for five minutes and all you can find to talk about is Hamas?!'

'He wanted to know about the intifada,' said Laila.

'So that's it is it? I'm out of ear shot for less than a few minutes, so it's safe to talk about the situation? In case either of you hadn't noticed, it's all around us – the security guard stationed outside the café across the street, the bar that was blown up on the seafront.' He paused. 'I live with what happened to Moshe every bloody day. There's not a day that goes past when I don't physically ache with missing him.' He stopped and rested both arms on the chair in front. 'Laila was right, David. There is no God. What kind of God would allow any of this to happen?'

'Yossi – Please! Not in front of David.'

He turned to me.

'You want to know what the situation's really like? Go, see for yourself. Were you aware Palestinian children sing songs about killing Jews on Palestinian Authority T.V shows? Or that celebrations are held on the streets of Gaza after every rocket attack or suicide bomber kills one of us? Have you seen the cartoons they have of us in their newspapers? Have you?'

'Yossi, enough!' said Laila.

'- Hook-nosed Jews with Swastikas, Christ killers, snakes and vampires drinking Palestinian blood. That's all we are to them!' He stormed back inside.

Later that night, curled up on the sofa with Yossi, I watched the documentary about the gay Palestinian asylum seeker and began to think about what it would be like, growing up gay and Arab in the Middle East. What of the gay men in the Arab world who remain invisible to their society because they're married and have children? And what of Ahmed? For all I knew, he could be one of them – living a double life: back in the United Arab Emirates, married to Fatima and already on the way to fathering his first child. But I couldn't allow myself to think about that. I reached for Yossi's hand. Everything was infused with a hyper reality – the banana tree outside the open window, his grandfather's clock, the warm night air. A reality I would be leaving behind in just a few days time as I headed back to London.

Chapter 9

Samba music suddenly blared from my mobile phone. 6.30am and the alarm had just gone off. I rolled over and hit the snooze button, wishing I was back in Tel Aviv and that Yossi was lying next to me. But it was Monday morning and the start of the summer term.

I hadn't slept well because the crazy neighbour from hell and her drunken pals from the local hostel were slamming doors and shouting on the stairwell, well into the early hours of the morning. I'd even seen one of them through the letter box, mouthing off with a hammer in one hand and in the other, a can of White Lightening. Still, the court case was pending. We'd waited nine months and given written evidence to the Housing Association, chronicling each and every incident of antisocial behaviour. Most of the neighbours were scared of reprisals, but half of them came on board at the last minute and agreed this was the only way of getting her evicted. She'd cornered me on the stairwell shortly after I arrived back from Israel, called me a 'fucking cunt' and said I 'aint seen nufing yet.' I just noticed the bruises on her frail and emaciated forearms.

I groaned as I forced my body up and out of bed, suddenly remembering the imminent Ofsted inspection. The day stretched ahead of me and all I really wanted to do was climb back into bed and hide under the covers for another couple of hours. Everyone's entitled to a duvet day every now and then but today wasn't it.

Judging from the deep guttural noises, Michael was already up and chanting to save himself from the perils of samsara. He'd started meditating with a new found gusto since I'd got back from Israel and was in one of his holier-than-thou Buddhist phases, extolling the virtues of the eight-fold path at every available opportunity. While I was away, apparently he'd taken to hanging out at the Buddhist centre in Bethnal Green and catching up on the teachings of Nineteenth century Buddhist scholars. He'd even resurrected his Buddhist shrine, so out came the framed photograph of a rather young looking and bespectacled Sangarkshita in his saffron robes, which now stood next to a bunch of wilting carnations and a trail of ash from burnt incense sticks.

At school, Caroline stormed into my classroom during morning break, looking stressed out and flustered. 'You'll never guess what's just happened.' She was wearing a new outfit she'd bought during the holiday, a strappy green dress and looked gorgeous. 'I've just had my pupil progress meeting. They pored over my kids' exercise books with a fine tooth comb. Wanted to know why three of them hadn't made the expected progress for this time of the year. I mean, Jesus, I've already got intervention programmes coming out of my arse! They've got in-class support and I listen to those kids read every day but oh no, it's always what more can I do to make sure they reach these arbitrary bloody targets! Am I value for fucking money?! Do I know each of my kids is worth five grand a year? I mean who does she think I am? Rumpel-bleedin'-stiltskin?'

I looked at her blankly.

'Do I look like I can spin straw into gold?'

'No, but you look like you might start stamping you foot in a hissy fit! Look, don't take it personally. Schools are run like businesses these days. You know that,' I said.

'But I try so hard and nothing's ever good enough.'

'Look hon, with the best will in the world there will always be the odd kid who doesn't make the grade. You can throw all the money into extra resources, support and intervention programmes. Kids just don't always perform to our expectations. You're doing your best, that's all any one can ask.'

'And to top it off, we've got a staff meeting after school. Something about 'stakeholders in the local community.' Expect loads of sugar paper, political correctness and group discussion. I can't bear it!' She dumped a pile of half marked exercise books on a child's desk and slumped herself in an orange plastic chair three times too small for her adult body. 'So, how was Israel? Did *Mossad* finally manage to recruit you?'

I told her about Yossi and what had happened in Tel Aviv.

'Oh my God, that's awful. How is he?'

'Blames himself. I'm worried. Worried he might do something stupid.'

'I'm sure you were fantastic. Still, it must be said, Israel has committed appalling atrocities against the Palestinian people. It does make you wonder who the real terrorist is.'

Before I could appeal to Caroline to stand down from her political soap box, the classroom door suddenly opened.

'There you are David, did I make you jump?' It was the Head teacher, Linda Ardent. We nicknamed her the Sergeant.

'Linda, did you have a good break?' I always made sure my classroom door was firmly shut when Caroline came in just in case we were slagging The Sergeant off or passing on some hot piece of gossip.

'Wonderful, thank you! Still, it's back to work now and we all have to change into a new gear! I can see you're both chomping at the bit!' She laughed nervously.

Ofsted was due near the end of term. Not that I could give a flying fuck. I'd been through two inspections before and swore I wouldn't bust a gut for the next one. During the last one, we'd all been expected to stay until ten at night and come into school over the weekend. One teacher, with over twenty years experience under her belt, fell apart, had a nervous breakdown and never came back. I swore I'd never go down that road.

'By the way David, could I have a word when you have a moment? Say lunchtime?'

What did she want now? 'Ok. I'll pop by your office.' I dreaded it when she said 'could I have a word.' It usually meant something ominous.

After teaching Maths or 'Numeracy Hour', as it had been rebranded by the Department for Education, to eleven year olds at the usual break neck speed, I knocked on Linda's door. She was at her computer as usual, immaculately dressed in a sharp designer suit, set of pearls and not a hair out of place. A shoulder-length bob framed her dramatic features: a nose that turned up slightly at the end, high forehead and strong jaw line. She looked up over the rim of her trendy, wide-framed spectacles. Her office was austere and businesslike. Not a child's drawing, card or painting in sight. Instead, just timetables, memos and directives from central government and the local authority.

'Take a seat David. We've had a complaint.'

I think she expected me to register shock or at least show some curiosity. I chose to remain calm and didn't give anything away.

'Well, two actually. From one of the parents. It's actually quite serious.' I could tell she expected me to rise to the bait. "*Gloria Goes to Gay Pride.*' Ring any bells?' She sounded peeved.

'Well, I've heard of Gloria Gaynor, but despite the anthem 'I am, what I am', I hear she's a notorious homophobe. She's the last one I'd expect to see on a gay march!'

'David, this is a serious matter. I take it you actually read this book to your class at some point before the Easter recess?'

I shifted uncomfortably in the chair, desperately scrabbling about in my brain for bits of argument to defend myself. I knew I hadn't done anything wrong but she obviously thought I had, so I needed to present my case reasonably and rationally.

'The book does actually belong to the school library. It's stamped with the name of the school.'

'Well, I certainly don't remember ordering any books like that. We can't be in the business of promoting teaching materials like that in schools.'

'I think you'll find that clause twenty eight was repealed back in 2003.'

'That may be, but this is a primary school David, in a predominantly Muslim area, which makes it even more of a, how can I put this? A culturally sensitive issue. Do you know how many prospective parents come here thinking this is an Islamic school?'

'And that's my problem?'

'I'm just saying we have to be sensitive, that's all.'

'We're learning how all families are different. Why shouldn't children learn that some children have two mummies or two daddies for that matter?'

She looked shocked. "Do I tell everyone I meet I'm a divorced woman? Do you see me going round shoving that down everyone's throats? It's completely inappropriate!' A red flush was spreading like a forest fire upwards from her chest to her neck and throat. I'd clearly hit a nerve. A homophobic one.

She tried to regain her composure. 'I didn't mean... What I mean to say is... As you know, David, this is a very trying time for the school. I have a senior member of staff who's been off work for more than a year, two five year-old children on Zimmer frames because of some apparent incident in the playground, and to top it all, one of the families is suing the school. If that isn't bad enough, three members of staff will shortly be on maternity, the attendance figures are down and Ofsted's just around the bloody corner!'

She clasped both hands together and tried to regain

her composure. 'Anyway, the point is, I can see you had good intentions and your value as a teacher is not in question. However you were, in my view, misguided. Just make sure I have the book by the end of the day.'

It saddened me. The children's reaction had been fine. They enjoyed the story and marvelled at the idea of Gloria having two mummies and going on a gay pride march. For them it was just one big party with balloons, banners and friendly policemen. The truth was kids just loved anything larger than life, camp or flamboyant. It was grown-ups that had a problem with it.

'As to the other complaint, may I remind you that nudity at *William Booth School* has never been school policy for display boards.'

I remained silent, contemplating my fate.

'I am referring to the print of two semi-naked females, holding hands and dancing together, which is currently displayed on class 6's Art display board.'

'You mean the Miro painting?'

'I don't care who painted it. The parent in question came to see me this morning extremely angry and upset. She said the children had viewed the painting and then modelled as the dancing females, whilst other children in their group sketched them.' She was making it sound pornographic. I took a sharp intake of breath.

'Linda, we're learning about relationships in Art. It's a classic portrayal of a joyous partnership.'

'But each of them is exposing a bosom!'

'Western Art is full of nudes and parts of the body being exposed. There's nothing sinful about the human body.'

'Try telling that to the parent who came to see me this morning.' She deliberately softened her voice. 'You do see my difficulty David?'

'And who might this parent be?'

'She'd prefer it if her identity was not disclosed. Anyway, Mustafa will be coming later this afternoon to replace the painting with one more suitable. It's vital we are all seen to be singing from the same hymn sheet, as it were. I need you on board, David.'

Mustafa was the Art co-ordinator - Turkish, in his mid-fifties and happily married to his boyfriend, Amir, for seventeen years. He'd been working at the school since the year dot and was hanging on in there, serving time, until he could retire and supplement the meagre state pension with his gold-plated teacher's pension. On the odd occasion, he could still be seen, sweating it out in Vauxhall in the early hours with Amir, stripped to the waist, hands in the air. At school he referred to me, John and himself as the gay mafia and would often joke in the staffroom that us gayers at *William Booth* would be the first teachers to produce a third or fourth generation of camp Bengalis.

At lunchtime it was just me and Caroline in the staff room. The place was the usual mess, covered in half empty coffee mugs, past copies of 'The Times Educational Supplement' and post that had fallen from overstuffed pigeonholes. Caroline would joke that having school dinners was the highlight of the school day. Today that seemed true enough, even though it was just fish fingers, chips and beans and some kind of congealed pink ice cream in a polystyrene cup. I told her how the meeting had gone with Linda this morning.

'God that just makes me deliberately want to read *Gloria Goes to Gay Pride* to my class, just to piss her off. Doesn't she realise homophobic bullying in schools is rampant? That kids today basically use the word 'gay' to mean crap? And how dare she decide what we can and cannot read to our class. It's like Stalinist Russia! Who does she think she is, bloody Trotsky?'

'The thing is there's not a lot she can do. She has to follow through with the complaint.'

'It's not like she's going to have a fatwa issued against her from the Islamic Republic of Iran. I mean someone please tell her - it's not *Satanic Verses*, for Christ's sake!'

Caroline suddenly stopped talking. John, a stocky, middle-aged guy with a ginger comb-over, had come into the staffroom, cradling a piping hot mug of coffee close to his stomach. There always seemed to be some prop or other close at hand that could be used to cover up his ever-expanding waist line: a coffee mug, stack of exercise books, copy of The Guardian.

'Good holiday John?' Caroline was inclined to include people who she instinctively felt were left out.

'Oh, you know just a quiet one.' He attempted a half smile. It's the same answer he'd give if you asked him on Monday morning how his weekend had been. 'A quiet one.' He never gave much away, including the fact he was gay.

'Aren't you eating any lunch?' Caroline said, wolfing her school dinner down in the usual fashion, elbows jutting out, about to take off.

'As a matter of fact, I'm on a diet, so I said to myself, I'm not going to eat any lunch this week.' A smile spread across his face.

'You can't do that. Not eat any lunch. You'll feel faint,' Caroline replied.

'Oh no, I'll be just fine.' He had the touch of a martyr about him as he sat at the far end of the staff room table, sipping away at his school coffee.

After the terminally dull staff meeting (they'd wheeled in a couple of dinosaurs from the local authority professional development centre, or PDC) and filling out a rather lengthy evaluation form, me and Caroline met in the car park at the rear of the school gasping for a fag.

'Jesus, I feel like I've had a frontal lobotomy,' I said.

'I know what you mean. Did you check out the guy's trousers? Harry High Pants or what? They were practically under his armpits!'

'I did detect a little ankle swinging going on.'

'And the woman with the muffin top! What's with the goth look? I know the Eighties are making a comeback but someone should tell her, black's not always slimming!' She was leaning against her battered Ford Escort sucking all the goodness out of her cigarette.

'Well, you know the old adage. Those that can't do, teach -'

'And those that can't teach, teach teachers!'

'And those that can't teach teachers…'

'End up working for the Department of Education?'

'Touché! I don't know about you but I've had a shit day. What the hell's wrong with *Gloria goes to Gay Pride?* The kids loved it. Culturally sensitive issue – that's what she'd said.'

'Culturally sensitive issue – my arse. You know where this all leads? First it's banning the books then it's burning them and in the end, all there is, is one bloody book left. *Mein Kampf, The Communist Manifesto,* Chairman Mao's *Little Red book.* Hey, that's given me an idea. What we need is some form of protest. Let's throw a double sickie. She'll be farting round like a blue-arsed fly trying to get supplies in to cover.'

'We couldn't. She'd know we'd arranged it.' I said.

'Why would she? We haven't done it before. If we're both sick, she's less likely to challenge us about it.'

'I couldn't deliberately leave my kids with a supply,' I said.

'Come on, we could meet up in Soho, do lunch – have a few cocktails.'

'What are you like? We've only just come back.'

'Exactly and look at the state of us. After just one day. Both knackered, brain dead and counting the days 'til the next holiday.'

'I'm not sure.'

'I know. How about next Friday? It won't matter anyway. We're booked in to go to the PDC so it's not like the kids will miss out.'

'Isn't it some target-driven Nu Labour initiative? Let's all sing from the same bloody hymn sheet as we march inexorably to a rapidly dumbed down, production-line nightmare -'

'Come on then. We can set the world to rights over a cocktail. Weigh it up. Tower Hamlets or Soho? Instant coffee and digestives at the PDC or cocktails and luncheon in the gay village? Hot gossip and sex talk over a Manhattan or death by boredom in Jurassic Park? Sweetheart, we'll look back on it as a defining moment.'

'A moment defining what exactly?'

'The time we took a stand. Said no more bullshit, reclaimed the curriculum - that's what. Viva la revolution! Anyway you can help Mamma plan her great escape route out of teaching over a Manhattan.'

'Very *Sex and the City*. Well, I can tell you one thing for nothing love, if you 'aint got out it in five years, you know what they say.'

'You're in it for life!'

'I don't know. Politics and paperwork aside – we can still make a difference to these kids lives.'

'I see Tower Hamlets LEA has programmed you well, Mr.Born To Teach.'

'You can talk. At least I don't come from a teaching dynasty. Just watch that perfectionist streak of yours. It's a non starter so far as teaching's concerned and a sure-fire recipe for burn out. I've seen it happen to countless others before.'

She flicked her cigarette out onto the street. 'Yeah, yeah.

Another day, another dollar. See you in the morning, gorgeous!'

And with that, she sauntered off down the street. I knew she'd be marking and planning 'til gone midnight. But that's one of the things I loved about her. She pretended she didn't give a shit but deep down she cared more than most. And I'd seen her in action. She was one of a dying breed. A newly qualified teacher not afraid to take a few risks or be creative.

Chapter 10

That evening, I decided to surprise Michael and turned my hand to a new recipe from the Middle East. I'd tossed the chicken thighs in an assortment of spices, chopped the parsnips and celery and was just about to add the prunes and apricots. Things hadn't been easy since I'd got back from Israel. Michael would lock himself inside his room for long stretches at a time and had begun badgering me to go to the Buddhist centre. It felt like he had something to prove to himself and reminded me of when he first discovered Lord Buddha down at the revamped fire station in Bethnal Green, which Sangharakshita had now firmly established as the headquarters for the 'Friends of the Western Buddhist Order' (FWBO). It was as if he'd found the answer to Love, Life and the Universe again and it involved getting up at the crack, burning incense made by Tibetan monks in some remote part of the Himalayas, and sitting on his crack, crossed legged on a maroon-coloured cushion whilst chanting away in Sanskrit.

For desert I'd bought some sweets from an Indian sweet shop in Brick Lane and as ever had a large glass of chilled Pinot Grigio at the ready. I'd bought fresh mint so Michael could use the glasses I'd bought him from an Arabic market in Jaffa. The table was set, incense was wafting through from the lounge and a scented candle lit up the blue and green mosaics on the Moroccan kitchen table.

We'd lived here together for nearly two years and although we'd had our ups and downs I couldn't see us not living together. Michael was my rock - the one I turned to when I needed advice or just cheering up. When I split up with Ahmed, it was Michael who refused to let me stay at home wallowing in self pity. Instead, he took me out and we got hopelessly drunk. He listened for hours whilst I bored him with my idea of the 'Grand Romantic

Narrative', the pinnacle of which was meeting that elusive 'One' you wanted to spend the rest of your life with. And after I was queer bashed, he was the first one at the hospital, and the one who threw a surprise party in my honour when I got out, having invited all our clubbing friends and stocked up on essential supplies the night before. It was Michael I went to Brick Lane with when we first moved in, buying swathes of orange and gold sari material and garlands of paper flowers to drape from the ceiling of the hallway and living room. We were desperate to recreate the harem look, and had scouted round the markets of Camden Town and Portobello looking for anything vaguely ethnic to go with it: a table from Morocco, hand-woven rugs from Afghanistan or Persia and silk cushion covers from India. We never really pulled it off - it was more South East Asia meets the Middle East meets council flat in the East End, than authentic Persian harem. But we'd spent every evening for a whole week painting the walls bright pink, orange and yellow - transforming it from a poky housing association flat in the East end of London into our very own twenty-first century vision of bohemian hippydom. Even though the fabric on the ceiling kept falling down, and the Afghan rugs clashed with the 70's swirling patterned carpet, it was our home and we'd fixed it up ourselves.

When Michael arrived home, he looked tired and put upon; he'd just returned from the Buddhist centre. I poured some mint tea and we sat down to dinner.

'How was the session?' I asked.

'I struggled with it a bit, trying to cultivate *metta*.'

'Come again?'

'Loving kindness. Compassion. But Brahmadhvaja said it was a good sign.'

The people who ran the joint were all westerners and had changed their English names to Buddhist ones, usually ending in vaja, vajra or shita. I wondered how long before Michael went the whole hog and changed his, and began to serve the chicken.

'You never told me much about your weekend when I was away,' I said.

He looked edgy. 'What's there to tell?'

'You know exactly what I mean. Did you get your sorry arse down to Vauxhell? Any hot guys to report?'

He put his cutlery down. 'You may as well know. I ended up at *Fire*.'

'I knew it!'

'They had one of those themed nights. Emergency services. A few guys made the effort, casing the joint kitted out in police uniform. A couple of medics, the odd fireman.'

'I take it you took your rubber truncheon? '

'If you must know, I had my own kind of emergency.'

'You didn't end up in the medic's room?'

'A spiritual emergency, David. A dark night of the soul.'

'You're not making sense.'

'Are you sure you're ready to hear all this?'

'I'm all ears.'

He took a deep breath. 'I ended up taking this really strong speed. Base.'

'Never heard of it.'

'Neither had I. It's a sort of gooey yellow paste, stinks of ammonia, you know like babies' nappies. Pure filth. Anyway I end up taking some at the club. I couldn't stand still, couldn't talk to anyone, felt really edgy, trapped inside this speed bubble and really horny but my dick had shrunk to the size of a marble and my balls had migrated north.'

'Sounds like one hell of a testosterone booster! Babies nappies, shrunk dick, waiting for your balls to drop! Go girl!'

'Just listen will you. I drop a Viagra which does nothing,

then eventually the base runs out and I start to crash. You know the 'Down and Out' story, so I won't elaborate. Anyway, so what do I do? What any self respecting gay man in Vauxhall at five in the morning would do. I nailed it and started on the ketamine. So now I'm still horny as hell, impotent and half blind. I can't make out if I'm being cruised, if the guys are cute or mingin' and I probably look like a complete mong myself but-'

'But what?'

'I still can't go home so what do I end up doing?'

'More K?'

'You guessed it, sunshine. I don't have a key so I empty the rest of the packet onto the back of my hand. It's a fuckin' beach of ketamine, man. I stumble out of the cubicle and back onto the dance floor. Now the music starts to take on this weird twisted, deranged momentum and now I'm really fucked, my feet feel numb and I start losing my balance.'

'Probably not a great look if entertaining amorous intentions!'

'I can't even put into words what happened next.'

'Oh, come on.'

'You won't believe it.'

'Try me.' I poured some more mint tea.

'A few minutes later everything begins to slow down, the music, people dancing, as if time itself was stopping. And then I felt I was in this place that existed outside time, if that makes sense?'

'Not really but carry on.'

'I felt a real sense of dread and this cloud of dark light gathered suddenly and swept over the dance floor. I wanted to leave but at that point I was rooted to the spot. My legs were like concrete. I mean it's a fuckin' horse tranquiliser, man.'

'I hear they use it on elephants as well. But anyway, you

were still inside the club?'

'Where else would I be? But I may as well have been on planet Vulcan. One guy even looked like he was from Star Trek. The whole club seemed like this huge spaceship and a feeling of foreboding grew with such intensity I was certain some terrible chain of events was just about to unfold. Then I felt someone standing next to me. I turned round and it was this little old Chinese lady in a shimmering emerald green cocktail dress.'

It was too whacky. I couldn't take it seriously. 'Was she from the Star ship Enterprise?'

'Just hear me out, man. She appeared from no-where. She didn't say anything but she'd been waiting for me. And I just knew. And what I knew chilled me to the core.' He was gripping the edge of the table with both hands. 'I'd died, David. I was dead and I felt this crushing sense of familiarity. It was like, here I am again, out of my body, on the other side. It's happened before. Countless times. Don't ask me how I know. I just do.'

'But you were still in *Fire*?'

'Right.'

'Which was full of dead people?'

'That's what I said. Then it went even weirder. I could feel the back of my skull lift apart like the doors of a spaceship opening. David, I was part of the Quantum Mind. Can you imagine what that felt like? At one point, I was wrestling with the idea of predestination. It seemed all mapped out and yet -'

'You're kidding me, right? Quantum Mind?'

'I was in a parallel universe. I began to recognise people I knew in previous lives and one or two guys had, what I can only describe as the window of heaven shining inside them. You could see it through their eyes. They were connected to The Light that was finding its way into the club through cracks in the walls.'

'I thought you said it was a spaceship?'

'You know what I mean. Then it really sunk in. I was dead. The Chinese woman in the cocktail dress wanted to take me to the medic's room where the 'Other Me' was still fighting for my life but I couldn't handle it.'

'You used to joke about it years ago, wanting to die some day on the dance floor in *Fire*.'

'It was a joke, David! Do you really think I wanted to end up in some outer reach of the universe, trapped in a virtual reality version of *Fire*? It was like the fuckin' matrix!'

'A lot of guys out on the scene would only be too happy.' I suddenly heard some Bengali lads shouting outside in the park.

'No, I got what I deserved. In life I'd got stuck in a karmic groove of drug and sex addiction and was now living that same karmic vision, only a thousand times more intensely. At some point I walked into another part of the club, the music had started up again and there were half naked Adonises everywhere.'

'Babes, that's just *Fire* any night of the week.'

'But now it felt as if I was this sex-god in the land of the gods. Reality seemed more malleable, fluid. The concrete in my legs was turning to molten liquid, liquid gold, like in the movie *I am Robot*. I could read people's thoughts and felt invincible and incredibly horny. There was this guy. Hot and hairy with huge buns, covered in tattoos, piercings, giving off this pure unadulterated masculine vibe, like he was from some ancient warrior tribe. Imagine your ultimate fantasy and multiply it by a thousand. I was approaching my own personalised, tailor-made seventh heaven, only it wasn't God, Allah or the prophets waiting for me up there. I was being led up the garden path to the horniest, sleaziest energy exchange of man power I could handle. My balls were fit to bursting and all I can see is this tattoo of a scorpion on his lower back. I knew what he wanted to do to me and - '

I broke the wholemeal pitta bread in two and passed him a

piece. 'Right. Because of the telepathy.'

'Let me finish. So I walk up to the guy, grope his arse, tell him I want him to give me the seeing to of my life. He turns round mortally offended, tells me he's straight and starts barking back at me. Back off, fuck off, what the hell was I doing?'

'What the hell was *he* doing in a gay club more like?'

'The thing is did I somehow know he was straight? He was my ultimate fantasy, right. I mean, is the old cliché true? Does every fag want to shag a straight guy?

'Ok. I've heard it all now, Sigmund.'

I got up and looked out of the window. A group of hoodies had congregated near the park bench and were acting up. I spotted the leader of the pack immediately – punching his fists in the air, desperate to impress, the crotch of his jeans so low it was practically down by his knees. He suddenly starts thrusting his hips backwards and forwards, egged on by his mates – so it's now a violent frenzy of thrusting – pats on the back all round and now everyone's joining in, laughing and jostling in some weird mock fest-fuck. Then out of the blue one of them shoves his mate hard on the shoulder who responds in kind, sizing him up and shouting 'You want some do ya? You fucking want some? Come on then!'

'Are you listening, David?'

'Sorry? Yes, of course. Sexual fantasies and straight blokes – I'm all ears.'

'I saw my life in reverse going back to my childhood. All the moments when I'd brought happiness to others and all the times when what I thought or said or did had hurt others, and I asked for forgiveness and immediately felt scales of dense, dark matter lifting themselves off my shoulders. I was being prepared for something, recycled and it felt unstoppable. And then, to the side of me was a door and it felt like the light of heaven shining through.'

His eyes were beginning to glaze over but his hand movements were becoming ever more manic.

'Michael, come on. This really is a bit too much now. You're not telling me you believe this stuff. You were monged, out of it. K- holing. Darling, face facts. You were *ketaminized* to the core.'

'I'm telling you what I went through. It was real for me. And it was real when I saw that light behind the door. But it didn't lead to a heavenly realm. I began to hear the noise of two people having sex - a man and a woman and I felt my disembodied self being propelled towards them and the overwhelming attraction for them changed into an all-consuming desire to be reborn.'

'Ok, nice one, Michael. The game's over. Do you really think I'm that gullible?'

'It was an N.B.E.'

'Come again?'

'A Near Birth Experience.'

'I thought you said near-death?!'

'Keep up, David. I was about to be reborn. Then I saw all the people I loved in my last lifetime and I imagined them being torn apart by my death and I thought of all the things I still wanted to do as Michael back on earth. With all my heart I wanted to go back.'

I'd heard enough. He might have disappeared into a K hole in the club but right now he was disappearing up his own arse hole.

'Why didn't you just click your red ruby slippers, Dorothy?'

'I summoned all my will power but it was like smashing my head against a brick wall, only it wasn't a brick wall. It was the new dimension of the afterlife. Then a voice told me to sit down. And the voice said 'the spirit is strong but the flesh is weak'.

'Very biblical.'

'There was a way I could go back and resume my life as

Michael but it meant making a promise. Avoid all drugs. It was pure revelation. Avoid all drugs or continue to struggle with the same issues of drug addiction in my next life. God was all-forgiving and all merciful. Then I looked up and the heavens opened up. It was raining, broad day light and I was sitting outside at the back of the club, listening to the sound of traffic passing on the Vauxhall Road. '

I watched from the window as one of the guys in the park jabbed his finger in the air and shouted 'you're fucking dead mate!' Maybe it was a drug deal gone wrong, maybe they were just play-acting. He limped away and I couldn't tell if it was because he'd been hurt or if it was just another show of macho bravado, a Bengali imitation of a gangster, Kingston, Jamaica style. I turned and looked at Michael.

'So basically, in a nut shell, you didn't die. You weren't transported to another dimension beyond time and space to the outer reaches of some parallel universe. The Chinese woman in the cocktail dress was a figment of your imagination and the grunting and groaning you heard did not signal your own rebirth back on planet earth. It was probably just two guys in the corner getting down and dirty. But knowing you, you probably did try and grope some random guy's arse and were unlucky enough to get knocked back, that's all.'

'No David, I had a genuinely mystical experience.'

'Oh come on, don't give me all that psychonaut rubbish. It was one massive hallucination induced by copious amounts of ketamine. And not a very interesting one at that. You didn't even leave the confines of Vauxhall. Surely you could have conjured up something better than that.'

'I did die. It was a psychic death. Death of who I thought I was and what I thought I wanted.'

'Face facts. You were a greedy-guts drug-whore who

spun out of control and suffered a brief but intense paranoid schizophrenic episode. You were in a K hole. Don't dress it up to be something it's not.'

'I call it a miracle. I don't care if it's the voice of God or my own subconscious, a hallucination or communication with another world. I experienced that higher power. And I'm going to use the experience to help me change my karmic vision.'

'So you're telling me it's the end of the road? After all these years, you eventually found salvation in the arms of lady Ketamina?' I began clearing the dishes away.

'I'm telling you I've definitely been beeped. I understand where the phrase 'dying for a shag' comes from. For me, the drugs were only ever about one thing. Getting my rocks off, searching for that elusive shag of my life and it was always tantalisingly just out of reach, but I was risking everything. My health, my state of mind and for what? Instead of a temple, my body and mind had become a trashcan. They don't call it 'trashed' for nothing.'

I called out from the kitchen. 'I know you, Michael. You'll be back on that dance floor in next to no time. Saint-sinner-saint-sinner. Eeny, meeny, miny, moe!'

'I mean it. I was lost in a shitstorm of intoxicants for years. And now...well it's like I'm coming out of the closet all over again, only this time the closet door doesn't open up to gay sexual liberation. It opens up to The Ground of Luminosity. My very own enlightenment and salvation.'

I stood in the doorway.

'Earth to Michael! You've got to get a grip!'

'Oh, I've got that all right. It's never been firmer. For the first time it all makes sense. I'm focussing all my energies on my Buddhist practice now. I now know I need to devote myself to something much bigger than myself and my own desires if I'm ever to be really happy.' Then he looked at me with renewed intensity. 'The question is David, when will you be beeped? And when you are, will you take the call?'

I'd pushed the boat out, brought a taste of Middle Eastern cuisine to the table and broken bread with him - all in the hope that we'd get things back on track. As it turned out, we'd never been further apart. Michael was now part of the 'Quantum Mind', whatever that was, spinning out of control in his own orbit that far exceeded any previous drug guilt-trip. This was a one-off. He'd opened Pandora's Box and there was no going back.

Chapter 11

I'd managed to secure a table by the window at *Balans* restaurant and had spent the last half hour waiting for Caroline, watching the rich tapestry of Soho life pass by. Some down 'n out crusty with dog on a string suddenly veered from one side of the pavement to the other clutching a can of Tenants Extra, and on the other side of the street, wearing a crop top so his midriff and pierced navel were exposed to all 'n sundry, a cocky queen, all of about nineteen, strutted by. I even spotted Yvette stumbling out of someone's front door across the street - drag queen and compere extraordinaire, who, on a Saturday night in the early nineties, would cavort on stage with a group of pumped up, naked muscle Marys at a night called 'Love Muscle' at The Fridge in Brixton. Still caked in foundation and wearing the trademark elbow-length, black gloves, and dark glasses, she didn't look a day over sixty.

'Sorry I'm late, babe.' It was Caroline, clutching her fake Marc Jacobs handbag, all buckles and straps of red leather.

'Can you believe we're doing this?' I said.

She giggled like a naughty school girl and sat down.

'Well I must say it's a refreshing change of scenery. I propose a toast. To education. Fuck New Labour's constant bombardment of new initiatives, fuck S.A.T's and teaching to the test, and above all fuck Ofsted!'.

'I'll drink to that! Education, Education, Education!' I said.

Balans was filling up. During the evening it was always jammed to the rafters but I guess it did a good business at lunchtime, either with the local Soho crowd, tourists passing by or office workers sneaking off for a boozy lunch. Michael used to joke that the 'Tango Brigade' could easily be spotted, hanging out at 'Balaaans' (which he'd always say, for some reason, in a phoney

American accent.) In other words, gay men of a certain age, who'd either spent far too long on the sun bed, or had overdone it spraying fake tan, and were now glowing a rather unhealthy shade of orange. They'd been 'tangoed' and either Clinique or the Tanning shop had a lot to answer for. A guy, just to the left of me had definitely been tangoed. I'd clocked him as soon as he walked in. Not in a sexy way. More in a way that jumps out at you but for all the wrong reasons. His skin had turned an unnatural dirty orange, and his neck, which was beginning to sag, was chained in a noose of heavy silver. His receding hairline was disguised by a closely cropped skinhead. We'd had the seventies clone: hairbrush for a moustache, checked shirt and cowboy boots. Well, this was the noughties clone: fake tan, shaved head, ultra tight T shirt and dripping in silver jewellery, courtesy of Gucci or D&G.

Still, the waiter was cute. Tight-fitting black trousers, which showed off his more than ample package. Dark brown eyes and skin and the distinctly soft, yet slightly nasal tonal sound, of Brazilian Portuguese. I wondered if he doubled up as an escort. It was a cliché, but the pages of QX and Boyz magazine featured many a well-endowed Braz boy from Rio or Sao Paulo, who'd heard the streets of London were paved with gold. But who was I to judge? Despite my run in with Ricardo last year, I could still understand the temptation of making a quick buck in Europe, especially if I'd come, as he did, from a sprawling favella in the heart of Rio de Janeiro and needed to send money home each month.

'Are you ready to order, Sir?'

I fought hard with myself to stop staring at the bulge in his trousers. We ordered our food and another champagne cocktail. A world away from Tower Hamlets and the PDC. I just hoped it was some nice Ozzie supply teacher rather than the sergeant covering my class. Where would we be without our noble army of Ozzie,

Kiwi and South African supply teachers?

'I didn't get a chance to show you something that was left on my desk after the kids had gone home,' she said.

'No, I made a quick get away. I was doing the big peace-offering meal for Michael, only it didn't quite work out.'

She undid her handbag and produced a magazine. 'Feast your eyes on that!' And with that she held up a centrefold of a woman dressed in a red basque, suspenders and black stilettos. I peered closer and saw she was wearing a headscarf and sunglasses courtesy of Dior.'

'Caroline why are you showing me this? Are you getting into soft-core lesbian porn in your old age? '

'Oh, you know me, sweetheart. Always partial to a bit of muff diving and the odd flick of the bean given half a chance! No, sorry to disappoint, love. I may be a jaded old fag-hag, last year's fag-bangle if you must, but I have no intentions of venturing forth into anyone's lady garden! Anyway, you're side tracking me. You rushed home early yesterday after school. I didn't get a chance to tell you.'

'Tell me what?'

'About the brown envelope. After I took my kids down to the playground at home time, I went into my classroom and there was this unaddressed envelope on my desk. So I opened it and inside was this magazine. But that's not all. Look at the front cover.'

There was another woman with long dark hair wearing a full piece swimming costume. The title was foreign. For a moment I wondered if it was an Israeli magazine.

'*Eastern Promise.* It's Arabic. I showed it to Sabina in the office who translated it for me. You know her. Always up for a bit of gossip and intrigue.'

'But why show me that particular centre fold?'

'That's where the post-it note was stuck with the mysterious ditty.

'Scratch the surface
And what do you find?
A rebellious glamour girl,
She's one of a kind.'

'The plot thickens! Guess it must be one of the kids in Year six playing a joke. Not exactly a Shakespearean sonnet but credit where credit's due. I guess they're getting to grips with the iambic pentameter. I'll have a word on Monday. Oh, and don't forget, we're covering sex and relationships next week, or rather skirting around it. The school governors, in their infinite wisdom, have drafted a Sex and Relationships policy. The first commandment – thou shalt not mention sexual intercourse, erections or sexual orientation.'

'Fat lot of good they'll learn about sex and relationships then.'

'I've got an hour to do it. You know what it's all about. Ticking boxes. It's the tick box culture in over-drive. Sex and relationships. Tick. Life? Tick. Death? Tick. A twenty minute slot in a crematorium, then its…Tick. Next! It's culturally endemic!'

'I can see you're on flying form today! But I guess you have a point. Why the government can't legislate across the country for proper sex education in every school. It's madness.'

'Anyway, what are you going to do? About the magazine?' I asked.

'What do you expect me to do? Start playing Miss Marple?' She handed me the magazine. 'Look, just take it off my hands for me. I feel like I'm already implicated in some weirdo's mind games. It gives me the creeps.' I took the magazine and put it in my rucksack. 'Anyway darling, enough about little 'ole me. How about you? Have you heard from Yossi recently?'

'He phoned yesterday. Said he missed me.'

'Well, that's a good sign.'

'I know. It's just -'

'What is it?'

'Well he doesn't exactly live a stone's throw away. Can you really see a future in it?

'Well that's up to you.'

'How do you mean?'

'If you want there to be.'

'I like him. A lot.'

'So what's the problem?'

'Um... let me see. He lives in Israel...I live in London. He's probably still in love with Moshe. He's -' I paused.

'What? There's something else isn't there. Tell me.'

'It doesn't matter.'

'Come on. I tell you everything. I told you all about Rich and his sordid little affair.'

I knew she wouldn't give up until I told her. 'He's taking anti-depressants.'

'Is that it? Sweetheart, he's bound to take medication after something like that happens. He's probably suffering from post-traumatic stress disorder, as well as depression.'

'I know but sometimes he can't, you know...'

Our food arrived. Rocket salad and chicken for Caroline and Toulouse sausages and mash with gravy for me. I always had the same thing. I really should try something new off the menu.

'He can't always get it up.'

'Oh sweetheart. I wouldn't let that worry you. It happens to the best of them.' I stared out of the window as two bearded guys on the other side of the street in matching Doc Martin boots, jeans and checked shirts walked hand in hand.

'That's not the full story is it?'

'It's not about the sex. I didn't want to think about it before.'

'What is it then?'

'I'm scared he'll do something stupid.'

'You're over-reacting. I can't begin to imagine what he's going through but it doesn't mean to say he's going to top himself.'

'He took an overdose. After it happened.'

'Oh darling, I'm sorry. I had no idea. Look, if there's anything I can do?'

'I don't know what to do myself. I feel completely out of my depth. He seems fine but who knows? Underneath I'm not sure if he's coping.'

'Remember, you've only just met him.' She flicked her strawberry blonde hair extensions and carried on eating, elbows jutting out, ready for take off. I stared out of the window. A transvestite (or was it a transsexual?) passed by. Six foot tall tottering in six inch white stilettos, huge Afro wig and leopard skin micro skirt. She was handing out flyers, no doubt to one of the clubs down in Vauxhall.

'Just take care, sweetheart. It isn't long ago you broke up with Ahmed.'

'I did go off the rails a bit, didn't I?'

'So would I if Richard ditched me for a young slip of a thing from Saudi. You were head over heels with the boy for god's sake.'

'I still think about him.'

'Of course you do. Oh well, we can't choose the ones we fall in love with, but thank god we can choose our friends.' She paused. 'What is it?'

'Nothing.'

'I know that look. David?'

'How's your salad?'

'You don't get away with it that easily. Tell Mamma!'

'It's nothing.' I knew she wouldn't get off my case until I told her. 'Ok you win. Ahmed, he, well he texted, a couple of days ago, that's all. Said he misses me.'

Her voice gradually crescendoed. 'Oh no! No,! No, No, No, No, No!!'

'Can you believe it? After three months!'

'Well, you know what that means?'

'What?'

'It can only mean one thing! He wants you back.'

'Just one problem. There is the small matter of his bride to be. And anyway, for all I know he was texting from the Middle East. Who's to say he isn't out in the Emirates right now and that his text was just a bad case of pre-wedding nerves?'

'I know that look, David. Don't even think about it. You have enough to contend with flying off to Israel without jetting off to Dubai in between!'

'Well I think the Israeli stamp on my passport would put a stop to that. Anyway, you'll be pleased to hear I didn't rise to the bait.'

'Glad to hear it.'

I decided to tease her. 'Now hopping on the first Air Arabia plane flying to Dubai tomorrow morning – now that's more my style!'

She laughed. 'You men. I give up! Straight or gay. You're all the same. Rushing in where angels fear to tread.'

I smiled with real affection for my friend. 'Only you could say that, Caroline.'

Her tone turned suddenly serious. 'But I'll tell you something for nothing Mr Climb Any Mountain. I bet my bottom dollar he's already shacked up in marital misery, be it Highgate Village, Dubai or Kuwait City. And if you see that boy again, you'll get hurt all over again.'

That evening Yossi phoned. He was coming to London in a couple of weeks. The production team he was currently working for were shooting a new jeans commercial in London to be broadcast on Israeli T.V. I couldn't believe it. I thought I was going to have to wait for the six week summer holiday before I could see him again. I decided then and there to take Caroline's advice about Ahmed. She was right; he was probably already shacked up in post-marital misery with his new wife. It was time to move on.

Chapter 12

I was woken up early Saturday morning by the sound of Michael banging about in his bedroom. I wouldn't have minded so much but I'd drunk a whole bottle of Pinot Grigio the night before and was now lying there in the dark with a thumping headache, willing myself back to sleep. No doubt he'd soon be at it again, chanting away the perils of Samsara, summoning the Bodhisattva of Compassion to lift the heavy burden from humanity and ease all our suffering. I just hoped he'd put in a special mention for me. Something along the lines of sparing David the agony of yet another pre-dawn chorus of guttural groaning in Sanskrit.

I hadn't mentioned his K-hole experience nor the voice of God he claimed was urging him to give up the drugs. I thought it best. The last thing I wanted to do was to be seen encouraging it. After all, who knows where those sorts of holy rantings might lead? A possible trip to the local psychiatric ward, dosed up on lithium and sedatives so you barely knew who or where you were?

I could hear coat hangers clanging in his wardrobe, his chest of drawers opening and closing, keys rattling, his bedroom door creaking open and then shutting. It would be impossible to fall asleep again so I forced myself up and out of bed. He was wearing a string of wooden beads round his neck with an orange tassel dangling at the bottom.

'Oh hi. I didn't mean to wake you,' he said sheepishly.

'Michael, do you know what time it is?'

'I'm sorry. I meant to tell you last night.'

'Tell me what?

'Where I'm going.'

'You're leaving?'

'Only for a few days. Well, maybe longer. I'll see how it goes.'

'How what goes?'

'The retreat.'

'What retreat?'

'Rivendell.'

'I thought that was the elfin kingdom in *Lord of the Rings*.'

'You can mock. It's a Buddhist retreat in the Sussex countryside as well you know.'

'Jesus, when were you thinking of telling me?'

'Someone cancelled at the last minute, which means there's a space for me.'

'It's the weekend. I thought we could do something together. Just the two of us.'

'Come on, you buggered off to Israel and left me on my tod. I'm sorry mate. Now it's my turn. Anyway, I need to clear my head. Sort a few things out.'

'I'll miss you.'

'I need some support staying off the drugs. I thought it might help.'

'Well, make sure you say hi to Gandalf for me.'

He grinned. 'I'll be home before you know it.'

And with that, he dragged his suitcase off the bed, kissed me on the cheek and slammed the front door behind him. I stared at his little make-shift shrine he'd erected in the corner of his room. Incense was still burning and petals had fallen from the single rose he'd placed in a vase.

The following week at school, I was handed a cheque by Linda for fifty quid. I thought she'd lost the plot until I discovered what it was for. To spruce up our drab classrooms with plants and bouquets of flowers ready for the inspection. I wouldn't have minded but it had nothing to do with the kids and everything to do with impressing the bureaucrats from Ofsted. Traditional wooden toy boats and musical instruments from Bangladesh had also sprung up around the school overnight, the senior management team obviously flapping over whether the school reflected the pupils' cultural background. Posters of Bengal tigers and Bangladeshi villagers in the paddy fields harvesting rice, or dredging water from the well, had also suddenly mushroomed in prominent positions across the school. I guess this was Linda's idea of 'changing into a new gear', along with walking into each classroom unannounced on the off chance of catching you 'off message'. I just found it all a tad tokenistic and more than a little offensive.

On Friday afternoon the girls and boys in Year Six had been split up to receive their one hour of sex and relationship education. Caroline had stepped in to teach the girls and it fell on me to skirt around the business of the birds and the bees with the boys, mindful of what the Koran and the dictates of the recently drafted school policy said on the matter. It would certainly be a challenge as we had no recourse to educational resources such as videos, books or posters and sexual intercourse itself was completely off limits.

When I walked into class, the boys were already in high spirits and helping to push the desks against the walls. We formed a circle with the chairs and I cleared my throat. 'Ok boys, as you know we're going to be learning about something of a personal nature today so it's important we all show sensitivity to each other.'

'Sir, is it we're learning about sex?' asked Hussain, a boy who had only recently arrived from Bangladesh and was already beginning to pick up the East-end lingo and mannerisms of the other boys. A few of them started to laugh.

'Good question, Hussain. And I'm afraid I can't really give you a straight answer. What I can say is, you *will* be learning about how your bodies change in puberty. Oh, and I want to say from the outset, I expect everyone to call the different body parts by their proper names.'

'You mean 'dick' sir?' said Jabil.

'Cock innit.' said another boy.

'Well, as you know boys, it has many names, but the name we'll be calling it this afternoon is 'penis'.'

'Sir, what's...fingy...what is it, fingy...wanking?'

'Jabil, do we say 'what's fingy wanking' or 'what's wanking?''

'What's wanking Sir?' The boys erupted into laughter.

'Thank you Jabil. It takes courage to ask a question like that. Maybe we can have a question and answer session at the end. Ok, let's crack on, shall we?'

They went back to their desks and drew two pictures. One of them as they see themselves now and one of what they think they'll look like in a few years time. It was surprising how many of them had drawn something resembling Popeye the Sailor man - all bulging biceps, tattoos and knee length donkey dicks. Were all males, men or boys, gay or straight, now aspiring to the same ideal? A cartoon-like, donkey-dick/bubble butt version of male beauty. Was it all part and parcel of the cultural drift towards the 'super-size society? Super-size Big Mac, super-size fries, super-size shlong, pecs, tits, lips – the bigger the better. But where did this obsession for freakish-sized body parts all end? With a pair of silicon injected bangers exploding at 35 000 feet over the Atlantic Ocean or penile extension surgery gone seriously wrong?

'So guys, have you got any questions you'd like to ask at this stage?'

'Sir, why does my dick, sorry, my 'penis' like go hard when I look at, you know...those magazines.?' asked Hamza who was Mr Popular to his class mates, given his talent at football and lack of Boffin credentials.

'I think he means when he looks at pussy sir, innit?' said Habid to more laughter.

'And what magazines would they be Hamza?' I asked

He immediately clammed up.

'*Playboy*, page three of *The Sun* or could it possibly be *Eastern Promise?*'

He still wouldn't budge. Just sat there with his feet stretched out in front of him, arms folded.

'Is that what you read, Sir?' asked Habid.

'All right, joking aside boys, pornography is a serious issue but not something I can really go into here. Hamza, I'd like to see you after class.'

Mrs. Begum's son, Mohammed, who rarely spoke, put his hand up.

'Ah yes, Mohammed. It's nice to see you with your hand up. Everybody, can we all look and listen to the talker please. Thank you.'

'Sir, can you ask a question?'

'Go ahead Mohammed. Anything you like.'

'Sir, is it you're gay?'

The room fell silent. All I could hear was the sound of the traffic outside the classroom. It was the question I'd never been asked in my entire teaching career and never expected to have to answer it. All I could think of was the stock, standard response: 'I don't discuss my private life at school.'

'Sir, is it you're gay?'

That question again. It brought back my own memories of being a pupil back at school and putting up with the litany of abusive names that came my way. Queer, faggot, gaylord, shirt-lifter. The thought of these kids going through anything like that made my mind up for me.

'Yes, Mohammed. I'm gay.' At first there was a stunned silence, then whispering and a ripple of sniggering that went round the group.

'That's *gunnah*, Sir!' said Ashraf.

'My dad says all gays are paedophiles,' said Habib.

'What's a paedophile?' asked Jalil.

'What is a gay?' asked Amir.

'Like that one off the telly in 'Little Britain'? The only gay in the village. Are you the only gay at school, Sir?' said Ibrahim.

'Sir, you can't be gay, in the Koran it says -'

I deliberately looked at every one of them. 'Yes, in the Koran and the Bible and the Torah, it says all sorts of things. But it also teaches love and compassion and that means respect. This might come as a shock to you but the fact of the matter is some people are straight, some people bisexual or transgender and some people are gay. The important thing is you treat people how you wish to be treated.' I was aware that not only had I broken every rule book in the newly drafted Sex Ed. Policy, I'd also outed myself. I was entering unchartered waters.

'Sir, what's transgender?' said Ashraf.

'Sir, Sir - what's those, thingy, … that's it. Them tubes babies grow in. Is that like for real?' said Ibrahim.

And they were off, wanting to know about IVF, transsexuals, wet dreams – the works. The fact that their teacher was gay was no longer headline news. The natural curiosity of youth demanded answers to an as yet strange and bewildering adult world just out of reach.

After the lesson and the boys had raced excitedly out to the playground, I talked to Hamza who assured me he'd only looked at porno mags in his dad's garage and wouldn't dream of bringing anything like that into school.

Caroline came up at break to let me know how her lesson had gone. 'Well, I think I kept safely within the parameters of the new policy. Not a mention of S.E.X. Just periods and the menstrual cycle. I couldn't believe how many girls were completely ignorant of the facts! I had to talk to one of them after class and reassure her everything was perfectly normal. She'd just started her period. How did the boys get on?'

'Naturally they were quite boisterous. Curious, understandably excitable. Oh, I had a word with Hamza. I'm going to keep an eye on him. We may well have found our phantom porno distributer, but I'll need to collect hard evidence. Catch him at it.'

'What is it David? You look a bit subdued.'

'Oh, it's nothing. Probably just the pressure of Ofsted catching up with me.'

'Come on. I know you. You're not one to let those old dinosaurs get to you.'

'If you must know, one of the kids asked if I was gay.'

'I hope you told him it was none of his business. David?'

'Actually, I told him I was.'

'Oh my god! You're joking me!'

'How else are these kids going to learn its ok to be gay? I doubt they'll learn it during Friday prayers at the mosque, or after school when they're learning Arabic at the madrassa.'

'But David -'

'What?'

'I just -'

'Just what?'

'I think you're very brave but look what happened in the eighties when ILEA stocked school libraries with *Jenny lives with Martin and Eric.*'

'I thought you were all for me reading *Gloria Goes to Gay Pride.*'

'I was. I mean, I am.'

'But coming out to my kids is another matter?'

'I didn't say that.'

'You don't have to. We've been censoring ourselves ever

since clause 28 came on the statute books. Even though it was repealed a few years back, its shadow still looms large across playgrounds up and down the country.'

'I know that. But this is Tower Hamlets, not some middle class, liberal enclave in Hampstead.'

'How many gay teenagers have attempted suicide, how many died of HIV and Aids as a result of that rather spiteful and pernicious piece of legislation? If people like me don't fight back, who will?'

'I don't know. It's just… It could turn ugly.'

'I thought you'd be proud of me.'

'I am sweetheart. What you did, it takes guts. Coming out in any school, but especially a school like this, you deserve a fucking medal. The kids have got their gay role model. Lord knows when some of them grow up gay they'll need it more than most. But I care about you. You can't take on a moral crusade single-handedly.'

The door to the classroom suddenly opened. It was Linda. She was wearing yet another new outfit with matching accessories – a navy blue pinafore dress and orange shoes and necklace. I guess she was going for the hip and trendy look but didn't quite manage to pull it off.

'Ah David, there you are. How did the Sex. Ed lesson go? I know how boys of a certain age tend to have furtive imaginations.'

'I like to think of it as a natural and healthy curiosity.'

'Well, I'm sure you do. I trust you stayed within the parameters of the school's agreed sex and relationship policy?'

'Let's just say it proved challenging.'

'Well, that's why we're all here. To rise to the challenge! Anyway the reason I'm hunting you down is because we need a drama performance. For Ofsted week. After all it's your forte. No point in reinventing the wheel. I was thinking along the lines of last year's show 'Into the Woods.' All the children involved should pretty much remember it from last year so no need for lots of full-scale rehearsals. One or two should do the trick.'

'I'll help him with it,' Caroline butted in.

'Fantastic, Caroline! That's sorted then. Another thing I can tick off my list. I'm sorry I didn't think to say before but you know how it is. Anyway, must dash. I'm forging links with the local business community. Swiss Bank over at Canary Wharf.'

Caroline closed the door.

'Why did you volunteer?' I asked.

'Oh darling, you love putting on a show. Come on, admit it, you missed your vocation: *'into the woods, without delay, but careful not to lose the way, into the woods, who knows what may be lurking on the journey!'*

'It's not for the kids. It's just so she can show off to the inspectors and take all the glory. Sondheim would turn in his grave.'

'Come on, they'll love the chance to perform it again. You could give it a cockney spin. *'Hoods in the Wood.'*? or maybe even *'Into the Hood'*?'

'If she wants to resurrect a ghost from the past, why doesn't she appear in it? I'm sure she'd be very good as the evil stepmother.'

Caroline started singing again. *'The cape as red as blood, the cow as white as milk, the hair as yellow as corn, the slipper as pure as gold.'* You could do a gay version.'

'Caroline, musicals are gay! Especially *Into the Woods*. Over the top, camp as can be, all singing, all dancing. That's why kids love 'em. They're larger than life. Believe me, there's no need to change a thing.'

She gave me a look.

'Ok, you win. I'll get my lesbian friend to come up from Brighton and vamp it up on the piano,' I said.

'You still haven't told me - if Sergeant's the evil stepmother, who are you?'

'Well I 'aint Red bleedin' Riding Hood – that's for sure!'

'Oh I don't know. I think you'd look quite fetching in a red cape and basket.'

'Now give me a pair of glass sling-backs and a handsome prince…'

She grabbed me by the waist and, started up a waltz round the classroom, knocking over pencil pots and banging into desks and chairs whilst singing at the top of her voice. 'Some day my prince will come, some day we'll meet again. And away to his castle we'll go. To be happy forever I know.'

Chapter 13

We started rehearsing excerpts from Sondheim's musical the next day, where well-known fairy tale characters take their own journey into the woods, each in search of the thing they think will bring them happiness. Caroline was more than happy to help out with making a few extra costumes and to be honest, it was a relief to focus on something other than targets, testing, data analysis and preparing to impress the clipboard carrying brigade from Ofsted.

Michael arrived back from *Rivendell* later that week, his head now completely shaved and a Tibetan Buddhist tattoo etched onto his left arm. White Tara: a half naked woman, seated cross-legged on a lotus flower, with a halo of red light behind her. Apparently it was a *Bodhisattva*, a Tantric deity with the power to heal and protect the believer from danger. One of the guys he'd met on retreat was a tattooist, and much to Michael's admiration, had moved into the Buddhist commune at Bethnal Green. Michael wouldn't stop ranting about him or the retreat; I think it was a serious case of hero worship.

On Friday I left on the dot to get the tube out to Heathrow and waited at El Al Israeli Airlines arrivals for Yossi. His plane was delayed but when it finally landed and I spotted him coming through customs, I couldn't quite believe he was back in London again. As soon as I saw him coming through the arrivals lounge, I ran up to him, dodging trollies and other new arrivals, until he was in my arms. I was going to be thirty five on Sunday and it was the best birthday present I could have wished for.

When we got back to the flat we'd barely got through the front door before we started tearing each others clothes off and having sex on the kitchen floor. Sharing a post sex cigarette, he told me he'd decided to come off the antidepressants. It wasn't just because of his sex drive, or rather lack of it. He was tired of how the pills cut him off, numbed everything. He didn't want to be wrapped in cotton wool anymore. It felt like he was ready to face what had happened to Moshe and I knew he'd need all the support he could get.

On Saturday we went to a Vivienne Westwood exhibition at the Victoria and Albert museum in South Kensington. It was a retrospective of her designs, beginning with the punk influenced years and moving through to the tartan look and her historical English coutre evening gowns. Yossi was clearly a fan, taking endless photos and eulogising over the use of tartan fabric. It wasn't really my scene but I was happy to be doing whatever he wanted, as we passed mannequins dolled up in bondage gear and safety pins, happy that he was here with me in London for my birthday.

That evening we were all meeting up at a new Italian restaurant in Soho that Caroline had recommended. I'd already done the drugs run to Old Street and waited long enough for what I was assured would be top notch Columbian cocaine. In reality it wasn't that glamorous a mission. There were no dark sun-glasses or Havana cigars, just some dodgy side street near Old Street roundabout and a red Fiat Uno to look out for. But after waiting nearly an hour, I had secured the goods. If I'd really thought about the bigger picture, I'd have realised that some poor girl from South America would probably have swallowed packets of the stuff to get it through customs, a drug mule risking life and imprisonment for a little extra cash for herself and her family. As it was, I was more concerned about any overhead CCTV cameras recording me handing over the readies to the weedy looking guy with a baseball cap behind the wheel of the Fiat Uno.

The restaurant was packed and one of the waiters was mopping his brow as he dashed from each customer serving seafood risottos or pasta and topping up half empty glasses of wine. Caroline was sitting all by herself looking a little twitchy. She was glammed-up for the occasion though, a glittering silver camisole top and short white skirt which showed her tanned legs off. Her feet were perched in killer high heels with rainbow coloured straps which sort of tied up around her lower leg and she'd just had her hair done. I know she was curious to meet Yossi and I was beaming as we pushed past seated diners and those still waiting for a table.

'Sweetheart, you made it! I've been sitting here on my lonesome for what seemed like forever!' She air kissed me and Yossi then gave an approving glance at my new T shirt. 'The devil may wear Prada, girlfriend, but her minions are clearly D&G devotees. Work it, bitch!' She put finger to nostril, tilted her head upwards and snorted. 'This place is buzzing isn't it, darling? And so many gorgeous men! I swear I'm in fag-hag heaven!'

We sat down and Yossi started to chat about the Westwood exhibition and how he loved her knitwear collection and the way she used eighteenth century cutting principles. I could tell Caroline really liked him. If she didn't like someone, they'd know instantly. I suddenly felt a kiss on my neck and turned round. It was Michael and he'd brought along a tall Scandinavian looking guy with a rather unkempt looking ginger beard. He must be Padmalokha, the Buddhist tattooist he met at Rivendell.

'Hello gorgeous, I brought a friend with me. I hope there's enough space,' said Michael.

'So Michael, tell us about your new fella. Where did you first meet?' asked Caroline.

Padmalokha cleared his throat. 'Well, just to put the record straight, he's not my boyfriend. How can I put it? At times I wish I was gay. I mean, I've dabbled - with guys in the Buddhist centre, that is. I call it 'sexual acrobatics'. For me, it's just a safety valve.

Of course there's none of that neurotic attachment, that obsessive romantic love I feel for a woman.'

'Personally, I'm all for neurotic attachment, in fact, the more crazed and zany, the better. Allrighty, anyone for a Margarita?' Caroline seemed to take an instant dislike to him and I must admit he gave me the creeps. It was something about his smile. It lingered just that little bit too long and underneath that calm, New Age exterior I sensed a pent-up passive aggression just waiting to assert itself.

After our main course, to my embarrassment, they all sang happy birthday even though it wasn't until tomorrow and gave me presents: Harvey Nicks vouchers from Caroline, incense and a book on Sangarakshita from Michael and return air ticket to Tel Aviv from Yossi. I couldn't wait to visit him in Israel again and was beginning to think that despite the distance, it might just work out. We ordered desserts then made a bee-line for the toilet, to sample the coke. Yossi declined our offer, saying he was saving himself for later so me and Caroline left him with Michael and Padmalokha upstairs discussing the difference between Mahayana and Theravada Buddhism. We pushed our way into the women's, diving into an empty cubicle, giggling like naughty school kids.

'I love doing coke in a toilet cubicle. It's downright sleazy,' I said.

Caroline looked twitchy. 'You always were a naughty boy! I just hope it's not cut to fuck,' she said.

I was already feeling pissed, having had one glass of champagne too many. I took the wrap out of my wallet, closed the toilet seat and scraped a generous sample onto the lid of the toilet. All this was part of its appeal. It was naughty, I know. But the ritual of chopping the lumpy white powder, dividing it into lines with the edge of your credit card and rolling a crisp twenty pound note between your fingers, was a definite temptation to be succumbed to. It still felt highly decadent, even though everyone was at it these days and the price had tumbled from around £70 a gram, right down to forty quid. Caroline rolled a tenner nice and tightly.

'Hold my hair back, hon. God forbid it all ends up on the fucking floor!'

I grabbed her strawberry-blonde hair extensions with one hand and held onto it as she snorted the fattest line. We must have looked pretty ridiculous! She stood up, dabbing at her nose.

'Wow, Daniella Westbrook eat your heart out! I can really feel it hitting the back of my throat. It's surprisingly good shit.' She started laughing.

Having sampled the goods, we bundled out of the women's cubicle to the surprise of a woman with brown, leathery skin applying hairspray and lipstick at the mirror. Back upstairs Yossi ordered yet another bottle of Bollinger, despite me protesting it was all going to cost too much.

Caroline was in her element. 'Champagne, champagne! Champagne for everyone!' She raised her glass. 'And a toast. To David. Happy birthday, gorgeous! You don't look a day over thirty!'

Everyone raised their glasses and it was then that I thought I heard his voice. Or was it just someone who sounded like him? I couldn't be sure but then again I couldn't chance it. The slightest possibility that he might be right here in this restaurant had already put me on edge. I reached for my glass of champagne and downed it one. Then the people at the table next to us suddenly erupted into laughter. It couldn't be him, could it? Surely he would already have had the big wedding back home and be shacked up with Fatima. It was probably just someone with a similar accent. Either that or the coke was just making me a bit edgy and paranoid. One thing was for sure, I couldn't relax until I knew for certain. As I turned round a waiter moved just in front of me obscuring the view. When he finally moved away, I could hardly believe what I was seeing.

It *was* Ahmed, smartly dressed in his Paul Smith pale blue jacket but with a fully grown beard and sitting across from him, a woman I hadn't seen for nearly a year. Fatima. They looked like they were both deeply engrossed in conversation. And then I couldn't be certain but I thought I saw her reach for his hand. I caught Caroline was staring at me.

'Darling, what's the matter? You've suddenly turned all white.'

'I'll be fine.'

Yossi passed me some water. 'Do you think it's the seafood?' he asked.

I was beginning to feel really hot and my heart was racing but how much of it was down to the shock of seeing Ahmed and how much was down to the line of cocaine I'd just snorted? I looked across at Yossi. Why was I even letting the fact that Ahmed was sitting at the far side of the restaurant even bother me. I'd moved on. It was over, water under the bridge. But telling myself that didn't help one iota.

We ordered coffee and I sat there the whole time wondering if Ahmed had actually seen me and was pretending he hadn't or whether he was completely oblivious to my presence in the restaurant. I wasn't coping well with the situation and, in my infinite wisdom, decided that maybe another line wasn't such a bad idea after all so I made a quick escape to the toilets for the second time that evening, with Caroline in tow. I slammed the cubicle door shut.

'Jesus, David, you're sweating buckets. Look at you. What happened up there?'

'What do you mean? It's nothing. I'm fine, really.'

'You can't fool me. What's come over you?' She reached for some toilet paper and wiped my forehead. 'What is it, darling?' There was no getting away from her when she was on my case.

'Oh, alright. You may as well know. You'll probably see him soon enough anyway. Ahmed is sitting there at the front of the restaurant, in the corner, with his wife or bride to be or whatever claim to him she think she has.'

'Oh my god, not Little Lord Fauntleroy? You're joking me!'

'No - I mean yes. I mean...but please, don't call him that. What am I going to do? I thought he'd upped and left for the Emirates. I can't believe he's up there with her, chatting away, happy as Larry, on my birthday of all days. The happy fucking couple! I can't do it Caz. I can't go back up there. I can't sit in this restaurant knowing full well he's here with her!'

'Calm down. Jesus, if you go on like this you'll give yourself a coronary! And trust me, being carried out of this restaurant on a stretcher in full view of Yossi and Ahmed is not exactly the kind of look that will impress either of them. Look, you'll just have to ride this one out. You've got your gorgeous Israeli boyfriend upstairs, who's not only flown all that way to see you on your birthday, but bought you a fuckin' air ticket to Israel, and you're freaking out because Little Lord... sorry, your ex shows up. Forget him. He binned you. For a woman. He made his bed and now he has to lie in it.'

'Can't we go somewhere else? Maybe I could just slip out the back?'

'David, get a grip of yourself! They'll probably have left by the time we get back upstairs. Now serve me a line of coke, bitch! On second thoughts, make it a fuckin' beach of coke.'

'God, you're one hell of a drug whore!'

She clenched a fist and I poured a generous amount onto the web between her thumb and forefinger then served myself.

Again the familiar bitter numb feeling at the back of my throat but this time it hit the spot and I felt a sudden sexual stirring in my groin. We climbed the stairs back up to the restaurant and I could feel beads of sweat dripping off me. Caroline was in front, her strappy high heeled shoes stomping up the wooden staircase. I looked at a reflection of myself in the mirror. It gave me a necessary confidence boost. When Caroline turned left at the top of the stairs, I suddenly found myself facing him and attempted a smile. Ahmed looked genuinely shocked then confused and unsure of himself. He stood up.

'David, I didn't know... where are you...... how long have you been here? This is a complete surprise.' He just stood there staring at me and then Fatima coughed politely into her hand. 'Ah, yes, sorry. You remember Fatima, David?'

I smiled again but it felt more like a grimace. She looked thinner than I remembered but still as young and beautiful – long brown hair and emerald green eyes. On her left hand, I glimpsed what I presumed was the engagement ring.

'Of course. Hashida's friend,' I said.

'David, you must join us,' she said graciously.

I could feel the coke dripping down the back of my throat and sniffed. Ahmed looked nervous. I sniffed again. 'I'd love to but I'm with a few friends tonight.'

'Well, another time then. But before you go, you simply must see my engagement ring. I take it Ahmed has told you the good news?'

'I'm sure David has to be getting back to his friends, Fatima,' said Ahmed.

She held out her hand and flashed the rock on her ring. 'Isn't it divine! Ahmed has such good taste, especially when it comes to jewellery, don't you think?'

A completely irrational voice inside my head was screaming

for me to rip the fucking thing off her finger, put it into my mouth and spit it into her pasta. I should have felt sorry for her but instead I wanted to tell her right there and then in full view of the waiters and other customers that he didn't love her, that he would never love her, that he was incapable of loving her in the same way as he'd loved me. I had visions of lunging at Ahmed, snogging the mouth off him in full view of his fiancé, declaring my undying love for him to the whole restaurant. I took a deep breath and managed to resist the urge.

'It's beautiful,' I said, practically choking on my words. 'Lovely to see you both again.' I could feel my heart pounding as I backed away from their table and towards the back of the restaurant. I sat down next to Yossi and began playing with the cutlery.

'Could we get the bill?' I asked.

'We haven't had our coffees yet.' Michael interrupted.

'You shouldn't keep snorting that stuff,' Yossi said. He placed a hand on my knee under the table.

'I'm sorry.' I put some cash on the table. 'I'll be back in a bit. I just need a breath of fresh air.'

'He's not worth it,' said Caroline.

'I can't breathe in here,' I said.

Yossi looked confused. 'Who's not worth it?' he asked.

'I can't fucking breathe!' I said and stood up nearly falling backwards over my chair. 'They seriously need to get some air con in here.'

'Sit down, David. Don't be such a drama queen!' said Michael.

I could feel everyone's eyes on me. I had to get out. I pushed my way past diners, dodged a couple of waiters and managed to avoid all eye contact with Ahmed. Before I knew it, I'd stumbled out onto the street and found myself caught in the middle of a hen party, all bunny costumes, fishnets and stilettos, and their wolf whistling admirers. Could it get any worse? I headed for the nearest gay bar, ordered a bottle of water and fiddled in my pocket for a Marlborough Light.

Chapter 14

I couldn't have stayed in that restaurant a moment longer. I thought I was over him but just seeing Ahmed sitting there with her made me want to throw up. I sat at the bar and lit a cigarette. My hands were shaking. I knew I was being ridiculous; I should have just stayed at the restaurant, stuck it out, pretended he wasn't there. It's just that seeing him brought it all back: being wasted at his flat, the bomb-shell about Fatima, being asked to leave, waiting for the bus to take me to Archway station.

I looked around. There were dozens of flickering candles dotted about the bar, friends chatting, a couple in the corner smooching away. What was I doing here? I was just about to stub my cigarette out and go back when the door to the bar opened and in walked Michael, looking hot and flustered.

'Are you ok? I thought I might find you here.'

'I'm sorry I rushed out like that, I saw Ahmed,' I said.

'Your Saudi prince? Your Fashion Mister?'

'You can joke about it now. She's in there with him. Flashing her engagement ring like it's going out of fashion.'

'Oh David, what are we going to do with you? You have to accept, rightly or wrongly that he's with her now.'

I felt my eyes well up but I was not going to cry, not here, not in front of Michael.

'You know, Yossi's worried about you.'

'I just needed some space, Mike. Sort my head out. It's the first time I've seen Ahmed since that night.' I thought of Yossi and wished I hadn't left so suddenly. He'd come all that way to see me and here I was ruining everything by letting Ahmed get to me.

'I guess the coke wouldn't have helped with that,' Michael said.

He was right. I couldn't believe it was the first time I'd seen

Ahmed since the break up and I was wired on Charlie.

'Listen to you, mister high and mighty. It wasn't so long ago when you would've been right in there snorting the Devil's Own.'

'The Devil's Own alright. Promises the Earth and takes away your soul. A truly Faustian pact!' He laughed out loud then suddenly looked serious. 'Seriously though, David, it hasn't made you happy, has it?'

I started singing: 'It's my birthday and I'll cry if I want to, snort coke if I want to! You would do to if it happened to you!'

'I can't believe you're pissed and high already! Your birthday's not until tomorrow remember?'

I'd known Michael for years and he would occasionally take a break from drugs and go all 'anti' on me. But this was different. This time he'd gone the whole hog – shaved head, retreats at Rivendell, strange new friends.

'So, you're definitely giving them up then?' I asked.

'Never say never. We'll see. I'm just trying to take each day as it comes.' He sounded like someone from Narcotic's Anonymous. But he didn't need a 'Ten Point Plan' or whatever it was. He already had his Higher Power.

'Look, I've been meaning to tell you. I know it's your birthday and everything. I tried to tell you before –'

'What is it?'

'David, I don't know how to say this… I know how much it means to you – us living together but you need to know. I'm going to live in the Buddhist Centre.'

'Sorry?'

'Just for a few weeks. Sort of like an extension of the retreat. But if I like it-'

'Buddhist centre?'

'In Bethnal Green. The one in Roman Road.' I stared in disbelief at him.

'Michael, I know where it is. You're moving out?'

'I tried to tell you before. There just never seemed to be a good time. I didn't want to upset you.'

'So you decided to leave it 'til my birthday? Great timing, Mikey.'

'When you split up with Ahmed, you really needed a friend.'

'So, that whole time was just one big act. You were just humouring me?'

'It wasn't like that! Sometimes you have to put another person's needs before your own.'

'How very noble of you!'

'David, you mean a lot to me.'

'We made that place our home and you're just going to give it up for some pseudo Buddhist cult!'

'Calm down. It's not a cult.'

'Do you really know what you're getting yourself into? Have you read the FWBO files? Have you? Have you seen the Guardian's article about it? *The Dark Side of Enlightenment?*'

'I'm warning you. Don't even go there,' he said.

'Why not? Are you afraid your little sanctuary isn't all that it's cracked up to be? You do know there are serious allegations of sexual abuse against senior Order members there.'

'You're just jealous that I've finally found something. '

'I care about you, Michael. We're family. I don't want to see you lose yourself, your identity. I've seen that glazed-over look. I don't want it to happen to you.'

'I'm learning how to find peace with myself.'

'You're being brainwashed! You may as well opt for electro convulsive therapy.'

'I'm trying to find a new direction in my life. Something I can value, aspire to - something real.'

'I know you are. I know you want to move away from the

whole drug scene. If I'm honest with myself, part of me does too. But you can do that without giving everything else up. You don't need to beat yourself up and dedicate your life to Buddha.'

'What is it you dedicate your life to, David? Getting so wasted every weekend that it takes you the rest of the week to recover? Or is it fetishising any bloke with a foreign accent and chasing them half way round the world? I mean, is there any Middle Eastern bloke or South American left in London who hasn't sampled your unique blend of *Poor Me* Bridget Jones and *Fly Away For A Bit of Foreign* Shirley Valentine? Any Brazilian just off the boat who hasn't tasted the delights of your Essex rosebud?'

'Congratulations! The inner bitch is at long last unleashed.'

'You asked for it, mate.'

'You know, Michael, believe it or not, I care what happens to you. I just don't want to see you replace one addiction with another. They don't call religion the opium of the masses for nothing.'

'I've found my one true salvation, my Unifying Principle. Can't you, just for once, be happy for me?'

'Unifying principle? Oh, please – save your personality by-pass jargon for the dipsters down at the processing plant! Better still, why don't you go the whole hog? Wear the saffron robes, dance in the street playing the tambourine with an inane grin plastered across your face. Go God-bothering members of the general public. I hear there's a great place near Tottenham Court Road!'

The door of the bar opened again and in walked Yossi, Caroline and Michael's little friend. I bet he put him up to it.

Yossi looked concerned. 'Are you ok? We didn't know what happened and then Michael told us you were probably here.'

'I'm sorry. It was sweltering in there. I had to get out for a bit. I'm fine.' I was anything but. This was rapidly turning into the night from hell but I was determined to not let it get to me.

'Are you sure you still want to go clubbing?' asked Caroline. I looked at Michael and at Padmalokha, his sanctimonious, lanky New Age sidekick. I couldn't bear to think of Michael morphing into some spineless, softly spoken clone, the rank and file of Sangharakshita's Brave New World.

'I can't think of anything better I'd rather do. Let's nail it!'

Michael looked at Caroline. 'I think we'll just leave it tonight actually. There's a late night meditation and puja session back at the centre.'

Caroline rolled her eyes to the ceiling.

'You guys go out and enjoy yourselves. We'll get a night bus and head down to Bethnal Green,' said Michael.

Padmalokha piped up. 'I think what Michael is trying to say is that he has evolved beyond the neurotic desire for narcotics. The roots of suffering – '

'Roots of suffering?! Oh shut the fuck up, you freak!' said Caroline. She turned to Michael. 'He's your best friend! You can't just bugger off now. It's David's birthday. You remember David? Your right-hand man, partner in crime? You can't leave like this.'

Michael shrugged and looked at me. 'Why don't you ask *him* why I'm leaving?' Then he made his way to the door of the bar with Padmalokha in tow.

'What on earth's got into Michael? Normally he'd be well up for a clubbing sesh in Vauxhall.'

'Don't even go there,' I said.

For a moment Caroline looked dumbfounded, then her face lit up. 'Well, you know what that means, don't you? More bugel for us lot!' Her brightly red lacquered nails scraped the denim on my jeans. 'I could just die for another line, darling. Come on. Let's try my shit. Follow Mamma!'

I decided against telling them about Michael wanting to

move out. It was a major downer and tonight I would do my best to forget I would soon be on my own and my best friend would be shacked up with a bunch of navel gazers just round the corner. Yossi gave me a look and we followed Caroline to rack up just one more line of Charlie.

Chapter 15

Maybe the coke was helping to blot things out but I was certainly feeling a lot better. Yossi was holding my hand and Caroline had craned her head out of the cab window as we sped past Big Ben and crossed Westminster Bridge. I loved crossing the river at night and taking in the view - the Millennium Bridge and Tower bridge to the left and the dome of St. Paul's, The London Eye and the revamped south bank, now all lit up against the night sky. I held Yossi's hand and refused to allow Michael, Ahmed or anyone else to spoil my night out. Caroline pulled back from the open window.

'God, it's exhilarating! I love it when it's this hot. I feel like I'm in some sweltering Mediterranean city.'

Once inside the club I made a mad dash to the toilet. Not to do another line of coke, but because I desperately needed a shit. I slammed the cubicle door shut and no sooner had I pulled down my pants than my bowels opened up and forcefully ejected a series of cow pats. Clearly one of the grams of coke was cut with laxatives and god knows what else – insecticide maybe, worming medicine?

'This is not a council flat! This is a public lavatory! Please do not take drugs in this establishment. I repeat, no drugs are allowed,' said the toilet attendant with a heavy Ghanaian accent and he proceeded to bang on every cubicle door with his broom handle.

I didn't know whether to take it seriously. After all, ninety percent of clubbers at *Fire* were on some form of narcotic or other. I opened my cubicle door to see him standing there, holding a megaphone in one hand and lighting a stick of incense above the cubicle door with the other. He was dressed in Bermuda shorts, a baggy Hawaiian short-sleeved shirt and sporting a pair of rather snazzy sunglasses. I went to the sink and splashed my face with cold water, graciously declining the assortment of aftershaves, deodorants and cologne. Then I felt a slap on my back and a familiar face staring back at me in the mirror.

'Hey David, what's up? How's it going dude?'

It was Sergio - an Algerian drug dealer, supposedly straight but not averse to having his cock sucked by the odd gay bloke when the opportunity presented itself. He'd just been granted full British citizenship. I'd been at the party to celebrate, somewhere out in Leytonstone - very random. All I remember was being coked up, very much on edge and listening to the new Madonna track which had just come out - *Time Goes Past So Slowly* and it certainly did. They kept playing it the whole night interspersed with sudden bursts of Arabic music and hip thrusting belly dancing.

'I'm good. You seen Naeem?' I asked.

'He's back in Morocco, man. Getting married to Doreen. The English girl. Remember? At my party.'

Unfortunately I did. Doreen, or 'Dor' for short: dyed blonde hair like straw, mid forties, tweeked off her titties with a Meth mouth to show for it. In other words, most of her teeth were either missing or had turned black from too much crystal. She was supposedly a drugs counsellor but in serious need of counselling herself to overcome her own spiralling addiction to crystal meth. Still, Naeem, god bless him, was desperate for a British visa.

He slung an arm around my shoulder and whispered in my ear. 'Hey, you want any stuff? I got what you want. I got what you need, man. It's your lucky night. I got every fuckin' letter of the alphabet. E's, C, T, K, G? Take your pick.'

Despite banging on about the evils of GHB, part of me had always been curious to try it. I knew the stuff was potentially lethal and I'd seen enough Gina casualties to put me off but then I'd also heard it made you feel relaxed and incredibly horny. And it was my birthday and what with Ahmed's sudden reappearance and Michael's revelation of moving into the revamped fire station in Bethnal Green, I was in need of a little diversion, a little transgression.

'How much for G?'

'You're after G?' He looked furtively around. 'Five quid one dose.'

'It's just – I've never taken it before. What do I do?'

'You A G virgin?! First time, eh? Look man, don't mix it with downers. No alcohol, ket, tranks. You know the score.' He winked at me.

'I'm not sure.'

'You'll love it. It's a real buzz. Give me five.'

He told me to wait outside. What was I doing? I wanted to back out but it was too late. It was just being greedy - having more drugs just for the sake of it. But then, I guess, that's what *Fire* was all about. A few minutes later he came back from the toilet with what looked like an empty Evian bottle of water and slipped it into my hands.

'What's that?'

'Your G, man. Mix it with a bit of water or lucozade and drink. You're gonna be horny as hell! Enjoy!'

And with that my fairy god-mother for the evening disappeared into the throng of Muscle Marys, Barbs and chemed-up club-kids. I went back into the toilet, half expecting the spoonful of corrosive liquid to have eaten away at the plastic and poured some tap water into the bottle. Then I swigged the lot and nearly vomitted it back up. Jesus, it tasted like something you'd clean the drains with. I couldn't believe it was still legal. I mean you could even get hold of the stuff by the litre on the internet. I went to look for Yossi and Caroline.

The main dance floor was packed. A Lebanese Go-go

dancer, bulging out of his Adidas shorts with a tattoo of a crescent moon and star across his back, was dancing on a podium, giving it some. I'd cruised him before and been pleasantly surprised when he'd taken me up on my offer. I looked up from his knee-high leather boots, taking in his hairy thighs and meaty bubble butt. The music surged through me and it felt like my cock and balls had been given a new lease of life. I could feel them rubbing against my jeans, giving me the Horn. I pushed my way through the dance floor, when all I really wanted to do was get lost in it. But I had to find Yossi and Caroline. Passing the bar near the entrance to the club, I saw them both sitting down engrossed in conversation - Caroline with a fag in one hand, water bottle in the other.

'Where did you get to?' asked Yossi. He was wearing the same white and blue tight fitting T shirt as when I met him. The only difference was I now knew what the Hebrew letters on his T shirt meant.

'Bad case of diarrhoea. London coke for you – cut with laxatives,' I said.

'Just like Israeli coke. Same the world over! Except, I guess, for parts of South America.' He was laughing and still looked as sexy as when I first met him.

'Caroline was telling me all about her boyfriend.'

Poor Caroline, she was a party animal but sadly her boyfriend, a solicitor for a family firm in Walthamstow, didn't share her love of drug-fucked clubbing sessions.

'Here open your mouth,' she said. 'Something to make you fly, sugar.'

I swallowed and took a key out from my pocket. 'Come on, I can't be arsed going to the toilets any more.' I took the coke out from my wallet and unwrapped it from its little paper envelope. I dipped the key into it, like a kid with sherbet dip, and passed it to Yossi and Caroline who each snorted a bump. Then I served myself. Drug taking here was pretty blatant and security would usually turn a blind eye to a bit of nose in the corner. It was G casualties they were really on the look out for.

Caroline went to the bar to get some more water. Yossi took my hand.

'David, I know it's not been long... but I know how I feel. I think I'm falling in love with you.'

He was beginning to blur at the edges.

'You don't have to say anything,' he said.

I tried to focus.

'What's up?' he asked.

'It's just ...we've taken drugs. They change everything.'

'Not for me. I know the difference. I know how I feel about you David. What's up?'

'I felt the same with someone else once, went round to tell him, drugged up to the eyeballs and ruined everything.'

'So you don't feel the same way with me?'

'I didn't say that. I just don't trust myself on drugs anymore.'

'So why take them?'

'Why does anyone take them? To get out of it, go a bit crazy, forget.'

'Forget what?'

'Does it matter?' I guess we all have our own shit to deal with but I certainly wasn't going to go into any of that now.

Caroline came back from the bar.

'Look, you guys wait there. I have to go to the toilet again,' I said, troubled by a pang of guilt over not giving Yossi what he wanted to hear. When I got to the toilet, the Algerian guy who'd supplied me with the G was standing outside and sold me another dose.

'Hey, go easy on that stuff,' he said squeezing my nipple

then walking off.

I swigged it back, retched again then went to pee. I didn't know what all the fuss was about. Standing at the urinals, I unzipped and took my cock out. I felt it as it began growing hard again. I was ashamed and turned on at the same time but I desperately needed a piss. I closed my eyes and focussed all my attention down there, urging my bladder to open up but I couldn't even feel my feet. I placed one hand on the wall above me and took some deep breaths. Nothing. I was just about to give up when I felt a thin trickle of urine passing out through my urethra and opened my eyes. It was like having an orgasm. I could see how people could get into 'water sports'. The relief was incredible. I also felt someone standing close beside me.

'I swear to god you're stalking me,' he said

I looked up. For a moment I thought I was hallucinating. I took in his shaven head, golden brown skin and beard. It rather suited him. Then my vision started to blur again. 'Ahmed! What on earth – '

'David, you're out of it again. What are we to do with you?'

The drugs had taken away all that up-tightness and anxiety I'd felt before. 'It's my birthday. I'm allowed to be.'

'I hadn't forgotten. Happy birthday, birthday boy.'

'What are you doing here? I thought you hated this place.' My eyes lingered on his lips.

'Something told me you might end up here. And I guess I wanted to see it for myself. See what all the fuss was about.' He smiled sweetly.

This shouldn't be happening. I imagined bumping into him maybe months later somewhere in Shoreditch or Soho, but off my tits at *Fire* of all places. It didn't make sense. I felt his gaze drop to the level of my cock which was now a semi hard-on. I made a conscious effort to stuff it back into my pants and began to zip up.

'But where's Fatima?' I asked.

'At an aunt's in Mayfair.'

'You're still going ahead with the marriage?'

He didn't answer.

'Look this is all a bit weird. It doesn't feel right. I came with some friends. They're waiting outside.' He grabbed my arm.

'Not so fast, mister.' His face was up close against mine. I felt messed up and confused yet really turned on. I should never have taken that G. It was then that I felt his lips kissing me. I suddenly came to my senses and gently pulled away. What was I doing? Where was Yossi? My eyes darted round the toilet then back to Ahmed. He looked disappointed.

'Was that your boyfriend I saw you in the restaurant with?' he asked.

'Yes, and he's waiting outside.'

'It didn't take you long to find someone else.'

'What did you expect me to do? Sit at home and twiddle my thumbs? It was you who didn't want to see me, remember?'

He looked sheepishly at me and began to do up the buttons to his jeans. 'I'm just saying.'

Then I felt my arm being grabbed and he was pulling me towards an available cubicle. I heard someone shouting out. 'Hey, there is a bloody queue you know!' Ahmed shouted back 'Fuck you and lighten up!' I'd never heard him speak to anyone like that before. He bolted the door behind us.

'Please Ahmed, don't.' He was trying to take off my T shirt, undoing my zip. 'You're getting married.'

'Don't remind me.'

'What about Fatima?'

'It's you I think about at night. It's you I want in my bed. I can't take it anymore.'

I felt his hands searching for my cock, reaching in between my thighs, freeing it from my briefs. I tried to push him back and then I felt his wet mouth on my cock. I heard myself groaning and he was kneeling down, looking up at me. Jesus, I was so fucking high and he looked so fucking hot sucking away at my cock. At that moment, I wouldn't have cared if the cubicle door was wide open and the whole queue could see. I was too far gone and the music being pumped into the men's toilets was taking me to a different dimension. The DJ out on the main dance floor was creating a wicked fusion of Arabic music and dirty-electro House and Ahmed kept on sucking. Fragments from the past flashed before me and began to merge: waking up next to him on Sunday morning, kissing in Kew Gardens, the Hand of Fatima, kneeling down to wash his feet in the shower, the pine tree outside his flat. I just wanted to fuck him right there, bend him over and give it to him, nothing else mattered - shit, I was gonna cum - he was looking right up at me, I could feel the point of no return, the ache deep inside my belly - then it came, that squirting sensation, and I shot my load all over him. His face was covered in splashes of milky white cum and some of his own juice had spilt onto his jeans. I felt like I was going to pass out and he just kept looking up at me grinning. I stuffed my cock, still dripping with cum, back inside my pants, and belted up, giving Ahmed some toilet paper to wipe his face with.

'I don't understand. This isn't you,' I said.

'Well, if the mountain won't come to Mohammed, Mohammed must go to the mountain.' He was still grinning. 'You didn't reply to my message. What's a man supposed to do?' He suddenly looked sheepish. 'I'd like to see you again. I mean it. I'm miserable without you. Anyway, I have something for you. I think you'll like it. Think of it as a belated birthday gift. My painting, it's finally finished and I'd like you to have it.'

'Ahmed, I can't.'

'Of course you can. If it wasn't for you, I wouldn't have finished it. I don't know. Not seeing you – somehow I found myself getting up in the early hours of the morning again to paint.'

'But I'm seeing Yossi,' I said.

'I don't care if you're seeing the fucking queen of Sheeba.' He grabbed me by the wrists and kissed me. 'I want you,' he said. 'I want you, David. That's all there is to it.'

There was a sudden thump on the door and the familiar Ghanaian accent. 'Hurry up in dere. This is not a council flat! No Jiggy Jiggy! No funny business!' The toilet attendant proceeded to bang on all the cubicle doors with his broom handle.

'Look, I've got to go,' I said.

His hands were under my T shirt again. 'Are you ok?' he asked.

I was breathing heavily.

'We've got to get you off those fucking drugs,' he said. 'Look what they're doing to you.'

Again the broom handle. 'Oi guys, the game's up.' I suddenly saw the toilet attendant's shocked face, replete with huge sunglasses, peering over the top of the cubicle.

'What are you doing in dere? Is one man, one cubicle. Outside!' he boomed.

Ahmed turned round. 'What the -? Can't you give us some privacy? We're just coming,' he shouted then turned to me. 'Don't tell me he saw us mid-action? That he was perched up there with a bird's eye view!' He started to laugh and hugged me. 'David, just promise me you'll take it easy. I hope whoever you're with is looking after you. Because if he isn't, he's got me to answer to.'

'I've got to go.'

'Call me. I'm serious. Just do it or I swear I'll arrive on your doorstep in the middle of the night and throw stones at your window until you let me in.'

'All right, all right, I'll call. Let me go. I'm sweltering. It's like a sauna in here.' I opened the cubicle door. It was then that I spotted Yossi. Standing by himself at the back of the queue, waiting to get into the loos. It was too late. He'd spotted me. What had I just done? Ahmed followed me out. I felt terrible.

'Is that your man?' said Ahmed. I could tell he was jealous as Yossi squeezed through the buffed-up naked torsos in front.

'*Motek* where have you been? You keep disappearing!'

'This is Yossi.' They shook hands.

'Look after him for me, he's a bit far gone,' said Ahmed.

'Do you two know each other?' asked Yossi.

'You could say that. I'm Ahmed.' There was an awkward silence.

'*As – Salamu' Alaykum,*' said Yossi.

'*Wa-Alaykum As-Salam.* Well, you boys have fun,' said Ahmed. 'I think I'm ready to make a move. Not really my kind of place. But feel free to join me for champagne in Shadow Lounge if you're still around later.' And I watched him disappear into the crowd.

'What were you doing with your ex. in the toilet?'

'What do you think we were doing? He wanted a line.'

'Why didn't you give him some outside? You gave it to us out there.'

'That was out there. Look in here. There's security everywhere.' I pointed to the tall black guy dressed smartly in a black suit with the ear piece then closed my eyes and leaned against the sink. All I could see was a vision of Ahmed kneeling down inside the cubicle sucking me off. I looked at Yossi and imagined both of them kissing each other and I started to get hard again. I went to the sink, splashed my face with cold water and stared at myself in the mirror. My whole body was tingling and awash with a cocktail of drugs - and my mind? It wasn't my own, that's for sure. It was like some form of psychic possession by a demon sex god– and all I could do right now was surrender to it.

Would all this have happened if I hadn't taken GHB? I'd lied to Yossi and had sex with my ex in the toilet. I wasn't even sure if Ahmed was still in the country. And what was he doing here of all places? He hated it. And did he mean what he'd said in the cubicle or had someone spiked his drink? Maybe the whole marriage thing had served to send him completely over the edge. None of it made any sense. I grabbed Yossi's hand and pushed my way past a transsexual checking her cleavage out in the mirror and back to the main dance area.

'Are you ok?' asked Yossi.

I'd lost my balance and stumbled, losing my bottle of water in the process. He picked it up for me, just as he'd done the first time we met. 'I'm fine.' I was actually beginning to feel dizzy and a bit nauseous but I didn't want to worry Yossi or start panicking myself. I probably just needed to sit down for a minute.

'I'll get you fruit juice.'

As we pushed our way to the bar, the waves of nausea were beginning to take over and I had to force myself to keep my eyes open. I told Yossi I was going to the toilet again. Instead I just went to sit down in a corner, away from the mayhem on the main dance floor and away from the prying eye of security. I knew what was probably happening and it wouldn't be pleasant. I'd taken too much GHB but I didn't want to attract attention and get chucked out or sent to the medic's room at the back of the club. I sat down and started to retch. My stomach spasmed painfully, a sudden violent contraction forcing the poison up and out of my body. But all that I managed to bring up was a bit of bile and strings of saliva. My head was hurting somewhere deep inside and I suddenly wished that Yossi was with me but I was too sick to stand up or open my eyes properly. The last thing I wanted was to collapse and be dragged under in a sea of Muscle Maries and pumped-up beefcakes. Why had I taken GHB on top of drinking champagne and then been greedy enough to take a second dose? I'd poisoned myself and for what? To reach that elusive new-found high? Well, I'd found a new-found low. I saw a vision of myself collapsing and being carried off by a medic. I fought hard against the vision becoming reality and faced the wall. My stomach muscles contracted again and my mouth released a sudden gush of projectile vomit and more saliva.

I couldn't focus my eyes. Everyone and everything was looking strange and a long way off. My eyes were becoming heavier and I just wanted to fall asleep but I forced them open knowing only too well where that might lead to. The music was making it worse. It was like a sick fairground ride and I couldn't get off. I forced myself to focus all my energy on sitting up and staying conscious. Just to the left of me I saw three guys all in sports gear - white shorts and football socks. One had wrestling boots and gloves and a jockstrap that was visible under his shorts. They were all getting off with each other and despite myself, the GHB was still working its sex magic, and I began to get turned on. Seconds later, I turned to the wall again and projectiled again.

After another ten minutes, the worst was over. I still felt dizzy and a bit nauseous but the vomiting and violent contractions had stopped and I could just about open my eyes. I was left feeling shaken, physically weak and strangely sober but the overwhelming feeling I had, was one of sheer relief that the worst of it was over. It was at that point that it really dawned on me what I'd done. For a few minutes I'd turned into one of those Vauxhall clones, who, hell-bent on getting trashed, end up having sex with their ex whilst their boyfriend's still in the club. But then did Ahmed think of himself as my ex? From what he'd said, it sounded like he wanted to get back together. And was Yossi my boyfriend now? We'd never used the word but he'd told me he was in love with me. I felt so confused about everything.

'Where have you been? I went to look for you. You've been gone over half an hour!' he sounded and looked really pissed off.

'I'm sorry. I'm all yours now. I won't disappear again, I promise.' I didn't want to tell him what had really happened. It was over now. It's something that had happened and wasn't going to happen again.

I took some more coke and started to come back up again. It felt as if the bad experience on GHB had actually happened to someone else. Caroline left the club a few hours later, worried what her boyfriend would say if she left it any later. I was ready to carry on partying but after a few more hours Yossi wanted to go. So we left, but not before I'd bought some more GHB from Sergio.

Chapter 16

When we arrived back at the flat, both trashed and horny as hell, there was no sign of Michael. I guessed he'd decided to stay the night at the Buddhist centre, which in a way was a relief because it meant we had the place to ourselves. But it was also a painful reminder that he was in the final stage of a full-on conversion to Buddhism. I went straight into the lounge and put on a dirty-electro house C.D. Yossi went to the fridge and was just about to open a bottle of wine when I stopped him.

'I've got a better idea,' I said and rummaged around in my dirty jean pocket, pulling out bits of old tissue, a few coins, a folded-up flyer to another club, some chewing gum and then found it. The plastic vial of G I'd bought from Sergio just before I left the club. In fact, I'd bought two, the other vial was in my wallet. They were both in the shape of a small fish. Normally they'd contain soy sauce and come with a Chinese take-out or take-away sushi, but I guess were ideal for smuggling into a club, small enough to go undetected and no pipette required to measure out the dose. I poured some coke, unscrewed the little red top and poured in the offensive liquid.

'Here - try that.'

'*Goodnight Cinderella*?' He shook his head. 'I've heard stories about that drug.'

He took some persuading. I told him that bad stuff only happened if you mixed it with downers like alcohol or ketamine and eventually he agreed to take it, but just half the dose. I took another full dose, retched slightly on taking it down then swigged a mouthful of coke to take the taste away. Sergio called it a 'chaser', which makes you forget you're swallowing an industrial solvent that corrodes your insides. But God, did I love how it made you feel after you recovered from retching on the stuff - relaxed, horny and high as a kite. A David Guetta track was buzzing round in my head - *The World is Mine.*

'Look, I've got something to show you.' Yossi led me into the bedroom and began to unfasten his suitcase. Out of it, he pulled a contraption made of bits of leather and metal. My vision was becoming a little blurry. 'Put it on for me. It's a leather harness. I'd really love to see you in it.'

I wasn't entirely convinced but Yossi was already helping me into it which was quite tricky because there was a strap I had to do up right in the place where my arse crack met my balls. And then I had to somehow squeeze both balls through a metal ring. It was whilst I was trying to squeeze the second ball through the metal ring that I felt something wet begin to explore my arse: his tongue, then his fingers gently probing, then tongue again. He was kissing me everywhere, working up from my arse to the small of my back, all the way to my neck, ears, and my mouth, which greeted his with insatiable desire. I felt his hands pressing and massaging my scalp then cover my ears and eyes, relieving me momentarily of my senses. Suddenly his arms were around me, holding me tight. When I struggled against him to test his strength I felt his vice like grip tighten then just as quickly release me. I looked back and saw him reach for the tube of lubrication, apply it to his fingers and then my arse. It felt cold and sticky. He tore open a condom and rolled it onto his large, circumcised penis. Then I felt him - at first just a sharp, stabbing pain. I gripped the pillow with both hands and buried my head in it. He was fully inside me now and as he began to fuck slowly, gently, the pain disappeared and in its place that familiar feeling. I didn't want it to stop. Then a brief moment of panic before a feeling of complete calm washed over me.

The first thing I felt was a slap on my face.

'What's his name?' said a voice I didn't recognise.

'David,' said Yossi.

What was happening?

'David, can you hear me? I'm Pete.' I could feel someone shaking me. I didn't want to wake up. I felt a slap on my face again. My eyes struggled to open.

'He's coming to.' I felt someone holding my wrist then made out two figures in green and white uniform.

'David, we're from the London Ambulance.' He looked at Yossi. 'Your friend called us. He was worried. You lost consciousness.' I looked at Yossi standing there just in a pair of jeans. I looked down at myself. I was lying on my side wearing some kind of leather harness. It was then that it all came flooding back to me.

'David what have you taken?' I struggled to put my thoughts into words. My mouth was dry. I wanted water.

'Ecstasy, cocaine, GHB.' I rattled off the list.

'It looks like you boys had quite a night.' Pete, the medic, smiled and looked round the room. The other one asked Yossi where we'd been. Yossi told him we'd been to *Fire* in Vauxhall. I heard the other medic's voice:

'Really? We were there last month. It was heaving. Personally I just stick to ecstasy myself. Not one for the drug cocktails.'

'David how much GHB did you take?' asked Pete.

I couldn't remember.

He took my pulse. 'Well, your pulse is fine. Breathing's fine. Your friend did the right thing putting you in the recovery position. Do you want to come to hospital to get checked over?'

The thought of being wheeled into the Royal London Hospital in Whitechapel on Sunday morning on my birthday was more than I could handle.

'I'll be fine.'

'David, I really think you should get checked over,' Yossi said.

'I'm fine. I've just really over done it haven't I?'

Pete smiled. 'You could say that.' He took my blood pressure, which he said was on the low side but not dangerously so.

'A word of advice. Stay clear of GHB. It's dangerous stuff. A guy died at *Fire* a couple of months ago. I was there when it happened. I happened to be working that night.'

Yossi thanked them. Then they packed away their medical equipment and left. I heard the front door slam shut and forced myself to sit up. Yossi came back into the bedroom. He didn't say anything.

'It was the first time we'd fucked. You passed out.' He looked like he'd been crying.

'I'm sorry.' Again the silence.

'I told you that stuff was dangerous. I said I didn't want to take it but you insisted. You didn't listen. How much did you take?'

'A full dose here.' My voice was flat, I felt washed out. 'I also took some at the club.'

'Jesus, David why didn't you tell me? So that's why you kept disappearing all the time. How can I trust you?'

'I got carried away.'

'You sure did. You nearly got carried away on a stretcher! David, I thought you'd died. One minute I was fucking you and the next you collapsed and wouldn't wake up.'

I felt ashamed and at the same time I was thinking I could really do with a line of coke. What was the matter with me? 'I'd never done the stuff before. I took too much. I'm sorry.' I felt like a kid and just wanted him to hug me. I wanted him to take the leather harness off.

'I've had one boyfriend die on me but that wasn't his fault.' He started crying. 'After you collapsed... your mouth was half open. You looked like a corpse. I'm sorry. I can't go through this again.'

'I've fucked it up haven't I?'

He didn't answer. 'Let's just try and get some sleep.'

I don't know if he slept or not. I eventually managed to get the leather harness off then lay awake thinking about the last twenty four hours: about Michael, Yossi, Ahmed, my job, the fact that it was my birthday and I'd promised myself I wouldn't be doing this stuff once I'd hit thirty five. My brain just wouldn't shut down and the more I thought about it, the more I saw my life as one big mess. Everything I touched, I fucked up. Michael couldn't even bear to live with me anymore and I'd given him such a hard time about going to the Buddhist commune. At least he was doing something to stay off the drugs. What was I doing? I was just another silly, synthetic queen overdosing on GHB, only I wasn't fitting uncontrollably on the dance floor; I'd passed out in the middle of the act. I wanted Yossi more than anything right now. But even though he was here in London, lying right next to me in bed, he felt the furthest he'd ever been from me. Later that evening, he began packing his suitcase.

'I'm sorry. I think it's best if I spend the night in a hotel tonight.'

His flight back to Tel Aviv wasn't until late the following afternoon.

'Yossi, don't be crazy. You can't leave now.'

'No-one should have to go through what I did. When I called the ambulance - I thought you were going to die.'

'Well, I didn't. I'm here. It's me. Don't go. Not yet. Please. Lie down.'

'I can't. It's all too much. I don't know. Maybe coming off the antidepressants – it was too soon.'

'Please, don't go.'

'I just want to be alone right now.'

'Come back to bed. We can fall asleep together. I'll fix us some breakfast in the morning then we can go to the airport together.'

He went to the bathroom and came back with his toiletry bag in his hand. 'I can't do this. I thought you were dead. I threw a glass of water on you, I slapped you. You were out cold. I shook you, yelled at you. Nothing! What you put me through - it was a living nightmare.' He zipped his suitcase. 'You knew that stuff was dangerous. Why? Why take it to the extreme? Why play with your life like that?' He put on his white leather jacket.

I could hardly string two sentences together let alone analyse the whys and wherefores of my reckless drug taking behaviour. 'Please, for now – let's just forget about it.'

'Take care of yourself, David.'

'Don't go. Please Yossi!'

'Goodbye motek. *Laylah tov.*'

He kissed me on the cheek and on my forehead. I stood at the front door and watched him walk down the stairwell struggling with his luggage. I walked to the landing and stood at the window. He put his luggage in the boot, got into the taxi and I half expected him to look back. But he never did. I watched as the taxi drove off in the direction of Whitechapel road. I went into the kitchen, leaned against the sink and stared at the garbage that had spilled out of the bins below, at the battered wooden door and the padlock broken by local gangs trying to get in at the rear of the building. I remembered how I felt when I arrived in Tel Aviv for the first time - so excited to get away from all this and I remembered how happy and surprised Yossi had been to see me. In a strange way it had felt like coming home. How could it end like this? It was all so sordid – me passing out, having no recollection of what had happened in between Yossi fucking me and the ambulance arriving.

It felt like someone else picked up the empty bottle of beer and hurled it into the hallway. It smashed against the wall, just above Michael's framed photograph of the Emerald Buddha, and the broken glass scattered in all directions across the laminate wood flooring. The silence was palpable. A rage was building deep inside me that for years had lodged itself in the pit of my being, had solidified somewhere inside me like a fist of rock. I remembered it now, that long-forgotten place and in the remembrance it began to turn to molten lava – an intense, smouldering heat, a liquid-yellow glow radiating outwards as it moved slowly inside my gut. I looked up at to the Royal London hospital. The hands of the clock were now showing half past eleven. I couldn't believe it. After months of it being stuck at quarter past four, someone had finally come to fix it!

I turned to a kitchen cupboard next to the boiler, opened it, picked up a plate and smashed it as hard as I could on the kitchen floor. A loud explosion took me for a split second out of myself and I stared at the pieces of broken crockery. My whole body was now beginning to shake and the room was spinning. I felt like I'd been carrying this rage inside me all my life. It was ancient, primal, unstoppable. It didn't want to negotiate or reason or listen. It had had enough of being told, of compromise, of being meek and mild of manners. The meek shall inherit the earth? What bullshit! What had I inherited? A world that revolves around clubs and drugs? A scene that sucks you in and spits you out the other side? Or a world where it's still ok to beat the living crap out of a dirty queer? And you still have to take it, still have to wait for the next kick in the ribs, in the stomach, in the head.

My thoughts turned to Ahmed. How he still dared not come out to his parents for fear of being taken back to the Emirates and forced to undergo therapy by a father who still thinks homosexuality is a mental illness, an aberration of God's will, something that hormone replacement or aversion therapy will sort out. And I thought of school - how they'd really rather prefer it if you played their game, if you didn't kick up a fuss and went along with their politics of the invisible.

But most of all, I was angry with myself - for needing to suppress this anger with enough drugs to knock myself unconscious. I'd popped so many pills over the years you could literally pick me up and rattle me. Go on shake me, why don't you? Pull the cord on my back. You know you want to. That's it: 'Come on Barbie, let's go party! Yeah, Yeah, Yeah, Yeah!' You got yourself a walking, talking, pill-popping, techno dancing, living gay doll – a gullible, passive, queer consumer. I consume therefore I am. I consume and am consumed. Amongst other things, I consume large doses of homophobic bullshit often coming at me from several directions at once, elements of the 'gay lifestyle' including periodic obsessing over body image, copious amounts of pills and powder (it's funny how the enduring myth of fairy tales remain – the magic wand, potion or flower…) to suppress all the homophobic bullshit, some of which must have stuck (it tells me so on occasion) so it begins to feel part of me even though it's alien and stinks like fuck – like the little fuck who pretended to come on to me then beat the living crap out of me.

But I didn't think about any of this, or maybe I did and then I forgot. I forgot how it wormed its way in, how it filtered down from on High, festering as I looked the other way, as it corroded my insides just like the mouthful of ball bearing cleaning fluid I'd gladly swig in the cubicle toilet of a club, like a fucking homeopathic remedy – like treating like. Only get the dose wrong and you puke your guts up. Get the dose wrong and you end up in A & E. Get too close to the source and you end up in a body bag in the morgue awaiting identification.

PLEASE – JUST MAKE IT STOP!

It was then that I heard a strange yelling, a guttural animal-like noise. It didn't sound entirely human and seemed to be coming from some way off. Then I realised it was me and I couldn't stop. The insides of me had come out. I felt my feet go from under me and fell to the floor, cushioning the blow with my hand.

Lying in the dark amongst the broken crockery, I watched the blood trickle slowly down the palm of my hand and felt strangely elated as if something had been lifted from me. I'd come back to myself, to a part of me I thought I'd lost for good. And in the acceptance of this, I heard my voice and understood. It was breaking me and releasing me at the same time and I cried properly for the first time since I was queer bashed coming out of a gay club in Kings Cross.

Chapter 17

I woke up before the alarm. The first light slowly gave form to my computer, book shelf and heap of dirty clothes in the corner. The sound of a lone vehicle passed by outside on the road. I began to make out empty beer bottles, packets of condoms and old copies of QX and Boyz magazine strewn across the floor. An upturned ashtray had left cigarette butts and ash marking the faded, beige carpet. The broken glass still covered the floor in the hallway. Monday morning already hung oppressively in the air and my body lay like a dead weight, unable to move. Dead to the world, facing the day felt like a task of Herculean proportions.

After a mammoth club/drug binge, Monday morning was at the same time both a shock and yet all too familiar. The longer I lay in bed, the more I prolonged the agony of finally getting up and facing the day. The temptation to phone in sick and lie in bed all morning was growing by the minute and I felt myself just wanting to give in to it. But I'd already taken Friday off a few weeks ago with Caroline and spent half of it wining and dining in Soho. The guilt kicked in. With a groan I pushed the duvet off and forced my body off the bed and into standing position. Zombie-like I shuffled to the bathroom. The piss was dark yellow, almost orange. My eyes, heavy and aching, had still not opened properly and I rummaged through the mountain of dirty clothes half blind, searching for clean underpants and socks. Under an empty packet of cigarettes I found half a gram of coke and a small bag of pills. I picked them up then saw the cut on the palm of my hand and the events of last night came rushing back. I went back to the bathroom and did something I'd never done before. I emptied the coke and pills into the pan of the toilet and pulled the flush. I then got a dustpan and brush from the cupboard under the kitchen sink and swept up all the broken glass in the hallway and broken crockery in the kitchen. I showered, ironed a shirt then sat at the kitchen table drinking my coffee and smoking my first cigarette of the day.

I made it to school just in time, clocked in with my fob key at the metal gate and walked through the playground. In my absence, the walls had received a fresh lick of paint. Dick Whittington now had both his legs, Red Riding Hood was more than just her cape and basket, and Cinderella's fairy god-mother now had her wand back - all just in time for Ofsted.

I thought of all the life that had passed through the school gates, now overlooked by CCTV cameras twenty four hours a day, ghosts from another era: the poor blighters of Victorian England who'd otherwise have faced a life of back-breaking labour in the workhouse, the children of Jewish migrants at the turn of the century and the white working class from the East End of the forties and fifties. Now a second or third generation of Bangladeshi kids were passing through, many of whom now lived in the dilapidated tower blocks opposite the school, in bedrooms which slept siblings and parents together. I slowly climbed the stairs to my classroom on the third floor, all the life of me left back on the dance floor south of the river.

When I opened my classroom door, Caroline was sitting on one of the desks chatting away on her mobile phone. She saw me, quickly finished her conversation then was all ears. I told her about Michael.

'What do you mean he's leaving?' she said.

'I think they call it 'going for refuge.''

'Sorry?'

'He's moving into the Buddhist centre down in Bethnal Green.'

'You're joking! Jesus, why doesn't he just go to the third world and do something useful if he's got a guilty conscience?

But, tell me, what happened after you left the club?'

'I over did it a bit this time round, even by my standards. Let's just say I've fathomed the anagram of GHB: Grievous Bodily Harm.'

'Oh darling, you know how I hate the idea of anyone taking that stuff. It's a dirty drug, really scraping the barrel. You may as well be sniffing glue on the outskirts of some council estate in Glasgow.'

'Well, I won't be going there in a hurry again.'

'I should hope not.'

'In fact, I won't be going there ever again, if I can help it.'

'What do you mean?'

'That's it Caz, no more G, no more pills and potions. I've had it.'

'Sweetheart, you just overdid it. You'll feel differently next week.'

'That's what I said to someone myself, and he didn't and he stopped.'

'Michael?'

'Who else? I wasn't going to tell you but I OD'd on G, passed out. Yossi called an ambulance.'

'Oh my god! Why didn't you phone me?'

'I'm fine now, but I mean it. Taking drugs - it's like the Midas touch, but for me it's the opposite. Everything I touch turns to nothing. Ahmed disappeared, Yossi's gone, Michael's going.'

'What do you mean, Yossi's gone?'

I filled her in and she gave me a hug.

'I'm still here, gorgeous, and I'm not going anywhere.'

The rest of the day passed by uneventfully enough and at 3.30pm the kids rampaged their way down the stairs and out into the playground. I stood and waited for their parents to pick them up. Quite a few of the dads wore the black and white chequered scarf round their shoulders, originally Bedouin headgear and now a symbol of Palestinian resistance against the Israeli occupation. It had also been adopted by most of the high street stores as the latest fashion accessory, and in certain quarters of the capital was almost as ubiquitous as the imported 'rude boy' get-up - baseball cap, gold jewellery and low-slung trackie bottoms.

A few of the other dads had taken to wearing the red and white chequered Saudi scarf, short trousers that came to just below their knees, and sported huge bushy beards. I was told by John that they belonged to JIMAS, which stood for the 'Movement for the Revival of the Prophet's Way.' Some of the mums wore the pinned-down-tight, face-grabbing style of headscarf and a few had adopted the Saudi or Afghani look and were completely covered up. Many others wore the traditional Asian salwar kameez.

'Can I have a word with you when all your children have gone?' It was Linda. She looked even thinner out in the playground than she did stuck behind her desk. Her arms were folded over a skimpy peach blouse and I wondered if the rumours were true, that she had turned into an 'orthorexic', obsessed with the purity of her food and convinced she had every food allergy and intolerance under the sun. After the last child had been picked up I climbed the stairs to the third floor and knocked on her door.

'Come in.'

They were all sitting there - the three stooges. Linda, Jane, the new Deputy, even John had been drafted in for moral support and sat at the side, a rather reluctant recruit to the senior management team. Jane gestured for me to sit down, eager to assert her authority, being new to the job.

'Take a seat David,' said Linda. She put on her spectacles and opened a note book, then looked at me. 'In a meeting scheduled for after school, did you or did you not ask a parent to remove the niqab?' She saw it wasn't registering. 'The niqab, David. The veil.'

All I could think of was how I'd screwed things up between me and Yossi. Right now he'd be on an El Al flight half way back to Tel Aviv. I really couldn't be bothered with all this.

'No. Why?'

'Well, just to jog your memory -we have a written statement here from the parent in question,' said Linda. 'Do you want me to read it out? Apparently the incident occurred nearly four months ago. The parent in question is a Mrs. Begum?'

'Four months ago? So what stopped her from making a complaint back then?'

'A complaint is a complaint, David. We are just following procedure,' said Jane.

'Well maybe if we used a bit of common sense instead of blindly following 'procedure' we might get somewhere,' I said. 'She claims I asked her to take it off?'

'Those were her very words.'

A vague recollection of meeting a parent to discuss an incident of bullying came to mind. 'I remember asking a parent if she wouldn't mind lowering her veil, so I could at least see her eyes. But isn't the real question – why she's decided to complain about it now?' I had a sneaking suspicion that her complaint had nothing to do with the veil and everything to do with her son's teacher being a poof. But I didn't want the senior management team to get whiff of the fact I'd outed myself in a sex education lesson.

'I fail to see why you risked offending her over something so trivial,' said Jane, notebook at the ready.

'She didn't seem that offended about it at the time.'

'You are aware that what you did is not school policy?' said Linda.

I was past caring. Michael had turned into a religious fanatic, Yossi had upped and left in the middle of the night and I was in the grip of a most horrendous come-down.

'Look, this is political correctness gone mad! Would you allow a teacher to teach swamped in a full-on Afghan burqa? Of course not. It's about what sort of dress code is appropriate in a public place. I mean, headscarves, turbans, swinging crucifixes, the Jewish skull cap – it's a different ball game. I completely get it – but to sit opposite someone covered in a black shroud who refuses to talk to you, well, to be perfectly honest, it's bordering on the surreal and pretty spooky.' I'd clearly spoken out of line and it was clearly not what they wanted to hear. Why did I always do that? Why couldn't I nod, smile apologetically and give them what they wanted?

Linda looked at Jane. As far as I was aware there was not a school policy on the issue but you could bet there would be now.

'You contravened our equal opportunities policy. Everyone is to be treated equally regardless of their religious affiliation or expression of faith. Women of a Muslim background are entitled to wear whatever they want, the *hijab, jilbab, niqab* or traditional *burqa* for that matter.' She sounded like she was reading from auto-cue, the cue being political correctness.

I was nearing the end of my tether. 'Tell that to the women of Saudi and Iran who risk the wrath of the religious police if they're caught uncovered in public.'

'But we don't live in Iran, David. This is the London Borough of Tower Hamlets. We have to be sensitive to the needs of the local community,' said Jane.

'It's not a *need* to be fully burqared up. It's a political act. A Saudi cultural import. A symbol of defiance and rejection of the West. But no-one dares say that. We're too busy pussy-footing around.'

'I'm sorry, but that attitude is completely unacceptable at William Booth school,' said Jane. 'I wished you'd raised your issues around Islam at last year's cultural awareness and diversity workshop. Islamophobia is best dealt with out in the open,' said Jane.

'Islamophobia? Oh, please! You can't play that card with me. If someone wants to believe in mythical horses flying to Jerusalem, the inspired delusions of some guy hanging out in a cave hundreds of years ago, or, for that matter, some old guy talking to a burning bush – that's their prerogative. But to pretend communication isn't affected when you're sitting opposite a faceless wonder – it's ridiculous.'

'I'm glad you seem to see the funny side in all this! Do you really think I want the Local Education Authority breathing down my neck, accusing us of institutional Islamophobia?' said Linda.

'And how about institutional homophobia? We can all play the 'phobia' game, Linda. Oh, I forgot – that's still the acceptable face of discrimination in certain quarters of the education system isn't it? We can't even mention the word 'gay', least we upset the faith community. For Christ's sake, gays and lesbians now have the right to marry in this country!'

'Calm down, David. Are you aware that the parent in question has talked to many of our other parents? Our parent school governor informed me today. She also let it be known that some of the mothers are organising a petition,' said Linda.

'You are joking?' I said.

'The parent who complained about your trip to the Tate Gallery and Rodin's statue also complained when you read *Gloria goes to Gay Pride*. The same parent complained about Miro's print you had displayed in the classroom.'

John was tapping his pencil.

'You picked on the wrong parent. Mrs. Begum. A devout British convert to Islam with a degree in Arabic from the university of Birminham. She's now a member on the council of The East London mosque and has expressed an interest in becoming a parent governor of this school. David, she's a prominent member of the community.'

'She converted to Islam? She's not Asian?'

'No David, she's white. I told you she's a British convert to Islam,' said Linda.

'I don't see why the colour of her skin should matter,' said Jane.

'I'm just surprised that's all. I've never seen her uncovered. I presumed -'

'Well, that's where all the trouble starts. When people start presuming,' said Jane.

'Look, I just asked her if she wouldn't mind lowering the veil. I thought it would aid the channels of communication. If she wants to kick up a storm that's her problem.'

Linda spoke very slowly and deliberately, as if talking to a child. 'But don't you see, it's not just her problem. It's our problem now. The school's being inspected next week and they'll be canvassing parents views about the school and their children's education.'

'I fail to see what you want me to do now.'

They both looked at one another. Linda spoke. 'We would appreciate it if you would speak to the mother in question. Apologise unreservedly for having upset her, something along the lines of it being a cultural misunderstanding. Offer an assurance that it will never happen again - that you now realise you were in the wrong. We would be there of course to facilitate the meeting.'

So that's what they wanted - their hidden agenda. I had to apologise to a parent over something that had happened over four months ago and who clearly had it in for me because I'd finally decided to come out of the closet to my class.

'We have arranged for the meeting to take place on Thursday to give you some time to think about what you're going to say.'

Linda gave me a look which dared me to challenge her.

The whole thing had been blown out of all proportion and I was beginning to feel like a scapegoat in a much bigger conflict of interests. There was no other option. I'd have to turn up to the meeting scheduled with Mrs. Begum. But there was no way I was going to apologise to a woman more censorial than Mary Whitehouse. Right now *Gloria Goes to Gay Pride*, Rodin's *The Kiss* and surrealist Spanish painters were in the firing line. Who knew what it might be tomorrow?

Chapter 18

I stood in the gravelled forecourt; the Jaguar and Mercedes Benz still parked in the drive, and looked up to the top floor of his apartment bloc. I was half an hour late but nearly didn't make it this far. Undecided at Kings Cross, I didn't know whether to take the Northern line on to Archway or just head back home. The sun cast a warm, orange glow, which filtered through the branches and foliage of neighbouring trees. All this was a far cry from Whitechapel, with its sprawling council estates and concrete tower blocks sprayed with graffiti. Flower beds that bordered the expanse of lawn at the front were bursting with colour, vibrant pinks and purples shooting up from the earth, rhododendron bushes aflame in red, all basking in the last few evening rays.

I knew I could still turn back, even now, make some excuse and head back home, pretend the desperado who came drugged up to the eyeballs to tell Ahmed he was in love with him didn't exist. Pretend that he wasn't engaged to be married to Fatima or that he might not be whisked off to the Emirates at any moment. I walked up the drive, the pine tree still standing magnificently at the entrance, its branches reaching all the way up to the nineteenth floor. I buzzed from outside, walked in and waited for the lift, listening to the familiar clunking of the lift shaft. Once inside, I was thankful this time I wasn't smelling like a farmyard animal or verging on near collapse.

He was standing at the door without a T shirt, in white linen shorts and sandals, a tea towel slung casually over his shoulder. The smell of cooking wafted through from the kitchen. I hugged him. His skin felt deliciously warm and my body remembered how his felt, how it always felt when I held him. I sat down on his sofa and he poured me a glass of wine. His apartment hadn't changed much but he'd hung a new black and white photograph of a mosque surrounded by mountains, just above the sofa.

'They look incredible,' I said.

'Thank you. When my parents came over, they bought a few photographs of Ras-al-Kaimah. Look, that's the local mosque I used to go to as a child and these are the Hajjar mountains, right in the middle of the desert.' He sat down at the other end of the sofa.

I wasn't quite sure how to broach the subject but I needed to know. 'Is it going ahead? The wedding. You didn't mention it at the club.'

'We didn't do much talking at *Fire,* remember? You were with your new boyfriend and then you couldn't keep your hands off me.' He held my eye and started laughing.

'I must have imagined you dragging me to a cubicle then.'

'You *were* pretty wasted.'

'Don't remind me.'

'Hey, come with me. I have something to show you.' He took my hand and led me to the spare room. His paints and brushes were as usual on the shelf near the window and in the centre of the room was his easel and the painting I'd only seen the early stages of.

'It's for you,' he said. 'Think of it as a belated birthday present.'

'Ahmed, I can't.'

'Of course you can. I want you to have it.'

The open palm of a hand nearly filled the canvass. I walked closer and examined the intricate design on each of the fingers. Around the contours of the fingers was the unmistakable Arabic script and in the centre of the palm, replacing the eye, was a flower with delicate pink petals, just like the orchid I'd bought for Ahmed when we first started seeing each other. I turned to him. He was still standing in the doorway.

'It's beautiful,' I said. 'What does the writing mean?'

'It's a fragment of one of my favourite love poems. 'Show me your face, I crave flowers and gardens. Open your lips. I crave the taste of honey.' Did you like the orchid?' he asked.

'It reminds me of us,' I said.

I walked over to him and hugged him. 'Thank you. I shall cherish it always. By the way, I want you to know. I've made a decision.' For some reason it seemed like the right moment to tell him. 'I'm through with drugs, the marathon clubbing sessions, the horrendous come downs.' I looked back at the painting. 'I've reached the end of the road.'

He raised an eyebrow.

'I mean it. I've had my road to Damascus, only there was no blinding light, no voice of Christ, just waking up from a deep sleep with a member of St. John's ambulance peering down at me.'

He looked shocked as I told him what had happened.

'You know this is your wake-up call. You might not be as lucky next time round. '

'I keep thinking back to when I was queer bashed. That's when the drug taking really got out of control. It's going to be a struggle but I've never wanted it like I want it now.'

'Maybe you've seen the light after all. You're finally understanding the nature of the greater *jihad. Jihad-Al Akbar*. The jihad of the struggle with the self. *Jihad-Al-Nafas*. The *jihad* of the heart and soul. The real battles we need to fight are not out there but in here. Just remember 'jihad' is not a one-off. Sometimes it's the work of a lifetime.' He took my hand and led me back to the lounge. 'I'll have the painting delivered to you.'

'Oh, I nearly forgot.' I opened my ruck sack and produced a rather expensive bottle of Pinot Noir. I also realised I'd forgotten to give the latest copy of *Eastern Promise*, to Linda. It was staring me in the face. Ahmed caught sight of it and took it from my bag.

'David, you surprise me. I thought you prefered your eastern promise with a bit more spunk!'

I tried to grab the magazine back. 'It was left on my desk at school.'

'Sure it was.'

'I'm serious. There's this freak who keeps leaving centrefolds of the same woman round the school with cryptic messages. Look, the latest one has a speech bubble graffitied onto it. 'I'm an internal exile."

'You're having me on.' He snatched the magazine from me. 'What is it?'

'It's uncanny. She does look familiar.'

'I was going to give it to the Head. She's gathering quite a collection.'

'Wait a minute. I know that woman. I'm sure of it. Photographed her in Birmingham. Tracy - Englefield, that was her maiden name. Knew how to say a few words in Arabic. She was studying it at the University there, I think.'

'Birmingham? Are you sure?'

'It was nearly three years ago. I'd just moved here and was a big fan of Hussein Chalayan's work. The Turkish Cypriot fashion designer. I told you about him. Created a storm with a collection called 'Burka' - models in various states of undress. I wanted to do a similar thing, you know – cutting edge but with photography. Impress my tutors at St Martin's. Someone gave me a contact of this woman in Birmingham, English, but willing to pose in designer hijabs, burkinis, the veil. Nothing too racy but sexy, provocative. I never knew the photos had ended up in a publication. She must have given them the negatives.'

'And you're certain she was studying Arabic?'

'The first thing she said was *As – Salamu' Alaykum.*'

'That's her.'

'Who?'

'It's gotta be. How many English converts to Islam do you know who've studied Arabic at Birmingham University?'

'David, you're not making sense again.'

'Mrs.B.'

'You've completely lost me.'

'I can't believe it. It's her! Mrs. Begum.' I filled him in on the story.

'I remember her well. We chatted after the photo shoot. I actually quite liked her.'

'She's a religious maniac with an axe to grind! You actually liked her?'

'Well, I guess I felt sorry for her. From what I remember her husband had just left her and certain members of the community wanted nothing to do with her. A single mother and white convert to Islam. Doesn't always go down that well. She was down on her luck, needed to make some money. I guess she also wanted to get back at her ex husband.'

'But why then come down to London and reinvent herself as a burqa wearing Islamic fundamentalist?'

'That's something you'll just have to ask her yourself. That is if it's the same woman.' He opened the bottle of wine and poured it into two large glasses. 'Good choice of wine by the way.'

He still hadn't answered my question about Fatima, so I asked him again. 'So you're still going through with things?'

'Do we have to talk about all that right now?'

'I have a right to know.'

'Look, after I've married Fatima, the deal is I can come back to London, further my studies, carry on with my work.' He paused. 'I've missed you, David. It doesn't mean we can't see each other.'

'You don't have to go through with it you know. It's not too late.'

'Family ties, loyalty, there's this huge expectation in Arabic culture, especially for the first born son. I don't expect you to understand but it's easier this way. My parents will be off my back, I can carry on with my life here, we can start to see each other again.'

'You've got it all worked out, haven't you?'

He went into the kitchen and started to dish up. I couldn't believe I was here. I never thought I'd see the inside of his apartment again. Yet the plants on his window sill seemed different somehow. I guess they were what they'd always been - terracotta potted plants. The only difference was one needed re-potting and the one in the corner looked half dead.

He came in with two steaming plates of lamb and rice covered in a rich creamy sauce then lit a candle in the middle of the table. 'When my parents were here, they told me about this group of gay Arabs who were arrested in a beach resort. They now face five years imprisonment and ninety lashes.'

I wondered if part of their punishment also included enforced hormone injections but remembered his father and thought better of it. 'Well, compared to Iran that's pretty mild. There they'd just hang them.'

'Unless you agreed to a sex change operation, of course. The Islamic Republic of Iran will gladly sanction chopping your bits of and stuffing you with silicon. They'll even fund half the cost of the surgery and turn you into a good, law abiding Muslim woman, but you're right, when it comes to a bit of man on man action…'

'It's not much of a choice is it? Genital mutilation or execution.'

'I blame the British myself. It if it wasn't for your laws on

sodomy you imported, the Gulf states wouldn't - hey, what's this?'
He'd pulled the Star of David out from under my T shirt.

'What do you think it is?'

'David, I know what it is but why are *you* wearing it?'

'Yossi gave it to me.'

'The guy you were with at the club?'

I nodded.

'I thought he was Arab. You're going out with a Jew?'

'Don't put it like that.'

'How else should I put it? I guess he lives somewhere near here. Golders Green or Muswell Hill by any chance?'

'Tel Aviv.'

'Tel Aviv!? David, what on earth are you doing with an Israeli?'

'What's wrong with Israel?'

'Where do you want me to start?'

'If it makes you feel better, demonise Israel. But I'll tell you something. If some of the Arab nations really wanted to do something about the Palestinians, they'd invest in the infrastructure of the Palestinian territories. But they don't care. They're too busy rewarding the families of suicide bombers with thousands of dollars.'

'Oh my god! You've been to see him there haven't you?'

'Tel Aviv's really gay friendly.'

'I'm sure as a gay tourist it's all very cosmopolitan and chic with its bars and clubs. Try telling that to the Palestinians in Gaza or the West Bank.'

'You haven't even been there.'

'No, David, and neither have you. For every Israeli that has died in the second Intifada, four Palestinians have died at the hand of Israeli soldiers. They have check points and road blocks everywhere in the Occupied Territories.'

There was an awkward silence.

'What is it?'

'Yossi. His partner was killed in a suicide bomb in Jerusalem last year.'

'Why didn't you tell me before?' He rested a hand on my arm. 'David, I'm sorry.'

We finished our dinner, managing to steer the rest of the conversation away from politics in the Middle East. But all I could think of was Yossi and his recurring nightmare: searching for Moshe amongst the debris, rubble and scattered remains of the dead. He was still searching for him, but now I'd never know if he ever managed to find him, if in the slumber of sleep, far from the living nightmare, there might be some place where Moshe would be, just as he remembered him.

I helped Ahmed clear the dishes away then we both sat down on the sofa. The windows of his flat were wide open and every now and then the candle would flicker madly in the breeze then all of a sudden, grow very tall and still. I watched as streaks of golden orange and dark pink outside merged and sunk further into the darkness.

'I'm sorry about Yossi,' he said. 'It should never have happened.' He placed his hand on top of mine. 'I did miss you, you know.'

'I was a mess. After we broke up I just remember having these horrendous withdrawal symptoms,' I said.

'You make me sound like a drug you needed to kick.'

'I mean it.' I looked towards the sun as it sunk beneath the horizon. 'It felt like I'd lost part of myself. I went crazy. I couldn't stop thinking about you. I would have done anything...'

'Then do it now. Stay with me tonight.'

He was about to kiss me and although it had already happened in the club, it was only now that it felt like it meant anything. And in that instant everything came flooding back: the intense rush I used to get just before I saw him, the physical ache inside my chest, the longing for a part of me I thought I'd lost, the disbelief and panic when it was all over.

'Ahmed, I can't.'

'It's Yossi, isn't it?'

'No.'

'It's because I'm engaged to Fatima. Look, I'll put it off for as long as I can. We can sort something out. Still see each other. I'm sorry I didn't want to see you before.'

'It's a lot of things but it's not Yossi and it's not you.'

'Then what is it? You're in love with him, aren't you?'

'Look, you may as well know. He left me. It's over. But all this – I can't. It's too soon. I need to be strong, sort myself out. I have to do it alone.'

'But that's crazy. I want to support you. When I saw you in the restaurant everything seemed clear. I want you. More than doing the right thing, more than marrying the woman I'm supposed to marry, more than pleasing my parents.'

'It's too late.'

'Once I'd said goodbye to Fatima and followed you to that club, once I'd stepped inside, it confirmed what I suspected. That place, it's a hell hole. I don't know about Islamic jihad – but there's a twisted kind of Homo jihad going on in our own backyard and it's not the jihad of the heart and soul. It's the biggest suicide cult in history, David. I won't let that happen to you.'

'I need to do it by myself!'

'I'm sorry I let you down before.'

'I can't be part of anything more right now.'

'Look, we can try. Work something out'

'Please don't, Ahmed.'

'It won't be the same as it was but I'm willing to try.'

'I can't.' I stood up.

'It's because you're still angry with me, isn't it?'

'No – It's because I'm still in love with you. But I love myself more. I need to do this alone. Sort my shit out. And so do you.'

I walked to the door. It was the first time in my entire life I was about to walk out on someone. He grabbed me by the arm. I could feel his breath on my cheek.

'Please, don't leave. You're all I've got.' He released his grip slightly.

I wanted to give in, say to hell with it, fall into bed with him, wake up the next morning as if the last four months hadn't happened.

'I love you, David.'

I could feel him trembling slightly and put my arms around him and held him tight. He buried his head into my chest but I hardened my resolve. 'I have to go now,' I said.

I stepped back, opened the door to his flat and called the lift. This time I didn't look back. I heard his front door gently close and wondered if I was doing the right thing. I knew that even though Ahmed's father was thousands of miles away in the Emirates, he still lived in fear of him. I also knew that he was under intense family pressure to marry but I couldn't just carry on from where we left off. It was too soon. And I couldn't be his bit on the side whilst he pretended to everyone else he was a happily married man. I knew myself too well. I didn't want to share him, even if it was with someone he would never find sexually attractive. But most of all, I needed to decide what it was I really wanted - a life driven by drug-fuelled weekends and all the drama and dead ends that would bring, or something more fulfilling, something that would enrich my life. And I had to do that by myself. Part of me didn't want to accept it, but maybe that initial high of being in love was a bit like the chemical high that keeps the junkie coming back for more: chasing the dragon, K-holing, the rush of your first ecstasy pill, a blissed-out warmth and enveloping haze of infantile contentment. Was it so far removed from the dizzy heights of being in love? I couldn't risk it. Gravel crunched under foot as I walked down his driveway and towards the bus stop.

When I got back to Whitechapel and entered the bloc, empty crisp and cigarette packets, rizzlas and beer bottles lined the stairwell. Somehow members of the local gang had got in again and spray-canned in black all over the newly painted white walls. *'Batty man, boom, bye bye'.* Next to it was *'We need no promo to rub out dem homo'.* Nice piece of cross-cultural homophobic fertilisation. Sort of Jamaican dancehall culture meets Bangladesh meets the East End. I could hear the thumping bass of House music coming from upstairs. There was no escape from its mindless monotony. The music was everywhere: bars, gyms, shopping malls and now on the stairwell of a run-down housing association block of flats in East London. I knew exactly which flat it must be coming from, just when I thought everything was beginning to quieten down. When I reached the second floor I knocked on number sixty five and managed to open the door slightly. They must have gone out and deliberately left the music playing. She knew we were trying to evict her. I pushed the door open a bit more and called out. I was in no mood to be kept awake half the night.

'Oi, can you turn the music down!' I shouted.

They hadn't even laid any carpet or flooring down in the hall – just thrown a couple of rugs over the bare concrete. I called out again. No answer. I turned the light on then went inside. The place was a tip. There were empty cans of drink in the hallway, and bags of rubbish everywhere. It stank of piss. A dog came from nowhere and started rubbing up against my leg. I went into the living room. A tube of florescent lighting fixed to the ceiling flickered on and off - cheap social housing fittings provided for by 'Tower Hamlets Community Housing'. There were half-eaten microwave meals in the kitchen area and empty bottles of vodka lying around. The sofa was threadbare and it looked like the springs had gone in it. I unplugged the stereo at the socket in the wall. Silence. That would show them. I went back to the hallway and saw that the bedroom door was slightly ajar. The layout of the flat was exactly the same as mine so I knew where each room was. It was dark but the glow from the street lamp outside lit up a single mattress lying on the floor and I began to make out an assortment of drug paraphernalia scattered round it: a small glass pipe, silver foil, a syringe. Something wasn't right. I had to get out. The dog began to bark loudly and was scratching at the bathroom door next to the entrance of the flat. They could be back at any minute. The dog managed to push the bathroom door open and it was then that I saw it. A bra and pair of jeans were on the floor alongside an empty bottle of vodka and syringe. I recognised her long ginger hair and track marks in her arms. She was floating in the bathwater, naked, mouth open, eyes staring up at the ceiling.

Chapter 19

After I made the call, I closed her front door and sat waiting on the stairwell in the dark. The lights were set on a ten second timer and had just flickered off. I peered through the stairwell railings to the ground floor and watched the elongated shadows on the wall of passers-by come and go. The dog was still barking and my hands were shaking as I lit a cigarette. It was little consolation that my neighbour would no longer be there to harangue, shout abuse and brawl well into the early hours. No-one deserves to die like that, alone and in squalor, whether by misadventure or by their own hand. I thought of her kids and how they'd probably be taken into care, how someone would have to go to the morgue and identify the body, how final it all was once you'd crossed that line. That was it - no second chances. I could've gone the same way. A few more millilitres of GHB and my internal organs might have reached the same point of no return, a chemical toxicity overpowering my body's will to live.

An image of my dead neighbour flashed before me, her red hair floating in the bath water, her luminous white skin pulled tightly across protruding cheek bones, eyes staring up at the ceiling. There but for the grace of God... The only difference was that I swallowed poison and she injected. I used to think class A's were glamorous and sophisticated, a walk on the wild side. There's nothing sophisticated about jacking up a syringe full of dirty brown liquid and jabbing it into an overused vein, nothing glamorous about knocking back a mouthful of ball-bearing fluid and going out cold in the middle of the act.

The police were there within minutes, unlike the numerous times when most of the neighbours, including myself, had reported her threatening behaviour or early hour drunken brawls. They took a statement from me then began interviewing the neighbour directly opposite, an elderly Jamaican woman who opened the door bleary-eyed in her slippers and flannel dressing gown. A yellow and black police cordon was set up at the front of the bloc and a policeman stationed outside. It was now potentially the scene of a crime. The guy who took down my statement said it looked like an overdose and sighed wearily.

'See a lot of it round 'ere mate. But then I guess you knew you were living above a crack den.'

When I got back inside my flat, I went into Michael's bedroom and was relieved to find it was just as he'd left it. His shrine, still in the corner: the maroon coloured meditation cushion, the black and white photograph of his elderly English guru, and the thin trail of ash from all the incense sticks he'd burned as he devoted himself to the practice of mindfulness and loving kindness. Above his bed, a poster of Green Tara, the Bodhisattva of Compassion, still looked down from her cosmic lotus flower. I opened his wardrobe. Most of his clothes were still there: the jacket he always wore to work, the tight-fitting designer tops he'd go clubbing in and a more recent addition – his prayer beads. I took out a Diesel jumper I'd given him a few Christmases ago, sat down on the edge of his bed and was reminded of a Buddhist parable he'd once told me that Christmas - the parable of the *Burning House*. And then it struck me for the first time. Was it just a coincidence that Michael had gone from serious clubbing stints at the nightclub *Fire* to a stint of community living at the FWBO headquarters, a converted fire station in Bethnal Green? Did the parable make sense to Michael on a symbolic, mythical level? Was the fire station some kind of metaphor for taming his own unbridled lust and desire?

I sat in Michael's room smoking the few remaining fags and my thoughts turned to Yossi. It must have completely freaked him out, seeing me like that, unconscious on the bathroom floor. I was meant to be helping him get over Moshe, not reminding him of death (lying there like rigor mortis had already set in.) I couldn't let go of the vision I had of him struggling with his luggage as he walked away and down the stairwell to get his taxi. Why had I taken enough GHB to knock myself unconscious? What if Yossi hadn't been there to call for an ambulance? What if I'd slipped into a coma and never woken up? The more questions I asked, the more I couldn't get the image of my dead neighbour floating in the bath out of my head. And why had her front door been open? Did she deliberately want someone to find her? When I did finally get to sleep, I dreamt of a corpse in a lake, face up in a full-length dress, a mass of pre-Raphaelite red hair entwined with pond weed and flowers.

When I passed her flat in the morning it was already boarded up. The police cordon was still outside but the policeman had gone. I guess they'd ruled out any potential foul play.

At lunch time, John was diligently marking a stack of maths books. He was the only one who brought any marking into the staff room at lunchtime and would often scribble frantically away in red biro, making copious notes that his kids would probably never read whilst pontificating on the absurdity of life and the human condition. John would let nothing pass him by and would have his own take on everything from the most recent educational initiative to foreign policy in Afghanistan or Burma.

Half empty polystyrene cups were dotted around the staffroom; a thick film of skin on each obscured the cold, instant coffee underneath. Old copies of 'The Times Educational Supplement' were strewn across the main table where we all sat, and where, every Friday lunchtime, I would flick through the international jobs section and fantasise of making a clean break and living somewhere exotic like Rio de Janeiro or Buenos Aires. Today there were only a few international teaching jobs advertised, mainly in Hong Kong and the Middle East: Saudi, Oman or Qatar. It would have been a good opportunity to make some quick money, tax-free. And I'd heard on the gay grapevine that Saudi Arabia, despite retaining its right to behead its citizens for a bit of man to man action, was rife with gay private parties in Jeddah and Riyadh, often attended by eligible, young princes from the House of Saud. But quite frankly, the prospect of living out my days, or even a few of them, in some compound for expats in the middle of the desert, with the occasional nocturnal excursion for a bit of Arab cock, wasn't exactly what I had in mind. That, and knowing Al-Qaeda had driven trucks loaded with explosives into a number of residential compounds a few years back.

Two gaping holes in the ceiling revealed thick electrical cables above our heads and a thin layer of green mould had began to form around the windows which looked onto the playground and nearby tower blocks.

'What's up John?' I asked.

'You know I hate it when people say that. I never know how to reply. Um.. everything's really up, or it's all a bit up or nothing much is up actually– I mean really, what does one say? To be perfectly honest, if the Gestapo stopped coming up with crack-pot ideas every couple of minutes, things wouldn't be half so bad.'

'I take it you're referring to the Sergeant and Jane?'

'Who else? I mean have you ever heard of such nonsense! They've decided, in their infinite wisdom, that they want to bring in yet another last minute pre-Ofsted whole-school policy. Headless chickens, the pair of them! Listen to this. Wait for it. The great new policy initiative is called, I kid you not, 'Meet and Greet.'

'You are joking!?'

'Anytime, anywhere we meet each other, dashing along the

corridor, sorting out a fight in the playground, desperately trying to hunt down some long-lost teaching resource, we are all now expected to stop, smile like a Cheshire cat and warmly greet each other. 'Meet and Greet.' What's the world coming to when even our facial expressions are up for grabs and policed by the powers that be. What's next? The Thought Police?'

'It is a bit Stepford Wives.'

'Just another example of the Nanny state and creeping feminization of the entire education system. It's not enough we have to fill out a bloody Health and Safety document as long as your arm just to go to the bloody toilet. We now have to smile sweetly, exchanging half-hearted pleasantries as we tiptoe on our way.'

'A classic piece of micro-management courtesy of Tower Hamlets!'

'So you're going ahead with seeing her?' he asked.

'Mrs. B? I've had a chance to cool down since the meeting. I want to clear the air. It's not fair on her kid.'

'Well, all I can say is, I'd like to be a fly on the wall.'

Caroline suddenly came waltzing in, performing a delicate balancing act, with a yellow plastic tray piled high with school dinner in one hand, and a copy of *Hello* magazine in the other.

'I swear to god, if I wasn't in it for the greater good, I'd be reclining on a tropical beach somewhere sipping caipirinhas and oogling the locals! Oh hello, John, darling. Didn't see you sitting there. Look at that, they keep piling more and more food on my plate. I mean do I look bulimic? It's disgusting.' I looked at the mass of congealed baked beans, child-size fish fingers and burnt chips.

'Still on the diet, John?' said Caroline.

'Oh yes. No lunch for the last two weeks but I must confess I wavered at the weekend and had a few chocolate biscuits.'

'Well, I must say you're looking a lot trimmer for it.' Caroline could charm the birds off the trees.

He beamed back at her. 'I've lost half a stone actually but for some reason it doesn't seem to be shifting from my mid-rift.' He patted his pot belly gently.

'I told you before John, be proud and work it. A bit of extra weight can work to your advantage. Some people love nothing better than grabbing on to a firm pair of love handles in the middle of the act,' I said, winking at him, but he chose to ignore me.

'I dread to think what they put in these fish fingers,' said Caroline. She played with the stodge on her plate, picking at the off-white filling under the layer of yellow breadcrumbs.

I finished my apple crumble, careful to remove the thick layer of skin over cold custard then stood up. 'Well, wish me luck. It's the Ninja verses the Gay Lord. Round one!'

'Always one to court controversy. Tread carefully young sonny-me-lad,' said John.

'Oh, I nearly forgot, sweetie,' said Caroline. 'All I can think about is bloody Ofsted.' Then I caught her staring at my T shirt. 'Oh my God!'

'What?'

'David, you can't wear that!'

They were now both staring aghast at my T shirt.

'What's wrong with it?' I asked.

'You are terrible. You're deliberately going to provoke her wearing that,' she said.

The word 'shalom' was written in Hebrew and English above a small picture of the Israeli flag. Yossi had bought it for me in Tel Aviv.

'If you must know, 'shalom' means peace,' I said.

John smiled wryly. 'And so, I seem to remember, does Islam.

Somehow, I don't think there's going to be much of that!'

I knocked on the Head's door and went straight in. Mrs. B. had toned down her attire somewhat and gone from full-on Afghan burqa, complete with face gauze, to a slightly more revealing hiljab and veil. Her hands and forearms were still covered in full length, velvet black gloves. For a change, Linda was not fixed behind her computer screen but sitting next to the parent in an armchair, her legs crossed in expensive looking slacks. Next to her was Jane, the new Deputy, her ample bosom and corduroy, full length dress contrasting sharply with Linda's rather flat chest and designer clothes. Linda was wearing one of her usual smiles for meeting parents.

'So, let's start with Mum, shall we? Would you like to tell me in your own words? What is it exactly that's upsetting you?'

A voice with a distinct Birmingham accent spoke from behind the veil and I watched strangely mesmerised. 'To be quite blunt, Mrs. Ardent, no-one has the right to ask me to remove my veil in a public place. I cover up because I feel closer to God. The more covered up I am, the closer to God I feel. And as a feminist, I reject Westernised beauty fascism. I want to be judged on what I do, not on what I look like.' She cleared her throat and continued in a strong Brummie accent. 'I don't dictate what he can and cannot wear in his job, do I?' She leaned forward and took a closer look at my T shirt. 'How can you possibly allow your staff to advertise the bastard state of Israel! Do you know how much innocent Muslim blood has been shed due to the occupation of Muslim land by the infidels?'

'We both know I never asked you to remove the veil – just lower it so I could see who I was talking to. And if it offended you so much, why did it take you so long to complain about it. This was over three months ago.'

Linda cut in. 'Well, I'm sure David's intention was not to

offend you in any way at all Mrs. Begum.' She paused and stared at me. 'David?!'

It was my cue for the apology. I cleared my throat and swallowed my pride. 'For the record, my intention was never to offend you, Mrs. Begum.' I found myself staring at Linda's desk. A book about the length of the Koran entitled 'Target Setting to Raise Achievement' lay next to her computer along with a bottle of organic carrot juice and a pile of forms and folders. On top of the pile was a letter with the school's motto 'William Booth School: Success Through Diversity.' There was an awkward silence.

'He doesn't care. He's clearly an outright supporter of the bastard state of Israel. Maybe he needs to take a closer look in the Jew book for personal guidance. It's the one thing Jews and Muslims do agree on. Read it carefully.' She paused for dramatic effect. 'It says Adam and Eve, not Adam and Steve!'

'Oh, very original. Like I haven't heard that one before!' I said.

'I'm not sure I follow, Mrs. Begum,' said Linda.

Mrs. Begum leant forward in her seat. 'Allow me to fill you in, Mrs. Ardent. My son came home last week, not only terrorised by what he'd learned in a so called 'sex and relationship lesson', but also informing me that his class teacher is an out-and-out homosexual. It would now appear that not only is he a sexual deviant of the highest order but a staunch Zionist!'

'And also, according to you – a terrorist!?' I said.

'David? What on earth's going on?' asked Linda.

'Well at least it's quite clear what you're main bone of contention is,' I said.

'David, we agreed you would stick within the parameters of the sex education policy. The senior management team have been through a lengthy and thorough consultation with parents and governors on the matter and did you or did you not agree yourself to adhere to the draft proposals?'

'To be honest, and with all due respect, I'm sorry but, how can I put this politely? Oh, what the hell – the policy sucks.'

'David! What's got into you?'

'What's the worst that could happen because I've decided to come out? Kids who turn out gay later in life, will have a positive gay role model to look back on. They might still grow up believing what their parents and society tells them - that they're unnatural, abnormal, but at least they won't think they're the only one.'

'It's an abomination, and you in a position of trust and authority working with young children,' said Mrs. Begum. 'It beggars belief.'

'You may have forgotten, but we actually live in a liberal democracy, not an Islamic Caliphate. The rights of gays and lesbian are protected and enshrined in our law.'

'Democracy? Democracy is *haram*! We don't rule, only Allah rules.'

'So that's the answer is it? Sharia law?'

'Allah's law in Allah's land!'

'You'd willingly drag us back to a Taliban dark age, where teachers who dare to teach girls are threatened with beheading, music and dance are outlawed and the country is run by despots?'

'David, that is quite enough!' said Linda.

'No, nothing is quite enough when confronted with narrow minded bigots and religious extremism,' I said.

Mrs. Begum was muttering something to herself in Arabic and Jane was giving me daggers.

'May we take this opportunity to state that what David requested, Mrs. Begum, in no way represents the view of William Booth school in any shape or form,' said Jane.

The phone suddenly rang. Linda reached across and picked up. Jane smiled apologetically at the mother whilst Linda drummed her fingers impatiently on the desk.

'No, I'm sorry, you must be mistaken. Are you quite sure you've got the right school?' said Linda. Silence.

'I have had no prior warning of such a protest.' I looked at the clock above her desk. In five minutes I should be in the hall rehearsing 'Into the Woods' with the juniors, a place I'd much rather be, and I began turning the chorus from one of the songs in the show into a fairy-tale mantra, repeating it in my mind ad infinitum: '*The cape as red as blood, the cow as white as milk, the slipper as yellow as gold..*'

'Did the parent in question leave her name?' Linda looked at Mrs. Begum. 'Well, you can tell the editor of 'East London Life' that Mrs Ardent wishes to speak to him personally. And you can also tell him from me that there never was a protest planned for outside my school and never will be. Is that clear?' She slammed the receiver down, a menopausal flush of fiery red spreading across her chest and throat like a forest fire.

'Is everything alright, Linda?' Jane asked.

'I'm fine. I just need a glass of water that's all.'

'I'll just go and fetch one.'

'Oh, and no tap. Highland Spring. Bottle's in the fridge.' Linda now turned her full attention towards the green eyes with long black lashes framed by a thin covering of black fabric. 'Mrs. Begum, you wouldn't by any chance know anything about a parent protest would you? Scheduled for the beginning of the Ofsted inspection?'

Again an uncomfortable silence. The bell was ringing outside and I could just picture the kids rampaging across the playground, charging to their lining up positions, jostling and pushing each other in line as staff issued the same tired commands.

'You need to understand this, Mrs. Ardent. Teachers who preach their own twisted homosexual perversion, have no right to be employed by the local authority. I cannot begin to describe my utter loathing and dismay that he is currently still employed by the school. It is *haram*. Intolerable! Something had to be done about it.'

For once, Linda seemed genuinely lost for words.

I decided to say something. 'Mrs Begum, I have sat here and listened to your tiresome tirade. You may have succeeded in banning *Gloria Goes to Gay Pride* and removing an art display inspired by Miro, but if a kid asks if I'm gay and I decide to tell the truth rather than brush it under the carpet like a dirty secret, that's my decision.'

For the first time in the meeting she turned round and addressed me directly. She practically spat the words out. 'You make me sick. You are not fit to teach our children. You're a pervert! If this country were to uphold Sharia law, you'd be thrown from the mountain top.'

'Oh, I've heard it all now. Darling, if this country upheld Sharia law, we'd all be fucked! Including you! Do you think Sharia law would allow women to congregate in public and hold an open demonstration?'

Linda and Jane both looked shocked. 'David, take it back,' said Linda. 'Take it back or I shall have no alternative but to issue you with a formal warning!'

'I'm just meant to sit here and take it? Is that it? Adam and Eve, not Adam and Steve, throw the dirty homo pervert from the highest mountain top? And I'm the one expected to retract what I've said?! She's a hypocrite. She wants Sharia law yet she still wants the right to demonstrate. She's a closet democrat!'

'Democracy is *haram*! Democracy is the work of the devil!'

'See, she can only talk in sound bites! She has more in common with the Nu Labour government than she thinks.'

'David, apologise for using inappropriate language at once!'

'This time I will not apologise. The gloves are off. And I'll tell you something for nothing, Ms. Englefield or whoever you really are. You can pretend you're holier than thou now, pure as the driven and all that, but you didn't look all that high and mighty posing half naked for a certain magazine.'

Jane was now standing in the doorway with a large glass of iced water, her mouth wide open.

'I have no idea what you're talking about. You're completely insane!' said Mrs. Begum.

'David, this has to stop right now. What on earth has got into you?' said Linda.

'Ask her, go on!'

'David! Enough! Are you having some kind of mental breakdown or something?' Linda's voice suddenly switched in a calculated bid to gain my sympathy and diffuse the situation. 'Under current legislation in the workforce, I have a duty of care to you. I think it's perhaps better if you go home.'

'Better for who?! You're not getting shot of me that easily! Ask her. Go on. Ask her how she reconciles getting her kit off for *Eastern Promise* with her new-found submission to the law of Allah.'

A flicker of recognition registered for a moment on Linda's face and then she stood up and opened her office door. 'David, the meeting is closed. Please leave.'

'I'm going remember, because there's a show to put on.' I stood up and turned to Mrs. Begum. 'Because there's a witch out there who has to sing off-key in D minor and can't quite get the whole discordant thing done well, there are still more trees to be made for the wood and the Baker and his Wife still don't know if they're searching for a red cape, gold slipper or milky white cow to lift the witch's curse!'

What I didn't say was I hoped, that if her own son turned

out gay, that she could see beyond the faith she'd converted to and could learn to love him for who he was. Her son was the kid, who, in Year 6 asked if his teacher was a poof and in Year two, could be found in the dressing up corner, donning the blonde wig, pink shoes and party dress, spreading a bit of fairy magic in his newly cherished role as Cinderella's God Mother. He'd need all the luck in the world with a mother like her.

I walked out and along the corridor, passing the R.E display outside the Head's office. Under a brightly coloured rainbow, Caroline's class had written prayers for a better world. I just hoped it was one that included the inalienable right to be gay, lesbian or any other colour of the rainbow for that matter.

I left school late that evening after rehearsing a tricky solo piece with the kid who was playing the witch and helping Caroline with some of the costumes. When I got back to my bloc of flats, I had to climb over the branch of a tree that had mysteriously appeared on the ground floor, to get to the stairwell. I passed my neighbour's flat, still boarded up, and wondered how long it would be before the housing association cleaned and repaired some of the damage to the flat, ready for the new tenants to move in. On my floor, an old broken-down washing machine was still there on the landing along with a scattering of kid's toys and an old pushbike. I turned the key in my lock, switched the light on and went into the kitchen, where I poured myself a large glass of wine. It was then that I noticed Michael's bedroom door was shut. Thank god – he'd changed his mind and moved back in. I knocked softly. No answer. I pressed down gently on the door handle, just in case he was deep in meditation, and opened the door.

His room was bare. He'd obviously cleared out when I was at work and taken everything except the single bed and Formica wardrobe provided for by the landlord. The mattress had been stripped of its sheets and an empty nail protruded from the wall where the clock had been. It had left a pale round imprint, untouched by the sun. The wardrobe doors were open and the plastic hangers were empty on the rail. And then I noticed something in the corner, near the window where he used to meditate. I switched the light on and walked up to it. Above the place where his shrine used to be was a postcard stuck to the wall. Looking closer it seemed to show a wheel, divided into different sections by the spokes, with all sorts of creatures coming onto it and off it: monks, women, animals and there were rivers and mountains and houses and it was all being devoured by a black monster with human skulls imbedded in its head.

I took it from the wall and went back into the kitchen, sat down and lit a cigarette in the dark. I didn't even get a chance to tell him - that he was right. That, taken to the extreme, messing around with drugs was like playing Russian roulette with your life. Whether the gun pointing to your head was loaded was anyone's guess. I should have been there to support him with his decision but I was too caught up in the delights of gay club-land south of the river, too enraptured with all the fun of the fair, too busy putting off my own inevitable departure

I stared out of the window at the clock on the Royal London hospital which had been fixed a few days ago and then at the photos and magnets on the fridge-freezer: Mardi Gras in Sydney, Acid-house foam parties in Ibiza, full moon parties on the beaches of Koh Samui, Thailand. It was the end of an era. No more gallivanting round the globe on the international gay circuit, no more pre-club parties, just the two of us, dancing manically round the flat coked off our faces, before going down to the cab office in Whitechapel Road and heading down to Vauxhall. No more coming home mid-week, opening a bottle of wine and settling down on the sofa for a DVD session. No more Christmases spent together, hiding out in London with enough food, booze and drugs to keep us going into the New Year. It was gone, all of it. Michael had never been close to his own family, and relations with mine had been decidedly frosty after I came out at University. Michael was more than my best friend. He was my family. But it was too late. He'd found a new one – one that revolved around communal living and early morning group meditation. He was never coming back.

I remembered when Yossi first met Michael here in the kitchen and what he'd said to him - home is everything. Without it, you have nothing. At the time he'd meant Israel. He was right. I looked at the star-shaped Moroccan light-fitting hanging in the hallway and the walls we'd painted bright orange after moving in, the deep red sari material embroidered in gold thread we'd bought in Camden Town, now draped across the ceiling and gathering dust. Without Michael it wasn't much of a home. I picked up the strange postcard of the black monster and the wheel and knew that it wouldn't be long before I left as well.

Chapter 20

It was the first day of Ofsted. Mrs Begum was at the front of the school, blocking the entrance, covered as usual in black from head to toe which gave her body a shapeless, ghoul-like appearance, but I guess that was the general idea: to hide any womanly curves and female attributes from the prying eyes of predatory men, although I did wonder if this always had the desired effect. You know what they say about forbidden fruit.

Ahmed once told me, a friend of his back in the Emirates used to find the whole veil thing a bit of a turn on. In fact, the more covered up they were, the more of a turn on it was for him. And a woman swamped in the full-on Afghan burqa used to send him into fits of frenzy. I'd heard of weird fetishes on the gay scene – rubber hoods, leather harnesses, even gas masks but never came across an outright niqabi fetishist before.

She was standing holding her son's hand, and in the other, held a white placard: 'THE VEIL. A WOMAN'S RIGHT TO CHOOSE !' Two fellow niqabis, stood by her side in solidarity, their black wings of fabric gently billowing in the summer breeze, each with their own banner. One said: 'HOMOSEXUALITY IS AN ABOMINATION!' The other had a rather interesting take on the Nazi death camps: 'ISLAM, THE FINAL SOLUTION!'

It was then that I spotted Linda marching through the playground, no doubt already high on adrenaline and her morning intake of vegetable juices and dietary supplements. She arrived at the same time as me and managed to squeeze past Mrs Begum, who was still blocking the main entrance. I was somewhat confused because I'd expected her to glam up for the first day of the inspection, show who's boss. Instead she'd deliberately dressed down for the occasion, wearing a blue A-line skirt and white frilly blouse. There wasn't a spot of slap on her and her face looked quite gaunt without it.

'As you can see, Mrs. Ardent, I am a woman of my word. This is a matter of principle. You were warned.'

'I think, Mrs Begum, considering how important this day is for our school, your actions are morally reprehensible.'

'Morally reprehensible? What's morally reprehensible is a member of your teaching staff insulting what the prophet has decreed as acceptable female attire. What's morally reprehensible is continuing to employ a teacher who is clearly pushing the gay rights agenda to impressionable young children.'

It was surreal. Linda, looking like she was auditioning for the part of *Miss Jean Brodie* and Mrs. B. swathed in layers of black fabric, ranting on about morality when I'd seen her in all her glory in the centre fold of the 2002 July's edition of *Eastern Promise*.

'In twenty minutes more parents will be arriving to block both the front and rear entrance of the school. We're aiming for maximum impact,' said Mrs Begum.

I had no doubt that Mrs Begum would have contacted a range of newspaper proprietors over the weekend, whose reporters would later on be descending upon the school in droves. The press would have a field day! I could just see the headline in the Daily Mail: 'Gay Primary School Teacher in Muslim Veil Row!' It would make the furore over the banned ILEA book *Jenny Lives with Martin and Eric* look like a storm in a teacup. I looked at her bewildered son, smartly dressed in school uniform, and could hardly believe she was willing to use him as a pawn in what was bound to become a media circus.

'If that's your decision, Mrs. Begum, you need to know that I've already made a phone call to a certain proprietor of an adult-only publication,' said Linda.

'I fail to see what good that would achieve,' said Mrs Begum haughtily.

'Do I have to spell it out?'

Mrs. Begum leant her placard against the wall.

'I have no idea what you're talking about.'

'Two can play at your game, Tracy Englefield. The press are due to arrive in a few minutes. Unless you go home and leave us to get on with the job we're employed to do, I shall have no hesitation of naming and shaming you to any journalist who comes knocking on my door. I'm more than willing to dish the dirt!' said Linda.

'There's no dirt to dish!'

'We both know what's at stake here and I don't think you'd be too happy with the before and after pictures if the press ever got hold of it.'

'You wouldn't dare!'

'You may not have realised it, but this school is a beacon of hope in an area of great social deprivation. The majority of our parents are in full support of what we are trying to achieve. Against all odds, we work hard to ensure all the children achieve to the best of their ability. That is the school Ofsted will be seeing, Mrs. Begum, not one besieged by religious extremists holding the school to ransom. We take the views of parents very seriously but religious extremism has no place here. I suggest if you're not happy with the education your children receive here, that you send them to an Islamic school. Now, if you'll excuse me I have other matters to attend to.'

Mrs Begum moved aside and Linda marched back through the playground. I followed closely on her heels, leaving Mrs Begum's mates to discuss the fallout in their mother tongue.

'Linda, you were great out there,' I said.

'Yes, well, we're not out of the woods yet, pardon the pun. I'm sure Mrs. Begum isn't one to back down easily. Either we've just turned a corner or all hell's just about to break loose.'

We both made our way up the recently carpeted staircase, passing welcome signs translated into different languages and awards for being an inclusive and emotionally literate school. Linda then disappeared into her office, closed the door and I went to reception.

'These are for you, David. Who's the secret admirer? Is it Tel Aviv calling or someone closer to home?' said Sabina, the school secretary, who was wearing a new, pink Calvin Klein headscarf and handed me a bouquet of dragon flowers and pink lilies. I opened the small, white envelope.

'They're from Ahmed.'

She knew all the ins and outs of my torrid love life and would constantly ply me for details, listening to each new development as if she were tuning into her favourite soap opera.

'I can't keep up with you, David. Does that mean the wedding's off dear?'

'Your guess is as good as mine.'

'Well I hope for you he finally sees sense and does the decent thing. I'd like nothing better than to see you settled down with a nice Muslim boy from a good family. You deserve it, love.'

The phone suddenly rang. Sabina leant across her desk, picked up and spoke in her trademark sing-song voice. 'Hello, William Booth Primary school. Can I help you?'

I blew her a kiss, walked down the corridor then into my class and read the card again: 'Good luck with the inspection. Love A.' I got a sudden urge to call him but needed some time to think it through. Instead I braced myself for the first day of the inspection and found a vase for the flowers then placed it on my desk, which was for once cleared of all the usual junk that would slowly and steadily collect over the week. I then started to manically sort some brightly coloured 3-D shapes ready for the first lesson of the day when I caught sight of a figure in a black burqa standing at the door. Mrs. Begum must have followed Linda and myself into school but something was different. She was stockier than Mrs. Begum with broad shoulders and a wide gait. Then I looked down at her shoes. She was wearing brogues.

'Can I help you?' I asked. And with that she vanished from my doorway. But was it a she? What woman in her right mind, burqared or otherwise, would take to wearing brogues? I left the shape sorting and dashed to my classroom door only to see the figure clambering in a rather ungainly fashion down the stairs.

Seconds later Caroline marched in, her four inch strappy high heels and mini-dress discarded in favour of elasticated brown trousers, a non-descript jacket and sensible shoes. 'Jesus these shoes are killing me! I can't remember the last time I wore flats.'

'I can't take much more of this,' I said. 'The world's gone mad! Everyone's in drag! I'm half expecting the lead Ofsted inspector to come waltzing in as a femme fatal – blood red lipstick, cigarette holder, serious sling-backs...'

'Oh come on darling. It's all about image.' She twirled round to show off her new look. 'Have you seen Linda? I'm going for the dowdy yet earnest look. Forget 'dress to impress'. This is all about out-frumping the competition and the gloves are off.'

'Translation please!'

'Don't worry sweetheart. It's a girl thing. And talking of girls, or rather glamour girls, another edition of *Eastern Promise* has just appeared in the women's loos – with another post-it attached.

'Hoist up that burqa
And what do you see?
Stockings, suspenders,
Yes it's Tracy!'
And the same edition arrived by post this morning with yet

another post-it.

'Englefield, Begum
Cast off your veil
Birmingham's calling you,
But to no avail.'

It's so frustrating. We know it's her but we still don't know who's behind it all. Oh my god, I just thought – do you think she might be doing it herself? Sort of split personality disorder type thing?'

'It's her – I mean him,' I said.

'Him?'

'The guy with the brogues.'

'I think the stress is already getting to you. You're not making sense.'

'Well at least I think it's a guy.' I quickly filled her in on the mysterious figure in the brogues and the burqa. 'So you see Miss Marple, we're still none the wiser. So far, all we know is it might be a transvestite Islamic fundamentalist with a penchant for pornography from Birmingham,' I said.

'Darling, it's clearly a bloke. I guess if you think about it though, it's the perfect disguise. I mean didn't some news reporter don a burqa when travelling across Afghanistan? And I heard of some anthropologist bloke going on Hajj to Mecca wrapped in the shroud.'

'Darling, this is not Afghanistan or Saudi Arabia! It's a bloody primary school in Tower Hamlets!'

'Come on – think! Stocky, broad shoulders, wears brogues, clearly a man with an eye for classic, traditional footwear.'

'I can't. It's bloody Ofsted. I can't think straight. For all I know Mrs B, I mean Tracy, is out there on the picket line dishing the dirt to a host of tabloid journalists!'

'Come on think. Who could possibly know her maiden

name? Who would know she was called Englefield?' she said.

'A spurned lover from Birmingham? Someone from the local community with an axe to grind? After all she is a convert. They're not always taken into the fold with open arms.'

'I guess we'll never know.'

It was going to be another hot day, so I decided to open the classroom window, half expecting to hear shouts of 'Islam, the Final Solution' or 'Adam and Eve, not Adam and Steve!' echoing across the playground but the only sounds were passing lorries and the siren of a police car. I couldn't quite see far enough to the entrance of the school and wondered if Mrs Begum was still there, a beacon of hope in a world overshadowed by sexual licence and immorality.

That morning, I was observed by the lay inspector who'd spent most of her working life as a nurse in a suburban hospital. She wore a mummsie dress with heavy floral print and sleeves that sort of puffed out at the top and sat at the back of the class making copious notes as the children got to grips with making their own 3D shapes. After the lesson she stayed behind and seemed more interested in the noise of the traffic outside and why there were still scraps of cut-out paper on the floor. I looked at her dumbfounded and explained that a classroom was a place of learning and not a museum of fossilised exhibits. She seemed somewhat taken aback so I refrained from telling her she should have stuck to bedpans and caring for the sick and infirm in hospital; clearly she didn't have a clue when it came to education. But that paled into insignificance, when later in the day, I heard that the Literacy co-ordinator had complained to the lead inspector and been upgraded from satisfactory to outstanding. The Golden Girl who couldn't put a foot wrong; I guess she intended it to stay that way.

The next few days went relatively smoothly but on the

last day of the inspection in the early afternoon, a sudden roar of fighter jets past overhead. The Red Arrows had clearly been on stand by and were now hurtling through the skies of East London. For a few minutes the whole school came to a complete standstill, I stopped teaching, the children dashed to the windows and then the cheering started. I couldn't quite believe we'd won the Olympic bid. I looked out of my seventh floor classroom window at the vegetable patch and garden area below then across to the 1970's tower blocks on the other side of the street. The sky was streaked in red, white and blue. By 2012, this part of London, just on the doorstep of the proposed site for the Olympic village in Stratford, would be transformed. Maybe even some of our kids would get a chance to compete in The London Games.

Caroline and I stayed behind at the end of the day to set up for the evening performance of 'Into the Woods', Caroline making last minute adjustments to the costumes whilst I finished off painting Rapunzel's tower. At six o-clock the hall was completely packed out, aunties, mums and grandmas in brightly coloured saris or traditional *salwar kameez*. And there, right in the front row, a veiled Mrs. Begum.

I decided to risk it and braced myself for a show down or, at the very least, an icy rejection. 'Mrs. Begum, glad you could make it.'

'Yes, well, if I'm to be successful in my bid to be a school governor I need to show my moral support.' She gestured for me to sit in the empty chair next to her and lowered her voice. 'I may have been a little harsh in my judgement of you, David. How can I put this? I think that perhaps it's time we put our differences to one side.'

For a moment I was stunned and left wondering what might have caused this sea change in her opinion of me when we were interrupted by a man dressed in a pin striped suit striding down the aisle of chairs towards us. Mrs B froze. He shook my hand firmly and introduced himself in a strong Birmingham accent. 'You must be the Year Six teacher. I've heard a lot about you.' I turned to Mrs B who now looked like she was eyeing the back of the hall. Then my gaze dropped to his feet. Large brown leather shoes with the unmistakable stitching and wingtip toe cap pattern. I could hardly believe my own eyes. The man with the brogues! They were exactly like the pair I'd seen on the first day of the inspection. Only this time they weren't poking out of a full length burqa.

'I've come to see my nephew, Mohammed,' he said. 'You've done a marvellous job with the set, by the way.'

Before I'd had a chance to reply, Mrs. Begum was standing up and hissing at him under her breath. 'How dare you turn up like this! You don't belong here, do you hear me? If you so dare to come within an inch of me or my son –' She turned and made her way to the back of the hall.

I turned back to the guy in the pinstripe suit unable to take my eyes off his shoes. Could this be the same person I'd seen loitering at my classroom door dressed in a burqa? Was this the man behind the spate of centrefolds and cryptic messages that would suddenly appear at random places around the school? Was this really Tracy Englefield's brother? It wasn't as if I could even tell if there was a family resemblance because, away from her husband, Tracy's face never saw the light of day. Anyway I couldn't confront him about it now, not in front of all these parents. I didn't want world war three to suddenly kick off. I'd just have to look for him as soon as the performance was over. I was lost for words. 'Well, I hope you enjoy the show,' I mumbled.

I looked back at the brother then at Tracy, who was now standing in the back row near the exit. I knew part of me would never understand why someone would want to hide away under a shroud of black fabric. And I was certain she'd probably never change her views on homosexuality and I certainly wasn't going to change my views on certain aspects of Sharia law. Yet we weren't completely dissimilar. We'd both taken a walk on the wild side - her appearing in the centrefold of *Eastern Promise* and me losing myself in the labyrinthine clubbing corridors of my own craving. Only unlike Tracy or indeed Michael, I was in no hurry to embrace a whole new religion and way of life. I wanted to make it on my own, step by step, but with myself essentially still intact by the end of it.

My friend from Brighton, wearing dungarees and sporting a new spiky haircut, was already seated at the piano, the lead Ofsted inspector was loitering at the back of the hall with Linda and even a journo from *East End Life* was there to take photos. I was just relieved it was this story that would be going to press and not one about the gay primary schoolteacher and ex glamour model turned Islamic fundamentalist.

In the end, the witch stole the show, and bravely managed to pull off her discordant solo in D minor whilst hobbling across stage with her staff.

> *'Princes wait there in the world it's true*
> *Princes, yes, but wolves and humans too.*
> *Stay with me*
> *The world is dark and wild*
> *Stay a child, while you can be a child...'*

After the children had delivered an epilogue on the dangers of casting spells and making wishes, everyone stood for a standing ovation and Linda, in yet another fashion u-turn, appeared in high heels and a strappy, black dress, that wouldn't have looked out of place on a catwalk in Milan or Paris. She clearly revelled in the role and made her victory speech.

'I'd just like to say a few words. First of all I'd like to thank all the parents and everybody for coming tonight and celebrating in your children's success. Without your help and support, an evening like tonight would not have been possible. On a slightly different note, it gives me great pleasure in informing you that *William Booth* school has gone from strength to strength and I don't think it's premature to say, and I hope the inspectors won't mind, when I tell you that our school has been awarded the honour of the 'O' word.' She paused for dramatic effect. 'Outstanding.'

There was a round of applause then gradually everybody started leaving for refreshments provided in the upper hall. I scouted around, looking for Mohammed's uncle and eventually found him talking to Linda.

'Congratulations, David, it was a resounding success. A real event for the whole community. Oh, by the way, let me introduce Mr. Englefield. He works at Swiss Bank in Canary Wharf and it's our good fortune that on behalf of the bank he'll be making a rather generous financial contribution to our new computer suite.'

I shook his hand, making a determined effort not to stare at his shoes.

'David can tell you more about the drama work we do at *William Booth*. We pride ourselves in harnessing the creative talents of our young people. Anyway Mr. Englefield, it's been a pleasure,' said Linda.

I couldn't be sure but there was something different in her manner. Something almost flirtatious. Was it the relief that the inspection was over or could it be that she had the hots for Mrs. Begum's brother, the investment banker?

'Anyway boys, must mingle!' She then sauntered over in the direction of the chief Ofsted inspector.

I decided it was now or never. 'It was you, wasn't it?' I said.

'Sorry?' said Mrs B's brother.

'The other day. Hovering by my classroom door.'

'I don't know what you're talking about,' he said.

'Your shoes. They're the same shoes you're wearing now. You were dressed in a burqa and legged it but not before leaving another centrefold of your sister in school.'

He looked at me somewhat bewildered. 'I'm not quite sure where you get your information but you're barking up the wrong tree, mate.' He put down his cup of coffee and was just about to leave.

I couldn't let him off the hook that easily. 'Look, I don't know what you're game is but just to let you know – if it happens again – we're calling the police.'

'Is that a threat? I'm sure your head teacher wouldn't take too kindly to members of her own staff threatening private investment opportunities from the local business community.'

'I'll leave the threats and blackmailing to you.'

'Keep your voice down.' He took me to one side, gripping me firmly by the elbow. 'I heard the protest was called off,' he whispered.

'It was you!'

'I said keep your voice down!'

'You're hurting me.'

'Have you any idea what it's like to lose a sister? One minute she's into celebrity culture, clubbing and reality TV and the next she wouldn't look out of place on the streets of Afghanistan. I tried everything.' He released his grip.

'So that makes it ok to creep around leaving half naked photographs of your sister round the school. That's brotherly love?! That's your idea of winning her back?'

'I got her off your backs, didn't I?'

'But disguised in a burqa! You're completely insane!'

'You haven't got a clue have you? I left a fantastic job in Dubai to relocate over here and find my sister. I was the one who hired a private investigator, tracked her down. The rest of my family didn't want to know. That's when I found out she'd remarried some guy from Hizb ut-Tahrir and taken to wearing the shroud.'

'But I don't understand. Why did she pose for *Eastern Promise*?'

'You really want to know?' He whispered in my ear. 'The first bloke she married liked to take it up the gary.'

'You mean he was gay?'

'If that's what you call it. She found him in bed with another man.'

I couldn't quite take it all in.

'It sent her over the edge. She'd always been a bit unstable, easily led but that-'

I imagined Tracy's reaction when she found her husband at it with another man and thought about Ahmed and Fatima. How it was just a car crash waiting to happen. 'But why the photographs, creeping round school in a burqa?'

'I wanted my sister back. I'd tried everything. I thought if I could remind her of her own past, put some pressure on without completely outing her, I might stand a chance. Then I heard about the protest. It was a step too far. I warned her I'd go through with it. I told her I'd do it.'

I began to wonder if Tracy's brother shared the same propensity for mental instability as she did. 'Look, you'll have to accept it. She's converted. I know it's hard. But what you're doing now – you're just pushing her even further away.'

He suddenly turned. 'What the hell do you know about it? From what I hear you and my sister's first husband have quite a lot in common.' His lips curled into a sneer. 'I bet you're just his type too.' And with that he released his grip on my arm and walked off.

I almost felt sorry for Mrs. B. Held to ransom by a brother

clearly as close to the edge as she was, married to a man and father of her child who turns out to be gay and rejected by both members of the local Muslim community in Birmingham and by her own family. It certainly went some way to help explain how she may have then found a sense of belonging in the arms of Islamic fundamentalism.

My mobile suddenly started bleeping. It was Ahmed. I walked through the hall, into the corridor and Caroline's classroom.

'You got the flowers then?'

'They're lovely. I'm just not sure -'

'How did the play go?'

'Oh, you know, curses lifted, giants falling from the sky, the usual stuff of fairy tales.'

'I've got a surprise for you,' he said.

'What sort of surprise?'

'Just be at Waterloo on Friday by five o'clock.'

'Ahmed. I don't think -'

'That's decided. See you there.' He then put the phone down.

I looked around at the empty hall: at the cardboard cut-out trees and multi-coloured leaves the children had painted, red-riding hood's basket of apples, the Baker's hat and the witch's staff - all abandoned in a rush of excitement as parents and staff came to congratulate them on their success. We'd certainly turned a corner and for the first time in a long time I was beginning to see the wood from the trees in my own professional life. Michael may have packed up and left, my neighbour may have OD'd on heroin, and Ahmed, as far as I knew, was still engaged to be married but seeing the excitement and pride on the faces of the children in the school play was more than anyone could wish for.

Chapter 21

I woke the next day with a slight hangover. We'd all met up at Canary Wharf the previous evening to celebrate a successful inspection, stuffed ourselves with pizza then gone to a swanky wine bar. The place had been packed with city workers and filled with red, white and blue helium balloons. Every now and then the sound of an uncorked champagne bottle and resounding cheer would shoot across the bar. The T.V was on with wall to wall news coverage of London winning the Olympic bid and Linda was becoming steadily more drunk, singing 'The Only Way is Up' and yelling out to all these city types what a wonderful staff we were and how no-one could possibly replace us.

That morning I downed a couple of paracetemol and left for work later than usual. Still, Ofsted was over so I was sure it would be wind down time until the end of term. I contemplated taking the tube to Aldgate but ended up walking along Whitechapel Road instead, passing market traders fixing metal poles together and unloading vans full of fruit and veg. The Met had erected another sign outside the tube station, appealing for witnesses to a violent physical assault in the area and the Chinese illegal immigrants were already out on the streets desperately trying to flog their illegal DVD's of just released movies and hardcore straight porn.

I arrived at school just before nine, falling over myself as I dodged a surge of little people all in post-Ofsted non-school uniform, as they bundled through the old Victorian entrance for Boys and charged up the stairs. When I made it into class, I was bombarded with the usual questions. Did I know when it was their birthday? When could they do P.E? Had I played the new *Power Rangers* game on Play Station?

At just after ten a.m, Linda appeared in my doorway and asked if she could have a word. I assumed it had something to do with Mrs. Begum or the inspection. She gestured for me to come to the doorway.

'Have you heard the news?'

'Sorry?' I looked at her blankly.

'The news. David, there's been multiple terrorist attacks on the transport system. They think six explosions have gone off on the underground. One at Aldgate East.'

For a moment I couldn't take in what she was saying.

'We've decided not to tell the children. If they ask anything just act like nothing's happened.'

I felt sick. 'It's Al-Qaeda'

'We don't know who it is at this stage.'

'They've attacked more than one target?'

'David listen, it could be any one of a number of groups. The G8 summit is going on in Glen Eagles at the moment. They don't know who's responsible.'

I couldn't believe it was happening.

'Are you ok? You're in shock. I think you'd better sit down.'

She took me along the corridor to her office. I sat down in the same place where Mrs Begum had been during that meeting. The office door was open and I could see the office staff, site manager and a parent watching the breaking news on Sky TV in the office next door. A reporter was somewhere in central London standing some way off from the wreckage of a Double Decker bus. Then it flashed to Edgware Road in West London. Linda put an arm round me.

'It's happening all over the world. New York, Madrid, Israel, Palestine. I guess now it's our turn,' she said.

'It's complete madness. If it is the work of Islamic extremists they've targeted their own people. We're right in the middle of one of the country's largest Muslim populations. And Edgware Road - it's the heart of London's Arab community.'

'I've just been on the phone to the police. Their message is to stay put.'

I looked out of the window and saw people in the offices piling out onto the street. At that point, it felt like a city under siege. They'd bombed four different underground stations and a double-decker bus. What would be their next target? I remembered a full scale rehearsal had been carried out a few years ago by the emergency services to see how they'd cope in the event of a dirty bomb going off somewhere in the Square Mile. What if this time it wasn't a rehearsal? What if, this time, it was the real thing and we were about to be caught up right in the middle of it?

Sabina, the secretary, was in the office staring at the TV screen. 'Whoever did this, they should bring back the death penalty. That could have been any one of us down there.'

I had no way of knowing what would kick off next. I walked back into class and as a precaution closed all the windows. It was completely surreal and the classroom was now unbearably hot. I decided to read the kids a story. My hands were beginning to shake. News of what was happening was still sinking in. The worst part was having to pretend everything was fine and not knowing how events were developing outside of the four walls of my old Victorian classroom. One of the children asked what the noise was outside and why they weren't allowed out to play. Overhead I could hear helicopters and the sirens of yet more ambulances arriving around the corner at Aldgate East underground station. I could only imagine the living nightmare those poor people stuck underground just yards away must have endured. For most of the morning, the sound of ambulances and helicopters carried on. In the afternoon there was an eerie silence.

At break time I tried to phone Ahmed but I couldn't get through. I immediately started to panic. Why wasn't he picking up? Where was he? Was he trying to get hold of me? I asked a colleague if I could borrow her mobile phone but I still couldn't get through. Someone suggested that the whole mobile network was down and I prayed that was the real reason I couldn't get through. I just wanted to know he was safe. I'd heard one of the bombs had exploded on the Piccadilly line. He could have been on that train on his way to St. Martin's college. I tried to focus on teaching a lesson on equivalent fractions but my mind was elsewhere.

By lunchtime, the news had been confirmed. One bomb had exploded on a Circle line train travelling from Liverpool Street to Aldgate. The second bomb went off on another Circle line train near Edgware Road and the third exploded somewhere between Kings Cross and Russell Square on the Piccadilly line. The last bomb had been detonated on a double-decker bus at Tavistock Square near the headquarters of the British Medical Association. I knew the park there. I'd been with Ahmed shortly after we first met. Rows of Georgian houses looked onto a bronze statue of Mahatma Gandhi who sat cross-legged in a loin cloth right in the middle.

After a terminally long afternoon trying to deflect the children's awkward questions and the last child had been collected, we were free to go. Many members of staff shared lifts back home or prepared for a long journey by foot. It was the first time I'd stepped out of the building all day and I was greeted by the yellow and black stripes of police cordons and armed police guarding Aldgate East underground station. Police with shot guns were stationed at the end of Brick Lane and Whitechapel Road was practically deserted. There was an eerie calm as I passed the East London Mosque.

Once inside my flat, I opened the window and turned the TV on. I still hadn't heard from Ahmed but I was not alone. A lot of people at work had been unable to contact loved ones. I tried not to think the worst. All the channels were still showing wall to wall coverage of the atrocity: images of the medics at the British Medical Association helping the injured from the Nos 30 bus at Tavistock Square, the wreckage of the bus with its roof blown right off. I didn't want to imagine the chaos and destruction on the carriages that had been blown up deep underground. Reports were coming through of forty or fifty dead and hundreds injured. The ringtone to my mobile suddenly went off. It was Yossi.

'*Motek*, are you alright?'

'I'm fine.'

'It's on all the news channels in Israel. I can't believe it. What has London ever done to deserve this?!'

'It's been a nightmare at work. One of the bombs went off at a station just round the corner to the school. All you could hear all day were helicopters and ambulances taking the injured to The Royal London.'

'You're ok though?'

'I'm fine.'

'I miss you.'

I didn't know what to say. All I could think of was Ahmed.

'I'm sorry how things ended when I was in London. I hope you're still going to use the ticket I bought for your birthday.'

I'd forgotten all about it after he' d left in the middle of the night the last time he was in London. I presumed he had too. The image of the number thirty double-decker bus with its roof blown off kept flashing up on the T.V screen. 'I'm sorry. I can't.'

'Come on, I could do with a friend right now. I never showed you Jerusalem, remember. You always wanted to go there, right?'

'It's ok. I understand why we didn't go.'

'Look, we need to talk. I can't do it over the phone and you've already got the ticket. It was your birthday present. It would be a shame if you didn't use it.'

Why hadn't Ahmed called? It was nearly seven o'clock.

'When I left - I just needed some time,' he said. 'That's all. But I don't want to go into all that right now and I'm sure you don't today.'

More T.V footage of medics helping those passengers injured or burnt by the bombs that morning; someone being led away from the scene of the crime, their face now a mask, hidden beneath layers of bandages.

'I don't know, Yossi. It just feels like it's -'

'You have to see Jerusalem.'

'I can't.'

'David, I wasn't going to tell you. You must have enough on your plate right now, but you may as well know. Laila's in hospital.'

'Are you ok?'

He didn't answer. Someone being interviewed was talking about the carnage in the next carriage and how he was one of the lucky ones.

'Yossi, are you ok?'

'I'm snowed under with work at the moment. It's a busy time. You know how it is.'

He didn't sound good. Laila was his life-line. His own family had disowned him when he told them he was gay but she was always there to pick up the pieces when things ever got too much. And now he was off the anti-depressants who was there? His therapist?

'I'll come.'

'Sorry?'

'I said I'll come.'

'Are you sure? Great. That's settled then.'

When I put the phone down I wasn't sure if any of it was such a good idea but I knew he wasn't ok. He was probably still going over and over in his head what had happened to Moshe and on top of that Laila's cancer had taken an obvious turn for the worse. I turned the T.V off because I couldn't bear seeing the same images and commentary being replayed over and over again. It was like the planes going into The World Trade Centre. Twenty four hour, wall to wall coverage on all the channels that made you feel a mixture of morbid fascination, disgust and outrage all at the same time.

I decided to try Ahmed again. This time I did get through but it went straight onto voicemail. I left a message for him to call me. Surely he wouldn't still be at St. Martin's. Everyone would have been sent home. But what if he was helping someone else who'd been injured? Or maybe he'd lost his mobile, got caught up in the commotion trying to get home and dropped it. But it was ringing – at least that meant it hadn't been vaporised in the blast. Suddenly the thought of staying in the flat all evening - the same horrific images beamed into my living room – filled me with an impotent rage. I had to get out. I had to do something. And the only thing I could think of was getting to Highgate. There were no tubes or buses and I was sure it would be virtually impossible to hail a cab. I looked at my bike in the hallway. One of the brakes wasn't working properly and I didn't really know the route but I had an A-Z. I carried my bike down three flights of stairs and set off in the direction of Highgate.

Parts of Whitechapel Road were still cordoned off so I rode on the pavement. A police helicopter flew overhead. I cycled through the city, passing Liverpool street and Moorgate which would normally be packed with city workers on their way home, but was now practically deserted and packed instead with police vans and armed police on the streets. I hit Kings Cross and there were more police cordons and large numbers of police on the street. The world's press seemed to have descended on King's Cross station with journalists, reporters and camera men camped outside. Bunches of flowers had already started to arrive and had been laid just in front of the police cordon. I cycled down the Caledonian Road to Holloway and then up Hornsey Road. I kept having to get off my bike and get the A-Z map out of my rucksack to check I was heading in the right direction. I was exhausted and sweat was dripping off me. Traffic lights, cars and lorries, road signs to different parts of London - it all passed me by in a daze. Nothing seemed real. What was real, what kept me going, was the idea of seeing him, safe, unharmed, at home.

I had it all sorted out in my mind. When I got there, we'd cook dinner together, I'd sleep over, then get a cab into work the next day. I just had to see him. The harder I cycled up Hornsey Road, the more I realised what a mistake I'd made, walking away from him the last time I was there. What was I thinking? He was never like a drug. Even when I first fell in love with him, I could see through the haze of serotonin and dopamine - nature's own conjuring trick. I could see him for who he was. It was more than a feeling, more than attachment, it was a knowing and deep understanding I'd never had with anyone else. I pressed down even harder on the pedals and leant forwards in the saddle.

I cycled along Hornsey Road, then continued into Hornsey Lane and eventually came to his block. I dragged my bike up his driveway and left it leaning against the wall outside, then buzzed his door number. No answer. I buzzed again. Nothing. I walked back and looked up to his apartment. There didn't appear to be any light on. I called out. No response. I tried again. At that point a neighbour leaned out of their window. I explained the situation and she immediately buzzed me in. This time I took the stairs, leaping up them, two or three at a time. When I got to the top I was seriously out of breath. I banged on his door - nothing. I opened his letter box. It looked just as dark as it did from the outside. I sat down, leaning against his front door, hoping against hope that it would miraculously open and Ahmed would be standing there. I'd just cycled half way across London and I still had no idea where he was. I tried not to think the worst but the more I tried, the more I thought about what had happened to Moshe. But surely this was different; this was London, not some war-torn part of the Middle East. I had to find him. I wrote a quick note and posted it inside his letter box.

Ahmed, please phone me. Just let me know you're o.k. David. X

When I eventually got back home I was absolutely shattered. I kept telling myself he was probably ok but part of me wasn't convinced. I just wanted to see him, touch him, to know that he was unharmed. I was going out of my mind with worry. I looked at The Royal London clock. Ten thirty. I poured a small glass of wine, lit a fag then went into the living room and turned on the T.V: footage of Tony Blair getting into a Royal Air Force helicopter, ready to take off and fly back to London from the G8 summit in Scotland, a sombre Tony Blair in Downing Street doing what he always did best - addressing the nation in a time of crisis. Then a telephone number for concerned relatives flashed across the screen. I rushed to the kitchen and rummaged around in kitchen drawers trying to find a pen but when I came back they'd already cut to the scene in Tavistock Square with the roof of the double-decker bus peeled back like an orange.

I reached for the remote, turned the TV off then grabbed my jacket and keys. Ahmed was still out there somewhere. I had to find him. Cutting through, behind the bus depot at the back of Whitechapel station, I crossed into the side road, and peered down through the metal grill onto the empty tube tracks and tubes, backed up and stationed at the platform. I carried on into Whitechapel Road, eerily quiet for this time of the evening. The Royal London Hospital was right in front of me.

Chapter 22

I ran across the zebra crossing then stood at the front entrance of the hospital, undecided which entrance I should take. Despite having lived just across the street for the last couple of years, I'd never been inside before. Ambulances were, as usual, parked back to back at the Accident and Emergency side entrance. I took the steps, two at a time then quickly stepped into the revolving doors. There was no one at reception. I rang the bell. No answer. I called out - still nothing. I looked around. It was remarkably calm. I didn't know what I expected but it certainly wasn't this. The place was deserted. Suddenly the double doors which led away from the main reception area opened and an elderly patient, fitted with what looked like an oxygen mask, was pushed in a wheel chair being by a male nurse.

'Can I help you?' he asked.

It was at that point that I wasn't quite sure what good it was me being there. 'I can't get hold of someone. I wanted to make sure he hadn't ended up here.'

'I'm sure he's ok. Try not to worry. Are you a relative?'

'Where did they take people who were injured?'

'Are you a relative?'

'You don't understand.'

'Look, why don't you go back home. They're advising people to phone the helpline.'

'Where is he?'

'Look, I don't think-'

It was useless. I decided to find out for myself. He called out after me but it was too late. I'd opened the double doors and was walking away from reception. I walked down a corridor. There was that familiar disinfectant smell I remembered from childhood and that claustrophobic feeling. I passed an empty trolley and a doctor in a white coat carrying a clip board. Her footsteps echoed mine as we walked in opposite directions. Bright fluorescent lighting lit the way to the different departments: Haematology straight on, Dermatology to the right, X-rays to the immediate left. Maybe I should have entered in the side entrance to A & E. But then, even if he was here, he could already have been transferred to a ward. I turned right and walked down another corridor. No windows, just endless doors, one with the name *Dr. Shah M.D* typed in bold lettering across it. A cleaner in a green uniform was pushing her trolley of cleaning products slowly across the lino floor. A random painting of a tree in autumn hung on the wall and next to it someone had scratched the outline of a star and written 'shit, cunt' inside. I turned left and suddenly saw a large sign above, pointing in the direction of the Accident and Emergency department. I walked to the end of the corridor then pushed the swing doors.

It was a scene of chaos. Phones were ringing, a woman in her mid fifties was crying inconsolably and being comforted by what I took to be a male relative, someone was shouting at the nurse behind the reception desk, a doctor was telling a young couple that they were doing the best they could, but they had to be patient. I walked up to the reception desk and waited behind an Asian guy and his two kids.

'Mr. Jalil, the doctor will be with you shortly.'

'But I've waited two hours. I have two small children. They want to see their mother.'

'I'm sorry.' She turned to me.

'How can I help?' I told her Ahmed's name and address.

'Wait there.' A few minutes later she returned.

'I'm sorry. No one of that name has been admitted.'

I left the side exit, weaving in and out between a row of ambulances that stretched all the way up to Whitechapel Road. A nurse with her red hair tied up underneath her nurse's cap hurried through the revolving doors and the image of my dead neighbour floating in the bath suddenly flashed through my mind. I made my way to the Whitechapel Road, now deserted of traffic except a lone double-decker bus that pulled up just outside Whitechapel tube station. No-one got on and no-one got off; just two armed policeman stood guarding the tube station which had been shut down since the atrocity earlier that morning. I walked up the cobbled slip road and over the bridge that led to my block of flats. The horror of what had happened that day was still filtering through. I prayed Ahmed had not been caught up in it, but even if he hadn't, other people had and other people had died. Lives had already been destroyed, loved ones left behind.

I was exhausted and couldn't bring myself to trudge up the stairwell to my empty flat so I walked into the park and sat down on the bench where the dealers would normally be hanging out. Parts of the grass had been scorched into a patchwork of yellow and brown by the sun whilst other parts had completely worn away, kicked and scuffed by local kids playing football or cricket. Now the place was deserted, not even the local winos or resident bag lady were there.

Looking up at the rear of my block of flats, I could just make out the shoots of the cuttings I'd planted earlier in the year poking through the railings on my balcony and remembered how different everything was back then. I was with Ahmed, that's all that mattered. There was no doubt in my mind that it would ever change. But even now, after everything that had happened, sitting alone in the park as the first stars began to appear in the sky, I felt my love for him just as strong as before. Not knowing if he was dead or alive, injured or unharmed, I prayed to a god I didn't believe in. I prayed that he was still alive, unharmed, somewhere safe, that, even if I never saw him again, he would be ok. Some time later I made my way to my flat, trudged up the stairwell in the dark, then crashed out on the sofa, wishing the day had never happened, that somehow it could be erased, wiped clean. That in the final moment the bombers had seen sense, thought of their loved ones and the mayhem and carnage their actions would cause to innocent civilians; that they'd suddenly realised how blind faith without reason or compassion turns into the upmost evil and backed out at the last minute.

I looked at the clock. It was four in the morning. The phone was ringing. I stumbled to the hallway and picked up.

'David?'

'Yes?'

'It's Fatima Hussain, Ahmed's fiancé. I'm afraid I have some bad news. Ahmed – he was in one of the train carriages that was bombed yesterday.' She started crying. 'He's at St. Thomas' hospital.'

I felt as if someone had punched me in the stomach.

'David? Are you still there?'

'Is he ok?' I asked.

'He's in a stable condition. He's been asking for you.'

'I'll be there as soon as I can.'

I scribbled down the name of his ward then phoned for a cab. I pulled on a T shirt and pair of jeans. What did 'stable' mean? I imagined him underground, the force of the blast, then wondered if they'd had to amputate a limb. I rushed to the toilet and threw up, and stayed there bent over, coughing and spitting sputum into the bowel. I sat down on the edge of the bath. Why hadn't I asked the extent of his injuries? I knelt on the bathroom floor, my head over the bowl and threw up again. I was washing my mouth out, my hands shaking as I cupped them together to hold the water, when the intercom buzzed. I grabbed my keys and ran down three flights of stairs, nearly tripping over myself half way down, as the stairwell light suddenly switched off.

The roads were virtually free of any traffic as we sped across Tower Bridge and into South London. At least he was alive, I kept telling myself. He's alive. He's not dead. Stable. That means not critical. It mean's he'll live. We sped along the South Bank, towards the houses of Parliament and through to Waterloo. Suddenly the cab parked outside St. Thomas' hospital, I was paying the fare and walking towards the entrance.

I walked to reception and spoke to the receptionist who told me how to get to the ward Ahmed was on. I walked away, towards the lift and waited. The lift door opened and a patient on a trolley was wheeled out. I stepped in and the lift stopped intermittently all the way to the ninth floor. I could feel my heart inside my chest and my throat was completely dry. I stepped out of the lift. The sister of the ward saw me approaching and came towards me.

'I'm here to see Ahmed,' I said. I could hardly speak.

'Are you ok, love? You look a bit peaky. Look, there's nothing to worry about. He's doing fine. I'll show you where he is,' she said then turned left down a corridor, towards the ward. We past a long row of beds, some had curtains pulled across. I watched as a nurse carefully dressed one of the patient's wounds and saw fluid seeping out through the burnt flesh. I heard the beeping of a machine and someone calling out in his sleep. And at the far end of the ward I saw him. A wave of sheer relief and gratitude passed through me. He was lying peacefully asleep, his beautiful face untouched. Then my gaze dropped slightly and I noticed a drip was by his bedside and his right arm looked badly burnt, and covered in a kind of gauze. There was a man and two women sitting next to his bed. I immediately recognised Fatima. She was holding his hand and looked up. It looked as though she'd been crying.

'David,' she said. 'I hope you didn't mind me calling you.

Ahmed was asking for you.'

Then a middle-aged woman wearing a loose fitting headscarf introduced herself. 'Forgive me. I'm Ahmed's mother. You must be a very good friend.' She spoke in a soft Arabic accent and had the same almond-shaped eyes as Ahmed. She stood up and hugged me. 'We managed to get a flight from Dubai to London late afternoon and came here straight from the airport,' she said.

I looked back at Ahmed.

'I'm his father.' A tall, thin man with a moustache stood up and brusquely shook my hand. I looked at Ahmed. I'd always wondered what he'd looked like, this man who Ahmed was so afraid of.

'He's sleeping. Heavily sedated,' his mother said.

'Have you spoken to the doctors? Is he going to be alright?' I asked.

'He was in the carriage that exploded near the tube station at Edgware Road and taken to St. Mary's hospital, then transferred here yesterday evening,' she said.

'Will he be ok?' I asked.

'He was in shock. They had to sedate him. He was suffering from smoke inhalation. His right arm was cut from broken glass and quite badly burned. They've put an antibacterial compress to prevent infection and are feeding him fluids,' she said.

'The doctor also said he's probably suffered a partial loss of hearing due to the blast but he thinks it will be temporary,' said his father.

I looked at him lying so peacefully in the bed, the drip attached to a vein in his arm and couldn't hold it in anymore. 'I'm sorry,' I said. 'Everything, it's just been such a shock.'

'You must be a good friend,' said his mother. 'But please, don't worry. Ahmed will be fine. There will be some scarring, especially on his arm. But he's lucky. We've been told if all is well, he can come out of hospital in a few days. He should be fully recovered just in time for the wedding. Then, God willing he'll be coming back to the Emirates to live.'

'The Emirates? I thought he was coming back to live in London.'

'Wherever did you get that idea? We've already bought them a house – seven bedrooms, swimming pool. I'm looking forward to becoming a grandmother at long last.'

I looked at Ahmed in the bed and knew that was the last thing he wanted; living out his days as a closeted gay married man in the UAE, with possibly a few hotel bars in Dubai to look forward to cruising at the weekend. I felt sick.

'We've decided. London is no place for a Muslim now,' said his father.

'But you must come and visit. Sharjah is no place for a young man to hang out but I'm sure Ahmed would love to take you to Dubai,' said his mother. 'He always goes there when he comes back home. He has many friends in Dubai.'

At that point I noticed Ahmed's fingers starting to move. His eyes were still closed and he began talking in Arabic. After an hour or so of Ahmed drifting in and out of consciousness, the sister came up to us and recommended that we go home, get some rest and come and visit later in the day.

'David, you must come back with us. We have reservations at a hotel in Russell Square,' said his father.

'I'm going to stay here for a bit,' I said.

'We wouldn't dream of it. In fact when Fatima told us you were coming, we booked a room for you. In our culture, extending the hand of hospitality is second nature.'

'I just want to spend a few minutes with Ahmed.'

His father looked at me strangely. 'He needs his rest,' he said curtly.

'I won't be long,' I said.

'Well, I suppose I could do with a cigarette.'

They left the ward and I sat down in the chair next to Ahmed's bed, relieved to have a few moments alone with him. I looked at the tube attached to his wrist feeding him a constant drip of saline solution from the inflated plastic bag at the side of the bed then touched the tips of his fingers. I placed my hand gently over his and leant towards him. His breath was warm and soft. ' I love you, Ahmed. I've always loved you, I won't let them take you away.'

As I walked out of the main entrance of the hospital, the sun had just appeared on the horizon and a black Mercedes drove up and a chauffeur opened the door. I climbed into the back seat. The windows at the side were tinted so it was difficult to see out properly. Ahmed's father sat in the front seat and said something in Arabic to the driver, who promptly drove off.

'Whoever did this to my son, will pay dearly,' he said. 'They may not value their own life or anyone else's but their soul will suffer great torment in hell,' An awkward silence followed. We passed the main terminal at Waterloo and I suddenly remembered Ahmed's proposal to meet there later today. Why was it so important I meet him there? What did he have planned? My thoughts were suddenly interrupted by Ahmed's mother.

'Thanks be to Allah. He is alive. He will lead a normal life. Our prayers should be with those who were killed or suffered horrific injuries.'

'The people who do these acts of barbarism, they're not Muslims,' said his father. 'They have perverted the true teaching of the prophet, peace be upon him.' He glanced across at me. 'The Koran clearly states whoever kills an innocent person, it's as if they have killed the entire human race.'

Ahmed's mother started to cry. Fatima remained silent for

the entire journey.

I turned to face the window but even though it was early morning, from inside the car, London was cast in shadow. No-one said anything until we arrived at The Hotel Russell in the heart of Bloomsbury and Ahmed's father got a suitcase out of the boot of the car. I noticed that the road that led to the tube station was cordoned off and two policemen stood in front of the closed street. We walked into the hotel and were greeted by the hotel manager.

'I'm terribly sorry Sir, but would you mind if I checked your bag?'

'But I'm a guest here. We have a reservation,' said Ahmed's father.

'I'm sure you understand the nature of the threat London is dealing with at the moment, Sir.'

He unbuckled and unzipped his suitcase and proceeded to rifle through his clothes and toiletries. He removed a cloth covering a hard-backed copy of the Koran, then covered it again and replaced it inside the suitcase. A framed photograph of Ahmed was removed and placed on the hotel desk.

I glanced across at Ahmed's father, who in turn averted his eyes and I thought about what Ahmed had told me. How he used to inject his gay patients with hormones to try and cure them of their homosexuality. But all I saw now was a rather old and tired looking man traumatised by what had happened to his son, and being singled out because of his Arabic appearance. 'Look, is all this completely necessary?' I asked.

He ignored me and carried on rooting through Ahmed's father's personal possessions.

I slammed my hand down hard on the desk. 'Do you know who these people are? Do you know they've flown thousands of miles to see their only son who right now is lying in hospital? He immediately stopped searching the bag.

'David, please. It's ok,' said Ahmed's father.

'No, it's not ok.'

'Sir, Madam. I'm terribly sorry. I had no idea. Please, allow me to show you your rooms.'

I said goodbye to Fatima and Ahmed's parents and agreed to meet up around midday to go back to the hospital. I phoned the school and left a message to say I wouldn't be coming in, then lay on my bed and looked across to Bloomsbury Park. The water fountain was firing jets of water into the air and I watched as a woman walked her dog. It was just another day and London was coming to life again, only for me, it felt as if things had changed forever.

Chapter 23

I didn't manage to get any sleep in the hotel. I still couldn't believe what had happened to Ahmed and to all those innocent people injured or killed in yesterday's atrocity. London winning the Olympic bid seemed like a million miles away.

We all visited Ahmed in hospital later that afternoon but he still seemed heavily sedated and spoke in broken English and Arabic. We were warned by the sister on the ward that we shouldn't talk about what had happened unless he wanted to. He didn't mention it once. In fact he didn't say much at all, then just before I was about to leave, he pulled me closer to the bed and whispered something in my ear - *Bahebak*.

That evening his parents took Fatima and me to a Japanese restaurant in Soho. We walked down Old Compton street and passed the *Admiral Duncan* pub that had been nail bombed by a neo-fascist a few years back. Once inside the restaurant, whilst we waited for our sushi to arrive, his father began talking about Al-Qaeda: Wahabiism, Saudi Arabia, the Muslim Brotherhood, Jamaat-i-Islami. I couldn't follow the gist of the conversation. All I could think of was Ahmed, all I could see was him lying in that hospital bed dosed up on morphine. And it was all I could do to stop myself from imagining what happened at 8:58 that morning on the underground train pulling out of Edgeware Road station.

A few days later, he came out of hospital and his parents moved in to his apartment in Highgate to take care of him. I visited a couple of times but Ahmed seemed a shadow of his former self – withdrawn and uncommunicative, sitting in the corner of his white leather sofa staring out across the large detached houses and lawns of Highgate and neighbouring Muswell Hill. His parents talked about the wedding, how it was a great blessing for the family, what a wonderful wife Fatima would make for their son, how he was the pride and joy of their lives. I got the feeling I wasn't entirely welcome.

The following week we arranged to meet outside Belsize Park tube station and go on to Hampstead Heath together. Ahmed had phoned to say he was desperate to get out of his flat and away from his parents. It took me twice as long to get to Belsize Park by tube because half the network had been closed down. And every time the tube stopped in between stations, I tried to stop myself from imagining the horror of what Ahmed must have lived through in those moments after the suicide bomber, strapped with explosives, detonated his suicide belt.

After waiting outside Belsize Park tube station for nearly half an hour, a black cab pulled up and Ahmed stepped out. He was wearing combat shorts, sunglasses and a white T shirt and I felt that familiar sensation, a hollow burning in the pit of my stomach. His right arm was bandaged up. He kissed me full on the lips.

'Sorry I'm late,' he said. 'Traffic was horrendous.'

We walked up the hill towards Hampstead Heath high street then veered off through a slip way lined with Edwardian street lamps to the Royal Free hospital. Ahmed slipped his hand in mine. We passed Hampstead Heath British Rail station and the huge oak trees that lined the path at the bottom of the Heath. We then made our way up the well-trodden footpaths towards the open expanse of Parliament Hill.

The sky was feathered with wisps of faint white cloud and an assortment of shapes and bright colours flying high under the expanse of light blue. Pieces of coloured fabric wildly flapping, attached to cords that pulled and tugged, would suddenly veer in one direction, cutting the air violently into a wild zig-zag of crazy, irregular shapes. As each kite cut through the air, you would hear a whooshing sound and see a figure down on the ground, running down the hill along the grass that had been scorched yellow by the hot summer. A father passed a billowing, pink kite in the shape of a parachute to his young son, two pairs of hands now steering the man-made, featherless pink bird. Ahmed turned to face me.

'I have two tickets to Paris sitting at home,' he said.

'You want to go to Paris?'

'I did. With you. That's why I planned to meet you at Waterloo last Friday. To get the Eurostar. I'd booked a hotel in the Louvre district.'

I squeezed his hand.

'We can go another time,' I said.

We carried on walking until we came to the top of Parliament Hill and sat down on a bench at the highest point. We watched as people passed by on the footpath that led up to the top. A family of American tourists were examining the metal plaque, trying to match the famous buildings on the London skyline: the dome of St. Paul's cathedral, the Post Office Tower, the Gherkin and Canary Wharf in the far distance, east of the city. It was a view I'd seen many times before and I listened to the gentle rustling of the leaves as I felt for his hand and interlaced my fingers with his.

I'd been here in the autumn, when the leaves had turned a deep red or gold, before they withered and were crunched under foot, and I'd been in winter, when the sun was a pale yellow on the horizon and the trees were quite bare, and in the spring, when the newly grown leaves were encased tightly in their buds. I remembered a day last November, when I came here alone. The earth was hardened with frost and fog had shrouded everything in a heavy mist that would not lift. I turned around and read the words carved into the back of the bench: 'To Esme, beloved mother and wife.' He turned to me.

'I'm going to tell them, David.'

'Tell them what?'

'I'm gay. I'm not getting married.'

I should have felt over the moon but instead I was taken aback. It wasn't what I was expecting. 'Are you sure it's what you want? What if your family disown you?'

'I'll take my chances. Those bastards from Bradford coming to London with the promise of paradise packed inside a device full of semtex and nails. I'm more of a Muslim than they ever were.'

I squeezed his hand gently and watched as a father lifted his little girl onto his shoulders to see the view. What did she see? What did her father see when he looked out across London, a city that was still reeling from the first suicide bombers to strike on British soil. What did any of us see? I turned to Ahmed but he wasn't there. He was standing up, looking out to St. Paul's Cathedral and the city of London. For a moment I thought he might just be admiring the view and then I heard his voice – yelling, screaming, shattering the peace.

'Fuck you, you bastards! Blasphemers! Murderers! You've lost. Everything! Can you hear me in Hell?' I stood up and tried to hold him but he pushed me off.

'Do you want to see it? See what they did to me?' he said.

I was aware that people were beginning to stare and I was concerned for Ahmed. I wanted him to unleash his anger and outrage at what had happened to him. But here outside on Parliament Hill – it didn't feel safe.

'Please Ahmed, just come and sit down,' I said.

'Look, look what they did!' He began to unwrap the bandages and dressing on his right arm and slowly revealed a layer of flesh that didn't resemble skin. It was a mixture of black and reddish orange which had sort of jellified.

'Touch it,' he said.

'Please Ahmed, don't.'

'Touch it!'

He started trembling. 'Do you know what hell is like? It's a flash of light. The window behind you implodes. Shards of glass are embedded in your arm, only you have no idea what it is, what's happened or where you really are. It's a burning sensation on your arm, like you've never felt before. Then the smoke clears slightly. You see that the roof has buckled, the tube doors are twisted off, there's a huge hole in the floor. When the tunnel lights eventually come on, people are covered in blood. There's an old lady on the floor. Someone's giving her mouth to mouth. When I close my eyes, I can still see that old lady on the carriage floor, the person further down ripped apart by the blast. They're all with me when I close my eyes at night.'

'It's all right. It's over. It's all over.' I walked slowly towards him.

'Why am I alive? Why me? Why didn't I try and help? I should have helped them.' He started sobbing.

I reached for his hand. 'You were injured yourself. You would have helped if you could. It's not your fault.'

'I can still smell that smell – as if the wiring in the carriage is burning.'

I was now holding him in my arms. He was still trembling. 'It's finished. They can't hurt you anymore. It's over.'

We stood like that on the top of Parliament Hill holding each other, neither of us willing or prepared to let go. And in those moments that passed between us everything else seemed to gradually disappear: the people around us, the trees, even the path we stood on, and I felt what I had felt before with Ahmed - the miracle of our love and for a few moments it seemed to obliterate the world of hatred and suffering. Then I felt his tears on my neck and I came to my senses.

Eventually I reached for his hand and we began to walk

towards an area of the heath which marked a Bronze-age burial mound. It was one of my favourite spots and was encircled by trees and benches inscribed with more messages of love to those more recently departed. We sat down on one which faced towards the lake and hues of pink and red that now stretched across the horizon.

'When will you tell your parents?' I asked

'I'm still going back to the Emirates. I'll tell them then.'

I wasn't so sure he'd find the strength to tell them - especially now. He was badly shaken by what had happened. And even if he did tell them everything there was no guaranteeing that he'd return.

'I need time, some time away. I can't be in London right now. Every time I hear a siren, every time I'm in an enclosed space - it brings it all back. Maybe if I spend some time with my grandmother... I need to go back home, David.'

As I held his hand, looking across to the huge detached houses and church spire in the distance, it felt like I was losing him all over again. But I understood he needed to go back home, get away from London for a bit. He might never come back but for now, even though it pained me, I had to let him go.

'I wanted to tell you before, but it didn't seem right, when you were in hospital,' I said.

'Tell me what?'

'I have a return ticket to Tel Aviv. Yossi bought it for a birthday present. One of his friends is in hospital. She has cancer. She said she wanted to see me.'

'You should go.'

'No, I'm going to cancel.'

'Don't do that. You should go. I'll be in the Emirates anyway. I want you to see your friend. I trust you.'

We stayed there, holding hands looking out across the

expanse of wild grass, golden in the late evening sun.

'When do *you* leave?' I asked.

'The day after tomorrow. I'm going to do it, David. I'm going to tell them.'

I remember thinking this might be the last time I ever see him. We stayed sitting there, for what seemed like forever, looking across the heath until tiny specks of white light began to form in the sky. At some point, we found ourselves walking away. He took a taxi back to Highgate and I headed east, but as I travelled back on the tube to Whitechapel, I felt as if I'd left part of myself on that bench, up on the hill with Ahmed, looking out into the night sky.

Chapter 24

Michael was walking towards me along the Embankment, his head still shaven and he'd taken to wearing loose fitting karate-style trousers. I clocked the tattoo on his left arm – White Tara, the Bodisatva of compassion, sitting on her lotus flower surrounded by a halo of red light. I'd wanted to meet him at the Buddhist centre in Bethnal Green to check out his new digs and Durdharsakumara, the guy he now shared his room with, but he wanted to visit a Tibetan Buddhist centre in Waterloo for some reason. I wondered if he was growing restless with Western Buddhism and wanted to branch out in a more esoteric direction.

School had broken up a few days earlier and the hot and sunny weather was forecast to continue for the rest of the week. We crossed the Thames at Westminster Bridge and walked towards the South Bank, with the resurrected Globe Theatre, London Eye and a growing number of cafes and restaurants spread along the river front. A boat ferrying passengers along the river left a trail of white foamy water and passed under the bridge. It was high tide and as we crossed to the other side the waves nearly spilled onto the promenade of the South bank. Later that afternoon, the tide would be so low that parts of the river bank would be entirely exposed, leaving beaches of mud and washed-up bits of rubbish on either side. St. Thomas Hospital was further down and I was still haunted by that dreadful night when I arrived there sick with fear, not knowing how badly injured Ahmed might be. On the other side of the main road, there was a sign for the centre: *Kagyu Samye Dzong London Tibetan Centre.*

We walked along a deserted side street monopolised by a mammoth council estate, the brain child of some naïve young architect from the 60's, the 'streets in the sky' now a hotchpotch of boarded up windows and wrought iron security gates. At the end of the street we turned up a long drive way. Pieces of multi-coloured fabric, threadbare and flapping in the breeze, hung in a zigzag formation from tall pine trees on either side, like the bunting to a village fete. Michael explained they were Tibetan prayer flags and that a special blessing or mantra was printed on each of them, and would be blown by the wind to the four corners of the earth.

At the end of the driveway were several outhouses with bright yellow and orange painted wooden doors that seemed to beckon you inside. Michael pushed the yellow door and we went in. The smell of incense greeted us and the sound of a deep, guttural groaning which must have been some form of Tibetan praying being played on a CD. At the window there seemed to be some sort of shrine. Sticks of incense, offerings of flowers and framed photographs of people were neatly arranged at the foot of a gold Buddha. A Tibetan Buddhist nun sat at reception, her hair completely shaved, wearing NHS glasses and dressed in maroon robes. She looked up from her paperwork.

'Can I help you?' She spoke with a lisp and smiled at both of us, her upper set of teeth protruding visibly, giving her a goofy kind of expression. I wanted to laugh.

'I'm looking for books on the history of Buddhist statues in central Asia,' said Michael.

She led him to a corner of the room. 'That's an interesting pendant, dear.' She looked at the Star of David around my neck.

'It was a gift,' I said.

'Are you familiar with the mantra 'Om Mani Padme Hum?'

I looked at her blankly.

'It's a Buddhist mantra associated with the Bodhisatva of Compassion. A prayer of compassion for all sentient beings.'

I was beginning to feel uncomfortable with her intensity and looked across at Michael, who was already engrossed in a book. 'Sorry, I'm not really into all that.'

The nun smiled again at me flashing her set of gnashers. 'The six points of your star correspond to the Tibetan syllables of the mantra of compassion and enlightenment.' Again the smile and the teeth. It was as if she didn't belong to this world, but hovered slightly above everything, smiling benevolently at anything that happened. I didn't know what to say so smiled back and went over to Michael. He was still deeply absorbed in his book. I began reading the titles on the bookshelf: *The Bodhisattva of Compassion, Finger Pointing to the Moon, Collected Verse by Tibetan Buddhist Monks*. I then looked to my right and saw an intricately detailed painting that looked strangely familiar. It was the monster with fangs biting into the wheel, the same image as that on the postcard that Michael had left behind on his bedroom wall, only this time I could quite clearly see what was painted in the hub of the wheel.

'Michael, what's that?' I asked, pointing at the painting.

He looked up from his book. 'Sorry? Oh, that? It's The Wheel of Life. Those are the different realms, look - the animal realm, human realm, those beings with the swollen bellies, they're from the hungry ghost realm.'

'You're making it up.'

'Look, they have tiny necks – they want to eat but can't swallow. When they try to drink, the liquid turns to fire. They're tormented by their own desires. Does it remind you of anything?'

'A place in Vauxhall we both know only too well? And the animals - there at the centre of the wheel?'

'The three poisons. The snake represents hatred, the cockerel – greed, and the pig, delusion. According to Buddhism, they're the roots of suffering.' I must have looked puzzled. 'The people that exploded those bombs. They're not evil, David. They're suffering from the poison of hatred and deluded as to

247

the nature of true reality.'

I couldn't accept that. 'No Michael, they're not victims. They are mass murderers.'

'Keep your voice down. Look, you have to understand the conditions that gave rise to it.'

'Tell that to Yossi, to Ahmed, to the people who jumped from the World Trade centre.'

The nun had stopped writing and was looking over at both of us.

'I mean, look at the shit we've had to put up with for years. Being gay's still illegal in over eighty countries, even punishable by death, but do we set up a gay terror cell and start hatching plots to blow up the Vatican or local places of worship? Does Peter Tatchell issue fagwas to the Pope or the Saudi and Iranian regimes?' I felt as if I was about to lose it so walked away and pretended to show an interest in the section on Tibetan Buddhist literature, casually leafing my way through a book on the lineage of the Dalai Lama. Eventually Michael found the book he was looking for, paid for it and we left.

'What's the book about?' I asked.

'The Buddhas in Afghanistan. They were a UNESCO world heritage site.'

'Like the Bauhaus architecture in Tel Aviv,' I said.

'I guess. Only the Taliban didn't blow that up.'

Walking back through the long drive way, I looked up at the flags fluttering in the summer breeze and thought of the prayers on the Tibetan flags and the wind blowing their blessings all over London.

Nearing St.Thomas Hospital, my ears were suddenly assaulted by the sound of sirens. First ambulances sped past, followed by police cars. Since 7/7, I'd noticed the presence of a lot more police on the streets and especially outside tube stations, so I didn't think anything of it. Suddenly my mobile rang. It was Caroline.

'David, where are you?'

'With Michael, walking back to Westminster. Why?'

'Haven't you heard? It looks like there's been another terrorist attack on the underground.'

Another police car came whizzing passed me at full speed, its blue light flashing on and off, its siren screeching. My stomach lurched. We were walking back over Westminster Bridge towards the Houses of Parliament and Big Ben. It was 12.50 pm. Two more police cars. Had something kicked off at Westminster?

'Where's it happening?' I asked.

'There are reports of four bombs detonating on underground stations but I'm not sure which ones.'

I could hear panic in her voice.

'David, listen to me. Just don't get on the tube.'

It felt like 7/7 was happening all over again. I looked up at Big Ben and for the first time it felt as if my home was about to embark on the same fate as Israel; where suicide bombs were seen as an inevitable part of everyday life. A helicopter veered over the Houses of Parliament and I felt a sense of déjà vu as I remembered the whirring sound of helicopters' propellers over Whitechapel only two weeks ago.

A crowd was gathering outside Westminster tube station. I walked up to a policeman who stood outside the closed gates of the station.

'What's happening?'

'They're evacuating certain stations and closing parts of the network. Three bombs have detonated on tubes but they're not sure if they detonated properly.'

I looked at Michael. 'Let's go home.' We tried to hail a cab but they were all taken so we started the slow walk back to East

London. It was a beautiful sunny day.

'Don't you miss how things used to be?' I asked.

'You mean a few weeks ago?' he said.

'No, I mean us two. Taking on the world together. The two musketeers.'

'I miss not seeing you, but to be honest, no, I don't miss the mammoth clubbing sessions, downing drugs like there was no tomorrow. And I certainly don't miss Suicide Tuesday or the relentless search for the perfect shag, treating the whole thing like it was the Holy Grail or something.' He started laughing.

He looked genuinely happy. Calm, relaxed, at peace with himself. He'd discovered an ancient philosophy and practice from the East and turned his life around. The 'One' he'd found might not be of flesh and blood and certainly wasn't a fulfilment of some conventional romantic longing, but he was in love - with himself, with life, with a search and quest for a deeper sense of meaning and understanding.

It was early Thursday afternoon and I'd never seen so many people walking along the embankment. I wondered if they carried the same sense of foreboding. Was this going to be a common feature to living in the capital? Martyrdom operations carried out by British-born Muslims, bomb scares disrupting the city's transport system, walking for miles because you were too scared to get on a tube or bus in case the carriage exploded deep underground or the roof suddenly blew off, detonated with home explosives. In the future, would riding a city bus be like flying El Al?

We eventually arrived back at the flat, hot, dehydrated and my feet having chafed from walking from Westminster to Whitechapel in Birkenstocks. It was the first time Michael had been back to the flat since he'd moved out and I wished it had been under happier circumstances.

Watching the news later that same afternoon, we realised

that all the bombs luckily had failed to explode. Even the bomb on board the bus in Shoreditch failed to detonate properly and was reported to have just fizzed away producing a foul smelling chemical odour.

The next day a man was shot dead by armed police at Stockwell station in South London.

Chapter 25

After Yossi left my flat on the night of my birthday and checked into a hotel, I didn't think I was ever going to see him again, let alone visit him on home turf in Tel Aviv. I spotted him in the crowd. He looked good - darker than before, in baggy shorts and the same T shirt he'd had on when I first met him. He hadn't seen me and was waiting anxiously in the arrivals lounge, alongside other Israelis, waiting to welcome family and friends back home. A pang of guilt kicked in. I knew this was going to be difficult and wished I'd made everything clear before I came - told him about Ahmed, let him know I'd be there to support him with Laila's illness but that I just wanted to be good friends. He suddenly turned in my direction and his face immediately lit up and broke into a smile.

'*Motek*. I've missed you,' he said and hugged me so tightly I didn't think he was going to let go. It was good to see him but it felt strange being at Ben Gurion airport after everything that had happened. Gone was the sense of adventure and excitement, when I had arrived for the first time in the Easter holidays, and in its place a nagging doubt, an unsettled feeling that wouldn't leave me alone. Was I doing the right thing? And how could I begin to tell him what had really happened since his last visit to London?

'I've hired a car and booked us in at *The King David* for three nights in Jerusalem,' he said.

I wasn't sure going to Jerusalem was such a good idea, given his understandable phobia of the place. 'Yossi, we don't have to go. I could quite easily stay in Tel Aviv, maybe go to Haifa for a few days.'

'You have to see it. I didn't take you last time you were here.'

'I mean it. We can stay here. Go and visit Laila in hospital, hang out on the beach, eat out in Shenkein. I still haven't been to the Diaspora Museum.'

He put an arm around my shoulder. 'It's ok. I'm not afraid anymore. I'm ready to go back. We're leaving tomorrow morning.'

The sliding doors at the entrance of the airport automatically opened and we walked from a cool, air-conditioned building and into the oppressive evening heat of Tel Aviv in late summer. An *El Al* plane was just coming in to land, the Star of David on its tail. I followed Yossi into the car park. He'd borrowed a jeep from a friend so he could take me himself to Jerusalem. I climbed in the front. Just before he turned the key to start the engine, he looked straight at me, resting a hand on my thigh. I knew I had to tell him, but he'd made such an effort booking the hotel and seemed so excited, it just didn't feel like the right time. He suddenly leant in to kiss me. 'What's the matter?' he asked.

'Nothing. I'm just tired that's all.'

'I hope you're not too tired for later.'

I attempted a smile but just felt even more uncomfortable about the whole situation. After a few minutes on the road, the jeep's headlights suddenly lit up a road sign to Jerusalem. Only fifty kilometres. We carried straight on to Tel Aviv, and soon enough, I began to make out the circular Azrieli tower and Dizengoff centre, where we'd both been swimming up on the roof on my last visit. Approaching the financial district of Tel Aviv, he took me on a different route, through streets I didn't recognise, until we pulled up outside a building, much closer to the seafront and built in the style of Bauhaus.

'A lot's happened since I last saw you, David. I've finally bought my own place.' He turned the key in the front door and we walked inside. The kitchen and lounge area was open plan, with huge cuboid pillars rising up to exposed metal rafters near the ceiling. Some of the walls didn't reach the ceiling but rather ended two thirds of the way up creating an opening near the roof into the next room. The overall feel was that of a converted warehouse or art gallery space. It was interior design, Bauhaus style - all clean, clear-cut sharp lines with lots of space between. I walked across the wooden floor boards to the patio window and looked onto a courtyard with an enormous banana tree, huge green leaves drooping downwards under their own weight and baby green bananas tucked snugly to the trunk. Unpacked boxes were everywhere, books and photographs, scattered over the floor.

'Let's go outside,' I said.

I pulled down on the patio door handle which nearly came off in my hand and stepped outside, breathing in the faintly perfumed air. Past the vine leaves that entwined around the roof of a wooden trellis and the thick cables and wiring that trailed and twisted across the top of the apartment block opposite, I looked up at the night sky, lit a cigarette and inhaled deeply. Under the scattering of luminous light, all the drama of a lifetime – the setbacks, unexpected surprises, the hurt and the joy – it all seemed to pale into insignificance. These were pointers to other worlds, other galaxies, suns in other parts of the universe, some dying out quickly whilst others continued to burn for billions of years to come. What did our individual lives – the day to day worries and concerns, the choices we made – what did it all mean, set against the fathomless eternity of the cosmos?

'So, you like my new place?'

'It's amazing!'

'The other apartment had too many memories. It was time to move on.'

'Why didn't you tell me?'

'I wanted it to be a surprise. I wanted to surprise you, like you surprised me, you crazy man, when you arrived on my doorstep straight from London. Do you remember?'

I did. Everything was different back then. It was one big

adventure. All I had to do was get on a plane and follow him out here - an extended holiday romance. He turned and looked at me.

'I have some bad news. I didn't want to tell you on the phone.' He fell silent. 'Laila - she died, shortly before you came out here.'

'But I thought -' I stared at the night sky.

'Somehow it didn't seem right telling you just before you set off.'

'Yossi, I'm so sorry.' Suddenly I wished I could see her again, hear her voice, angry yet full of compassion.

'She asked me to give you something, the day before she died.' He went inside and brought out one of her handmade denim shoulder bags with the trademark bright yellow sunflower sewn on the front. He opened it and took out a book. It was wrapped in a piece of silk splashed in shades of blue and purple.

'It's a book of Rumi's poetry. A thirteenth century Sufi Persian poet. One of her favourites. She wanted you to have it. Look. She earmarked one of the poems especially.' He handed me the book and I began to read.

> *'My mouth tastes sweet*
> *With your name in it:*
> *I turn my face to you,*
> *And into eternity:*
> *There is a growing taste I prefer*
> *to every*
> *Idea of Heaven.'*

I felt Yossi's shoulder around me and remembered what she'd said about the dead only being truly dead when they are forgotten. I looked out into the night sky, wondering, if somewhere, she might know we were thinking of her.

'When's her funeral?' I asked.

'It was yesterday. She was in a lot of pain at the end. It's better she doesn't have to endure all that pain, day in, day out, anymore. Don't you think?' He glanced down at my neck and toyed with the pendant.

'You're still wearing the Star of David then?'

'You mean the mantra of compassion and enlightenment? The Seal of Solomon?'

He began to laugh which helped lift the mood. 'And who told you all that? Have you been attending the local mosque in East London by any chance? David, you never cease to amaze me!'

'The Tibetan Buddhist centre in South London, actually.'

'Now don't start. You know what I think of all that.'

'I'm only expressing an interest. And anyway I know what you and your friends are like. Psychoanalysis seems much more in vogue than old school religion.'

'And I'm sure you can understand why.'

'Israel following in the footsteps of the U.S?'

He was prodding me playfully in the chest. 'Ok, enough Israel bashing for one night. It's about time we got you into bed, but before we do, I think you'll find the U.S followed in our footsteps. After all the founding father of psychoanalysis was Jewish.'

'Just one more cigarette.' I was stalling for time.

'Ok, no more than five minutes.' He went inside. I had time to think. Maybe I could just sleep on the sofa again? But we hadn't argued, so there was no excuse to pull that one off. I inhaled deeply on my cigarette and looked up at the apartment block opposite. The blue and white of the star of David flapped gently under the pale moonlight and I remembered Yossi telling me it was like Tel Aviv - the blue, being the sea and the clear blue skies and the white background, the city.

'David! Hurry up!'

'I'm coming.' I crept into his bedroom. Most of his clothes were still in suitcases or on the floor.

'Come here,' he said.

I undressed to my underpants then clambered onto the bed and rested my head on his chest. It seemed the safest place.

'When Laila died, something changed in me. I realise what's important in life. I was afraid before. Afraid you didn't really want me. Afraid I'd lose you, like I lost Moshe. But I'm not afraid anymore.'

'That's good, *motek*,' I said.

'David, I want you to come and live with me, here in Israel.' I listened to the steady rhythm of his beating heart. His chest slowly rose and fell with his breathing.

'David?'

'Let's talk about it in the morning.'

'You're tired. I'm sorry, motek. Sweet dreams. *Laila tov.*'

His breathing deepened and soon after a whistling, rasping sound started up at the back of his throat. I thought of Ahmed back in the Arab Emirates and pictured his slender frame and shaven head turned towards me. I got a sudden urge to book a flight, arriving in Dubai some time later that week, turning up at his parent's place in Sharjah. They'd invited me, after all. Then I remembered Ahmed's promise to tell them everything. I could just imagine the scene. 'Hello Mrs. Akhtar, remember me? Yes, that's right. I'm the one who fucks your son up the arse. I hear it's a time-honoured tradition in this part of the world.' But it was a crazy idea. Yossi needed me here and anyway my passport had been stamped by an Israeli official. There was no way I could enter the Arab Emirates. Like many of the surrounding Arab states, they refused to accept Israel as a sovereign nation and refused entry to anyone with an Israeli stamp on their passport. I didn't know what to do for the best. I gently lifted my head off Yossi's chest so as not to wake him and faced away towards the wall. Tomorrow we would be in Jerusalem.

Chapter 26

As I ate yoghurt and cereal under the shade of the banana tree, the shadows of last night were given form by the early morning sunshine. The garden had a wonderful overgrown, unkempt feel to it. Flowers had fallen from vines that twisted their way around the wooden trellis above and were now lying scattered over the patio in various states of decay, some still a pale shade of pink, others crunchy and dried up, burnt to a crisp by the sun. A lemon pulled at the bending branch it was attached to, as if just about to drop. The courtyard was enclosed by two brick walls at either end. At one end, the concertinaed leaves of a type of palm tree spread out like a fan, and at the other end, ivy had twisted and knotted itself over most of the brick work and was beginning to work its way towards the main apartment block.

A sudden scuttling near my feet alerted me to a small lizard darting from under the banana tree, towards the glass patio doors. Then just as suddenly, it stopped, waiting to make its next move. I listened to the distant sound of traffic and watched as Yossi drank coffee and read a copy of *Haaretz*. I remembered what he'd asked me just before falling asleep but all I wanted to do was talk about Ahmed, tell him what had happened, how I was woken in the middle of the night by a phone call from Fatima, how I was just beginning to understand what it must have been like when he lost Moshe, but I stopped myself.

'You didn't tell me that,' he said.

'What?'

'One of the 7/7 bombers was a teaching assistant.'

'You're joking.'

'Mohammad Sidique Khan. Says here, he worked in a primary school in Leeds.'

I thought of the kids back at school and wondered if

they were playing outside in a park somewhere or stuck indoors, sweltering in the over-crowded tower block across the street.

'It seems Islamic terrorists can be anyone. You name it. A poor, unemployed drop-out from the slums in Morocco, wealthy Arab from Saudi, or, in *Londonistan*, as they're calling it now - a British-born teaching assistant of Pakistani descent.'

Yossi was at the wheel, driving his friend's jeep whilst I stared out of the dirty window at a part of Tel Aviv I hadn't seen before. It was more built up and industrial on the outskirts of the city; factories, office blocks and towering new apartments all fighting for the same space. We drove alongside a railway track until we got onto the motorway and electrical pylons stretched across flat fields of crops and olive groves, as far as the eye could see. Every now and then, we'd come across a scattering of red roofed white houses, the type favoured amongst Jewish settlers in the Occupied Territories. And further off, a new motorway was under construction. Our road stretched ahead of us towards the holy city of *Yerushalayim*. Yossi called it J-town, a place of religious fanatics, the city that never wakes up, unlike Tel Aviv: liberal, secular and distinctly hedonistic. The morning sun was already streaming through the windows and two litre bottles of warm water were at my feet.

'I couldn't believe it when I saw the images of the red double-decker bus with its roof blown off,' he said.

'I guess that's what they wanted. An icon of British life blown to pieces and the pictures beamed all round the world.'

'Have you thought about what I asked you last night?'

I had hoped if I didn't mention it, he might just forget about the idea. I looked out of the window at a settlement up on the hills. There was a time when I would have been tempted, but I couldn't really see myself living under the Star of David now. The daydream of life in Tel Aviv, with its cafes, bars and clubs, good weather and hot Israeli men lying on the beach, was just that - a day dream: an exotic fantasy when faced with the daily grind of London life. I knew the reality would be far different. If I ever managed to find a job, I'd be on a third of the salary I was on back home, struggling financially, trying to get to grips with the Hebrew language and learning to cope with an altogether different kind of religious fundamentalism. I'd be stuck in a country with a siege mentality, surrounded by hostile Arab states. To the north was Lebanon and Syria, to the East, Saudi Arabia and to the west, Gaza. A few hundred kilometres away was Iraq, which had sent scud missiles across to Israel in the Gulf war and was now on the verge of its own civil war. Yossi had already told me before how he and his family had sat at the kitchen table, fitted with government issue gas masks, as scuds from Baghdad had rained down on Israeli soil. Saddam Hussein had promised to turn Tel Aviv into one big crematorium. Looking through a gas mask changes one's view of things. That's what he'd said. Now instead of scuds, the second intifada had created a new wave of suicide bombers, mainly from Gaza, intent on martyrdom operations inside Israel. It didn't feel much like the Promised Land or somewhere I could easily settle down and call home. But if I was honest, I still hoped that Ahmed would find it in himself not to go through with the marriage, to leave the Emirates and come back to London. But it wasn't looking good. I hadn't heard anything for more than a week.

'David, did you hear me?'

'It's too soon. I didn't think I was going to see you again after you left me in London.'

'I'm sorry, *motek*. It just upset me seeing you like that. You know that.'

'I just thought -'

'What?' He took one hand off the driving wheel and rested

it on my thigh. 'You were adrift. That's why we met. You reached out. You never said it but I knew you understood. Somehow I knew you understood. You have a Jewish soul, David.'

I didn't say anything. I couldn't. He'd touched a nerve. I felt choked up as the road began to swerve and cut through the steep rock face of the Judean hills. I fixed my gaze on the crumbling white rock as we took a sharp bend.

'I'm not expecting anything. I thought I'd ask you, that's all. I mean I have a beautiful apartment now, right by the sea. And you wouldn't have to teach, not if you didn't want to.' He made it sound like a holiday destination that I needn't return home from. He reached across and kissed me. 'Just think about it. That's all I'm asking.' He concentrated on the road ahead.

I looked out of the window at a shepherd and the goats grazing on the already parched land, the soil cracked and exposed to the scorching rays of the sun. 'So where are we staying?'

'I told you. *The King David Hotel.*' He paused. 'I wasn't going to tell you but you may as well know.'

'Know what?'

'My grandfather. He worked behind the scenes. David, he was in *Irgun.*'

He must have seen the name registered a blank look on my face.

'A militant Zionist organisation. They bombed the place just after the Second World War. The hotel was the headquarters for the British mandate of Palestine. Ninety one peopled died. Jews, Arabs, British.'

'Your grandfather was a Jewish terrorist?'

'Freedom fighter. On my father's side. He worked for the resistance. *Irgun* wanted the British out. We all did. They gave a warning thirty minutes before the bomb went off. Can you imagine *Hamas* or *Hezbollah,* doing that?'

'But it was terrorism. The IRA used to -'

'Terrorism?! Your fellow countrymen arrested and rounded up Jews in Tel Aviv, set up barbed wire interrogation cages, imposed curfews, refused entry to Jews from Europe. Do you know about *The Exodus*? It carried over four thousand Holocaust survivors from Europe to Palestine. It was turned back by the British, first to France and then incredibly to Germany.'

Whenever he bought up the topic of the holocaust there was nothing I could say. What can you say in the face of six million Jews dying in the camps? But we were going to stay in the hotel his grandfather had helped to blow up. I couldn't believe he hadn't told me about it before. Innocent people had died and I was entitled to an opinion on it.

'Ninety one people died, Yossi! You said it yourself.'

'And how many died in the gas chambers? If it wasn't for people like my grandfather, all hope for a Jewish homeland would have vanished into thin air. It was just three years after the liberation of Auschwitz. We owed it to ourselves and the Jews who died in the Nazi extermination camps. '

I didn't realise how close Jerusalem was to Tel Aviv. In less than an hour we were driving up King David's street, a street clogged with cars and coaches and lined on either side with expensive looking boutique shops and scores of Israeli flags. We pulled up outside the hotel. Opposite was the Jerusalem International YMCA, a place where I would have felt a lot more comfortable. I pulled my old rucksack from the boot of the jeep and Yossi took his suitcase. He told the doorman we had reservations and we pushed our way through the revolving doors.

I immediately felt dwarfed by the high ceilings and grandeur of the place and wondered how much it must have set Yossi back for both of us to stay here for three nights. After all, this was a bastion of privilege where Elizabeth Taylor, President Saadat of Egypt, the Clintons, Margaret Thatcher and countless other British P.M.s had stayed. Everywhere shone and glistened: the marble floor, wood panelling and brass fittings, the polished dark wood of the armchairs arranged around glass coffee tables, the ceramic vases, varnished and bursting with bouquets of dragon flowers, red roses and lilies. We were met at reception by Magda, a thin-lipped woman with sensible shoes.

'Welcome to The King David,' she said and beckoned to two porters in smart navy uniforms with brass buttons, who came and took our luggage. We went through the lobby with its tasselled, gold curtains draped across the rear windows and framed oil paintings, mostly portraits of stuffy old men, that wouldn't have looked out of place as exhibits in the Victorian section of *The National Portrait Gallery*. I got a glimpse of the reading room, and the long mahogany table that took centre stage which, according to Magda, had hosted key political conferences on The Middle East.

'Most people feel quite at home here,' she said with a wave of the hand and the assured confidence of someone who is a dab hand at this sort of thing. 'It has an old European charm, don't you think?'

I looked at Yossi who seemed to be taking it all in his stride. I felt awkward, all four of us now squeezed tightly together in the lift, our reflections staring back in the mirrored walls; Yossi in his expensive but rather crumpled linen suit, me in my khaki shorts and Birkenstocks that had seen better days, standing over the main emblem of the hotel that had been nailed into the floor. A silver crown, and above it, in gold, the letters: KD.

'Yossi, it's too expensive. Can't we stay somewhere cheaper?' I whispered.

'Just enjoy. It's my treat.'

I was beginning to feel increasingly uncomfortable, but it

wasn't just down to the grandeur and chequered history of the hotel. It was beginning to dawn on me that for Yossi, this was about much more than spending a few days in Jerusalem together.

The lift opened and we walked down a thickly carpeted corridor, with EXIT signs in Hebrew lit up in green showing the way down to the lower levels. We stopped outside our hotel room, Magda swiped the card and the door opened automatically.

Inside, we walked down a small hallway, covered in dark wood panelling, which opened into the main room and the king size bed, over which hung a floral tapestry on a brass pole. The room had an old colonial feel about it with its towering brass table lamps, dark panelling either side of the bed and the chaise longue near the window, embroidered in gold and green thread. On the glass coffee table, a bouquet of pink roses and lilies, a silver platter of fruit and tray of chocolates had been neatly arranged, all courtesy of the King David. Magda walked us over to the light, pulled back the curtains and opened the window. Suddenly the room filled with a cacophony of birds chirping, car horns beeping and a police or ambulance siren somewhere in the distance.

'The Deluxe suite! You have one of the best views,' she said.

I looked out onto the old city walls, turreted like the tower of a castle and the citadel that rose up and spoke of an entirely different age. Coiled tightly round the old city, like the body of a snake, an arterial road, clogged with a constant stream of cars, coaches and traffic fumes, wound its way around the limestone walls.

'See where the traffic is at a complete standstill? That's Jaffa gate and next to it is The King David Tower. But I will leave you now and wish you a relaxing and pleasant stay at The King David. If there's anything you need, don't hesitate to call me.' She was smiling to herself as she walked out.

I placed both hands on the marble window ledge and leant

out, looking up at the palm trees that stretched all the way to the fourth floor and then across to the landscaped garden below: rows of rose bushes, flower beds and hedges, neatly trimmed into shapes of birds and animals. I took in the hotel swimming pool, completely deserted, except for the pool attendant who was busy washing down the path around the pool with a hose, and the tennis court, topped with barbed wire and crowned with two flags, one, the star-spangled banner, and the other a ring of twelve gold stars, representing the different member states of the European Union. I looked out onto the Judean hills in the distance, stark and majestic under a cloudless sky. From somewhere not too far away, the call to prayer echoed across the city.

'It's beautiful isn't it?' Yossi was standing behind me, his hand lightly touching my shoulder. 'Some say Jerusalem is built on romantic longing and Tel Aviv on a yearning for that which does not exist.'

I didn't say anything.

'What's the matter?'

I stepped back inside the hotel room, turning my back on the view of the old city. 'I'm sorry, Yossi.'

'Sorry for what?'

'Sorry I came.'

'What do you mean you're sorry you came? You've made me so happy. Surely you know that.'

'It's just… we can't just pick up from where we left off. Things have changed.'

'Why not? I already explained what happened in London. I want you, *motek*. I haven't felt like this since Moshe died.'

I wanted so much to fulfil his dream of us both forging a life together in Israel, to give him back the love that had been taken from him in the cruellest and most untimely way. But I could never replace Moshe. And Yossi would never be Ahmed.

'It's too late,' I said.

'Listen to me. I want you. I want you to come and live with me here. You know that.'

I didn't know how else to tell him. 'I'm in love with someone else.'

He froze. 'What do you mean? You can't be in love with somebody else. You're with me.'

I sat down on the bed. My mouth felt dry and the room was beginning to spin. I forced the words out. 'I'm with Ahmed.'

'The guy you were with before me?'

'Yossi, *you* left me. You were the one who got a taxi to some anonymous hotel in the middle of the night. It was my birthday. Everyone left me that night. Michael left, you left- '

He muttered something in Hebrew. 'That was all rather convenient. I come back to Israel and suddenly the Arab is back on the scene. I'm sure his wife to be can hardly contain her joy.'

'Don't talk about him like that. He has a name.'

'Well thanks for telling me before you came out here.'

'You sounded upset over Laila. I knew how much she meant to you. I thought you needed a friend.'

'Please. I don't need your pity.' He was standing above me his arms folded. 'Why are you here David? Just tell me why you even bothered coming.'

'I want to be friends. I want to be there for you. Our friendship's more important than this.'

He looked like he wanted to hit me. 'Friends? You're going back out with that fucking Arab and you want to be my friend? He doesn't love you. His family will always come first.'

I stood up. 'Don't say that. Don't just ruin our friendship because I can't give you what you want.'

'Friendship? What friendship? Are you crazy? I'm fucking in love with you.' He paced up and down the room talking to himself in Hebrew again.

'Is he good in bed, is that it? Is he better than me?'

'That's got nothing to do with it,' I said.

'Tell me. What does he do that I don't? Does he rough you up, is that it? Does he take it that bit further?'

'Stop! Enough Yossi!'

'I haven't even started.'

'I thought you didn't want to see me again,' I said.

'Liar! You didn't even try. Not even a phone call.' The curtains were blowing straight into the room. 'Were you still seeing him when you first met me?' he asked.

'I told you I hadn't seen him for three months. He broke up with me.'

His voice went quiet. 'You were with him at that club.'

'Sorry?'

'On your birthday. You came out of the cubicle together.'

'I'd taken too many drugs.'

'For once, just take responsibility for it.'

'Ok, he blew me in the toilet. It was fucking great. Is that what you wanted to know?'

'That's the spirit! Did he spit or swallow?'

'You arse hole!'

'Fuck you!'

I stared at the embroidered flowers on the chaise longue.

'Why did you start seeing him again? What has he got? Tell me.'

'I don't know.'

'David, I pay for your flight to Tel Aviv, I bring you to the most famous hotel in the whole of Israel. I tell you I love you, that I want you to come and live with me. Is that not enough for you?'

'It's not about money. It's not about the grand gestures.'

'What is it about? Tell me. Has he told you he loves you?'

I remembered Ahmed taking my hand, pulling me towards the hospital bed. I remembered his words: *Bahebak.*

'Well, has he?'

'Yes.'

'And you believe him? Where is he now? Huh? Does he know you're in Israel?

'He's with his parents - in the Arab Emirates.'

'You're not making sense, David. He's not in London?'

'No.' I wanted to cry.

His voice softened.

'David, it's the oldest cliché in the book. You're not in love with him. You're in love with some idea of him. Some idea of the unattainable man, just out of reach who will never give you what you need.' He went to touch me.

I flinched. 'Don't. I can't anymore.'

He looked shocked. 'You won't even let me touch you?'

'I didn't mean for any of this to happen.'

'I don't believe you. You're angry with me for leaving you that night. Tell me now. Tell me to my face. Tell me that you don't love me.'

All I could think of was Ahmed. 'His arm was badly burnt,' I whispered.

'Sorry?'

'Ahmed. He was in hospital for three days. His arm was badly burnt.'

'You're not making sense again.'

'He was on one of the tubes targeted in the London bombing,' I said.

He leant back against the wall, folding his arms. 'Why...why are you telling me this?'

'I thought you should know. You told me about Moshe.'

'You're comparing this to Moshe?'

'They were both victims of suicide bombs.'

'You're comparing this to Moshe!?'

'Yossi, they were both innocent.'

'Moshe is dead! He's never coming back, David. They murdered him! They took everything I had! They ripped my world apart! Do you know what that feels like?'

'No. But I do know what it's like to get a phone call at three in the morning. I know what it's like to go to the hospital, not knowing if his leg or arm had been blown off. The not knowing. - I know that.'

'It was his sort that killed him.'

'His sort? How dare you! For Christ's sake. Not all Muslims are terrorists.'

'No, just the ones that murdered Moshe.'

'You have to forgive, Yossi. You have to let go. You can't go on like this.'

'That's all I have to do? Forgive and forget? It's that easy? That's what love means, does it?'

'It doesn't mean letting his death eat you up and poison you with hatred and guilt. You have to let go.' I said.

'Bullshit! Love means fighting - to the death if necessary, but you wouldn't understand that, would you, David?'

'That's completely unfair.'

'Unfair? Tell me why you love him.'

'What do you mean? '

'Tell me why you love him!' He was pacing the room again.

'I love him because... I don't know. I love him. That's all there is to it. There are no reasons in love.'

'And do you love me, David? Did you ever love me?' He stopped pacing and faced the wall. 'Well at least I know now. I think you'd better go.'

'Sorry?'

'You heard.'

'But I don't have a clue where I am.'

'I'm sure you'll find your way. Why don't you go to the Arab quarter in the old part of the city? I'm sure you'll feel completely at home there.'

'Please, Yossi. Can't we be civil about this?'

'You've told me everything I need to know.'

I looked round the room: the bed that had just been made, the bouquet of flowers on the glass coffee table, the incredible view looking out onto the old city. Everything was perfect. But even before we arrived, I knew I couldn't go through with it. If I'm honest I knew before I boarded the plane for Tel Aviv. Even as far back as the phone call he made on the day London was under attack, when I was unable to take my eyes off those traumatising images on T.V. His back was still towards me.

'Yossi?'

There was no emotion in his voice. 'Just go.'

I had no guide book or map with me, only a few hundred shekels and didn't speak a word of Hebrew or Arabic. I turned to the open window, the curtains still billowing into the room, Yossi still facing the wall like he wanted to punch his fist through it. I lifted my ruck sack onto my back and made my way to the door. I walked down the corridor and took the first set of stairs down to the ground floor, a collection of black and white photographs of Oscar winning actors and actresses smiling down at me from the walls: Ben Kingsley, Elizabeth Taylor, Richard Gere. I could feel more eyes on me as I walked straight back through the lobby, out through the entrance and into the glaring midday sunshine. I had no idea where I was heading. I only knew I had to get as far away from *The King David* as possible.

Chapter 27

I was on the street near one of the gateways to the walled city, a steady flow of traffic and exhaust fumes choking the main route around it. A bead of sweat trickled down the nape of my neck, sending a sudden shiver of goose bumps over my arms and legs. I shifted the heavy straps of my back pack and walked down to one of the main gates in the city's surrounding wall. A family of Orthodox Jews climbed the steep incline, the father wearing his hat with the brim down. There were about nine children altogether and I could hear Yossi's voice pitying the poor mother who had to give birth to so many children in the name of God's chosen people. I could still see his face when he asked me whether I loved him.

An Israeli Arab, wizened by the weather, as he sold his wares in searing midday temperatures, stood outside the gate to the old city, puffing on the butt end of a hand-rolled cigarette. He looked as if he'd been there all his life, standing outside this same gate, his brown skin etched in a myriad of deep lines, his head covered in the traditional white headdress, a black band holding it in place. To him, this was his city. He was calling out in English, French and German to a group of tourists being shepherded by their tour guide, his voice hoarse, no doubt with years of smoking unfiltered roll-ups. Under an umbrella on the ground, he'd arranged his merchandise: postcards and guide books to the city, nativity scenes and effigies of Christ on a wooden cross, in silver, bronze or gold. T shirts, baseball caps all with the image or photograph of the Old City and pendants in different sizes, bore the symbol of the Star of David.

The roof of my mouth was dry and I was feeling slightly light headed so I bought a litre bottle of water from another old guy further along. I crouched down and sat on a large rock on the edge of the pavement and felt the hot sun, now at its zenith in the sky, mercilessly beating down upon my head. I leant my head back, held the bottle above me and gasped as I poured ice cold water all over my face.

I was stuck. I couldn't go back to the hotel. I didn't know anyone in the country apart from Yossi and my flight from Tel Aviv back to London wasn't for another ten days. I didn't have much money with me and was maxed out on the credit cards and nearly up to my limit on my overdraft facility. I had visions of myself travelling north, joining a kibbutz and picking grapes or hitch-hiking further east to the Emirates to see Ahmed, spending the summer lounging by the pool and taking long walks with him in the desert at night. But there was no way of seeing Ahmed. Even if I did manage to hitch a lift, I'd be stopped at the border. I looked straight ahead, towards the heat shimmering on the edge of the horizon. I needed a plan. Maybe I could find a cheap hotel in Jerusalem for a few nights or would it be better to just head back to Tel Aviv? I couldn't decide and could feel my eyes wanting to close and my head beginning to loll. Suddenly a taxi pulled up and the driver inside shouted out of his window.

'*Beit Lahm.* I take you. *Beit Lachem.*'

I stood up. 'Bethlehem?' I knew it was in the West Bank and remembered what Ahmed had said about seeing the Occupied Territories.

I threw my backpack onto the back seat then climbed in, my legs sweaty and already sticking to the black leather. I noticed a sign hanging from below the driver's front view mirror. It said: 'Allah is Most Gracious and Merciful.'

'How far to Bethlehem?' I said.

'Sorry, no understand.'

He sped off and I watched as we passed alongside the old walled city before screeching to a halt at a set of traffic lights and then veering off in a completely different direction. What was I doing? I had no idea how far Bethlehem was. It could be miles from here. I started to undo the straps on my back pack, to fetch my guide book out, when I was suddenly thrown to the floor as we nearly collided alongside another taxi. I braced myself for the scraping of metal and heard my taxi driver shouting something out of the window in Arabic. My head was pounding and everything felt completely out of control, speeding towards Bethlehem with a crazy cab driver behind the wheel, who, for all I knew, could be taking me to Gaza. I turned round and watched as the golden dome on Temple Mount receded into the distance. I was about to make another futile attempt at engaging the driver in conversation, when the taxi suddenly came to an abrupt stop.

'You. Out here.' It looked like I was in the middle of nowhere.

'Is this it?'

'*Beit Lahm. Beit Lachem.*'

'Bethlehem?'

'Look. Israel Wall!' He pointed and I could make out some kind of check-point up ahead and an electrical pylon with barbed wire coiled around it, a twenty first century Christmas tree of steel and iron glinting in the early afternoon sun. I climbed out of the taxi and handed the driver a fifty shekel note.

Near to the check point, a bored looking Israeli soldier in green uniform, who couldn't have been more than eighteen, approached me carrying a gun and asked me to step through to have my passport checked. I did so. One of his colleagues, a girl dressed in the same Israeli green uniform, looked at my passport photo, then at me and brusquely waved me through. I stepped over rubble, discarded glass bottles and rubbish until I came up against the wall itself. Towering great slabs of concrete several metres high stretched in both directions as far as the eye could see. This is what Ahmed had wanted me to see. The wall they were building to partition Israel from the West Bank. Yossi called it the 'separation fence' and said it had prevented countless suicide missions planned out there. Ahmed called it the 'apartheid wall' and said it was against international law. Graffiti artists had made their own mark on the lower reaches of the wall: 'Israeli Apartheid' and 'US dollars fund the Israeli Occupation'. I crossed the border in a gap between the giant slabs of concrete. It struck me how ugly and obscene this wall was compared to the limestone wall, built by a Turkish ruler in the fourteenth century, which surrounded the old city of Jerusalem. It was an eyesore, a blot on the landscape, a symbol of division and separation just like the walls in Berlin, Belfast or Warsaw had been. On the other side of the wall, graffiti artists had spray-canned their anger and sense of injustice onto the great wall. 'Fear builds walls – hope builds bridges'; 'Jesus wept for Jerusalem, we weep for Palestine,' and 'Ich bin ein Berliner.' I was beginning to see why Ahmed suggested coming here. Further along, another graffiti artist had added her own splash of colour. An armchair faced a view of an idyllic, Alpine landscape.

A barrage of taxi drivers, clearly desperate for some trade, began beckoning and shouting at me to come to them. I was wary to say the least and determined this time to make it on my own. Bethlehem couldn't be that far and I scanned the horizon for any sign of a town, but could just make out a scattering of olive trees and rocks.

'Hey come with me. I show you church of Holy Nativity, Rachel's tomb, Milk grotto church. See the place Jesus born, the milk of Mary...I make you good price.'

I carried on walking, determined not to look at him.

'I make you good price.'

I looked up. He was leaning out of the car, smiling, a golden crucifix glinting in the sunshine. Damn, he was sexy. 'How much?' I asked.

'You give me how much you think. Now get in.'

I didn't have the strength to argue. I strapped myself in the seat of his car. I wasn't taking any chances.

'I am Wallid, pleased to meet you.' He shook my hand vigorously. 'This your first time in Palestine?'

'Yes.'

'Relax. You look nervous.' A crucifix on beads attached to his car mirror hit the dirty window screen as we bumped over a pothole in the road. 'Not many people come now. The wall is bad for business. Places closing down. No one wants to visit.' He smiled at me and I noticed one of his front teeth was missing. 'See what the Israelis do to our country?' He pointed at the wall. 'My children used to play in orange groves on the other side. Now is all gone. My neighbour, her house now in shadow of the wall. Her house this close to wall.' He took his hands off the steering wheel to show me. 'Before beautiful view. Now like prison! They say is for security. Is not true. They build it deep into Palestinian territory. When they move out of West Bank they still want bigger Israel than before.' He spat outside the open car window.

'You Christian?' he asked.

'No, not really.'

'You look Christian. What's your name?'

'David.'

'Maybe you're Jewish then.' He slapped my thigh laughing.

'You married?'

'No.'

He looked surprised. 'Not marry, no children – the life is cut!' His hand gestured a slitting of the throat.

'You like Arabic music?'

I nodded. 'I love Arabic music.' He looked pleased.

Suddenly Arabic music was blaring out of his car radio, he revved the engine and we sped off, I hoped in the direction of Bethlehem

'Welcome to Palestine, my friend!'

Crossing the border into the West Bank, I noticed how different everything was. The few shops and businesses there were seemed to be closed or shut down and a number of houses were half built, steel rods left jutting out of concrete plinths. There was hardly any traffic and dirt tracks veered off from the main road. On one closed shop front, a poster of the embattled Yasser Arafat smiled back under the familiar black and white chequered scarf. And next to him, another poster, the swirling dotted characters of the Arabic script below, and above, a photo of a young boy proudly holding a shotgun against the gold-coloured Dome of the Rock on Temple Mount. I could feel eyes following us as we passed by in the car and groups of young men congregated on street corners, an arm slung casually over another one's shoulder, a cigarette smoked down to its butt. Old men were sitting down on the pavement smoking shisha pipes, staring into the distance. No one seemed in a hurry to get anywhere.

'Why you not Christian? I am Christian, my family Christian. We are Arab Christians. We live near Bethlehem.'

'I guess I never saw the light,' I said and smiled.

'I pray for you, David.' He looked at my neck and started laughing again. 'I told you. You *are* Jewish. This is Star of David! Don't be ashamed! We can all be friends. Remember 'love thy neighbour.'

I laughed with him and wondered if that included homosexuals. Yossi had told me the one thing in J-town that had brought the priests, imams and rabbis together that summer, was banning a gay pride march through the streets of the city. Maybe the road map to peace did have a chance after all, if all the holy men could unite the hatred of their people against an age-old enemy – the queers.

'David, this is Church of Holy Nativity. Very important. Where Jesus born. I wait here. Fifteen minutes you come back.'

We both got out. He lit a cigarette, leant back on the car and pointed me in the direction of the church. 'Over there. Through the eye of the needle. A doorway. Remember. Bend down.'

I walked across slabs of white stone, passing a statue of Hieronymus holding an open book in one hand and quill in the other. Stooping through a tiny limestone doorway, I entered into the main interior of the church. Reddish columns with Corinthian capitals lined the aisles on either side as I walked down. The smell of incense was heavy in the air and huge brass lanterns hung from wooden beams on chains down the centre of the aisle. There was an altar at the end of the church, filled with hanging icons of the Virgin Mary and Jesus, where black robed priests busied themselves with ecclesiastical duties of some sort. I waited in line at the top of some stone steps, leaning against a grey, marble pillar and noticed someone had etched the mark of the cross deep into the marble. Holding onto the wall, I went down a set of narrow stone steps and was greeted below by the orange glow of hundreds of flickering candles, in what appeared to be a tiny grotto, crammed full with hanging fabric of embroidered silk in deep red and gold. The air was dank and musty and the candles gave a partial light to the dark hues on an oil painting of the Madonna and child. And there, framed in frayed, orange silk, a multitude of yet more hanging brass lanterns, and underneath those, a silver star on the marble floor that marked the place of Christ's birth.

I looked again at the painting of the Madonna and child and thought of Yossi. I felt the points on his pendant again and remembered when he'd clasped it in my hand at Heathrow airport, before disappearing through to passport control. I saw his face when he'd asked me if I'd ever loved him and I thought of Ahmed, lying there in the early hours at St. Thomas Hospital, heavily sedated, bandaged and hooked up to a drip. I turned and looked at the hundreds of candles flickering in the darkness and demanded an answer. Why did it have to be Ahmed who got on that tube carriage at Edgware Road? Why had Moshe found himself sitting in that café in East Jerusalem? Why was there so much hatred and insanity? I leaned back and felt the cold stone wall behind me. I could feel something inside wanting to give way, like a dam about to break, a pain in my chest, like it wanted to crack open. I slumped against the far wall and felt hot tears streaming down my face. The Madonna and child now blurred and merged with the light from the candles.

Then everything began to move in slow motion, people behind the lenses of their cameras jostling, straining for a glimpse of the silver star. I watched as one flame grew very tall and still, and for a moment, gave off a thin stream of black smoke. Gradually I began to feel more at peace and my mind began to clear. I closed my eyes and felt a warm light inside me, a space open up inside my head. Then I saw it, like watching part of a movie but being a really long way away. I saw myself dazed and confused, covered in blood in that side street in Kings Cross, then again, this time unconscious, lying on the bathroom floor and Yossi calling the ambulance, my neighbour strapping her arm with a belt, ready to inject heroin into a vein, someone helping Ahmed from the burnt wreckage of a tube carriage and Michael prostrating himself in front of a statue of the Buddha, then dedicating himself to the Dharma. *Not to do evil; To cultivate good; To purify the mind; This is the Teaching of the Buddhas.* And I saw the light change and become the blinding light of the suicide bombs in Jerusalem and London. I felt the bomber's blind faith bind him to the belief that men who kill and maim in the name of God are blessed martyrs. And I saw a man shaving his pubic hair in preparation for the act, reciting verses from the Koran, embracing his suicide mission as divine destiny, receiving it like a revelation. Searching for my own slice of enlightenment, the ultimate high, I saw my face distorted and fractured by the hundreds of tiny mirrors of a giant glitter ball on the dance floor of *Fire*. An explosion of light from behind filled the club with smoke, and silver stars rained down from the ceiling. Suddenly I was back on my bathroom floor again, naked, and close to death. 'You stopped breathing,' a voice said and I saw Yossi closing the bathroom window, as a cloud past in front of the sun. How easy it was to blow it all to kingdom come.

A bright flash of light brought me back to my senses, as another tourist captured their special moment inside the chapel of the nativity on the immortal reel of film. I wasn't quite sure what had happened and was feeling in need of some air. For a moment, walking back up the stone steps and away from the chapel, I had a strange feeling that none of this was real: the marble columns, brass lanterns, religious icons. Then gradually the feeling lifted as I left the grotto and the chapel of the nativity and walked back through the main body of the church.

Stooping down, I climbed back, through the eye of the needle, out of the stone doorway in the wall of the church, and into the blinding sunshine of our own burning star. I'd always thought of myself as a non-believer before, but forgotten that underneath I'd always believed: in the sanctity of life, in me.

Chapter 28

'Did you get what you came for?' asked Wallid. He offered me a grape inside the car. It was enormous and as I bit into it, the juice spilt all over my fingers. I spat the seeds out of the window.

'From my uncle's vineyard,' he said.

'Thanks. I don't know. I just feel dazed.'

He smiled. 'It's probably the heat. Here, take some water.'

My head was still pounding. 'I want to head back to Jerusalem.'

'But you haven't seen old palace of King Herod. I take you there and after I show you Hebron. Mar Saba Monastery. Only twenty kilometres by taxi.'

'I have to get back.'

'You are crazy. Come to my wife's house. She cook you great Palestinian food.'

We drove back through the same streets until we came back to the wall. Wallid left the engine running. I paid him and got out of his taxi. He leaned out of the car window.

'*Belsalama*. May God be with you, my friend.'

I waved and walked towards the border crossing and check point. I could hear Arabic music trailing off into the distance as he drove back towards Bethlehem.

After waiting for over half an hour in the scorching heat of the late afternoon sun, I boarded a bus heading back to Jerusalem. I knew they were an easy target for suicide bombers, especially in Jerusalem, but I was tired of being driven everywhere like a tourist and anyway I needed to save money. The bus was packed with Palestinians trying to make their way, like me, from the border back to Jerusalem. I headed for the back and squeezed in between two Arabic looking guys who were probably in their early twenties. I began to feel sleepy, as the sound of the engine and vibrations of the wheels under my seat lulled me to a peaceful inner calm. It was a struggle just to keep my eyes open and my head kept dropping onto the guy's shoulder sitting right next to me.

I suddenly woke up with a start, for a moment wondering where I was. The bus had come to an abrupt stop and two Israeli soldiers had climbed onto the bus, shouting something in Hebrew or Arabic. Passengers were frantically searching for documents to show them and then the shouting started up again. One of them pointed the barrel of his gun at an old man near the front. The woman sitting next to him began crying and shaking her hands in the air. I didn't have a clue what was happening. Then I felt the first soldier's foot land straight on mine as he punched the guy sitting next to me - the same guy, who only minutes before, I'd been fantasising about as I drifted off to sleep. The soldier grabbed him by his shirt and the Palestinian held his hands up to his face. For a split second, I thought there might be a suicide bomber on board. A baby started crying and the young man grazed the back of my neck as he nearly fell on top of me. He was dragged off his seat, all the time a rifle pointing at his head. His hands covered his head as he stumbled down the aisle of the bus and fell. The soldier's boot kicked him in the stomach and the man retched. And it was at that moment that my own *bu'ha* or 'bubble', burst. Was this what Palestinians had to put up with on a daily basis? Was this the side of Israel I'd been unwilling to accept? I remember both Laila and Ahmed talking about the Occupied Territories – the military road blocks, checkpoints, refugee camps. I'd blocked it out. I hadn't wanted to think about it before. It was enough trying to understand what Yossi was going through, how his loss had engulfed him, how there was the ever present danger it might engulf him permanently.

The bus drove off and I watched the soldiers snatch some papers from inside the guy's jacket pocket, roughly force his hands behind his back and handcuff him. One soldier was now pointing at the papers, pushing him and shouting in his face. Maybe his crime was simply not having a work permit to enter Israel from the West Bank. I felt the back of my neck. It was sore and painful and then I realised. Something was missing. My fingers searched around my throat, onto my chest and then again at the back of my neck. I lifted my shirt up and looked underneath. I looked on the floor of the bus. Nothing. The Star of David round my neck had gone.

When I got off the bus in Jerusalem, I searched all my pockets then opened up my back pack - still nothing. It must have come off on the bus when that guy fell on top of me - the bus, which would now be travelling back towards the West Bank. It was as if a piece of Yossi had been taken from me. I wondered if he was still in the hotel room. Maybe he'd already checked out. He might even be back in Tel Aviv by now. I couldn't leave things as they were - Yossi standing in front of the wall, unable to even look me in the eye. I couldn't bear the thought of him hating me for loving Ahmed, of that horrendous scene in the hotel being the defining moment of our brief relationship. I had to see him. I managed to hail a taxi, threw my back pack in the back seat and the driver set off in the direction of the *King David* Hotel.

We pulled up directly outside the revolving doors and the driver overcharged me sixty shekels, but I didn't have time to argue. I grabbed my back pack and walked in. This time I didn't care. I was in desperate need of a shower and badly underdressed but all that mattered now was finding Yossi. It was a different man at reception, bald head and glasses with a moustache that curled up at either end.

'Excuse me, has Mr. Mizrahi checked out?' I asked.

'Just a moment, Sir.'

I scanned the lobby for Yossi but there was just a group

of American businessmen seated round one of the coffee tables.

'Yes, Sir?'

'Has Mr. Mizrahi checked out?'

'Let's see. No Sir, but he has left the hotel.'

'Do you know where he's gone?'

'I'm sorry sir, he didn't say. And you would be?'

'We checked in together.'

'Just one moment. Ah, yes.' He gave me a spare card for the room and I ran across the lobby, passed the reading room, down the hallway and waited for the lift. On the fourth floor, the lift opened and I ran down the corridor to the room. I swiped the card and walked in. The lights suddenly flickered on.

His clothes were still in the suitcase and the windows were left wide open, the curtains still billowing into the room. The sound of opera was coming from the bathroom. I opened the door and saw his toiletries scattered all over the marble floor: toothbrush, deodorant, soap, shower gel. I bent over to pick them up and then saw empty packets of some kind of tablets. I picked the empty box up: *Lexapro*. The rest of the writing was in Hebrew. *Lexapro?* It could be anything. Then it hit me. Maybe it was a brand name for antidepressants. I suddenly remembered Yossi telling me about Laila finding him unconscious and taking him to hospital. It was antidepressants he'd taken.

I sat down on the toilet seat, still holding the empty packet of tablets. He'd told me he'd stopped taking them but maybe he'd started again when he came back to Israel or had he just stockpiled them just in case he couldn't take it anymore? But if he'd taken an overdose, why would he have left the hotel room? It didn't make sense. I went to the bedroom and grabbed my mobile which was still lying on the bed. The battery was almost flat. I phoned Yossi but it went on to voicemail. I couldn't just wait here for him to turn up because it might never happen. But I had no idea where he was. Suddenly my phone rang. It was Ahmed.

'David, how are you? Are you still in Tel Aviv?'

'Oh my god, it's so good to hear your voice.'

'Where are you?'

'Jerusalem. King David hotel. You?'

'Dubai. Is something up? You sound stressed.'

'It's Yossi. I'm scared something's happened. Ahmed?'

My phone suddenly cut out and I couldn't phone him back as I'd left my charger in Tel Aviv. I went back to the bathroom, splashed my face with cold water, grabbed the card and left the room. Yossi had said he wanted to take me to the Wailing Wall. Maybe he was there. It was a long shot but I couldn't just sit in that hotel room and do nothing. I walked back down the corridor, waited for the lift then went back down to the ground floor. The lift opened and I made my way towards reception to hand the card in.

'Sir, Mr. Mizrahi returned a few minutes ago.'

'Sorry?'

'He's in the restaurant outside Sir.'

'What restaurant?'

'Let me take you there.'

He led me through the foyer and into a restaurant, empty except a young couple enjoying a bottle of champagne together. I weaved in and out of tables laid in white table cloths and silver cutlery. At the far end, open doors led out onto a terrace with pillars painted with the images of Egyptian and Greek gods and there in the corner, seated at one of the tables overlooking a garden and facing views of the old city, was Yossi.

'Thank you,' I said and the guy from reception smiled and left. Yossi turned round.

'Ah, I thought you might come back,' he said. 'Would you like a drink?'

I nodded and he poured me a glass of white wine from the

bottle in the ice bucket. He carried on looking out at the view.

'Look. Up there.' He pointed to the rear façade of the hotel. In between the fourth and fifth floors was a kind of half floor lined with a series of holes. 'Bullet holes,' he said. 'The hotel used to lie on the Jordanian border. It was used as a strategic lookout point for the Israeli army.' He carried on looking up at the pockmarked rear wall of the hotel.

'I came here with Moshe,' he said. 'The summer before he died. We had the same views of the old city. The deluxe suite. He told me off for spending so much money.'

'Did you stay in the same room we're in?' I asked.

He didn't answer.

'I'm sorry Yossi. I should have told you everything before I came.'

He reached for his pack of cigarettes, took one out and lit it. 'Let's face it. We're both in love with someone else, David.'

I watched as a flock of birds flew across the sky, over the old city.

'But you were right about one thing,' he said.

'What's that?'

'When I went to the Botanical gardens near the Hebrew University -'

'I thought you'd taken an overdose,' I blurted out.

'An overdose?'

'*Lexapro*. There were two empty packets along with all your toiletries scattered on the bathroom floor. I kept thinking he's done it before. What's to stop-'

'Are you crazy?' He looked straight at me. 'I'd finished the course. I told you when I came to London. I kept them in my toiletry bag. I must have forgotten to throw the empty packets out.'

'But what was all that stuff doing on the bathroom floor?'

'When you'd gone, I had a shower and threw the stuff at

the wall. Then I left."

'But where did you go? '

'I was about to tell you. Back to the café in East Jerusalem. I hadn't been back since it happened. Not since I'd heard the news and got a friend to drive me down from Tel Aviv and seen the blood still on the pavement, the tables and chairs blown onto the street by the blast. Can you believe they used to call it Paris in Jerusalem?'

'If you'd have asked me, I would have gone with you,' I said.

'It was something I had to do on my own.' He paused. 'The front of the café had been completely rebuilt. It still bears the same name. I sat by the window and drank some coffee. I don't know what I expected to feel – some release, peace?' He paused. 'I felt nothing.'

'I thought you said you went to the botanical gardens?'

'I did, afterwards, the place where Moshe used to work. It was completely deserted. Apart from an elderly couple, I was the only one there. I followed the narrow stone paths through the cedar groves, the rose gardens and medicinal plants. I passed the lake, stopped near a bridge and watched the water trickling over rocks. I breathed in the air, felt the breeze on my skin. It was there that I found him again. I felt my love for him, untouched by what had happened and I felt his love for me. I felt him in that garden, David. He was all around me – in the water, the rocks, in the breeze.'

A shiver of goose bumps appeared on my forearms. 'It makes sense he'd be there. The café, it has nothing to do with Moshe, his life, who he was.'

'Yes, he was there in the garden. Before I left, I climbed the path to the conservatory. It's like a tropical rainforest, humid, crammed with exotic plants and trees from South America and South East Asia. And there, in amongst a mass of tree roots and moss, I spotted this delicate, blue flower. It was Moshe's favourite orchid. You were right, David.'

'What do you mean?'

'About letting go. I just didn't think I could let go and still love him. I thought if I just let go of all the hurt and the pain, I'd be letting go of him.'

'I didn't mean to hurt you. I just hated seeing you torn apart,' I said.

'Being there in the garden - it helped me decide. I'm going to donate some money to a school in Tel Aviv. It's what Moshe would have wanted. It's mainly Arab kids who go there. They only have a big concrete backyard to play in and very little shade. I'm going to help them plant some trees, create a little garden area. Moshe knew one of the teachers who worked there. It's what he would have wanted.'

I looked at him.

'What is it?' he said.

'It's love.' It felt like I had to dredge the words from a place deep inside of me or forever remain silent. 'It's... incredibly painful. It's sad yet at the same time -' I couldn't help myself and started to cry. '- it's intensely beautiful.' I looked at him as if for the first time. 'What you said before, that's love.'

'You should know. You helped me find myself again, *motek*. You helped me let go.' He smiled. 'And about love. Yes, it can be painful. But it's not always that way. You need to know that. I want you to know that.'

'I love you, Yossi.'

'I know. I know, *motek*. That's life. It is *bashert* – it's meant to be.' He inhaled on his cigarette. 'Go to him, David.'

'Sorry?'

'Find some way to be with him.'

That evening we ordered another bottle of wine and

ate some kosher sea-bream fish on the terrace and listened as musicians in a string quartet, bent over their instruments, played Mozart, bathed in the warm and enveloping light of dusk. I wasn't really a fan of classical music but sitting there with Yossi with the old city in the distance, I began to feel uplifted, taken briefly to another place as I recognised when certain musical phrases were repeated or was swept along in a gradual crescendo. After finishing the wine, we went for a walk in the old city passing through the gate of Zion and into the Jewish quarter.

The Wailing Wall lay on the foundations of Solomon's temple, the first ancient Hebrew temple. Yossi said it had been destroyed by the Babylonians then rebuilt, and this section of the wall represented the outer wall of the temple that Herod had extended. This was the spot in 1967, at the end of the Six Day War, where victorious Israeli soldiers laid claim to the Wall. To the Muslims, it was the *Al-Burq wall*, where prophet Muhammad had tied Buraq, the mythical white creature, that had carried him and angel Jabril on the 'night journey' from Mecca to Jerusalem. The wall was now lit up by floodlights and heavily guarded by armed Israeli soldiers.

After a quick body search, I was given a paper kippah to wear on my head and we approached the wall. Orthodox and non-orthodox Jews alike were standing and rocking in front of towering slabs of stone, reciting passages from the Torah or kissing the wall.

'Some believe when water starts trickling through the stones of the wall it will signify the advent of the Messiah. It happened once. Turned out to be a faulty water pipe.' he said.

I watched as prayers were written down on small pieces of paper, rolled up and stuck in crevices in the wall. In places so much paper had been pushed into the cracks, the prayers had merged together, creating one big mesh of paper. I didn't need to write mine down. As I looked at Yossi, and thought of the garden that would be built in Moshe's name, I knew it had been answered.

Chapter 29

In the morning we breakfasted at the King David like kings, feasting from mountains of exotic fruit, helping ourselves to sausages and scrambled eggs, muesli and yoghurt whilst our cups of coffee were attentively filled by hovering waiters. After breakfast, Yossi left to spend the next few days with Moshe's parents who lived in West Jerusalem, and at about midday I went down to the pool. I stretched out on a sun-lounger, listening to the sound of the gardener mowing the lawn and opened a copy of *The Times*. The second page carried the headline: 'We are at war and I am a soldier.' Next to it was a photograph of a bearded Mohammed Sidique Khan, the Saudi red and white checked scarf tied round his head. He was cradling a Kalashnikov. I wondered if this simple warrior of God had found his way to the garden of paradise.

'Living in the lap of luxury I see!'

I looked up and took my sunglasses off, squinting in the brightness of the midday sun. For a split second I thought I must be mistaken and that it might be a guest from the hotel being overly friendly. But there was no mistaking his voice, light and airy with a slight Arabic accent. He was smiling down at me, suitcase by his side, wearing army combat shorts and a baggy green T shirt with a crescent moon and star and the words, 'Don't Panic – I'm Islamic!' He'd let his beard grow even more and the bandage on his right arm had been removed to reveal heavy scarring. He was laughing like an over excited school boy. I stood up and hugged him.

'How on earth? I don't believe it! You're here in Israel?!'

'You know how it is. Just passing through. Thought I'd look you up.' He surveyed the hotel grounds. 'Not bad. Not bad at all for one of meagre means !' And he started to laugh.

'But how did you -? There aren't any flights from the

Emirates to Israel. Don't tell me you were smuggled across the border?'

'It wasn't easy. I flew to Cairo from Dubai and then on to Jerusalem – used my Egyptian passport. Dual nationality, remember? Egypt still has diplomatic and economic links with Israel. Still, that didn't stop them giving me hell at the airport.'

'You said there wasn't a hope in hell you'd ever come to Israel.'

'Well, things change.' He sat down on the sun lounger and I squeezed next to him. 'I told my father,' he said softly.

'About us?'

'He said if he knew you were my lover at the hospital, there was no way he would have allowed you to see me.'

'That figures.'

'He told me I needed treatment. I knew what that meant. I'd heard enough about his patients. Said I was suffering from a Western perversion, that it was un-Islamic. Called me *shaadh* – queer, said I'd bought shame to the whole family after everything they'd been through.'

I hugged him. 'I love you Ahmed. I've always loved you.'

He smiled. 'And I love you. It just took me longer to get there but I'm here now.'

'So how did you leave it?'

'He refused to talk to me - for days. Then out of the blue said I could do what I liked – go to the hamam, fuck other men, as long as I swore I'd never tell my mother, as long as I was discreet and never got fucked myself. For him, only women are penetrated. He said I could still marry Fatima. Suddenly having sex with men didn't make me gay – as long as I was the active partner.'

'So you *are* marrying Fatima?'

'How can I? I agreed not to tell my mother. But how could I go through with marrying Fatima? How could my father, who was there for me every day at the hospital – how could he expect me to? He forced me into a corner. I called his bluff and threatened to tell Fatima the real reason I couldn't marry her and eventually he agreed the marriage should be called off.'

'Would you have?'

'What do you think? If people in our community ever found out I was gay, do you know the shame that would bring to my family? My own sister would never find a husband, people would shun my mother, my father would lose his job.'

'Did you tell him you were coming to Israel?'

'Are you crazy? – I didn't want him to completely flip his lid. I'd just told him I liked sex with men – did you want him to think I was a raving Zionist as well?!'

Ahmed wanted to see the old city so we left his luggage at reception, jumped in a taxi and got out at Damascus gate. We walked down the steps, passing a market trader and his selection of toys and plastic ornaments that looked like they'd been shipped in from China or Taiwan, and entered the Arab quarter. We edged our way through a network of narrow, labyrinthine streets, thronged with tourists and groups of young Palestinian men who reminded me of the gay boys back home, kitted out in arse-hugging jeans, tight T shirts and heavy chains round their necks. Shopkeepers would call after the steady trail of tourists with 'Hello, welcome, where you from?' enticing them into their shops crammed with the usual religious bric-a-brac: menorahs, crucifixes, kippahs and prayer mats. An old woman, her skin wizened by the sun, was sitting on the street selling her wares; pulses, bulbs of garlic and bunches of herbs. A boy pulled a wooden cart full of oranges and heading in the other direction, the crowds parted for a small tractor, stacked with toilet rolls and sacks of flour. The air smelt of a mixture of spices, incense and animal blood as we passed carcasses of halal meat and mountains of yellow, green and red powder; cumin, falafel spice and paprika, displayed at the entrance to a shop. A group of tourists posed for a photo with an armed Israeli soldier, and further on a bus load of American tourists, shepherded by their Jewish tour guide and all decked out in yellow baseball caps, were desperately trying to avoid a Palestinian shopkeeper, who was laughing as he mopped the street outside his shop, deliberately splashing them with dirty water.

We turned a corner and suddenly had to make way on Via Dolorosa for a large procession of Christians from the Indian sub-continent, a colourful rainbow of saris, scarves and bindis, singing *Lord of the Dance* and clutching their hymn books with a ghostly image of Jesus looking up from the front cover. Behind them, another group of Christians, solemnly holding candles, were following in the footsteps of Christ, led by a Russian Orthodox priest swinging a lantern of incense and backed up at the rear by four pilgrims carrying a heavy wooden cross on their shoulders. Under a plaque on the wall with the Roman numerals VII, I stopped a man and told him we were lost. He stared at me for a moment, as if seeing me for the first time, then took a step closer so he was right up against me.

'No-one is ever lost, not if you follow the Lord.' he said with a thick Texan drool. 'Prepare yourselves, for The Rapture is coming and the Lord will descend from Heaven. It is foretold 'their flesh will be consumed from their bones, their eyes burned out of their sockets, and their tongues consumed out of their mouths while they stand on their feet.' Zechariah 14:12. As it is written, so shall it come to pass.' And with that he disappeared into the crowd.

'Well, at least we've only lost our way. He looks like he's completely lost the plot!' said Ahmed.

'Probably just suffering from a temporary bout of The Jerusalem Syndrome, that's all,' I said.

'Jerusalem Syndrome? You're having me on.'

'It's a recognised condition. Some tourists become so overwhelmed by the history of the place, they end up thinking they're the Virgin Mary or John the Baptist.' He slung an arm over my shoulder and started laughing as we passed an Israeli policeman in a padded bulletproof vest.

We eventually found our way out of the Arab quarter, and passed the plaza in front of the Wailing Wall. We both wanted to see the Dome of the Rock, so Ahmed waited in line with me at the entrance for non Muslims, as a young Jewish boy in his Bar Mitzvah outfit made it up the hill on the other side, carried on someone's shoulders, waving his hands jubilantly in the air. He was accompanied by a small crowd and the sound of drumming, wailing and clapping that got louder and louder as they approached the top of the hill. After passing through airport style security and armed police, we made our ascent to the Dome of the Rock, up a rickety wooden slope, peering down through wooden slats onto the Wailing Wall below.

Loudspeakers were mounted at every vantage point on Temple Mount, filling the silence with the call to prayer. As we passed the El Aqsa mosque, the Dome of the Rock suddenly came into full view, covered in thousands of arabesque tiles: azure, light blue, yellow and green, decorated with Arabic calligraphy and crowned by the familiar landmark of the gold-coloured dome. Ahmed looked up and translated for me.

' 'In the name of Allah, the Merciful, the Compassionate. There is no God but God. He is the one and Mohammad is his messenger.' It's the *Shahadah* – the declaration of faith.'

Only Ahmed was allowed to enter the dome and I wandered outside, across the main square and under olive trees, strangely moved by the tranquillity of the place and Koranic verses that filled the air.

We left the old city through a gate presided over by two lions carved in stone and walked in the direction of the Mount of Olives, drawn by the onion-shaped domes of the Orthodox Russian Church of St. Mary Magdalene, gold and glistening in the sunshine. We were both seriously out of breath, having to stop every few minutes, as we made the steep incline to the top.

'It's a struggle,' he said, stopping to rest his arm on my shoulder.

'You're telling me! Did you see that car try and change gear? I didn't think it was going to make it.'

'I mean my father, Fatima - the bombing in London.'

'You did the right thing.'

'Did I? His only dream for me was to marry, start a family.'

We carried on and I made use of the hand rail on the stone wall to stop myself from slipping backwards. Ahmed was in front. Had I done the right thing, wanting him to adopt a Western- style 'Come out of the Closet' liberation? But then what right did they have to pressure him into an unhappy marriage?

'You have a right to exist. Your love - for who you are, for me. It has a right to exist,' I said.

'I know. But it doesn't help what I've done to Fatima or what my father must be going through.'

'You're both struggling to rediscover who you are to each other. It will take time.' I looked back towards the old city and the Dome of the Rock, a golden shield reflecting back the light of the sun, and I looked at Ahmed, drenched in sweat. 'It's not easy but maybe it's the struggle that gives love its meaning - focuses the mind on what love really is.'

He looked uncertain. 'A jihad for love?'

'I don't know. Maybe there's a moment when the struggle just opens up and all there is, is the love.'

Eventually, we found ourselves standing next to a cemetery

that stretched right across the upper reaches of the Mount of Olives; a wasteland of rocks and white tombstones, some crumbling and in a state of disrepair, yet somehow growing in between them a forest of daisies and red poppies had burst from the ground. I walked closer and noticed that one of the tombstones was inscribed in Hebrew. Small stones had been placed on top of the graves, some as if arranged in a pattern around the Hebrew inscriptions, others seemingly scattered at random, like the wild flowers growing around them. I suddenly felt Ahmed at my side.

I looked again at the poppies scattered amongst the tombstones, their petals deep red, as if blood from the past had seeped through the desert of rocks and stones, in memory of the dead. Up ahead, conifer trees stretched towards the cloudless sky and led to a secluded garden. Ahmed unhooked a rusty padlock, pushed the gate and we went inside. I was certain the place had some important religious significance but the only reality now was this garden, Ahmed and the warmth and light of the sun: a holy trinity that seemed like it would last forever.

Ferns and shrubs were growing in the crevices of what looked like the ancient ruins of stoned walls. The green and yellow spikes of a yucca plant had grown sideways, edged in between two of the white stones, and its roots, exposed and bleached white by the sun, trailed down the face of the wall. And just above that, I saw it; stepping closer, until I was right up against the wall, I looked up. It was as if a liquid had seeped through a tiny crack, trickled down and was now giving life to a gentle opening of velvet petals, deep blue and purple, magnificent and defiant against the blinding white light of the sky. I suddenly felt Ahmed's hand on my shoulder and I did what I had longed to do in the old city; I turned round and kissed him. I felt the bristles of his beard, pulled out his T-shirt and felt the dip of the small of his back, hot and moist with sweat and breathed him in, intoxicated by his musky, sweet smell.

We continued past the ruined walls and alongside a barbed wire fence, towards a field of wild grass, long since turned into gold by the sun.

'Let's sit down over there,' he said, pointing to the shade of several olive trees, then offering his hand, as he squeezed through a narrow gap in the barbed wire.

We sat down under an olive tree and he kissed my forehead, then my neck and the hollow directly under my Adam's apple. I lay back on the earth and closed my eyes. Ahmed rested his head on my chest and I felt the light inside me once more, warm and welcoming, as the branches of the olive tree above turned shadow into sunlight.

Acknowledgements

I would like to thank Alex Dalton, James Kapalo, Henry Lawson, Michael Harth and Martin Ouvry for their help and support with editing and proofreading the text. I would also like to thank James Kapalo and Oliver Berman for years of stimulating discussion and David Nelson (Stonehouse Press), Richard Warden and James Kapalo for their technical support, and Lauren Winton for the art work. I am also grateful to Gay Author's Workshop for all their support and encouragement.

Lightning Source UK Ltd.
Milton Keynes UK
12 April 2011

170774UK00001B/25/P

9 781904 585152